- BOOK 3 -

MAHAYODDHA

KALKI

SWORD O

KEVIN MISSAL

FINGERPRINT!

Published 2024

FiNGERPRINT!
An imprint of Prakash Books India Pvt. Ltd

113/A, Darya Ganj,
New Delhi-110 002
Email: info@prakashbooks.com/sales@prakashbooks.com

Fingerprint Publishing
@FingerprintP
@fingerprintpublishingbooks
www.fingerprintpublishing.com

This is a work of fiction. Names, characters, places and incidents are either product of the author's imagination or are used fictitiously, and any resemblance to any actual person, living or dead, events or locales is purely coincidental.

ISBN: 978 93 8943 296 1

To the readers who have stuck by this story,
you all are the reason I continue to write.

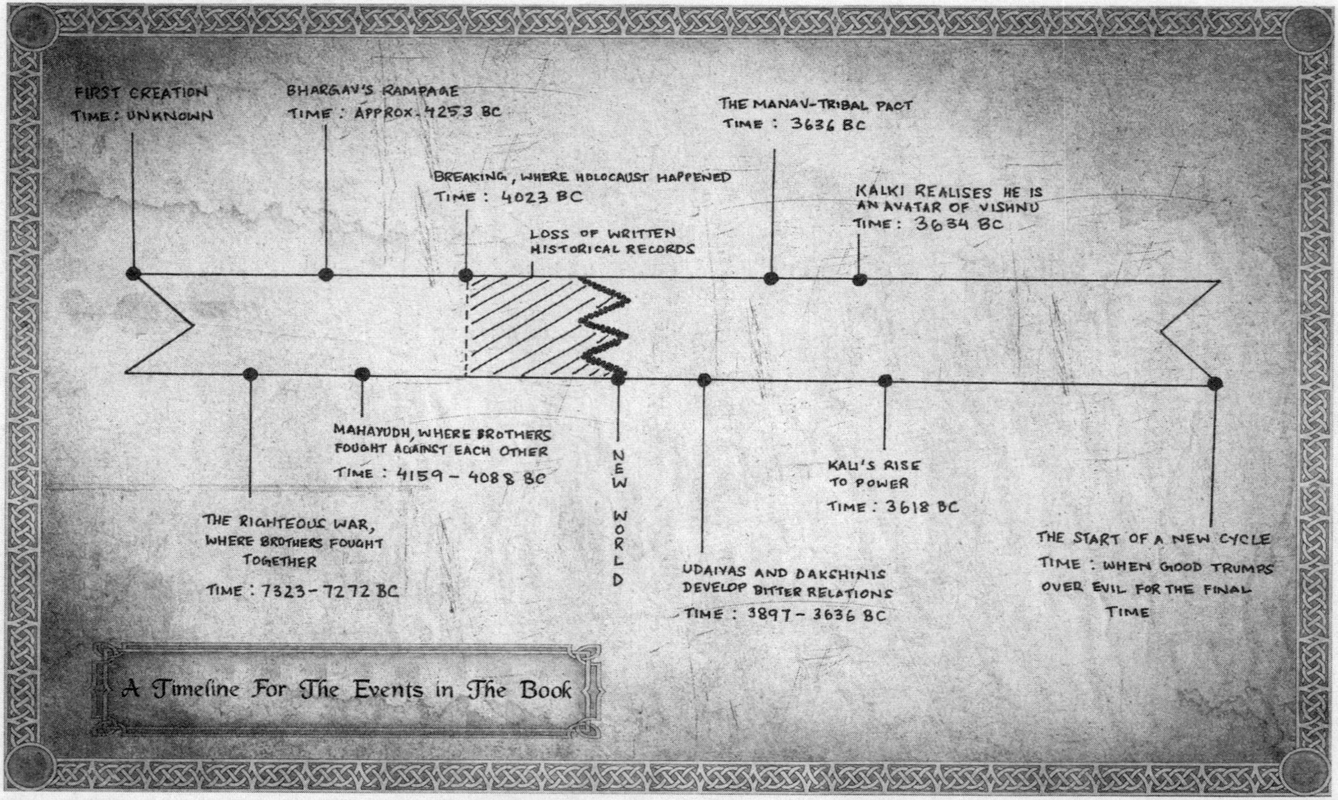
FIRST CREATION
TIME : UNKNOWN
BHARGAV'S RAMPAGE
TIME : APPROX. 4253 BC
BREAKING, WHERE HOLOCAUST HAPPENED
TIME : 4023 BC
LOSS OF WRITTEN HISTORICAL RECORDS
THE MANAV-TRIBAL PACT
TIME : 3636 BC
KALKI REALISES HE IS AN AVATAR OF VISHNU
TIME : 3634 BC
THE RIGHTEOUS WAR, WHERE BROTHERS FOUGHT TOGETHER
TIME : 7323 - 7272 BC
MAHAYUDH, WHERE BROTHERS FOUGHT AGAINST EACH OTHER
TIME : 4159 - 4088 BC
NEW WORLD
UDAIYAS AND DAKSHINIS DEVELOP BITTER RELATIONS
TIME : 3897 - 3636 BC
KALI'S RISE TO POWER
TIME : 3618 BC
THE START OF A NEW CYCLE
TIME : WHEN GOOD TRUMPS OVER EVIL FOR THE FINAL TIME
A Timeline For The Events in The Book

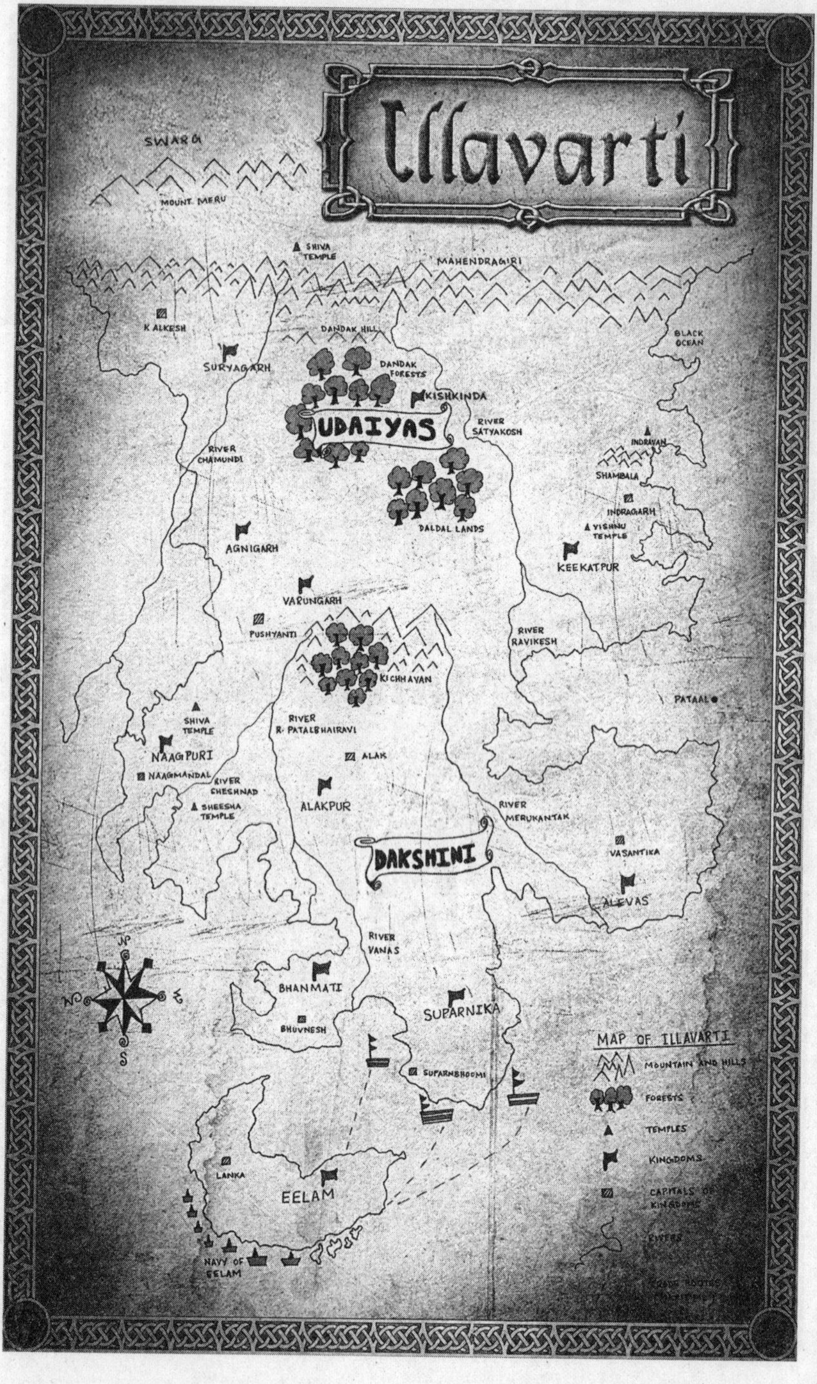
Illavarti
SWARG
MOUNT MERU
SHIVA TEMPLE
MAHENDRAGIRI
KALKESH
DANDAK HILL
BLACK OCEAN
SURYAGARH
DANDAK FORESTS
KISHKINDA
UDAIYAS
RIVER SATYAKOSH
INDRAVAN
RIVER CHAMUNDI
SHAMBALA
INDRAGARH
VISHNU TEMPLE
DALDAL LANDS
AGNIGARH
KEEKATPUR
VARUNGARH
PUSHYANTI
RIVER RAVIKESH
KICHHAVAN
PATAAL
RIVER R. PATALBHAIRAVI
SHIVA TEMPLE
NAAGPURI
ALAK
NAAGMANDAL
RIVER SHESHNAD
SHEESHA TEMPLE
ALAKPUR
RIVER MERUKANTAK
VASANTIKA
DAKSHINI
ALEVAS
RIVER VANAS
N
W
E
S
BHANMATI
SUPARNIKA
BHUVNESH
MAP OF ILLAVARTI
MOUNTAIN AND HILLS
SUPARNBHOOMI
FORESTS
TEMPLES
KINGDOMS
LANKA
EELAM
CAPITALS OF
NAVY OF EELAM

PART FIVE

THE CURSE OF AN **IMMORTAL**

1

Arjan woke up to screams.

Horrific, screeching yells and shrieks from outside could be heard in his room, followed by the boom of explosions. He instantly lurched from his bed, and went to the window to see what was happening.

Death greeted his eyes.

From the third floor of the fortress, he could see what was attacking the city of Indragarh, the place he had been living in for a month now with Lord Nalakuvera, the Yaksha king, a man who was considered a god in his Tribe.

Desperately scanning the dark purplish horizon, Arjan's eyes fell on the disturbed skies where the enemy soldiers were hovering. There were wings protruding from their backs, emitting blue flames. Armed with fire arrows and crossbows, they were shooting at the soldiers below in his city.

Close to the eastern gates of the city, multitudes of black-armoured soldiers toppled the city guard, slashing their way through, opening the way for an invasion.

What is happening?

He couldn't wrap his head around it.

Are these men flying?

They had chosen to attack in the dead of the night. Arjan knew about war strategies—attacking at night was a smart move, maybe even the best time to catch an enemy unawares.

Arjan heard someone knock incessantly at his door. Before he could reach it, the door swung open, and a dwarf-like man entered. Yakshas were of diminutive size, but regardless of that, they were exceptional in battle. The soldier had a bow and arrows tightly slung on his shoulder.

"My lord, the entire city is being attacked. Lord Nalakuvera seeks your presence in the armoury where the soldiers have gathered."

"Who's behind this? I don't see any banners or flags."

"It's an alliance. The flying warriors, they are Suparns. And the others, the ones on the ground . . ." the Yaksha soldier's eyes filled with hatred, "they are Nagas."

One week ago.

Arjan stood in front of the thorny, ornate, golden throne. It was the same one on which Urvashi had sat last month before he . . .

I killed her. I strangled her. I made sure her life ebbed away.

There was so much evil in him; he had realised it recently. But there was guilt too, pooled in the crevices of his heart.

"It'll be yours one day," a voice proclaimed.

Arjan turned to see a tall man wearing a golden coat. He had a goatee, and his hair was shaggy, and he was wearing a crown. The man was bare-chested, and wore his pants low, held in place by a belt that glistened under the silvery light of the throne room.

"I don't want it."

"It's not about wanting it, dear," Nalakuvera said with a smile. "It's about doing the right thing. This city needs a god. When I told you that I will be announcing you as a candidate in the council meeting, you were happy."

"I know. I'm just . . . scared."

"I understand. Fear is important." Nalakuvera's eyes widened. "They don't need just any king. They need *you.* You have powers that no other man possesses."

Except my brother.

"And you can lead this city. This entire empire will belong to you, once you sit on that throne. With my help, of course."

"The council wouldn't agree," Arjan responded.

"Gah!" Nalakuvera growled. "We strive for monarchy and yet we choose democracy to vote for our king."

"For me to sit on the throne, all councilmen will have to vote for me." Arjan knew this because he remembered how Urvashi had coerced these councilmen to rally behind her, so she could follow her father's legacy. "And no noble would vote for the killer of the queen."

Nalakuvera came to stand next to Arjan, and patted him on his bare-chested body. "Let me worry about that. That comes after you decide to sit on the throne. Have you made your decision?"

Arjan clenched his jaw and before he could respond, Nalakuvera planted a kiss on his cheek, while whispering in his ears, "Embrace yourself. You are the only person who can save this city, this world, my dear."

Present.

I don't believe I'm worth being a saviour.

Arjan had had this conversation with Nalakuvera about being the king a week ago, but he still couldn't make up his mind.

One part of him wanted to leave for Lord Bajrang's temple and hide with his mother, while the other wanted to be here in the midst of all this blood and gore to save the people.

The city was being attacked in front of him. It was plunging in darkness . . . he didn't know what to do.

But he had to do something.

He grabbed the spear lying next to his bed and said to the Yaksha soldier, "Tell Nala, I'll be late."

And then he jumped from the window, grabbed it from the ledge, and pulled himself up to the top of the fortress, where he stood on the strong, concrete floor.

He was at the top of Nalakuvera's fortress, and from there, he could see the flying soldiers, firing arrows at the people.

His long shoulder-length hair fluttered as the shine of the silver-dipped moon embraced his shadow, delightfully showcasing his chiselled body which had developed after a period of intense workout and training he did every day.

Looking at the flying soldiers' machines, Arjan deduced that the machines were burning Soma, since blue liquid was spraying around and thrusting the men in the air.

I never thought I would be fighting Suparns. The very Tribe I once wanted to study and learn about.

"Hey!" Arjan shouted at the four soldiers who had surrounded the fortress.

They instantly zapped towards him with their arrows, ready to strike. Arjan leapt high up in the air, his spear tightly clutched in his hand. He dodged the incoming attack from one of the soldiers and rolled over on the ground.

Another came flying towards him and instead of jumping this time, he knelt down and pushed up the spear high in the sky towards the soldier. It pierced the soldier's gut, pouring out his entrails on the floor.

Arjan looked at the three soldiers who had backed away. He ran towards them. The ledge was getting close now, and from its edge, he jumped—uncaring about the fact that if he didn't catch the soldiers, he would fall three floors down.

But he caught them.

He held on to one and stabbed him with the spear. From the

dead soldier's crossbow, he fired an arrow at the other soldier. The soldier clutched the arrow helplessly before falling to his death.

He jumped from one soldier to the other, using his fists this time to beat him. The soldier tried to stop Arjan, but Arjan hit him like a man possessed. Soon, the soldier lay dead on the floor. His skull had cracked.

Arjan kept hitting the soldier, not realising that the man was already dead. His punches were so strong that the floor cracked and they came crashing down to the ground floor. It was littered with rock and pebbles.

There were bruises on Arjan's knees but he didn't care. Now, he noticed that the soldier was already dead.

He came on his feet, dusted himself off, and held on to his spear, making his way to the entry gates of the fortress.

Arjan trusted Nalakuvera to handle the intruders in the fortress. He had to help the civilians in the city.

And as he exited the fortress, he turned back to give it one last look before heading out in the streets. And at that moment, close to the main door, stood the Yaksha king. As soon as the soldier had given him Arjan's message, Nalauvera had come out of the armoury and was on his way to Arjan's room.

A huge grin was plastered on his face, almost as if he wanted to say . . .

See, you *are* a god.

A few days ago.

Arjan strolled in the streets but no one took notice of him. Ever since Urvashi's death, things had been quiet. The Yakshas had been appointed as guards and the Manav soldiers were only tasked with protecting their noble houses and forts.

He was in the bazaar, and his eyes fell on a small stack of leatherbound books being sold by a kid. He had brown skin and dark eyes, and was wearing tattered, soiled clothes. All his books were spread out on a carpet.

Arjan smiled. It had been such a long time since he had picked up one of these and just rushed to read them in the comfort of his home.

Home . . .

But I have no home.

I am a killer. An angry madman with powers.

"You're him," the small bookseller said.

Arjan frowned. "I'm uh . . ."

"The man who killed the queen," said the kid. "There are rumours about you everywhere. People are scared of you."

They wouldn't choose a king they fear.

A king is supposed to be loved.

And I'm a killer.

"And you are walking like you own this bazaar." The boy gestured to the shops around him. There were carpets and low-hanging ceiling drapes in multiple colours in some of the shops. Snake charmers were sitting on the ground, ready with their pipes and baskets. A shopkeeper had displayed ornaments of value and a wide range of weapons, calling the passers-by to come and buy.

Arjan turned to leave. He was afraid someone would recognise him.

"Don't leave, my lord," said the kid. "At least buy something from me." He had a sparkle in his eyes that reminded Arjan of the way he used to be, once upon a time.

"I'm not a lord."

I'm a killer.

"Even though people fear you, they can't stop talking about you. You are so famous and yet many don't recognise you. I do. I butt in places I'm not supposed to. It will be an honour if you buy any one of my books. No, you should have my finest item." He presented a red-coloured leatherbound copy to Arjan.

"What are the people saying?"

"Some say the young queen was inexperienced and mad. The rich favoured her only because she was from a royal family. But no one asked us—the lower castes, the poor—what we wanted. We aren't even allowed to vote. What would a princess who has had everything know about our problems? Nobody cares about what we think. But you . . . you removed her from the throne for us. Rumour is that you can battle a hundred armies. Is that true?"

Arjan chuckled as he grabbed another book and flipped through it. It was a book about the adventures of an explorer. The author had exaggerated the traits of Tribes, describing Rakshas as blood-thirsty monsters and Pisach as ghosts and Vanars as full-blown monkeys. And Asuras were demons, with horns on their heads.

"Is it true then?" the kid asked. "You are the fiercest warrior, our saviour, a righteous hero?"

Arjan looked at the kid, thoroughly amused. "What's your name?"

"Amar."

"Amar," Arjan said, "I don't know. All I know is . . ."

I'm a killer.

Present.

Dead bodies were *everywhere.* Crimson threads of blood were seeping from them into the gutters. Tears welled up in Arjan's eyes as he walked through the bloody bazaar and saw the mangled faces of men, women, and children.

The night was a time to rest; it was when people slept. But the bazaar closed late at night. The enemy had not left a single person in the street alive. As he witnessed the carnage in front of him, Arjan remembered something.

No.

Arjan rushed to where the bookshop was and when he reached, his eyes laid on Amar, who was now just like the others. He had been stabbed multiple times.

Amar looked peaceful with his eyes closed, but the books around him had been sprayed with his blood. Arjan knelt, weeping as he looked at the young boy.

He thought I was his saviour.

Why would the Nagas and Suparns do this?

"Let's leave. Lady Manasa said to kill anyone we could find," a man said. He was walking with another man a few steps away from Arjan.

The other said, "The guards at the fortress are patrolling the streets, so let's make a move now."

Arjan saw the Naga soldiers walking about like mercenaries, as if they owned the street. They were heading towards the main city gates, where Arjan could see a huge mound of corpses of the Yakshas guards.

He had read about this kind of military attack. It was called the Night Combat—surprise the enemy at night and destroy them internally with a small band of soldiers.

I am a killer.

No.

Arjan sprinted towards the Nagas with his spear. He didn't give them the opportunity to even notice him as he swung his blade and stabbed all three of them in succession. They fell down, unconscious, unable to comprehend what had just happened.

Arjan panted, anger surging in him as he clenched his jaw and walked back to Nalakuvera's fortress, carrying Amar in his arms.

I'm sorry I let you down.

As he reached the fortress, he saw Nalakuvera waiting for him with the rest of the Yakshas. They circled around their lord like bees hovering over honey.

"We have gotten rid of them for now, killed most of the ones who had entered but some escaped. Intel says," Nalakuvera began, "it was Manasa, the queen of Naagpuri. She ordered this attack. Her camp is miles away from us and we don't know why she did it."

Arjan still held on to Amar, tightly. Nalakuvera looked at the dead boy but he didn't say anything. "How many have we lost?"

"Many. The nobles have called for a meeting in the next few hours. Apparently, they don't trust the city guard anymore. Yakshas are unreliable, they say. They also want to speed up in getting their wards to be king." Nalakuvera sighed. "I'll handle them. But this attack happened because the snake queen thinks we can't protect ourselves, because no one is sitting on that throne."

I am not a killer. Urvashi had been responsible for Rudra's death. I had a reason to end her life. But what excuse does Manasa have to slaughter hundreds of innocent people? Manasa is a killer.

Arjan handed Amar to a guard and ordered him to arrange a proper funeral for him. He squared his shoulders and looked at the worried Yaksha king, and said, "I'll contest for the kingship, Nala. I'll go to the council soon and make sure everyone votes for me."

Nalakuvera's face lit up. "Really? But I thought—"

"I know."

I am not a killer.

Arjan said, "I have changed my mind."

I am a king.

2

Narasimha . . . Varaha . . . Raghav . . .

Kalki felt like his head was splitting into two as he walked through mounds of cold, undulating snow. Along with him was Devadatta, majestically white, like the snow they walked on.

A shooting, searing pain went through his head. He instantly put his hand on his forehead, massaging it in the hope of reducing the pain.

It's been happening for days.

And he had been out here, deep into the hills of Mahendragiri Mountains for a month now. He had to seek shelter now. The cold had seeped in his body and chilled him down to his bones. He felt extremely exhausted as he rested close to the caves, away from the storm that was brewing in the skies.

Devadatta stood next to him, neighing.

You're lucky I don't eat that much. I usually have a good appetite.

Kalki sighed. *Well, you are a talking horse and you have a good appetite. Thank the graces of Lord Vishnu.*

I don't talk. I mind-talk. There's a difference.

Kalki laid back, massaging his head. *What's going on with me?*

Your powers . . . they are uncontrollable. Perhaps, you need to control them.

You don't say? Kalki scoffed.

As he blinked, he saw blurry images forming in front of him. Trying to make sense of what he was seeing, he squinted and focused on his surroundings, but the images had disappeared.

"Is there anyone out here?" he shouted and then turned to Devadatta. *Did you see someone?*

Nope. You are imagining things now. Great. I'm on a journey with a madman.

Kalki growled under his breath and pulled out a blanket from the horse's saddle bag, wrapping it around himself. An Avatar's body was such that even in extreme cold and heat, it would be unaffected, but Kalki had been travelling for a month. His body had given up, his skin had turned coarse, and he felt like the blood inside his body had frozen.

He looked back at what had happened ever since he had left Lord Bajrang and Padma and come here to the uppermost crust of the snow-capped hills, where an eerie silence engulfed the night and the harsh winds were his enemies. He missed Padma and her nonchalant attitude. He missed Kripa and his drunkard wisdom. Most of all, he missed Arjan. He hadn't received a reply from him since he had sent his message last month. Shuko had come back empty-handed, though Shuko was positive that he had delivered the message and said there was something off about Arjan.

Kalki had left Shuko with Padma so that he could be there for her in need. And if something happenend to her, he had been briefed to come back to Kalki and tell him about it. In some way or the other, Shuko always knew where to find Kalki, even in the worst of places. Perhaps because these three—Devadatta, Shuko, and Kalki—were somehow cosmically connected.

I hope this training is worth it.

It must be.

You don't know anything about it, horsey?

Horsey? Really????

I'm amusing myself.

Well, amuse yourself then, but not at my expense. And yes, I don't know anything about it. I just know you and I . . . we understand each other and we are meant to be with each other.

That's sweet.

Ew! It wasn't supposed to come off as cheesy.

A sound reverberated in the air. Kalki sprung up, throwing the blanket aside and reaching for his sword.

There's someone outside.

A snow monster? Who would live here in this cold?

You have a point. Kalki trudged forward, his feet sinking in the snow, his sword up high, when there was a squeak.

"Oh hello there. Please don't hurt me," the voice said.

Kalki turned his head to see a dwarf. He had a bald head, a saffron-coloured robe hung on his tiny body, and an umbrella was in his hand.

"I am quite queasy when it comes to these weapons. Never liked them. Though that sort of feeling comes from the fact that I don't know how to wield them." He began to hop away from Kalki, who sheathed his blade and furrowed his brows.

Who is this man? Isn't he feeling cold? And what in god's name is he doing up here?

The dwarf leaned on his umbrella, which was half his size, as he walked along with it. "So this is Kalyug, eh? Quite snowy, isn't it?"

"Who are you?" Kalki asked, frowning.

"Well, I'm you. And you are me. We both are the same." The dwarf smiled.

"Am I . . ." he looked back at Devadatta who had come out of the cave to see what was going on.

Do you see this?

Who? I see only a madman talking to himself.

Great. I am imagining stuff. He looked back at the dwarf who was standing with a huge smile on his face. "You are not real."

"Well, of course not, my dear friend. I'm a product of your Channelling."

Channelling was a power of an Avatar which allowed him to meet his past selves, his past forms, and learn from them. But Kalki always travelled to the past; no one till now had come from the past to the present on his own.

"How have you reached here? I mean—"

"Your Channelling is getting stronger, my dear friend. Initially, you could only see images, then you began talking to the Avatars, and now your Channelling selves can grow their own consciousness, like me, who hopped on here. This is the doing of your mind and it's doing wondrously. Soon, you'll be able to . . ." he trailed off. "Oh my my, I shouldn't be saying more than I'm supposed to."

"I'll be able to do what?"

"Do you know who I am?"

Kalki looked at the dwarf from top to bottom, but he couldn't figure it out. He frowned and was almost embarrassed when the dwarf said, "Oh, it's all right. I am not surprised. Why would you remember a person like me? I am not monstrously strong like Narasimha, neither am I as good as Raghav, or as cunning as Govind. No, wait. Maybe I am cunning. I should explain." He looked up at Kalki. "I am the dwarf who defeated the greatest Asura king, Mahabali. And I did it with this size. I made sure Asuras never came back after I made a pact with them. I am Vaman, the fifth Avatar of Lord Vishnu."

"You defeated an Asura? How did you fight?"

"Ah, well," he shrugged, "I didn't. I used my mind. Unlike you." He chuckled. "Everyone thought I would never be successful." He and Kalki began to walk. "But being underestimated is a blessing in disguise—when your enemy thinks that you are not good at all, you can surprise him. That is exactly what you need to learn."

They reached a cliff from where Kalki could see a village, which he had not noticed earlier.

Kalki beamed, seeing some life. He saw humans after such a long time, walking and doing chores, battling the wind and snow. "It was so close, but I didn't know."

"We often miss things when we don't look closely, and things often change when we do." Vaman looked grave as he turned to Kalki. "My dear friend, always remember that appearances can be deceiving. Don't forget that. My enemy did and look who conquered him." He grinned, before vanishing in a puff of smoke right in front of Kalki.

Kalki remained frozen for a moment and looked back at Devadatta, who began to neigh. His Channelling power was growing stronger and he hadn't even realised it.

Well, we should go to this village. By the graces of Vishnu, we need food.

I am also a grace of Vishnu, Devadatta said.

Kalki gave him a look of derision.

Kalki reached the village, and was hoping to obtain some food and shelter. But the people seemed weirdly quiet. And he also noticed that there was fear in their eyes. Most of them looked pale and a little bit sickly. Maybe it was the cold; they all lived so high up in the mountains, after all.

He walked on, noticing that the huts and shops on either side of the road were devoid of any sign of activity. Some villagers glanced at him and his horse, whispering to each other.

Kalki was searching for a tavern to barter a few knives in return for food, but he couldn't find one. He approached an old man who was busy talking to someone else, and said, "I am a traveller, Sir. I seek shelter and food."

The old man looked at him suspiciously. "We don't keep leftovers. We don't have anything left to feed a *traveller*."

It looked like a ghost town. And the old man in front of Kalki looked like a ghost himself—his skin was wrinkled, he was weak, and he looked exhausted, as if life had taken its toll on him and he was barely managing to stay alive.

"But . . . come." The old man moved away from the person he was talking to and urged Kalki to follow him. "Where are you going, lad?"

"Up."

Kalki had no idea where Bhargav was. He often met him through Channelling and Bhargav had said to keep going to the top, and he would eventually reach Lord Parshuram's temple. Parshuram was Bhargav's other name.

But it had been a while since Kalki had spoken to Bhargav through Channelling. Bhargav was the only person he could talk to right now. He was always to the point. Not like Vaman or other Avatars who spoke in riddles. Their conversations sounded more like recordings of wisdom and learning than actual conversations.

"I seek Parshuram's temple."

"Are you a pilgrim?"

Kalki nodded. "Of course."

The old man grunted at Kalki's response.

"And what kind of a pilgrim carries a sword?" The old man pointed at the scabbard hung on Kalki's waist.

"Uh . . ."

"You stay for tonight, boy. Only tonight. I don't like sheltering liars."

Kalki saw they were nearing a huge, bronze statue of a bear-like creature wearing a crown and around him, there were several plates of food, fruits, jars of wine, and drinks of all kinds.

"You are close to the temple. It's just a few miles away," the old man said. "But you look like you need some rest."

"What is this?" Kalki stopped with the reins of Devadatta in his hand, as he pointed to the statue.

"Lord Jambavan, the son of Lord Brahma, the mightiest

Rakshas lord of all time. He has been blessed by Lord Raghav with a long life and the strength of ten million lions." The old man bowed to the statue as he continued. "We are all his children and he protects us from the world."

"And you feed him . . ." Kalki lowered his gaze, "food?"

"Yes," the old man said, gazing reverently at the statue. "He comes when he pleases and he takes our offerings. It's usually every fourteen days."

"Have you seen him?"

"No. No villager has ever seen him. We think he doesn't want to show himself to any human . . . maybe. His blessings are enough for us."

Kalki had a hard time believing that an immortal would come here and eat food, but it made him wonder.

Immortals are real. And they die too. Can Jambavan be yet another one, who I am not aware of?

"Come, I own a small stable. You may find some room to sleep in for the night."

Sleeping with me tonight, are you? Devadatta asked proudly. *I'll make sure it stinks more than it usually does since I have a roommate tonight.*

Kalki frowned at the thought as they all moved away from the Rakshas lord's statue.

After the old man left, Kalki lay flat on the hay amidst the dirt, the smell, and the filth of the place. He closed his eyes, trying to sleep.

And when he opened his eyes, the wind howled and he found himself again in front of the muscular leopard-skin-wearing warrior. He was leaning on his axe, his hair was matted, and he was looking down at Kalki.

Kalki groaned as he stood up. "Why am I unknowingly Channelling people?"

"No." Bhargav stood close to Kalki now, towering over him. "It's not you who Channelled. It's me. And who Channelled you earlier?"

Kalki told him about Vaman, and Bhargav listened intently.

"Don't listen to him. He's a sly man. Also, he's not real. He's just a conscious projection of your Channelling. But it's also good that your powers are growing." He smiled. Kalki noticed that Bhargav's beard had grown since he had last seen him.

"So we can Channel each other whenever we wish to? Does this power act as a messenger?" Kalki had just figured it out and it was like being hit on the face by a brick. "I mean, since you said you Channelled me."

"This power can do a lot of things that you are not aware of." He put his palm on Kalki's shoulder. "Where are you? Why are you taking so much time to reach the temple?"

"I was exhausted, and then I found this village to rest."

His eyes narrowed. "What village?"

"I don't know the name. It worships Lord Jambavan. Do you know him?"

He pursed his lips. "Leave. Now. That monster is dangerous and if he learns an Avatar has taken refuge here, he will destroy you."

"I don't even know if he's real. He could be—"

"He *is*," Bhargav emphasised. "Leave for my temple at this instant. Do not wait or you will perish. Jambavan is stronger than you. And trained. He's the oldest living entity right now. He has witnessed the birth and death of all Avatars."

All?

Kalki had never met such an old immortal, and the very idea of being close to someone like him made him squeak in joy and excitement, but he didn't tell Bhargav any of this. He remained impassive and nodded grudgingly.

When the Channelling got over, Kalki looked around. He was back in the stable. He came on his feet and made his way to Devadatta when he heard something.

He pricked up his ears. *Was this a growl? Is there an animal nearby?*

As he came out of the stable, careful not wake up his snow-coloured stallion, he noticed a shadow lingering around the bear statue—a massive furry creature was noisily munching on the food.

It's him.

And Kalki did the worst thing he could have done in this situation—he yelped. The furry creature turned. His beady, sparkling eyes looked at Kalki.

Well, this is going to end badly.

3

Manasa knew her men must have killed hundreds of people in Indragarh.

But she was okay with it.

They were under Kali. They were supposed to die.

Shedding the blood of others didn't bother Manasa if it meant she could have her revenge. And she had realised that a long time ago.

"Your Majesty?" a sweet, familiar voice came from outside the crimson tent. She entwined her fingertips on the goblet from which she was sipping her wine.

"Come."

The man entered, and the most distinctive feature of his was the silver and golden beads that clung to his braided hair. He was wearing a breastplate with the symbol of Lord Shesh Naag on it.

"General Airavan," Manasa smiled, "how did our surprise attack fare last night?"

"Much better than expected," Airavan said. "Honestly, I thought it wouldn't work."

"You should have more trust in me."

"That's true. Lady Kadru had brainwashed all of us into thinking that you were weak," he said, lowering his head, making Manasa recall what had happened. After Kadru's downfall, Manasa had taken over Naagpuri. The commanders in the army who used to work under Kadru, had now pledged allegiance to Manasa. One of them being Airavan.

Manasa had initially noticed he had been slightly curt in his manner, but right now she knew that he respected her. He was willing to follow her orders. He had, in a way, just complimented her. And by the graces of the gods, he was a good-looking fellow.

"Kadru is dead." Manasa stood up, her jaw clenched. "I made sure of that. And I'm the reigning queen."

"Yes, Your Majesty."

"And this attack was important. It was a way to make Kali aware that I am here to end him and his people."

"Yes, Your Majesty. And we did that successfully."

"How many did we lose?"

"Very few compared to the number of people they lost. Apparently, the Yakshas work as city guards now."

Yakshas?

Manasa furrowed her brows. She had no idea what the political system was in Udaiyas. *How has Kali managed to rope in Yakshas?*

"Did you happen to get any intel on Kali?"

"He's nowhere to seen. We raided the bazaars, questioned the civilians, but nothing came out of it. Some say he was overthrown."

"Impossible! He wants us to think that."

"I hope so. Otherwise, we might have just killed innocents."

Manasa glared at her general. *Is he chiding me?* His face was impassive. She stood close to him now, staring at his deep, sunken, scarred face. "You don't agree with my actions, do you?"

"I do what my queen says, what she orders."

"Yes, you do. But you have a conscience now. And that, I'm afraid, would hurt me in the long run. What should I do about you?"

"I can be removed if you want. There are others—"

"Is that what you want? Why do you not want to serve me, General?"

Airavan looked at her, but didn't utter a word. *He thinks I'm no different than Kadru.*

"I want to serve you, Your Majesty. You have grand visions for the Nagas. Our Tribe will benefit if we control the North and after the peace treaty with Suparns, we certainly have an advantage."

"Thank you for saying those words. Not many Nagas agree that being friends with Suparns will help."

"No, they don't."

"Is there any internal dissension that I'm unaware of?"

Airavan looked at her sharply and nodded. "There has been an issue. I was going to tell you, but I thought this morning I will be the bearer of good news only."

"I don't pay you and give you that title to pamper me, General. What is it? What's going on? Are the two Tribes not mingling with each other?"

Manasa had feared that. Tarakshya, the king of Suparns, had given her half his army in return for saving his butt in Suparnika.

"It's not that. It's a minor issue. But, a grave one."

"Minor or grave? Make up your mind, General. What is it?"

He sighed. "The men . . . they are . . . unhappy."

"Why?" Manasa was confused. She paid all of them handsomely, and had also given them good tents to sleep in.

"Uh, it's kind of embarrassing, actually. Usually in long-drawn wars, soldiers seek female audience. Apsaras are hired by generals and captains for their squad, to pleasure the men who fight for the kingdom."

Manasa had no clue about this. She clenched her fist and said, "You want to turn this war camp into a brothel, General?"

"I'm no more interested in ladies. As you know, I had first served under Lord Vasuki. He had made me a lieutenant under General Takshaka." Manasa remembered the general. He had been murdered by the people who had killed Vasuki, one of them being Kali. It was the beginning of the end of the Tribal Truce. "So I am, well . . ."

"You are castrated, just like Vasuki wanted, to maintain discipline and avoid these kind of issues."

"Exactly." He blushed. "But you see, most of the soldiers you command, were under the leadership of Lady Kadru, who was anything but opposed to this. She made sure this castration rule for soldiers was removed since she saw it as inhuman, as one might put it."

"I see." Manasa ran her hand through her hair. "Now, they want ladies to pleasure their cocks. What is your advice?"

"Uh . . . I am as befuddled as you are, Your Majesty."

Manasa sighed.

"But," he continued, "most war camps *do* have Apsaras to help the soliders feel less *exhausted*. It's a tradition." Manasa noticed that he was using words carefully.

"A tradition that my brother opposed."

"And so, he imposed another tradition that led to many hating him. You don't want that, Your Majesty," he carefully added.

"So you want me to allow you to bring back slave girls?"

"Uh . . ." He felt embarrassed again. "I mean, it's good for the camp. What we started last night was the beginning of a war that might go on for months. The last thing we want is losing the war because of a rebellion amongst our men. But then, it's your choice. I leave it to you."

Manasa nodded. "Thank you, General. You may leave." She sat back on her cushion and velvet pillows.

Who can help me and give me some good advice?

And in this entire camp, she knew there was just one person who would do that.

My dear, cowardly friend.

She went to speak to Vibhishan, the son of Vibhishan the First who was brother to Raavan and the last king of Lanka.

Manasa walked across the war camp that stretched on for miles. Huge rows of tents could be seen till the forest at the back. Thousands of soldiers populated the plain area. Some were resting, others were eating. Manasa could see smoke coming from a tent nearby. She caught a whiff of a delicious roasted chicken and goat. As she walked on, she noticed that some soldiers were training. There was a clanging of swords as the soldiers practised. She passed by a huge tent in the centre of the camp where liquor had been kept. Some soldiers could be seen carrying out barrels full of wine and ale.

It was like a well-built city in itself, miles away from the city of Indragarh.

And another thing Manasa noticed was that all of the soldiers were men. Women were only here to serve, not fight. They were servants, not warriors. The Naga army used to have women warriors. But so many had died during the time Manasa had attacked Kadru, when Suparnika had fallen.

This had to happen.

Along with her two guards, Manasa crossed over to the side where Manavs had set up their tents. But what she saw inside, took her by surprise—there were more women here as compared to her camp. The soldiers were singing and dancing, their arms flailing in the air. It seemed more like a festival than a bloody war camp.

But then, this is Vibhishan's camp.

She set her eyes on Apsaras who were seducing the soldiers. There were some who were running around naked. At the sight of Manasa, they hid their bodies as she eyed them with disgust and hatred. This area had turned into a brothel, but then she was no one to tell Vibhishan how to control his camp.

Vibhishan had been resting in Bhanmati, the only Manav kingdom in Dakshini, for many years before Manasa brought him out in the open. And he had agreed to support her for he believed in her cause—to get rid of Kali.

She came close to the most flamboyant and majestic tent in the area. There were large stone pillars around it, orange in colour, that had beautiful, ornate engravings. Manav guards bowed to her before she went inside and found Vibhishan reading a few books.

"You should have sent a messenger," he looked up, alarmed. "My friend, you don't have to come. I should come to you. You are the queen here."

"And you are the king."

Vibhishan chuckled, and Manasa was instantly reminded of how he used to laugh when they were kids. Even then, he was chubby and round like a ball, just like he was now. "I am no king. How was the attack?"

"It was good. Went well."

He looked disappointed. "You do realise I don't approve of that, yes?"

"Of course. Your men are my stand-in army."

"Yes. I only help when you need it. The attack you conducted has displeased me. You were being extreme. I'm worried for you, my dear." He stood up. "I worry that you might lose yourself in this vengeance."

"My vengeance is the reason I control two kingdoms now," Manasa responded curtly.

Vibhishan shook his head in dismay. It was not the first time that he had expressed his disapproval of Manasa's war tactics, but he was here out of courtesy, and nothing else. And Manasa didn't like that.

But she wanted his help. Every bone in her body was telling her to scream at him, to tell him that he should be siding with her in each combat rather than just being present in extreme situations, that he should help her, assist her, be with her. But she remained silent. She had a pressing issue to deal with. "I got some news from my general," she said, and began to tell him what had happened. Vibhishan kept the book aside.

When she was done, he shook his head. "Vasuki should not have done that. Castration was a poor idea."

"It was not just Vasuki. It was a Naga tradition. Many rulers don't follow it, but some do. Vasuki just happened to be the latter."

"And which one are you?" Vibhishan asked.

"I meant to ask you."

"You meant to ask me what *you* would do?" He chuckled, smacking his stomach. "In my opinion, you should do what your general says. He's right. War amongst you and your men will only complicate things."

"How do you know? Have you experienced it?" And right after asking that, she felt stupid. Of course, he hadn't. He had been living inside his comfortable kingdom till now.

"No. But I have read a lot of books on war tactics and strategies. They were my father's, you know. Quite interesting. They talked about the time when the Ancients ruled—Raghav and Raavan and whatnot."

She didn't believe in Ancients. People talked about how supremely powerful they were, but Manasa thought of them as humans who had just been given a cool name. But she refrained from voicing it out loud. "I need your opinion on how to handle this situation."

"I'm sure you'll do a good job. And I hope you are doing the right thing by attacking innocents and the civilians of the city, too. You have angered Kali."

Manasa smiled. A few deaths would lead to her enemy acting reckless.

That is exactly why I had attacked.

That is the only way I can get to him.

4

Sickness spread in the Vanar camp as Padma went about packing. She was leaving for Indragarh to be with Arjan.

Oh, how much I miss him. Padma had met him for a brief while, but he had left an impression on her. She believed he was a good man, just like his brother. She wondered now if Kalki was okay. He had been away for a month.

Padma was stuffing her clothes inside her bags when Shuko squawked and signalled to her from the window of her hut. As she stroked the parrot lovingly, she swept her gaze across the snowy landscape. The men were coughing, and weak, frail women were being carried in cots.

What happened to them?

"You heard?" a voice came from the back.

She turned to see a bald-headed woman with a fur coat around her body, and a smile dancing on her lips. But it was more of a snarky smile rather than a pleasant one. "The monkeys are not well."

"How did this happen?" she asked Ratna Maru, the head of the rebel Apsaras. "They are Vanars led by the legendary Lord Bajrang." She revered the monkey god for he was an Ancient, a mighty but humble Vanar, full of goodness and nobility. She had read stories about him and even though so much had happened till now, she still got nervous while talking to him.

"Yeah, whatever. They went to collect some herbs and fell ill. Some kind of poison, the Vanar shamans say."

"Poison?" Padma was confused. "Who would poison herb collectors?"

"Who knows? And they are farmers, not just herb collectors." Ratna Maru's eyes fell on Padma's bags. "Are you leaving?"

"Yeah. What about you?"

"I am planning to," Ratna Maru said, sighing. "I'm still figuring out to where I should go."

Padma nodded.

"You aren't going to invite me to come to Indragarh?"

Padma clenched her jaw. As much as she admired Ratna Maru's quest to emancipate women, she didn't exactly like her as a person. Ratna Maru was headstrong and self-centred at times, and she had too much baggage from her past. She reminded Padma of . . . how she used to be. "Why would you want to?"

"Women slavery and prostitution is prominent there," she said, shaking her head.

I don't want you to come.

"You can start from Suryagarh. It's close by. Each city has the same issue."

"You really don't want me to come with you, do you?" Ratna Maru chuckled and then went out of the hut.

Padma couldn't help but feel embarrassed. Instead of finishing her packing, she whistled at Shuko, who flew inside and perched on her shoulder. Padma made her way towards the man she wanted to talk to one last time before she left.

Lord Bajrang.

Padma immensely respected this legendary warrior, this hero of an Age, this Vanar king. She wanted to pay him a visit and ask him how he was doing.

When Padma reached his cabin, she noticed that it was filled with Vanar soldiers. Lord Bajrang seemed disturbed. His face was pensive, and his hair looked dishevelled. He was observing something but she couldn't see who or what it was. Padma moved a little to her left and peeped inside his cabin. A Vanar was on the floor. He could barely keep his eyes open.

The Vanar was scarred and bruised. The pristine white fur on his body had smears of blood on it and the hair on his head had fallen completely. He lay there completely still, moaning every few seconds.

"You didn't have to bring him here," one of the Vanar soldiers said. "Lord Bajrang, you might get infected."

"I don't care. He needs to know that we are not abandoning him just because he is unwell," Lord Bajrang roared. "I'm here, my friend," he said, looking at the victim. "I'm here."

"Lord Bajrang, as you see," one of the Vanars said, "these marks, this redness, it's an allergy, but worse than a normal one."

"What do you think it is, Doctor?" Lord Bajrang asked in his husky voice.

"Wolfsbane, I presume. He's paralysed too. It's a miracle he's alive, but he's having a hard time staying conscious."

"Wolfsbane?" Lord Bajrang looked perplexed.

"The air . . ." the victim spoke, his voice barely audible. "Something . . . in . . . the . . . air." And then he fell silent.

The shaman instantly ordered the gloved guards to take the victim away. Once he was gone, most of the people moved outside, whispering amongst themselves. Reclining on his chair, Lord Bajrang closed his eyes, thinking hard about what he had just witnessed.

"Doctor, I think they might have been poisoned purposefully. That's if this man wasn't babbling because of being delirious," Lord

Bajrang concluded. "Wolfsbane poison floating in the air? Nonsense! The farmers must have had knowledge of how toxic wolfsbane is. They wouldn't even touch it, let alone take it. And if it was in the air, maybe someone took the time to condense it into a cloud of poisonous smoke. Someone . . ." He seemed lost in thought when his eyes met Padma's, who instantly went red. "Padma, my dear, how can I help you? Do you want my men to escort you?"

Padma remained frozen. Lord Bajrang spoke with such softness, it made her feel even brighter than usual, even though the atmosphere in the room was so tense. "My lord, what has happened?"

Lord Bajrang looked at his guards and then directed them to stand outside. Once they went, he told her to sit in front of him. "After Taar got defeated, I believed our worries were over. But now, I think we still have an enemy. Perhaps, an ally of Taar."

Taar was a crazy general. He had tried to kill Lord Bajrang, though he had had a good reason for trying to do so. And now he lay rotting in the Vanar prison.

"Sometimes I think I shouldn't have brought my men from the South. They were happy there."

"Why did you?" Padma asked.

"For a better land. After the Breaking, our home was ravaged with illnesses. And now we are facing the same thing. I'm beginning to believe that things have come full circle."

There was so much worry in his eyes and voice that Padma felt awful for him. But she restrained her emotions since she didn't like displaying them. "What can we do?"

"We?" He raised his furry brows. "You should leave, Padma. Kalki instructed you to be with his brother. He needs you more than we do."

"I have a fair knowledge about surprise attacks," she began, ignoring what Lord Bajrang had just said. "Whoever carried out this attack, he or she is clearly sending you a warning."

"About?"

"About the fact that he or she exists," she said. "The next attack will be worse and it'll impact deeply, if you don't do something about it."

"You are sure about this?"

"Sometimes I wonder, Lord Bajrang, how naïve you can be."

He chuckled. "I have lived amongst honourable men. And now I don't. Hope was what I strived for. Hope was what I saw amongst people. But this is Kalyug. Not a day goes by without something catastrophic happening. You are right. We have to take action."

"And I want to help."

"But your mission?"

"I want to serve you, Lord Bajrang. I'll leave after that."

Shuko, on her shoulder, squawked as if trying to convey that this will be a waste of time but she didn't care. She was sure about her decision.

"All right. What do you suggest we do now?"

Padma thought about it deeply. "Go where the farmers went, and investigate. The men who did this, they must have left something behind. I'm sure."

"You think they were reckless?"

"Everyone gets reckless when they try to kill someone. Even the professionals." She smiled. "And you must ask yourself, who would use the wind to poison people?"

Lord Bajrang thought about this for a few minutes. "That is a good question. I should do my research on this. I'll get back to you if I find something. So you'll be leaving to investigate?"

"Yes."

"Be careful."

"I'll wear a mask to cover my nose and mouth. I'll be fine."

Padma was about to leave, but then she looked back at the Vanar king. "I also wanted to ask you something."

"Yes?" He looked up with hope.

"Why don't you help Kalki?"

"Eh?"

"Once he returns, I'm sure he would need your help to defeat the Adharm."

He shook his head. "My time is over."

"But you live here. The world gets affected and in this world, your Tribe lives. By helping Kalki, you will be helping your Tribe."

Lord Bajrang was stumped. He broke into a grin. "You bring up wise points, Padma. Let me think about that too. I want to help him, but his journey is different and my journey got over a long time back. But let me think on it."

Padma nodded, smiling back, and went outside. Shuko squawked again, but she fed him some grain that she had put in her waist pocket.

Sorry, Arjan. You have to wait.

5

"Before you show yourself off to the council," Nalakuvera had emphasised, "you need to show your face to the public." The political system in Indragarh was such that the king was elected through votes—fifty percent came from nobles and the rest was from the public.

Arjan had agreed. He was on the chariot now; it was rocking on the ground. Men on the streets followed. Guards strolled on their mares. Men, women, and children watched Arjan in awe as the flutes played and the drums beat.

The public hadn't forgetten the massive slaughter that had taken place the previous day. People watched Arjan in silence, curious and scared at the same time.

"They don't like me," Arjan whispered to Nalakuvera. His sword was up and his eyes were darting towards the public. He had been instructed to pose in this ridiculous manner by Nalakuvera's wife, Rambha, who was very good at handling public relations.

"They are just concerned. They elected the last queen and it didn't go as they had hoped. Plus, you stand with a Tribal. The Manavs have always looked at us with condescension and disdain."

Arjan shook his head. "Did you hear anything more about the attack?"

"Nothing new. The Nagas had been commanded to attack the city by their queen, Manasa. They are very far from here, but they are dangerous. And I feel their aim is to usurp the kingdom, rule over Indragarh. All we can do till the king is elected is to bring up barriers, and make the security stronger. The councilmen have agreed on this, but that may be so only because they don't care much about the city being secure. Their minds are focused on bringing their sons to power."

Arjan nodded. He didn't like the sound of it. The councilmen seemed obsessed with getting the throne for their children. *Once I become king, I will set them straight.*

"Also, when I mentioned in the meeting you'll be a candidate, they weren't happy."

"Of course. I'm a plebeian trying to be a king."

"It's not that." Nalakuvera looked at the people as the chariot moved ahead. He smiled and waved at them. "In the council, the head priest Guru Narendra also holds a seat. And he knows something about you. In fact, I'm sure he has been the one to start that rumour about you."

"What rumour?"

"That you liked another man," Nalakuvera said, concerned.

Arjan gritted his teeth. "Why is that a problem?"

"Ah, well, no one wants a sodomite ruler," he said nonchalantly. For a moment, Arjan wanted to bash his head for saying this. But Nalakuvera added, "Those were his words. Not mine. He's narrow-minded. And why wouldn't he be? The religion practised in the city talks of homosexuality like it's a disease."

Arjan was outraged. One of the reasons he wanted to be a king was so he could pass a bill that would allow all kinds of people, all kinds of ways, to be free of any religious intolerance.

"Kali was right about one thing."

"Which is?"

"Religion will be the death of us."

Nalakuvera chuckled. "One might argue that religion gives us hope."

"And also crushes it." Arjan shook his head as he lowered his sword. His arm was hurting. "I don't like Rambha's plan. I feel like a fool standing like this. People want ideas, not false ideals."

"They *think* they want ideas, good man, but they just want a hero. Anyone. Even a villain can take the guise of a god. They'll worship him if he acts like one. What Rambha has asked you to do will shape your godly image in the public eye. You look ethereal and well-groomed, I must say."

Arjan hadn't liked being scrubbed harshly by soap and being left in the warm water for hours. He had even had his hair rinsed and gelled with sap to have a clean, glimmering shine to it.

"But you are right." Nalakuvera surveyed the land around him, watching the people and their grim faces. "They need more than just a poster boy. They need to see action. They need to see what I see in you."

And that was when Arjan saw them.

A bunch of men entered the parade on huge black stallions, stopping right in front of Arjan's chariot. They were carrying serrated blades and were wearing black cloaks. Arjan noticed their dishevelled appearance. He also noticed how they were speaking to the people, pushing and pulling them apart.

"You don't deserve to be here, boy. We don't need a king like you," the man in the centre of the hooded men said.

Who are they?

And then he realised that they were Mlecchas—the outcasts and the misfits. Arjan had had a good and a bad experience with them.

And this was going to become yet another bad experience.

"Am I right?" the man in the centre yelled to the people. "He's a smartass who thinks he can use this Naga threat as a way to shine like a hero. He can't even fight his own battle."

Arjan flared his nostrils and looked at Nalakuvera. "Why are they interrupting the parade?"

"One doesn't know what Mlecchas usually want. They are paid by men. Perhaps, our opposition wants to demean us publicly."

Arjan couldn't let that happen. If the public got swayed by this man's words, it will blow his opportunity to be the king.

"Stop them from embarrassing us, for my sake," Nalakuvera whispered, worried.

"Throw him out. He doesn't belong in this city. He belongs outside," the man said, wary of the Yaksha guards who stood alert, ready to strike at Nalakuvera's orders. "He's weak and frail." He pulled out his spear. "See, everyone, what he does now." And then he flung his spear towards Arjan.

Arjan didn't even flinch. The spear was now stuck in between Arjan and Nalakuvera, dangling at the back of the carriage.

"See, he can't even fight back—"

The man stopped speaking. People gasped.

And Arjan saw the spear puncturing the face of the man, the one he had just flung back with precision.

The man died instantly. His body fell down from the horse.

"Goodness gracious," exclaimed Nalakuvera.

Arjan came off his chariot, his hands clenched as he looked at the other Mlecchas. "You can't let my opportunity go away like this. I will not let you do this."

One of the Mlecchas lurched from his horse and grabbed the nearest woman. "Hurt us, and she gets hurt."

Arjan shook his head. "Leave her."

The Mleccha still clung on to her.

Arjan tightened his fist and before the Mleccha could do anything, he sprinted towards him with incredible speed and ferocity. Arjan twisted the Mleccha's arm, letting his blade fall on the ground. The woman rushed into the crowd, relieved that she had managed to escape alive. Arjan punched the man, held him by the throat, and smashed his head on the ground.

And when he did so, the man's skull cracked. A huge hole had formed on the ground.

"Dear gods," the other Mlecchas exclaimed, scared to attack. They kicked their horses and rushed from the scene, fearing for their lives.

Arjan smiled, and as he panted, he heard someone in the crowd clap. And that clap evolved into a deafening applause.

"You did it." Nalakuvera's voice came from the back, and he was beaming.

"Yes." Arjan smiled.

"Just like today," Nalakuvera announced to the crowd as the applause died down, "as Lord Arjan, a man from the small village of Shambala, a civilian just like you all, stopped these mercenaries, he will stop the army that stands outside our city. He will stop the enemy that's ready to pounce on us. We need an able ruler, a strong warrior to lead us in these dark times, my friends. Don't let this opportunity go away. Speak to your houses, your nobles, your ministers, and tell them that instead of being nepotists, let someone deserving win the throne this time." He pointed at Arjan, bowing to him dramatically.

Oh, he's good.

People applauded again and Arjan could see a few people tearing up. He made his way to Nalakuvera on the chariot. "I don't think the council will like that," Nalakuvera whispered. "We are trying to gain votes through grief and tension of this city. But . . . well . . . to hell with them."

"Thank you." Arjan smiled, patting his friend on the shoulder.

"No, thank you." He smiled back. "I wanted them to see how powerful you are."

"What do you mean?" Arjan gave Nalakuvera a quizzical look.

"You didn't think the mercenaries happened to just barge in like that? Unfortunately, they had no idea of how powerful you are. That kind of information was purposefully left out, otherwise they would have squeaked and ran."

"I thought they had been paid by the opposition."

"This is politics, kid. They were paid, of course," he smiled, "but by me."

6

Kill her.

He looked at her peaceful face. It was golden in complexion. So beautiful.

Kill her.

If only he could strangle her. No one will know. No one will suspect him.

Kill her.

Nalakuvera shook his thoughts away. "No," he whispered to the voice of his mother.

She's an impediment in our plan.

"She's helping us." He glanced at his wife again, who was snoring softly. Night had fallen. A ray of silver light filtered in the room, dancing on the granite floor. Lamps burnt in the corner. "Like today."

That was a bad plan, son. Yours though, was genius.

Nalakuvera smiled. He knew it was. But Arjan hadn't been happy with it. He hadn't like being deceived, but then Nalakuvera was not here to make friends. He wanted to fashion Arjan into a god. An actual god.

He's our saviour. The one from the books. The one I told you stories about.

Nalakuvera remembered. The legend was that at the beginning of Kalyug, a hero will rise to fight evil. And the hero would be from the village of Shambala . . . just like Arjan.

Once he becomes our saviour, he will fight the evil that stands outside our gates. That snake lady!

Nalakuvera hated the Nagas. They were evil incarnate. The Yaksha lore spoke of them as the harbingers of the damnation of this world. They were the people who would start apocalypse.

The stories he had heard about the Naga atrociousness were coming to life. Hundreds had been slaughtered in the attack, just so that Naga queen could gain Indragarh.

The council didn't like what you said.

"It's all right. I have paid a few of them to stay silent."

That's good, his mother's voice rasped. *Also kill those who oppose you.*

"I shall."

Rambha fidgeted on her bed and turned her towards Nalakuvera. She was naked. A purple shawl was draped on her body.

And she looked angelic.

What did they want in the recent meet-up?

"Most of them say that they don't care about who's crowned, for now. They want to decide on battle strategies." He sighed. "I don't believe them, Mother. They also say they don't care about the throne but I know they are grooming their children to be suitable candidates."

Yes, I've taught you well.

"Some of them even want to surrender, give up arms, form a treaty with the enemy."

And what do you want?

"I don't know. I'm confused." Nalakuvera shook his head. "We don't have enough manpower to kill the Naga army. Intel says there are thousands of them. My spies were shivering while apprising me about their vast army. Only a miracle can save us. It is wise, then, to surrender, especially when these nobles are not united. They all have personal grudges and agendas. Some want to give their men to fight, and some don't. Some want their children to have the throne, some want to focus on war."

THEN UNITE THEM!

Nalakuvera's hands instantly shot up to hold his head. The voice had screamed. He wanted to shout back at his mother, but he refrained. "How?"

Use the saviour. Show that he's someone you cannot trifle with. He's a good instrument for your prosperous future. OUR future.

It would be hard to use Arjan like that since Arjan was quite smart. He might catch on to what Nalakuvera was planning. Arjan was also needlessly noble, but Nalakuvera had observed that there was intense anger and darkness in him too.

And then Nalakuvera heard it. As the voice in his head died down, the voice outside rasped. It was the growl of a wild animal. He could hear it gnawing at the flesh of the men outside, who yelped in agony.

Nalakuvera instantly went for his blade that he hid under his bed. He tried to wake up Rambha, who was fast asleep.

And then, the door opened.

Nalakuvera had expected it to blow up, but it just squeaked. Two figures in dark cloaks came inside with their respective beasts—gigantic, furry hyenas, having sharp teeth, their red eyes glimmering in the dark.

Behind these ominous figures, the corpses of his guards lay.

Nalakuvera looked at the cloaked figures. His voice was stuck in his throat and his heart was racing. He wanted to hear his mother's voice, even though he sometimes wished that the voice would go away.

"Who are you? What do you want?" Nalakuvera asked, gulping nervously. "There's a treasure chest. You can have it."

One of the cloaked figures whistled and the hyenas sat down. The taller one said, "I am not here for your money, Yaksha King.

I come here to make you aware of my presence. I have been in the kingdom for a while and I see what you are doing with that boy."

Arjan?

"You train him well. I want you to continue that."

"So you killed my guards just to inform me of the obvious?"

The other cloaked figure whistled and instantly the hyenas glared at Nalakuvera, baring their teeth. The blood of Nalakuvera's guards could still be seen in their mouths.

"Don't be snarky with me," the man said. "I come here for his good and for yours."

"What kind of good can you provide me other than commanding the hyenas that you have?"

And at that moment, the man removed the hood.

Even in his wildest dreams, Nalakuvera would not have been able to guess that *he* would be here.

He knew him very well.

"Kali," he breathed.

"Yes." His previously bald head was now filled with golden locks of hair.

The former king of Indragarh stood tall in front of Nalakuvera. "And I can provide you with something very important. For the sake of this city. And for the sake of the man you train."

7

As morning dawned, the village witnessed the arrival of a bunch of white-cloaked men.

Kalki had been sleeping in the stable, hidden from the villagers and from the sinister furry creature. The night before, when he and Kalki had come face to face, the bear-man had looked at him intently, as if he was studying him. He hadn't even blinked. And Kalki had been petrified.

That *look*! It was as if Jambavan had gotten himself inside Kalki's skin, torn apart his soul, and then left. And then, the moment Kalki thought Jambavan would attack, he had sprinted away with his food.

It was strange. He hadn't done anything. Kalki had wanted to leave the village that moment but there had been a storm outside. Moreover, the bear-man could be anywhere. Afraid, Kalki had run back to the safety of the stable, and fallen into a fitful sleep.

It was morning now. The stable master was poking Kalki with a stick. It was the old man who had given him shelter the previous night. Kalki didn't even know his name.

"You can leave now, boy. My help only extends for one night," the man said, grunting.

Kalki thought of telling him what he had seen last night. *The old man deserves to know his god exists. He helped me, even though he didn't have to.*

"I saw him."

"Who?"

"Your god."

And at that moment, the old man's face went pale. "How is that possible? He never shows himself."

"But he did. I saw. He took some food too."

"Yes, our offerings to the statue have vanished." The old man had passed by the statue on his way to the stable. "Tell me more. What did he look like?"

"He . . . had black eyes, darker than the night." Kalki shivered. He had never felt so frightened by someone. He had fought in a couple of wars, engaged in battles with the mightiest men out there, but the very look of that bear-man brought some deep-seated fear out of him. He had felt like the frightened child that he once used to be.

People thought he had always been strong. But he hadn't. He used to be quite weak when he was a child, and he had had no friends. And he had been unaware of the power he possessed.

Things had changed when Kalki had become a big brother. Things had gotten better. Kalki had stopped falling ill, gradually, and began bossing around his younger brother, Arjan. He stopped feeling lonely and miserable. Though Arjan had been a cheeky brat, always getting praised by their father. Sometimes, Kalki had been jealous of him. He was the smart one, the responsible one. All Kalki had was brutish strength, and he hadn't even possessed this when he was a child.

And that look by the bear-man, brought all of this back.

"You have no idea what great news you have given me. For so long, we thought he didn't exist. Our faith had dwindled."

"But you offered him food."

"And we thought the robbers had been stealing it. Deep down, we had lost faith in his existence and now you have come as a blessing. You saw him!" He grinned and seeing the old, grunting man smile like that, brought a smile on Kalki's face too. "We are surrounded by marauders, by animals of all kinds, and we lack the weaponry to support ourselves. We can't even ask for the support of others since there is no other village in the hills. Even the weather is not kind to us—a storm rages here every other day." Tears brimmed in the old man's eyes.

Kalki smiled. The description of this village very much reminded him of Shambala, his homeland.

"If only Lord Jambavan had helped us, we would have prospered as a village. We would be safe. But he doesn't help. I'm sure he has his reasons. But if only he did it, it would be great." The old man couldn't contain his happiness. "Thank you. Thank you so much, son. I have to tell the village headman that you saw him. I have to tell everyone. It is a miracle! Do you know that?" The old man kissed Kalki on the forehead and fled.

Kalki stayed there for a while, thinking, when he heard Devadatta's voice in his head:

Your mission was not to save a village, kid. Let's leave.

But it feels nice to give hope to people.

Sure, but Adharm is rising and I don't want you to get lost in helping everyone on the way. We don't have that much time.

Kalki nodded. The white horse was right. He came on his feet and grabbed the reins. And as they departed from the stable and came outside, they saw the white-cloaked men were waiting.

They were standing at some distance from the bear statue, in a semicircle. The villagers were observing them curiously. The old man was not there, but Kalki was sure that he must be witnessing this strange spectacle from somewhere around.

The white-cloaked men had a strange circular symbol on their cloth and their faces were hidden under their hoods. All of them were carrying weapons—lances, to be precise—and they were directed towards Kalki.

Why are so many strange things happening to me?

Beats me, Devadatta answered.

"You are needed, Avatar of Vishnu," one man's voice boomed.

"By whom?"

"Lord Bhargav Ram. He mentioned you sought shelter here. We are here to escort you to his temple."

Kalki nodded, feeling secured. Perhaps, Lord Bhargav, after knowing about Jambavan, had sent his men to help Kalki in fighting the monster if he tried to attack him.

But yesterday, he had fled.

"Let's go."

On his way with the group of white-cloaked men, he felt something strange.

He had a splitting headache again, and he could see images of his previous Avatars being formed in front of him. The images appeared and then swiftly disappeared. The pain was getting unbearable.

This is killing me.

"Appearances can be deceiving," Lord Vaman's voice boomed in his head.

Kalki blinked hard, controlling himself, taking deep breaths, letting his mind calm down. He tried to focus.

Focus on what they are saying.

And slowly the pain began to reduce and he could feel his heartbeat slow down.

Focusing is important. Channelling must be controlled and contained.

He knew his powers were growing. No matter what, he must discipline his mind and control his ever-increasing powers. If he didn't, he was sure that his headaches would get worse. And the pain might even kill him.

I can't let the Avatars control me. I can't let Channelling do this to me. I should be the one contacting the Avatars, not the other way around.

And as they walked along the ridge, Kalki opened his eyes. He could see the path was steep. Horses were lined behind him. Standing near the ridge, he could see the wide landscape of the place from which he had begun travelling up the mountain.

Everything looked so small from here.

He couldn't believe he had travelled so far. Somehow, it made him feel successful. He was mentally patting himself on the back for being able to come so far, when he noticed something.

Some snow had fallen from above him.

He looked up to see the looming shadow . . .

. . . OF JAMBAVAN!

There was a deafeaning roar. The sound echoed in the hills.

Instantly Jambavan lurched from his position and onto the white-cloaked men, grabbing them and attacking them with his long claws. The men attacked him, but he overpowered them with ease. He pushed some of them from the cliff and threw their bodies against the ground. Kalki looked at Jambavan properly this time. He had a huge body—thick and furry.

The horses were riled up. They neighed and threw their masters on the ground.

Lances were pulled out and poked at the bear-man but Kalki saw Jambavan breaking them with his huge, strong hands.

He has come for me.

He wants to kill me.

Kalki instantly pulled out his sword and leapt from his horse towards the bear-man, even though his hands were shaking from fear.

"Come here, you!" Kalki yelled at Jambavan.

Jambavan turned to look at Kalki. His beady eyes watched him intently, and for a moment, he snarled. At that instant, the white-cloaked men began stabbing and slashing!

The attack came from the back and there was a loud cry from Jambavan, before he began to bleed. Blood sprayed on the snow, looking so pure and red.

Jambavan grabbed the lances and pounced at the white-cloaks, and then . . .

HE LEAPT!

He hurled himself off the cliff. Kalki instantly sprinted towards it, looking to see if Jambavan had fallen to his death. But he couldn't see his body anywhere.

Many white-cloaks had been severely wounded, while some had managed to run away when Jambavan had attacked. The injured ones were put on the horses. They would be tended to at the temple, and everyone got ready to continue their journey.

As Kalki peered down from the cliff, he wondered whether Jambavan was still around, waiting for another chance to finish Kalki for good.

8

She had planned for another attack at night. They were going to storm the fortresses of Indragarh, kill the bowmen who stood at the top, steal from their treasuries, and burn their shops.

Deplete them. Bleed them.

That was the idea.

Manasa's spies had told her that security had been beefed up but the western gates were still weak. She had studied the structure of the city with the spies who acted as traders in Indragarh, who provided her with information about the goings-on of the city.

A day had passed, and so far, there had been no response from the enemy. *Kali must be pacing around in his fortress, uncertain of what to do.* And before he could respond in kind, or parley for a peace treaty, she would attack again.

But as she was planning in her tent, there was another issue.

"My lady, it's happening. As we expected. Squad three, who specialises in night combat, is refusing to assist in the next attack. The leader of the squad wants an audience with you," Airavan said.

"General, it's not my duty to control your men."

He lowered his gaze. She could see that he was feeling angry because of the way she had just spoken to him, but he was trying to control himself.

Just like a true soldier.

"Who is this man?"

"He's a captain. Jaratkaru," Airavan said. "He's very talented. He has been a soldier since Lady Kadru's reign. I'm afraid he and his men are conspiring with other squads to rebel against you if you don't give them what they need."

"Where are they?" Manasa was fuming.

Airavan signalled her to follow and as she did, she walked with her head held high—like a queen. There had been a time when she had had to struggle to win the throne. She had to fight her cousin and overcome many obstacles. She had lost a loved one. Poor Nanda. She had labelled him a womaniser, but he had always been in love with her.

She had faced so much.

And now Jaratkaru was another one of her issues.

She waded her way through tents, and saw a lot of soldiers were training. And in the centre of the soldiers stood Jaratkaru—a small, young man with sleek black hair and a puffy moustache, directing his men to practise fighting with spears.

On seeing Manasa, they all sprang in attention. Jaratkaru did too. After all, he was a soldier. But he did not fear the queen.

"I hear you have an issue with me."

Jaratkaru shook his head. "Not with you, Your Majesty. We have an issue with rules. When we pledged allegiance to you, we thought we would get what we want, but we have been left high and dry here. The Manav camp is filled with Apsaras, while ours doesn't have a single woman. It is a war tradition to have—"

"Women as sex objects?" She raised her brows and he lowered his head.

"It's how it's always been. At least when Lady Kadru was queen."

Lady? She was a monster and Manasa knew that. "So if I don't give you that, you won't fight?"

Jaratkaru hesitated. "Your Majesty, we do as you please. All we need in return is a little bit entertainment. I'm sure you can help us so we can carry our attacks swiftly. The last one had been led by me and both of us know how smoothly it was executed."

Jaratkaru seemed like a driven, disciplined man to Manasa. But the men behind him, the men of his squad, were not like him.

Airavan stepped closer, whispering to Manasa, "Your Majesty, I can talk to the Manav guards to send some Apsaras here. It won't take a—"

She shot him a look as she began to round all the soldiers. Right now they were bare-chested, and were carrying spears and blades in their hands. Manasa glared at them, her big blue eyes shimmering in the daylight.

She wanted to say something. She wanted to yell and scream and put the rebels inside the prisons to rot. But Jaratkaru had a point. They were a *talented* bunch. If she enforced a rule they didn't like, she risked losing them, and the men would think she is a tyrant.

"Fine," she looked at Jaratkaru and Airavan, "if you don't want to help me in my crusade, then don't. I'll seek help from our ally."

A surprised look washed over their faces. All the soldiers had thought that she would agree to their demand.

And then she left, leaving the shocked, disappointed soldiers behind.

As Manasa entered the Manav camp for the second time in two days, she heard the Manav soldiers whisper.

"She's weak."

"Keeps coming to ask for help."

"Lord Vibhishan shouldn't have sided with her. We are on the losing side."

"It's good we don't indulge ourselves in petty fights."

The men didn't stop mumbling but she didn't say a word,

trying hard to keep a lid on her anger that threatened to burst out at any moment. She looked at Airavan, who rode next to her silently.

"What if I lock up Jaratkaru for insubordination?" she asked him.

He gazed at her, worried, but tried to voice his thoughts carefully. "Your Majesty, it would be a blunder. Jaratkaru is a talented fellow. And plus, a captain. Putting him in prison would affect us in the war. And what if the other soldiers rebel in anger? Jaratkaru is respected by them. What you say will be done. You are the queen, and we are the pawns. But the pawns, at the end, are more in number and the queen is only one. They won't follow you if they don't respect you."

Manasa was growing more and more angry as she heard Airavan speak, but she grudgingly had to admit that he had a point. All of these—the Suparns, Nagas, and even the Manavs—followed her because she had defeated Kadru, saved Tarakshya, and formed an alliance with Vibhishan.

She entered Vibhishan's tent after dismounting from her stallion, to find him yet again amidst his books. But this time, he was also feeding himself grapes as he studied.

"If only you fought in the war as intently as you read," she said and Vibhishan got alarmed. In his haste, he slipped and fell from his cot. Finally, he stood up and laughed at his clumsiness. "Well, I was deep into this memoir written by Lady Prameela which had been bought by my father. Lady Prameela had worked as a scribe after Lord Raghav had defeated Lord Raavan. She was the wife of Lord Meghnad, the son of Raavan, and she speaks at length about their relationship and his love for nuclear bombs. He was a physicist."

"I wonder if this Ancient even existed." Manasa had always been a skeptic. People talked of and read about Ancients and immortals, but they were only mythical figures according to her. "Isn't he considered a sorcerer of some kind?"

"People are mistaken about that, unfortunately. He was a

scientist, a brilliant visionary. Lord Meghnad was a bit of a maverick though, but a passionate lover and an ardent follower of Raavan. Apparently, he died fighting for him at the hands of Lord Lakshman. Quite a fellow, isn't he?"

Manasa smiled. Vibhishan always got excited discussing a book he liked. This had not changed in all the years she had known him.

Suddenly, he straightened up. "But I digress. You have come for the second time in two days, my dear. What is happening? Is everything fine?"

"It's the same issue." She reached for the wine bottle, and poured some wine for herself in a gemmed goblet. "They want Apsaras for their pleasure."

"Ah, well. I thought you must have given in. Why don't you?"

"Because . . ." she clenched her jaw.

"Because you are a woman, isn't it?" He smiled warmly. "And you don't like to do anything in your camp that degrades your sex."

Manasa didn't say anything, but she knew he was right. She had fought and clawed so much to show that a woman can be strong, that she can be a good leader. How could she condone other women being treated like sex objects then?

"The world is a dangerous place, my dear. There are things—traditions, rules, people—that you must learn to accept. Fighting them would only hurt yourself." Vibhishan looked at Manasa with pity. "That is why I think you should give the men what they want."

And it's safe. Vibhishan has always been about being safe and nothing else. But Manasa didn't want to say this to her only ally. She bit her tongue, quelling her frustration and anger.

"I want your help," she began. "It's a foolproof plan. I have mapped out—"

He shook his head, keeping the book aside. "No, no, my dear. I told you, I won't take your side on this. There has been no response from them. Not even a message. I won't send my men in a fight where the opposition doesn't even know what's happening. I'm sorry."

"But they could be planning something."

"Let them. I told you. I made it clear that I will only interfere when it's necessary and you agreed."

Manasa lowered her gaze.

"Did you or did you not agree, my dear?" Vibhishan asked, his voice firm. For a few seconds Manasa didn't speak. She was getting red with embarrassment, feeling like a child being reprimanded for making a silly mistake.

"I did."

"You *did* agree. So why did you think I would help you?" He shrugged, chuckling like a boy. "What you are doing is planning unnecessary attacks and we both know it will have devastating consequences. Now, do we want that?"

Exasperated on being talked down to, Manasa stood up, nodded at Vibhishan, and left the tent. Airavan stood outside, humming a song under his breath. She scanned the colourful, vibrant camp spread out in front of her.

Finally, Manasa made up her mind.

"Do it," she said to her general.

The general gawked at her. "Your Majesty?"

"Do it," she repeated. Manasa had decided to take Vibhishan's advice, even though she was far from okay with it. They had to win this war. "Get the Apsaras. Transfer them. I'll sign the papers and I'm sure Vibhishan would be very happy to oblige to it as well."

"I take it he didn't support you," Airavan added, carefully choosing his words.

Manasa clenched her jaw. "No, he didn't." She looked at her general and for the first time, she saw pity in his eyes. "But then, I didn't know why I expected he would."

9

Padma knew she would find something.

The moment they reached the area where the Vanars had gone to collect herbs, they could feel that the air felt . . . off.

Padma wrapped a cloth around her mouth and nose as she studied the air. Layers of fur coiled her body, keeping her warm as they waded through the snow. Majestic, snow-capped mountains loomed over the hill. The land was enveloped in greenery, with rays of the sun's golden light cascading on the grass. The pathway twinkled as if the stars were littered on the ground.

Padma's eyes were drawn to the never-ending snowy wasteland. The wind wasn't harsh in this area probably because of the trees.

"Dead horses," said Ratna Maru from the back, pointing at the carcasses of stallions on the ground.

Padma had not wanted Ratna Maru to come with her to investigate, but the Apsara had insisted. She wanted to see for herself how one could release poisonous smoke bombs in the air.

"I want to learn about this technique so I can use it myself someday," Ratna Maru had callously said, and Padma had grunted in response.

This was an important mission. Sometimes Padma felt that Ratna Maru was self-centred, focusing on only what was better for her Tribe. Padma had been like her at a point in her life, only thinking about herself, but she was not that person anymore. She had grown to be someone who would help others selflessly.

Kalki and Arjan taught me that.

A few Vanars had accompanied Padma. Smrit, Ratna Maru's right-hand girl, had chosen to come as well. They were all studying the campsite, hoping to find something.

Padma whispered to Shuko, who was perched on her shoulder, "Go, look for a trace of any other camp around us."

Shuko instantly flew in the air. He was a strange parrot with unimaginable powers. And Kalki had mentioned to Padma how to use him well—like sending him out to check for any enemies who might be lurking nearby.

"There's nothing of consequence here, girl," said Ratna Maru, her voice muffled against the shawl wrapped around her mouth. "I believe it's a fool's errand."

"You give up too easily, don't you?" Padma said, irritated.

"Me? Give up? Never!" she exclaimed. "If I gave up so easily, my mission would be futile."

Padma began searching the tents. The cots were empty as expected. "Your mission? What kind of mission do you exactly follow? All you are doing is poking your nose in other people's business. Have you ever asked the Apsaras what they actually want? What if they don't want to be free?"

Ratna Maru squared her shoulders and came close to Padma, her eyes menacing. "Be careful of what you say in front of me, girl. Do you think any woman *wants* to be a sex slave?"

Padma instantly regretted what she had said. She had spoken without thinking.

"We will separate our rucksacks. After this mission is over, you should go to Indragarh on your own. I thought it'd be nice to travel with you, but I've changed my mind." Ratna Maru clicked her tongue, muttering, "I thought we could be friends."

Padma sighed. "Sorry. I didn't mean what I said."

Ratna Maru gave her a sad smile. "It's okay. Whatever anyone thinks, I won't be deterred from my mission. There will come a day when I would have freed all Apsaras in Illavarti."

"And then what?"

Ratna Maru was silent for a few seconds. "What do you mean?"

"You have to stop somewhere, right?"

"I will. Once I emancipate all Apsaras and once I have my husband's killer's head on my lap. That is the day I will sit back and perhaps smoke some pipe and drink some ale. But till then, I fight. Each day."

"Husband?" Padma asked, surprised, and it sounded like she was thinking, *You don't seem like someone who would have a husband.* Though Padma didn't voice this out, it seemed like Ratna Maru understood what Padma meant.

"Yes, he was murdered. By his own brother. Nalakuvera. Engrave that name in your mind. One day, you will hear the news that he was butchered by me, that I paraded his severed head in the streets and distributed his money amongst the poor."

"Vengeance often ends up causing more suffering to the one who's executing it," Padma said. "I used to think like you, but I've changed."

"He *killed* my husband! It is only fitting that he pays for it with his life."

Padma wanted to change her mind, but knew that she won't be able to. She reminded herself that Ratna Maru was no one to her. *But then, hadn't Arjan helped me think straight even though I was no one to him?*

That was when Shuko appeared out of the blue, breaking through the clouds and sitting on Padma's palm.

"WEST! WEST! WEST!" the parrot squawked.

Ratna Maru and Padma looked at each other.

"Why would a camp be in the middle of nowhere?"

Padma smiled. "I think we may have just found our enemy."

They walked a few miles to the west and reached the tent. It was close to the Vanar campsite, where the towering trees ended. The tent lay abandoned. Charred fire logs were in front it, the tent itself was tattered in places, and a man's clothes were lying on the ground. As if this wasn't strange enough, a small hole had been dug on the left side of the tent, filled with wet hay.

"Seems like a hunter's site." Ratna Maru sighed. "Your parrot had a false alarm."

Shuko squawked at her, trying to convey that he hadn't.

Padma smiled when Shuko continued to squawk angrily at Ratna Maru, but then she directed her attention at the hole. There was some green pigment in it and it had a pungent smell. The smell got stronger when she pulled out the hay.

Ratna Maru groaned. The other Vanars backed off.

Coughing slightly, Padma looked down at the hole. There was some dry ice and water with strange leaves inside.

"I think I have figured out how they created the smoke." She pointed at the leaf, showing it to everyone. "It belonged to the culprit. This is wolfsbane. I remember it from one of my botanical courses."

"Botanical courses?" Ratna Maru asked. "Botany is taught to the nobles' children, as far as I know. Are you a princess?"

Damn!

Padma shrugged. "Of course not. I *stole* a book from a princess. I like to read." She had to lie. No one knew she was King Vibhishan's daughter.

"They took some dry ice, used some hot water, and voila! They got the smoke which they directed towards the camp of the Vanars.

It was close by." She pointed at the clothes. "Whoever did it, threw his stained clothes and left."

"Too much effort to attack a few farmers, don't you think?" Ratna Maru asked.

Padma shook her head. "It's not that. What worries me is that they knew that Vanars were resting here. That means they must have followed them. That means they *really* wanted to kill them."

"They? The hunt seems like a one-person job."

"Look at that." Padma pointed to the hoofprints at the back of the tent. "There are so many of them."

"Gods, this is troubling."

"You bet."

Padma straightened and looked around, scanning the place when she saw someone—a man atop a horse, far away from them. He was wearing a mask on his face that had horns protruding out of it. The mask was twisted and dark and had large, painted eyes. Everything about the rider seemed off.

He was staring at them.

He was staring at *her*.

Padma had returned to Lord Bajrang's cabin with the full story.

Ratna Maru was standing beside her as Padma described what she had seen. Lord Bajrang was sititng on his chair, listening intently.

"They know about us. They *wanted* us to find the tent." Padma gritted her teeth. "That's why they had a scout placed, to check whether we would come or not."

"You said he was wearing a horned mask?" he asked. "That's strange. It reminds me of something."

"What?"

Lord Bajrang stood up and walked towards his small, unkempt library. A lot of leatherbound books could be seen in it. He pulled one out and began to flip through it as he spoke. "Since you had asked me, Padma, to think of someone who would use wind as their weapon, I started researching. And now I believe, after your account, I feel we can come to a conclusion."

He showed her a page from the book which had a large photograph of a mask. It had grey fur around it, with the same painted eyes she had seen earlier, a jackal-like mouth, and large, goat-like horns.

"This was the mask. What is it?" Padma asked. "What does the book say about it?"

"This mask is worn by the Sons of Shiva. They used to be a majestic warrior class who worked as soldiers at Indra's palace in Swarg, until they became extinct and dispersed, forming small tribes of their own, growing insane after the Breaking. They are trouble seekers and worshippers of Virabhadra—the angry, fearsome form of Lord Shiva."

Padma pursed her lips. She looked at Ratna Maru who looked equally perturbed.

Lord Bajrang announced, "They were once called Maruts. But now, they go by the name of Rudras and if they are here in this part of the country, they *really* want something from us. And we need to figure out *what*, as fast as possible."

10

Arjan slammed his shield against his trainer.

The trainer fell back, rolled over, and then jumped on his feet. He leapt towards Arjan, who blocked his attack with his shield. Arjan brought his blade forward, trying to injure his trainer a little, but the trainer pulled out his sword to deflect the attack.

There was a huge clang as they parried.

"Hit me from the left," the trainer yelled and instantly landed a blow at Arjan's chest, pushing him back as he somersaulted on the sand. "You are distracted, child."

Arjan was on the ground just outside Nalakuvera's fortress with his white-bearded sword master, who was not really happy with his performance today.

"Can we take a break?" Arjan panted as he knelt.

The trainer nodded. "Five minutes." And then he went inside the fortress, perhaps to the bathing room.

Arjan wiped his sweat as he lay on the sand, wondering how he used to detest all of this, and now he was practising it. He was always buried in books back then. It had been years now since he had read one. The last one he had flipped through was the one that had been given to him by the street vendor, Amar.

I should read it properly.

"You look exhausted, my friend. Are you up for another match?"

Arjan straightened up when he saw Nalakuvera coming out of his fortress, looking royal in his golden-coloured overcoat. He was carrying a double-bladed spear in his hand.

"*You* want to fight me? A privileged brat who is busy playing god to his Tribe?" Arjan spat. He didn't want to see the Yaksha king's face. After the stunt Nalakuvera had pulled, Arjan had felt like a fool.

"Are you still angry?"

"You used me." Arjan got up, gripping his sword and flexing his muscles. "I am not some toy you can play around with."

"I just wanted the world to see—"

"You wanted to let innocents die!"

"They were Mlecchas, Arjan. They are . . . dispensable."

"No life is dispensable." Arjan yelled, furious. "Every life is important."

"I'm sure it is." Nalakuvera rolled his eyes. "Fight me."

"I won't."

Nalakuvera didn't listen or wait. He hurled himself forward, bringing his spear next to Arjan.

Arjan dodged, rolling on the ground. "You don't want this."

"I want to know why you keep practising day and night," Nalakuvera said. "Whenever I call you, you are here. What do you sweat out? Your frustration? Your anger? Towards whom?"

Arjan flared his nostrils. Ever since Rudra had died, he had liked being here. The sand . . . it reminded him of the first day Rudra had taught him how to wrestle.

Arjan had not mourned Rudra's death. He had not cried when he had lain his dead body on the pyre. The grief and anger he had felt then, that he still felt today, was forgotten whenever he fought.

"I don't have to tell you anything."

Nalakuvera aimed to attack Arjan with his blade again and Arjan couldn't dodge this time. There was a cut on his shoulder now.

Arjan gritted his teeth. He tried to attack Nalakuvera again and again, but Nalakuvera had nimble feet.

"I am not as privileged as you think. I lost my mother long time back. My father killed her."

"I'm sure you loved him even more after that."

"He did it because she was an Apsara. Dispensible."

"Makes you think if your mother is, so is everyone else, right?" And he instantly brought his blade forward. Nalakuvera rolled away, the sand falling on his back.

"I never thought about it that way. You may be right." Nalakuvera grinned. He started moving his spear from one hand to the other. Arjan looked at him, confused, trying to gauge how Nalakuvera was going to attack.

Nalakuvera brought the spear close to Arjan's abdomen, and pushed the spear up, letting the blade knock on his nose.

Arjan's hand shot up to his bleeding nose.

"The councilmen have called for a meeting. I'm going there now and I have a plan, Arjan. I plan to unite all the noblemen and convince them that we should fight the enemy lurking outside our city." He paused. "And I want you to stand there with me, when I formally announce my candidate—you."

"Not after the stunt you pulled."

"I'm sorry I went behind your back. I wouldn't do that again. I promise."

Arjan didn't believe a word of what the Yaksha king had said. Nalakuvera, like his father Kuvera, was a slimy fellow. "Why do you want to go in battle?"

"If we don't, it will be the end of us. The way the city was attacked, I don't think the snake queen will accept a peace treaty." Nalakuvera slid his hand over his spear as he said, "An eye for an eye. Though there is one issue."

"What?"

"The councilmen are divided on what should be done. Some

of them don't want a war, so they won't give us their men. If we convince them to unite, the probability of us triumphing over this enemy will increase. Our army doesn't have enough men."

"And uniting them is impossible," Arjan brought his blade forward and the spear and the sword clashed. "You know it. I know it."

"No, it's won't be impossible if you become king. If they have someone like you, scaring them, frightening them, they will bend the knee."

Arjan pulled back. *Will they fear me?* "What if they don't vote for me?"

"I don't think that will happen. I always see the brighter side of things, dear." He paused, panting. "The only way to attack the snake army is by uniting the banners. And the more we delay, the worse it gets. My spies say that the snake woman is planning another attack. Perhaps in a day or two. How many lives will we lose? I don't know."

Arjan didn't want that. He balled his hands into fists. He didn't want to see any more deaths. He was about to speak when Nalakuvera put the spear down and clapped his hands.

A guard appeared from the fortress with a cushion on his hands.

No. It can't be.

"I believe it's yours." Nalakuvera picked up the weapon kept on the cushion. "I remember you told me about it over dinner a few weeks ago. How you had lost it when Kali trapped you in his prison. I went through the prison and talked to the warden and got it for you. Your mother's gift."

Arjan came forward, dropping his blade and looking at the sickle his mother had given him. Teary-eyed, he picked it up, brushing his hand on the burnt edge.

Arjan clutched the sickle for a few seconds, remembering the day his mother had gifted it to him. He was about to express his gratitude when Nalakuvera turned to leave.

"If you believe in what I say, do come to the meeting," he said, and went into his fortress, sure that his play had worked.

11

Why isn't he here yet?

Nalakuvera waited for Arjan but the councilmen were getting antsy. They couldn't wait anymore.

The room was filled with many banners, many noblemen and their clerks and advisors. Some had even brought their sons and daughters.

They looked frantic with worry.

"Can we begin?" one of the nobles asked.

Nalakuvera nodded. A hush fell over the crowd.

He will come, his mother said. *Just go with what you have to say and don't let them know about Kali's plan.*

He won't. But he was excited for Kali had returned and he had something big planned for the city.

"Are you sure?" he said, his voice barely above a whisper to prevent anyone from noticing that he was talking to himself.

Yes. You continue.

Nalakuvera believed in his mother's words. They were right, most of the time.

He sighed as he looked at the people he was addressing. "Thank you everyone for coming today. We all know why we are here, in the council chamber, with our deadliest generals. An army that slaughtered the people of our city two days ago stands outside Indragarh. We have received information that they will attack again. It is imperative that we come up with a plan of action. And there is another matter that needs our attention—who will be crowned king?"

One nobleman said, "Of course you still care about the crown. We all know what you planned with that sodomite on the day of the parade. It was pure buffoonery, the wrong time to pull off such a stunt."

"I didn't do anything. People wanted a hero, so I gave them one."

The nobles began to whisper amongst themselves.

Don't let this get away from you, his mother's voice boomed.

"I fill the treasury with my coins. I should be worried about who rules over it."

"And we are grateful, Lord Nalakuvera," another noble said. "We truly are, but right now, dealing with the enemy takes precedence over deciding who should be king, don't you think?"

"Of course," he said, lowering his head. *Here we go.* "We should unite. Use our army and declare war."

The councilmen became quiet. They looked at each other, uncertain.

"But Lord Nalakuvera, son of Lord Kuvera, we are small houses. We have small armies and—"

"I don't think each house having two hundred men would be considered a small army." Nalakuvera grinned, cutting short the nobleman.

"But even if we give our men to the royal army, they still won't be enough," another noble said. "That's why we had requested that your men, the Yakshas, guard the city."

"Which went poorly," someone from the crowd mumbled.

Nalakuvera flared his nostrils, but managed to remain silent.

"And if we combine our armies," the nobleman continued, "we will be left dry in the city."

Nalakuvera recognised this noble. His name was Amreesh. He had amassed a lot of money by heading the gambling dens in the city. Not as much as Nalakuvera, of course.

"I propose," Lord Amreesh stood up and began pacing, his pot belly jiggling as he did so, "we surrender. Ask them what they want. If it is truly the land they are after, maybe they'll settle for ruling over a portion of the city. They might even back down if we give them money."

Nalakuvera didn't want that, but he could see people were thumping their table. Out of the corner of his eye, he noticed Guru Narendra, the head priest of the temples—a short man with flowing white hair and beard, and a fierce look in his eyes. Though he was not a noble, he was a councilman since he represented the religion of the city.

Guru Narendra didn't bang the table. He just looked at Nalakuvera, his grey eyes stony as ever.

"They want something," Lord Amreesh continued. "We ask what it is and we give. Sure, if we had still been under Lord Vedanta or hell, even Lord Kali, we could have easily fought them. But this city has been shifting rulers like a pack of cards. We are weak. The soldiers in Indragarh have tremendously depleted since all the previous rulers were hell-bent on carrying out their crusades, without caring about how many soldiers lost their lives. We are in no position to fight."

Nalakuvera knew that not having enough men was not going to be a problem. But he couldn't reveal this to anyone right now.

He was thinking of what to say when there was a loud bang on the door.

The door opened and Arjan entered the room. He looked beautiful in his pristine white tunic and a black dhoti.

"And what if this enemy destroys our land and the army that you so cling on to once you offer them something? What if they are just madmen? We can't predict what this enemy will do," said Arjan.

Lord Amreesh chuckled. "And a brawler enters. This is a council meeting, son. You don't belong here."

Arjan glanced at Nalakuvera and smiled. Nalakuvera could see the sickle dangling from Arjan's cloth belt.

"I called him here. I thought it would be a good opportunity to tell you that I would like to nominate Arjan as a contestant for the kingship, for the crown."

"And why is he fit to be king?" Everyone turned to look at Guru Narendra. His loud voice reverberated in the room.

"Frankly, Guruji," Arjan said, "I was adviser to the last queen. And I come from a small village, so I know the grievances of the people, even the minute ones. I'm even morally corrupt to please all of you." He chuckled.

They all gasped in horror for being called corrupt. But Nalakuvera looked at Arjan approvingly. He was speaking with such confidence.

He was being . . . himself.

"But most of all, I want to protect the people of the city. During Queen Urvashi's reign, the people had suffered so much. Her stringent policies and the hike in taxes had filled the coffers but robbed the common man. And I just can't bear to let some outsider, some Naga, a *Tribal* of all people, threaten *us*. I say we come together and we fight." There was a broad smile on Arjan's face as he said, "And I would like to remind everyone that the treasury is filled with money; it is only fair that if you decide to give us men to fight, you be handsomely paid." Arjan looked around the room, noticing that some of the nobles were nodding vigorously at this statement.

"Let me lead you. Not as a king, but as a probable one. And let me prove it to you that I have it in me to be an able ruler."

All the councilmen were looking at each other. Lord Amreesh stood still, unsure of what to say next. Guru Narendra remained impassive. There was complete silence for a few seconds. But then Guru Narendra spoke up. "You killed the queen, Arjan. The councilmen had prospered during Queen Urvashi's reign."

Nalakuvera spoke up promptly. "Let bygones be bygones. Arjan is right. We need to unite. And we need to not worry about being threatened but focus on being a considerable threat to our enemy."

Lord Amreesh scoffed. "I still believe we should extend an olive branch. And I certainly don't want to be led by a sodomite. He has no experience, and frankly, he seems like a weak fellow. Who is with me?"

Before anyone could bang on the table, Arjan ran to Lord Amreesh and pushed him away. Surprised, the noble lost his balance and fell on the floor.

Lord Amreesh's son yelped in horror. The guards now closed around Arjan, ready to attack.

Arjan was quick to pull out his sickle and put it close to Lord Amreesh's throat. "Move closer and I will kill him."

The guards stepped back.

"Still think I'm weak?" Arjan darted his eyes at everyone, but Nalakuvera noticed that his gaze lingered on Guru Narendra. "I have powers greater than Kali. All you great nobles witnessed my match with him. Not only was I bold enough to challenge him, but I almost defeated him that day. My strength and agility are unmatched." Arjan paused for a few seconds. He had to address the elephant in the room.

"Some of you see me as a killer. And it's true, I did strangle Queen Urvashi, but I did it because she had killed someone innocent. And after that I realised that for there to be justice, talking or asking *nicely* wasn't going to work anymore. If we surrender to this threat, we might not lose but we would be losers because we would not be avenging the innocent souls who were slaughtered by the enemy. The person who led the attack deserves to die. Understood? We can worry about who becomes the king after we kill the snake queen. Who's with me?"

The nobles nodded in unison, afraid.

"Good." He turned to Nalakuvera, who was grinning from ear to ear. "How do we proceed, my lord?" Arjan winked.

Nalakuvera nodded. "We combine our armies . . ." and he began to tell his plan, all the while knowing that Guru Narendra's cold, unwavering gaze was on Arjan.

But Nalakuvera couldn't help but be ecstatic. His mother was feverishly applauding him, saying, *I told you he will do it. He's the saviour. And you made him one.*

12

That night, a feast was organised as the Apsaras were brought in the Naga camp.

Manasa was present at the feast, but she kept her distance from the soldiers. They were dancing, playing music, beating drums, and revelling with Apsaras. Manasa could clearly see the women were uncomfortable. But she could do nothing to help them and it was driving her crazy.

The soldiers clearly had no respect for her. Manasa felt like they had agreed to serve her just because she had given them what they wanted.

She tapped the wine glass in her hand, and one of her guards came forward to refill it.

Manasa was standing under a giant oak tree, observing the spectacle in front of her. The war camp had finally come alive, much like Vibhishan's camp.

Did I do the right thing by getting bullied?

Her eyes fell on Airavan. He stood at some distance from her, away from all the hustle-bustle, quietly observing all the men.

She walked towards him. When she got close, he instantly bowed.

"At ease," she said. "Everyone seems happy."

"Except you, Your Majesty, if I have the liberty to say."

"You don't. And yet you did. You are a sly man, General." A smile appeared on her face. "You remind me of my husband. He always got what he wanted."

"Pardon, Your Majesty?"

"You wanted this, didn't you?" She clenched her jaw. "For your soldiers."

"I wanted what was best for them."

She shook his head. "I feel they are more distracted now. We attack tomorrow night and today they are getting drunk. What a sight." She groaned.

"You shouldn't have done it then," he muttered.

"What?" Manasa stared at him, gobsmacked. "What did you say?"

"You shouldn't have . . . erm . . . done it, Your Majesty," Airavan said cautiously. After all, you are the queen. They have to listen to you, no matter what. The best leaders are the ones who keep everyone under their thumb but also pat them on their head once in a while to show their respect towards them."

"That's how dogs are treated, General."

"And by the looks of it, what do you think Jaratkaru is? He may be a captain, but he's a slime. He got what he wanted from you—women." Airavan directed his gaze to the moustached men who had two Apsaras in their arms.

Manasa noticed that unlike the Nagas, who were enjoying themselves thoroughly, the Suparns were disciplined, eating at their tables away from the Apsaras.

"That wretched Kadru spoilt them," Manasa said, shaking her head.

"I couldn't agree more. If she would have ruled any further, things would have gotten even worse. She had been too liberal. We live in Kalyug, Your Majesty. Tyrants are everywhere," Airavan responded confidently now.

"And you say all of this *now*? When it's too late to do anything?"

He chuckled. "I am just being the devil's advocate. Nevertheless, I apologise for being so brazen. I realise I may have said too much. Please know that I am here to do as you command, and on occasion, offer advice."

"You are a strange, complex man, Airavan. What is your story?"

"My father is a fisherman, Your Majesty. I joined the Naga army when I was eighteen. And I first served under Lord Vasuki."

"No wife?"

"Never got the opportunity. I was castrated before I could even think of marriage." He laughed, as if it was a joke. "I had a girl though, once. She was beautiful. We were so smitten with each other. We even promised to stay together for the rest of our lives, but then I was enlisted in the army. We parted ways then. I still think about her sometimes, but I don't regret my decision. Even though I am not with her, I know she is happy now. She got married a few years ago."

Manasa shook her head. "Vasuki shouldn't have had the soldiers castrated."

"Lord Vasuki was a good ruler, but he ran a tight ship. And he made a poor choice of following Lord Kali. We call him the Oath Breaker now. He destroyed the Truce."

"I hate him. I want to do everything to make sure his empire crumbles." Manasa looked at the dancing soldiers again. "And I don't think these . . . these drunkards would be able to deliver."

She heard an Apsara yelp as Jaratkaru tore her clothes. She was trying to push him away. Irritated, Jaratkaru slapped her in front of everyone. The Apsara started crying but Jaratkaru didn't care. He began to undress her without even caring that the others watching. In fact, most of them had started to cheer.

This is exactly what I feared.

Airavan sighed. "They are strong, capable men, even though they are behaving like monsters right now. Just show them the direction. If you want to be a leader, a queen that they will follow . . . then I suggest you show them who's the boss."

His words were like a splash of cold water. He was right. She was their queen. It was time she started acted like one. No matter how talented this captain was, he was not going to bully her ever again.

She pulled out a sword from the belt of one of her guards who had been standing behind her and then stormed towards Jaratkaru, breaking through the dancing and singing.

Everyone got silent as they saw Manasa entering the circle where the fire logs were burning.

And before Jaratkaru could even notice her presence and react, she swung the sword right between his legs. Blood poured as he fell on the ground, his hands clasping his bloody robe. His face lost all colour. The Apsaras shrieked, horrified. The Apsara who Jaratkaru had been holding, looked at Manasa gratefully, finally free from the clutches of the monstrous man. She ran away and hid herself in a tent.

Jaratkaru looked up with tears in his eyes and blood on his palms, confused. "Wh-Why?" he asked.

She didn't say anything and then the captain fell on the ground, unconscious. A smile danced on her lips as she saw the look of her startled soldiers. "Don't worry. I'm not going to castrate all of you like your captain. I just wanted you to know that you shouldn't mess with me. Don't bloody bully me. I'm your queen. You are under me. I'm not under you. From now on, there will be no consumption of alcohol in this camp, and no other distractions. Women are not sex objects and everyone should realise that. The captain apparently needed that lesson." She looked at Airavan, who had a soft smile on his thin lips. "General, please escort these ladies from this camp. Pay them well. Pay them full."

"Back to the Manav camp?" he asked loudly, still a smile on his face.

She had to make changes. *Major* ones. "No. Away. There will be no pleasure squads for *any* soldier in my war. Not Naga. Not Suparn. Not even Manav. Send this message to the other camp as well. Everyone should know. *Everyone*."

And now, she had one more thing to do.

Manasa entered Vibhishan's tent. The man was eating this time instead of reading. His dinner was on a table in front of him.

A handkerchief lopsidedly hung from his throat so as to not let the spilled food fall. With a spoon and fork in his hands, he was about to dig in when Manasa alarmed him by picking up one of his books and throwing it on his food.

There was a huge clanging sound when the soup bowl fell, splashing its content on Vibhishan's face.

Vibhishan looked at Manasa, dumbfounded. "What was that, Manasa?" he shrieked.

"I thought since you like books so much you wouldn't mind eating them."

"Are you okay?"

"I'm not."

"Is it the—"

"I got rid of the Apsaras."

"You transferred them here?"

"No. I sent them *away*." She glared at him. "And they won't be returning. Not in your camp. Not in mine."

"Frankly, my dear, this is my camp."

"AND THIS IS MY WAR!" she yelled. "And you promised to help me, not spend all your time reading books. I want your soldiers, your support." Her voice broke and her eyes glistened with tears. "And you didn't give any and it hurts me. It really does, old friend. You know how much I've lost. You know my journey and now I need your help."

"I uh . . ." Vibhishan used the handkerchief to wipe his face. "Oh dear, you remind me of my daughter. A lot. Dear me. She was a rebel too. She left the comfort of her home with her rebellious brothers."

Manasa was surprised. Vibhishan never discussed his personal life with her. He had always been very secretive about it.

"I think she's dead. Just like her brothers." He shook his head. "I could have stopped her, but I didn't. I chose to let her go. What a spineless man I was."

Manasa knelt down next to his childhood friend and warmly smiled at him. "Please help me, Vibhishan. Your soldiers don't respect me. They think I am using you. They think you are wise to keep your army away. But we are not in a bloody reading contest. We are at war. We need to fight." She paused for a few seconds, and then said something she never thought she'd have to say: "Or else, if you don't, you can go. I don't want your help even in extreme situations. You have to be all in or out."

"Sounds like gambling, oh dear." Vibhishan wiped the beads of sweat on his forehead. "I never liked gambling. Ah, my, my. Well," he looked straight at her, "I can't lose you like my daughter, like my children. You are the only good thing in my life right now." He smiled. "What do you want me to do?"

Manasa smiled back and embraced her friend, even though he still had tomato soup all over him.

But it felt good.

It feels good to make people understand that I am not a pushover.

But their moment of friendship was short-lived. The sound of horns reverberated in the campsite.

Manasa pulled away from the embrace and, with Vibhishan, instantly rushed outside to see the commotion. Men were running in every direction, grabbing their swords and spears, bows and arrows, axes and hatchets, shields and helmets, wearing their armour of iron and bronze in haste.

Manasa and Vibhishan now heard the sound of drumbeats. They knew what this meant.

"Oh dear," Vibhishan drew a sharp breath, "I believe you wouldn't be needing that night attack that you had planned any longer."

Yes. She knew that now.

Manasa reached the watchtower from where the soliders kept an eye on the wasteland in the front. She pushed a scout to the side and grabbed his binoculars to see the impending army that was marching forward with two men at the front.

She recognised one of them. It was the king of Yakshas. And the other . . . he was young and handsome. But didn't look like a warrior.

Where the hell is Kali?

It didn't matter where he was.

She knew he will show up soon.

The war has begun.

13

Kalki had arrived at his destination, finally, after walking for hours.

Having near-death experiences, fighting in wars, meeting men from the legends, losing love and finding it again—he had been through so much to reach here.

He had done it.

In front of him stood Bhargav Ram's temple. The fatigue he had been feeling up until now, vanished. Kalki felt immensely relieved; it felt like the most important thing that he had to do was over.

By the graces of Lord Vishnu, it feels so good!

Wondering about the training he would receive from Bhargav Ram, Kalki circled around the temple, studying its architecture—the ornate walls were lined with glyphs and symbols that belonged to an ancient realm, the tall long gate to enter the temple was fixed and frozen, engulfed in ice as if by magic, and the stone pillars around the temple were gigantic, majestic. Even the granite floor was as white as the snow outside the temple.

The temple seemed vast, unending. It was a sight to behold.

The white-cloaked men went inside. The gate had been opened by the guards in the front. The ice sheet on the gates cracked when they pulled at the gates with bamboo ropes.

Inside, Kalki noticed a long golden path embedded with jewels. There were pillars on both the sides of the path. He could see a lot of scrolls crammed in shelves on the wall. At the end, he could see sunlight filtering through the open ceiling in a bright chamber.

He looked at the white-cloaked man on his side, the one who had ridden beside him and had managed to save himself from the bear attack. "Why does Jambavan want to kill me?"

The man didn't say anything.

Ah, great.

"We are worshippers of Lord Bhargav Ram," said the man after a few seconds, breaking the silence as they walked inside the temple.

Kalki noticed that there were many more white-cloaked men inside the temple, their faces hidden. Kalki wondered why.

"Our ancestors have worshipped the great lord," the man continued. "We have devoted ourselves in priesthood to take care of him."

Take care? Bhargav was a strong, healthy young man. Kalki had noticed that in all his Channelling sessions. *Why would he need people to take care of him? But then, Kripa had been an immortal, and still grown weak and died. I need to ask Bhargav about how an immortal can die.*

Kalki was excited about his training, and about gaining knowledge on this topic as well.

"Someone said to me that Lord Bhargav can't leave this place because of a curse."

The priest nodded. "Yes, he can't. The last two times, he failed—the first time had been during Lord Raghav's time, and the second time had been during Lord Govind's. But this time . . . this time the plan is foolproof." And then he muttered, "Until the bloody creature attacked." He directed the wounded priests to the infirmary.

Failed in what?

Kalki wanted to ask more questions when Devadatta nudged him.

Human?

Yeah?

Devadatta neighed. *There's something wrong with this place. I can feel it.*

What do you feel?

Danger.

Kalki's hand immediately went to his sword. He was fully alert, ready to attack if anything untoward happened.

They came to the end of the pathway which opened to a long, snowy clearing. The space was empty except for a bronze statue in the middle. For a moment, he thought he would see the idol of a god or goddess, but the statue was of a man holding a bow and an arrow.

"Who is this?" Kalki asked, getting off his horse.

"Jara," the man said, taking the hood off. He looked extremely old. His sunken cheekbones, grey, fish-like eyes with huge bags under them, made Kalki feel as if he had seen a ghost.

"Why do I feel I've heard this name somewhere?"

"Jara was the hunter who killed Lord Govind."

Kalki's face lit up. "Yes. But it was an accident."

"That's not true. The arrow had been aimed at Lord Govind. It was an assassination."

Why is an assassin's idol placed here?

"Lord Govind was a brilliant strategist, but he didn't do good work. Lord Bhargav would have done better and prevented the Mahayudh and the Breaking. All Lord Govind managed to achieve was getting his home, Dwarka, and his people, the Yadavs, to ruin." The old man stopped and said, "You have to leave your animal here."

Animal? Who are you calling an animal? Devadatta neighed.

Kalki patted him. *Ease up, fellow. I'll be back.*

Stay safe. There is danger here. I can feel it.

Kalki nodded. He didn't want to dismiss the notions of his talking horse for he had saved Kalki's life at a point. He would have died that day, drowing in that cold lake, had Devadatta not arrived at the right time.

The other cloaked men took the horse to rein it in as Kalki followed the old man to another spacious complex ahead. There were innumerable books, scrolls, and papers lining the shelves here. Fire lamps had been hung on the ceiling. There were huge portraits of old kings on one side of the wall. But the portrait that stood out amongst all was of Karna, the low caste warrior.

"Lord Bhargav's favourite pupil. He was the first assassin that had been sent to kill Lord Govind but he had failed," the old priest added.

"What?" *Bhargav had trained Karna specifically to kill Lord Govind? Does that mean that the stories I have heard, we've all heard, about Bhargav and Karna are not true?*

"Why did Bhargav want to kill Lord Govind?"

"Look where we are. Don't you think it would have been better if he had died early?"

Kalki had no idea how to respond to that. *Why did Bhargav, an Avatar of Vishnu, want Lord Govind, another Avatar of Vishnu, dead?*

"Lord Bhargav had come to know the secret of a god—the god you know as Surya. The god cursed our lord in anger. Our lord was doomed to see every hero of every Yug fail, to be unable to do anything substantial to save the world. Our lord could only watch. As time passed, he grew old, weak, frail. He was close to death, he suffered every day, but he cannot die. His immortality is his curse." As they walked in a dark circular chamber, a fog enveloped them. There was a tomb in front of them. "Lord Vishnu keeps blessing each Yug with an Avatar, and yet evil exists. All our lord wants is to eradicate evil from this world."

The priest brushed his hands over the tomb.

"But the curse also stated," the priest continued, "that if he wanted to save a Yug from Adharm and be his young self, he would have to be the *only* Avatar of that Yug. Unfortunately, during Lord Raghav's time, he was afraid to do anything to him. Lord Raghav was a good man. And by the time he finally went out to kill Lord Govind, he had already died. But now . . ."

Kalki's hand was close to his blade. He had an idea of where this was going, but hoped in his heart that he was guessing wrong.

No. It can't be.

"He's right on time." A malicious smile came on the priest's face who was staring at the tomb.

And from there, came out a strange, twisted creature. Skin hung loose on his thin, pale body that was covered in a leopard's skin. His shaggy white hair and beard were covered in dust, and in his right hand was carrying a heavy axe.

He looked like a lost, dead remnant of Bhargav Ram.

He didn't look anything like this during Channelling. He was masking his true self. He had been the one to tell me that I didn't know what things could be done through Channelling.

The figure contorted his face into a smile. "Kalki," the man rasped. "Oh, how long I have waited for you."

14

Padma had a plan. It was simple but effective. And yet she was scared, for she was venturing into the unknown.

I have gone through worse.

She remembered how lonely she had been after her brothers had been killed, hunted by King Vedanta and how she came to work for a Naga queen as an assassin. She had even journeyed into the depths of the swamp lands of the Pisach and battled in the war of Vanars.

I have gone through a lot. I deserve a pat on the back.

Padma was on foot, following the hoofprints left behind by that Rudra scout, along with Ratna Maru and a bunch of Vanars. They had chosen to not bring any horses with them since the hoofprints they had to follow would have mixed with the prints of their own animals. As they waded their way through a forest, they saw a clearing where the grass was covered with a thin sheet of ice. Padma couldn't help but be awed by the dove-white mountains searing into the sky.

The place was beautiful, yet Padma could sense something dark, something sinister here. The trees around this clearing had completely frozen, from the root to the branches. The flowers in the shrubs around had fallen, dead from the cold.

"I gotta confess something to you, girl," Ratna Maru said. She was a few steps behind Padma.

"What?" Padma asked without turning back. She was focusing on the ground, studying it.

"I know I was being selfish before. I had wanted to find out how the poison was working so I could use it in the future, you know, against the people who had enslaved Apsaras. But . . ."

"But?"

"But please don't think any less of me because of my motives. I am just looking out for the people of my Tribe. And now, I'm here only because I want to help you. I have realised that it is important to help others, to do right by others. Kalki taught me that."

Wow, that was sweet.

"I understand, Ratna. I shouldn't have been so quick to judge you. And Kalki can be irritating at times, but he has taught this to me, too."

They had reached the clearing now. Standing atop a slope, they saw fire logs burning and large tents set up. Strange men with masks were walking around with long spears.

"Found them," Padma said, gazing at the Rudras' campsite.

"I see." Ratna Maru surveyed the area.

As Padma surveyed the camp, she knew she had to act out her plan that she had made with Lord Bajrang.

A few hours ago.

"Are you sure about this?" Lord Bajrang asked.

Padma had just told him her plan. "I'm sure, my lord. If we capture one of them and interrogate him, we might get some answers. We might find out their purpose for going after the Vanars."

"But they are Rudras. They are not some . . ." Lord Bajrang looked worried.

Padma had not seen Lord Bajrang so scared even during the battle with Taar. *What do the Rudras possess that is making even the great Bajrang afraid?*

"Can I ask you why? Why risk your life in Vanar affairs?"

Padma smiled as she glanced at Ratna Maru, who had been quietly listening, standing at the back. "My lord, I respect you, and it would be an honour to serve you. You deserve a stable rule. And I will do anything to make sure it happens before I leave this place."

Lord Bajrang pursed his lips. "I'll send my army with you then. And thank you for the kind words, but I must tell you that I'm not perfect. The stories about me make me seem like a perfect Vanar, but I too make mistakes, Padma."

Padma didn't believe him. The king of Vanars was just being modest. "I don't need an entire army. If we do that, the Rudras will know we are coming. This has to be done quietly."

"So I'll send my captain—"

"Just a few soldiers. And, well, Ratna should come along. She has the right amount of cynicism needed for the job."

15

The Nagas stood ready with their weapons as Arjan's men attacked.

Arjan was still on his horse, witnessing the spectacle in front of him. The Naga soldiers had formed a barrier through their thorn shields by lining in front of the Indragarh army. Arjan's men were trying to break the line to enter the battlefield but the Nagas remained unmoved.

A catapult was brought from the back, and Arjan's men hurled a fiery boulder at the barrier. The line of defense broke, and Arjan's men charged in.

Arjan stood at the back with Nalakuvera. He didn't have to enter the battle for now. The Manavs and the Yakshas were managing on their own. He had appointed Manav soldiers as the infantry, and the Yakshas had been tasked with firing arrows from the back.

Now, the Naga army also began firing huge boulders from their catapults.

"The boulders are killing our men," Arjan said. "I must join."

"Never send your champion in the first wave of attack," Nalakuvera said as he directed the cavalry to enter the battlefield.

Arjan saw the archers firing their arrows to shoot the flying Suparns. The Suparns were trying to dodge the attack by firing arrows of their own.

Nalakuvera ordered the elephants to come forward. Their trunks had been covered with an armour made of iron, and thorns were protruding from it. The earth shook as they ran wild, crushing the soliders under their feet. Some began moving their trunks, injuring the men around them.

The air turned red and dusty, infused with the smell of fresh blood.

"You seem confident." Arjan saw the Yaksha king smiling to himself.

"Oh well, I always have a back-up plan, as you know."

"Care to inform me or will you keep me in the dark this time as well?"

Nalakuvera looked at him and his face softened. "It doesn't have to do anything with you this time. All you need to do is attack at the right time . . ."

At that moment, a javelin was flung towards them, piercing Nalakuvera's chest. He fell from his mare and groaned. Arjan leapt from his horse and came to his friend to comfort him. Nalakuvera looked pale.

"Don't worry about me. I think it's time for you to enter the battlefield."

And before he could do anything further, the Yakshas came and put their king on a cot. The infirmary had been set up at the back.

Arjan was worried for a moment, but then, he knew that his friend would get the right medical treatment. He directed his attention to the front. It was clear that the Indragarh army was vastly outnumbered. No one would have guessed that the snake queen had Manav soldiers on her side as well.

Arjan pulled out his sword.

And he *stormed* in.

The battle was intense.

Arjan had practised every day, but this was the first time he was fighting in a war. He had fought relentlessly, but the enemies had still managed to stab him a couple of times. Arjan's hands and legs were bleeding.

God. This is not going the way I thought it would.

He recalled how he had barged in the council meeting in the morning and showed his dominance. He had taught those petty rich councilmen the value of innocent lives, just like he had planned.

But now he felt . . . weak.

He didn't understand why he wasn't winning. Where was the power he used to feel while training with the swordmaster?

As Arjan wondered what to do, a Naga galloped towards him and threw a javelin. Arjan managed to roll aside, missing the blade by inches. It took him a few seconds to grab the javelin and throw it back at the soldier.

The javelin reached its target—the wheel of the soldier's chariot. It somersaulted and broke into pieces.

At least I have done something.

And instantly he felt a shooting pain in his stomach.

Arjan had been stabbed. He looked back at the Naga, who was grinning at him.

Even though his chariot broke, this bloody Naga managed to throw a dagger at me!

Arjan pulled out the blade as he groaned in pain.

I need to believe in myself.

I need to.

The power comes from within.

He let out a bellow of rage and ran towards the Naga with the blade, plunging it deep in his chest.

The power . . . it comes from self-belief.

Arjan recalled this fact as he looked his men. They were dying. The snake queen was winning.

He felt weak. He had lost too much blood.

I have to get back to the camp.

Arjan started limping back towards the camp, when he felt the ground shake. A roar resounded in the air.

Everyone stopped fighting.

What is happening?

Arjan looked up at the sky. The entire battleground was enveloped in a huge shadow . . . of a giant.

16

Within seconds, Kalki was surrounded. White-cloaked priests began to circle around him. They were carrying short but sharp daggers. And in the middle stood the weak, ghostly Bhargav Ram.

All my journey . . . was in vain. Bhargav had been lying all along.

"So you called me all the way here to just kill me, is that it?" Kalki asked, furious. "Why didn't you just kill me before?"

"Because I don't have men. I don't have warriors anymore. I have grown too weak and these men . . . they worship me but they can't fight. Most of them don't know how to wield a blade except for the bunch you see here. Also, you had to be an Avatar for me to sacrifice you to the god who cursed me. And you became one, fortunately, in the process of finding me. That symbol on your chest defines you as my next target." Bhargav signalled his priests to get closer to Kalki. "I was living under their care when I began to grow old and weak."

"But you are immortal."

"Yes, a weak one who feeds on the energies of the Avatars." Bhargav was leaning on his axe. "And I thought what better way to bring my prey right at my doorstep—by using a bait of giving you training."

"So there will be no training?" Kalki was severely disappointed, but he tried not to show it. He had taken his sword in his hand, ready to defend himself if the priests or Bhargav attacked.

"No. Your journey ends here. I will kill you so I can finally save the world."

"Save the world? By killing the Avatar?"

"I AM THE AVATAR!" he yelled. "I am the saviour. Not some bloody cowherder. Have you seen yourself? You are weak. You need someone's help all the time. You take time to realise the truth; that's how foolish you are. Compared to you, I am wiser. I have lived hundreds of years and I have mastered all the weapons. I have the Axe of Shiva and I have the powers of Vishnu. I will—"

"You are cursed. Your time is over."

"You don't understand, do you?" Bhargav laughed. "I am the saviour. I am the real hero of this entire story. Come here, boy. You have to be sacrificed so that I can return to my younger self again."

"And then what? You'll fight in that form?"

"Yes. I'll be myself again. The real me. The one you saw through Channelling. And then I shall kill the Adharm." He directed one of the priests to come forward with the dagger.

Kalki slashed him with his sword and stabbed him in the back. Blood sprayed out from the priest's body.

Another priest came forward and plunged the dagger in Kalki's shoulder. Kalki screamed. He pulled the dagger out and then kicked the priest away.

"And Kripa knew this?"

"Of course not. No one did. Everyone thought it was legit training. Everyone." His eyes shone maliciously. "I fooled them through Channelling that I was waiting for you. But there was one I couldn't fool. The one who waited for you in the hills."

"Who?"

"Jambavan."

Kalki's eyes widened. He had been trying to run away from the bear-man. But Jambavan had been trying to help him all along.

That's why he had attacked the white-cloaks. He was trying to save me.

Kalki clenched his teeth.

So, that's it. Everything I have done to get here has been for nothing. My friend Kripa died for nothing.

"How did he die?" Kalki screamed as another priest came at him. He instantly deflected the blade and then cut the priest's leg.

"Who?"

"KRIPA!"

Bhargav's expression changed. "He died?"

"Yes."

"How is that possible? But . . . wait. My father did tell me there was a myth about the people endowed with immortality dying once their duty was complete. If the Trimurti agreed that the purpose for which the Endowed had taken birth had been achieved, their life will end. But I've never seen this kind of thing happen . . ."

"So you can't even say for sure why Kripa died, you wretched old man?"

Kalki clenched his jaw. Before he could even move, two priests appeared at his side and stabbed him.

The pain was so intense that Kalki came to his knees. Blood was oozing out of his stomach. Bhargav came forward, grabbed Kalki's hair, and made him look up.

"There is another way by which Kripa could have been killed—the Sword of Shiva. It is the mystical sword that can slice skin like butter. It was made from the very hands of Lord Shiva for the purpose of killing evil warriors and warlords with extraordinary powers. Even the gods fear this sword. And we all know that if Lord Shiva has created something, it must be the strongest weapon out there."

Bhargav Ram coughed vigorously. Speaking for so long was exhausting him.

"But I don't care about it. I don't even know where it is. Though I do feel sad my puppet has died. But now's not the time to grieve over a puppet's death."

Everything he had said to me was a lie.

Bhargav continued. "I will be the hero. I will finally be the hero and the world will see. I will reclaim what I lost."

"You don't get it," Kalki managed to speak even though he was in agony because of the pain. "A hero doesn't want to do the right thing just because he wants to be a hero. He does it because it *is* right, and if he doesn't then he wouldn't be able to live with himself."

Kalki stood up, feeling his power come back to him. His belief grew strong as he held on to the weak, frail hands of Bhargav. Bhargav began to groan as Kalki twisted his hands.

"In all your efforts to be a poster boy, you forgot one thing. It's about doing the right thing."

"SEIZE HIM!" he yelled to the priests as he freed himself from Kalki's tight grip.

The priests closed around Kalki, ready to stab him when Kalki heard a voice.

Human, I have returned.

Dashing like a hero himself, Devadatta smacked the priests with his tail and his fine ass and said, *Jump! We need to leave.*

Kalki kicked and punched the priests around him and ran towards the horse. Together, they escaped from the chamber and started racing towards the temple gates.

The door was about to close when Devadatta swung his majestic legs and propelled them out of the temple gates. They heard Bhargav yelling, "STOP THEM! STOP!"

I always save your ass, human.

Ah well. Get used to it.

Kalki's relief was short-lived. The priests had followed them outside on their stallions. And a few seconds later, Kalki heard a clanging sound.

One of the priests had aimed his lance at Kalki, but missed him by inches.

Buddy, we have to go faster, or we'll die.

At that moment, he heard a roar.

The sound was very familiar.

Kalki instantly halted his horse. He turned and saw Jambavan hurting the priests. Most of them had fallen from their horses in their haste to run away. He was saving Kalki.

You sure you can trust him?

I don't have a choice. Apparently, he had been waiting for me in the hills and he knew what Bhargav was planning. That's why he tried to save us.

Ah, well. Appearances can be deceiving, you know.

And that's when Kalki realised that Lord Vaman had uttered the same words. A chill ran down his spine.

What else can Channelling do?

Jambavan got up after beating the priests and walked like a gentleman towards Kalki. He noticed now that the Rakshas lord was in fact a human, wearing a thick fur-like costume over his muscular body. He looked at Kalki with a feral grin on his face.

"Thank you," Kalki broke the silence. "I didn't know you were trying to save me that time."

"You hurt me."

"What? No, I didn't. It was the—"

Jambavan growled. "You bleed. Will cure. Much to learn. Less time. Come," he said and started walking down the hill.

"You'll be my teacher?"

"Agh. Don't want. But will do."

Kalki followed him on Devadatta, all the while thinking that at least his journey had not been for nothing. He had managed to find a reluctant but a great teacher.

17

Padma was perched on an oak tree with a rope in her hand. One end of the rope had been tied to the branch she was standing on. And on the tree opposite hers, stood Ratna Maru. The Vanars were hidden behind bushes.

And now we wait.

Padma looked down at the ground where Smrit, the Apsara under Ratna Maru, was pacing frantically towards the guard who was standing at the entrance of the Rudra camp. He had a spear on which a red handkerchief had been tied.

Padma strained her ears to hear the conversation.

"What are you doing here?" the guard yelled. "You are not allowed to enter."

"Please, Sir, my carriage has broken. And I just need some help."

"I can't help."

"Please, Sir. I just need some help lifting jars."

Smrit was playing her part well. Padma was amused to see her act like a helpless woman when she was anything but that.

The guard agreed and began to reluctantly follow Smrit to the spot where Padma was waiting.

As soon as the guard reached the oak tree, he turned to Smrit and shouted, "There's no carriage here!"

Padma didn't waste any time. She jumped to the ground, clutching the rope. Grabbing the guard, she swiftly tied the rope around his throat. At that moment, Ratna Maru came down and took away his spear.

"Why did you attack the Vanars?" Padma asked, tightening the noose around the guard's throat.

The man began to choke.

"He can't breathe, Padma," Ratna Maru said.

Padma loosened the noose a little bit for him to breath. "Why did you attack the Vanars? Tell me and I will let you live."

The guard didn't open his mouth.

Padma instantly jerked the rope and it tightened around the man. "It hurts, doesn't it? I'll do more of it if you don't tell me." Out of the corner of her eye, Padma saw Ratna Maru look at her with a worried expression.

Am I going too far?

The guard tried to loosen the rope. Padma gritted her teeth and before she could tighten it further, she heard a voice from the back.

"Leave him, girl."

They all turned to see a crowd of Rudras. All of them were wearing monstrous masks with red eyes painted on them. They had come armed with spears.

The man in the front, perhaps their leader, was the one Padma had seen last time near the poisoned area. Padma released the rope and the guard fell on the ground, gasping for air. At that moment, the Vanars came out of the bushes. But they were no match for the Rudras.

Right in front of Padma's eyes, the Vanars were killed ruthlessly. All of them died within minutes.

The leader of the Rudras stared at Padma, Ratna Maru, and Smrit—the only survivors left. "That was a stupid plan. Was it yours, girl?" he asked, his face inches away from Padma's.

Padma didn't say anything. She looked at Ratna Maru.

Their survival depended on how fast they could run.

"You are his new pawn, right?" the leader asked. "You should not follow that meglomaniac. He is a hypocrite."

Padma flared her nostrils. "Do *not* speak badly about Lord Bajrang. He's a hero."

"Would a hero abandon his pregnant lover?" the leader shouted.

"Lover?" Padma snarled. "You might have mistaken Lord Bajrang for someone else. He is celibate."

"Sure, that's what he wants the world to believe." And then the leader removed his mask, revealing a white-furred Vanar.

The resemblance was uncanny.

"And if he's celibate, who the hell am I?" he asked.

Ratna Maru stepped forward, confused. "Are you—"

"Yes," the white-furred Vanar nodded, "I am Macchanu, the son of Bajrang and the heir of Kishkinda."

18

Manasa had planned for everything, but not even in her wildest dreams would she have guessed that Kali would manage to rope in Danavs.

They were huge. Manasa estimated their height to be around twenty feet. And their cold, red, monstrous eyes were giving her goosebumps.

They had come out of nowhere.

Where the hell is Kali?

The ground shook with each step that the Danavs took. One of them was crushing the Suparns in his palm, and another was crushing the Nagas on the ground.

"Your Majesty!" called Airavan from the horse next to her. He was wounded. "We need to retreat."

"We . . ." *can't.*

She didn't want to. But her men were being massacred by the Danavs. So many of them had been crushed under the giant's feet.

"We need to go back to our camp. We are not adept in dealing with such giants. Heavens and gods, the demons are upon us," Airavan exclaimed, worried as the Danavs' roars filled the air. "I thought the Danavs were just mythical creatures."

Danavs . . .

If they are real, so are the Ancients.

Manasa took a deep breath and looked at the Danavs. There were four of them.

I can't let this happen.

In front of her, a few steps away, she saw the soldiers who were going to face the brunt of the Danav's feet. The soldiers threw away their weapons, begging for their lives.

Manasa leapt from her horse. With her spear in hand, she raced towards the soldiers and pushed her spear inside the giant's foot.

The giant yelled in agony.

"RUN!" she ordered her Naga soldiers. They thanked her and began to run towards the camp. As soon as they fled, Manasa sprinted away from the Danav. In her haste to get away, she collided with a few soldiers and fell down. But when Manasa looked up, a horse was standing in front of her. And Airavan was on it.

He extended his hand and she took it, jumping on the horse. She sat behind him as he began to ride away from the Danav.

Manasa had lost her only weapon.

"General, order the retreat. Raise the flag."

"Are we surrendering, Your Majesty?"

"By heavens, no! We are retreating for now."

As they galloped towards the camp, there was only one thought in Manasa's mind.

I might have to use the Fourth Shard of the Eye of Brahma.

19

Kalki sipped his soup from the terracotta bowl. A lot of questions were running in his mind.

They had walked for a few minutes and reached Jambavan's cave an hour ago. Utter darkness and absolute quiet in the cave had made Kalki uneasy. But after walking a little further inside, a few fire lamps had been hung here and there on the ceiling. Jambavan had then treated Kalki's wounds. The bleeding had been stopped and Kalki had been asked to rest. As Kalki lay on the ground, Jambavan had busied himself in making some soup for Kalki.

Kalki looked at the mighty Rakshas lord as he sat munching on the food he had taken from the village.

"How did you know I would be here?"

"Smell," he touched his nose, "strong. Very strong. Got a whiff."

Must be quite a nose. He looked at Devadatta who was fast asleep. The horse had saved his life once again.

"Didn't know you come to this side of mountain," he shook his head, "until saw you."

"I'm glad you did."

Jambavan finished his food and belched loudly.

"Knew slaughterer was up to something. Can't believe what all planned."

Kalki had told him what Bhargav had said. All of it. And Jambavan had listened while making the soup.

"What should I do now?"

"Learn." He nodded vigorously. "Learn, you must."

"You'll really train me?"

"Yes. Must control your powers. Very important." Jambavan took a deep breath. "Chakras. Control the chakras and you will be stronger. Learn that."

"And you will teach me?"

"Yes. To defeat slaughterer."

"And what about Adharm?"

"Him, too. Not easy, but you use Sword of Uncle."

Uncle? Oh, he means Lord Shiva. Kalki remembered that in some cultures it was believed that the Trimurti were brothers.

"Kills and slashes all, even immortals, but only if wielded by true Avatar of Yug."

"Why?"

"Tainted, it was. Long time back by an Asura. Used for killing an Avatar. After that Uncle fashioned it so only Avatar can wield it. No other can."

"Should we go fetch it now? Where is it?"

He shook his head. "Learn, you must. Control, you need to. Your emotions and yourself too."

Kalki nodded. His headaches had been increasing every day. And he had tried so hard to control his Channelling powers, but the Avatars had been appearing to him on their own.

"Why are you helping me?"

"Father told me to wait. Gave me instructions. I'm supposed to be your teacher."

Is Lord Brahma really this bear-man's father? Kalki looked suspiciously at Jambavan. *Well, he has no reason to lie to me.*

Bhargav had had no reason to lie to Kalki either. He had said that Kalki always needed other people's help. That he was weak.

Kalki pursed his lips. Self-doubt began to creep in his mind. "What if Bhargav is right?"

"About?" growled Jambavan.

"About me. I do feel that I'm weak. And if you and Devadutta had not appeared at the right time, Bhargav would have succeeded in killing me."

Jambavan looked at him with a quizzical expression. Kalki tried to figure out what he was going to say.

But what Jambavan said next took Kalki by surprise.

"All Avatars stupid, weak. But they train from me."

"You? You were their guru?"

"I trained most. Only for control of chakras. Rest trained themselves."

"This is great. We should begin the training now."

Jambavan growled. "No. You rest. You travelled for long. Not for nothing. But something. And your journey still incomplete. You have grown but must grow further."

Jambavan is right. Kalki had grown. He wasn't naïve anymore. He wasn't full of himself. And he had realised that he should be selfless.

I wouldn't repeat the mistakes I made in Shambala.

"You are stronger now. And wiser," Jamabavan said earnestly. And then he belched loudly.

Kalki wanted to laugh at his teacher. He wasn't like the godly-looking Bhargav he had seen during Channelling. He was a strange, bear-man. Kalki hadn't even known Jamabavan existed until he had come here. "I still feel I'm not meant to be a hero." Kalki wrapped his arms around himself. "Do you have a blanket?"

Jambavan nodded. He pulled out one from his rucksack and tossed it to Kalki who wrapped it around his body. Feeling cold and drowsy, he lay down to sleep.

"I want to go back home."

"Return, you must. But not without control. Headache?"

Kalki's eyes widened. "Yes, I have been having headaches every day for weeks."

"Many do, few conquer. Headache, lack of control. Chakras," he said, taking a deep breath, "the secret to your strength."

Kalki shook his head. "I have no strength. I'm weak. Bhargav was right." His heart was sinking. He felt he had lost. *It was such a fruitless journey.*

Jambavan couldn't listen to this anymore. He grabbed Kalki's shoulders and pulled him up. Kalki just looked at Jambavan, unsure of how to react.

Looking Kalki in the eye, Jambavan said, "Bhargav weak, not you. Believe in yourself even when everything goes against you. True heroes born from that. Remember."

The claws of the bear-man began to pierce Kalki's skin. Jambavan's words had woken him up.

I can't just give up like this. If I've come here, all this way, I might as well learn something.

I can't give up.

"All right, all right."

Jambavan backed off. He was no longer angry. A smile crept on his face.

"Okay, then. Where do we begin?"

20

Manasa could feel her consciousness melting with that of the Shard of the Eye of Brahma. Her vision had turned blurry. As Manasa began to think of the battle she had retreated from half an hour ago, the Shard began to show her an image—a vast area filled with dead bodies of her soldiers.

What if I fight again? What will happen then? she asked the Shard and let the images form in front of her.

The Fourth Shard showed her what will happen if she attacked Indragarh again—the Danavs were trampling over the Nagas and crushing the Suparns in their huge hands. And in the centre of the Danavs stood Kali.

He was no longer bald; he had curly, golden hair and golden irises. Ecstatic on witnessing the carnage in front of him, he danced in the battlefield. Then, noticing Manasa, he pointed at her and began to laugh.

She didn't understand why he was pointing at her when she felt the Danav grab her. And as she closed her eyes, the image began to dissolve.

What should I do?

She had never asked this kind of question to the Shard.

To her surprise, an image began to form in front of her. Manasa saw a narrow lane. Someone was running towards her. A woman.

One of her hands was limp, and in the other she was holding a scroll.

It's me. Who am I running away from? And then she noticed a bunch of hooded men were following her. They had blue eyes and cobras were coiled on their arms, ready to pounce at her.

Who are they?

The image dissolved and now, Manasa was back in Vibhishan's tent. She felt an intense pain in her head. Using the Shard had affected her. Her nose was also bleeding profusely.

Airavan rushed to Manasa with a handkerchief. Vibhishan looked worried.

"Are you okay?" the Dakshini king asked.

"It hurts but I'll be fine." Manasa touched her forehead and groaned. She tucked the Shard inside the pocket of her overcoat and put her palm over her eyes.

"What did you see, Your Majesty?"

"That we will die if we attack again," Manasa confessed.

"Oh dear," Vibhishan said and sank in his chair.

"The Danav attack . . . Kali was behind it."

"Dear goodness, I should have thought so." Vibhishan looked horrified. "They are monstrous abominations that used to exist long ago. I don't understand how Kali has managed to bring them here."

"They are our enemies now and we are going to lose if we don't come up with a plan. And when I asked the Shard about what should be done, it showed me a vision—I was running away with a scroll in my hand. But I was being chased by Nagas. It's strange that my own men were after my life." Manasa sighed, straightening her posture and looking at the two men in front of her. "I wonder what it all means."

Airavan and Vibhishan looked at Manasa, uncertain. For a few minutes there was complete silence in the tent.

"My dear, I think I understand what the Shard is speaking of," Vibhishan suddenly spoke up, startling Manasa and Airavan. He went to the corner of the tent and brought a book back with him. Flipping through its pages, he said, "Do you remember that I had told you about a book I was reading—the one on Meghand written by Lady Prameela? Well, I happened to read a passage in it that was about Lord Raavan. During the time of his triumphant conquest of Illavarti, he had ended up defeating a lot of Danavs. He had even conquered Narak, and you know what it is—the kingdom at the edge of the world where the Asuras and Danavs lived together. And the way he had defeated Danavs was . . ." he began to read, straining his eyes as Manasa and Airavan waited eagerly for his response, " . . . through bombs made of Soma."

"Bombs?" Manasa exclaimed, shocked. "Is it going to be another Mahayudh?" She shook her head.

"My dear, I am sure that might have been the only way. Danavs are incredibly strong. Even the Rakshas and Asuras don't stand a chance against them."

"No, I know." Manasa nodded. "How did he make bombs during his conquest?"

"He had worked with his engineers on them. It is believed that Lord Raavan laid out the process of making Soma bombs on a scroll and then instructed the men he trusted to pass it on to posterity."

Manasa smiled. "You must be having it."

"Unfortunately, my dear, I have nothing. You see, my father and Lord Raavan didn't see eye to eye on certain matters. After a huge fight over whether a war should be waged against Lord Raghav or not, Lord Raavan had declared that he no longer considered my father his brother. I came to know of the scroll only because I read about it. It has not been passed on to me."

"Your Majesty, may I?" Airavan had been itching to speak.

"Of course, General."

"When I was serving under Lady Kadru, she had once spoken about a scroll that she was going to take from Lord Raktapa, the ruler of Eelam, who now sits in Varungarh. She had said that this scroll would make our Tribe invincible."

"You mean to say that Kadru already knew of these bombs?" And then she recalled that Kadru had told her about wanting to create Astras out of Soma. This was why Kadru had gone to Suparnika—to steal the Soma plants to make the bombs. But Manasa had stopped her.

"She knew of these plans. I believe Lord Vibhishan is right."

"And why hasn't Lord Raktapa done anything if he has the scroll?" she asked.

"Maybe he just didn't want to attack Suparnika. He doesn't need bombs right now, at least. The Rakshas men are already strong enough to win a war if there is one."

I have to get the scroll. It may be the only thing that can help win this war.

"When do you think the next attack will happen?" Manasa asked Airavan.

"I don't know. They have lost a considerable number of men, but who's to say they won't bring more Danavs into the battlefield? They might attack us tomorrow morning."

"Damn. Going to Varungarh itself will take me a day. General, please arrange a *vimana* for me," Manasa said, referring to the flying chariots the Suparns had been using. "And Vibhishan, will you hold the fort while I am away?"

The fat man nodded, wiping the sweat on his forehead. "How will you convince Raktapa to give you the scroll?"

Manasa smiled. "Well, my friend, I'm going to ask him *nicely*."

21

Arjan woke up with a start. His body was aching everywhere. And his head was about to explode because of the headache.

What has happened? Am I in the infirmary?

He couldn't move a muscle. Helpless, he closed his eyes and fell back to sleep.

The next time Arjan opened his eyes, he saw sunlight filtering inside his room. He was back in Nalakuvera's fortress. Smell of Ayurvedic creams permeated in the air. Bandages had been wrapped around his wounded body.

Arjan was covered in a blanket. And beside him sat Nalakuvera. His chest had been bandaged. Nalakuvera didn't look like he was in pain. A huge grin was plastered on his face.

"Did we win?" Arjan asked softly.

"Yes, my friend."

"The giants . . . who were they?"

"My secret weapon," Nalakuvera said, laughing.

"I don't get it. How did you—"

"You'll know, all right? Stop worrying about it." Nalakuvera suddenly grew pensive. "Do me a favour. Tell people it was you. Tell them that you were the one controlling them."

Arjan looked out the window near his bed. A Danav was sleeping on the ground in front of the fortress, like a guarding dog.

"The people . . . they must be afraid."

"Yes. Fear is good, Arjan. Fear has made you king." He clapped his hands in excitement. "The people think you are some kind of god. You cannot be hurt. You breathed life into creatures that were believed to be dead. The nobles and the public believe in you now."

He should have been elated, but he didn't feel good about lying to people. "I didn't do anything last night. I collapsed."

"And the world does not know that, my friend. This is politics, all right?" Nalakuvera got up from his chair. "Do not screw this up with your nobility, Arjan."

Arjan shook his head as he straightened on the bed. He looked at the sickle that had been kept at his side. He hadn't brought it to the battle, afraid that he would lose it.

I should have.

"It's all right." Nalakuvera shrugged. "I am not a noble man, but look how far I've come."

Arjan shook his head.

"You are their only hope, Arjan. Remember what you said in the council meeting. You have proven that you are worthy of being king in everyone's eyes. Do not hesitate. The coronation is tomorrow and then we shall continue with the war against the Naga queen. I didn't want to attack them again since you were wounded. You have to be at the forefront of our next attack."

Arjan knew that the Yaksha king was a sly man. But that didn't change the fact that he was right. And he had managed to procure Danavs to help defeat the enemy. "They were Danavs. I've read about them. According to legend, they had been put to sleep forever by Asuras. How did you manage to bring them to life?"

"Don't freak out. But I wasn't the one who brought them here. The one who brought the Danavs is standing outside the room right now. He wants to have a conversation with you."

A chill ran down Arjan's spine.

Nalakuvera walked to the door. He opened it slightly, saying, "You both have a lot to catch up on. He's the one who helped us, helped you. And Arjan," Nalakuvera turned, "there are things you should you know about yourself. Things he will tell you."

The door opened and a thin man entered. He had blonde hair and sharp features. But the first thing that Arjan noticed was that he had golden irises.

No.

It was Kali.

22

"Hello, Arjan." Kali entered and stood beside Arjan's bed, his hand extended.

Arjan got up and moved away.

The tyrant, the previous king of Indragarh, the maker of Truce, the killer of Arjan's friends was right in front of him. Just a few steps away from Arjan's grasp.

He could choke him. And hold him down.

Control yourself.

Nalakuvera had left. They were alone. There was complete silence in the room. Kali nervously scratched the back of his head.

"I hope you liked my gift."

"I don't want it," Arjan snapped. "I would rather die than be helped by you."

Kali wasn't hurt. It was the reaction he had expected. "I know I have done some horrible things, so I want to redeem myself. Give you the title you deserve. You understand these people. You need to be the king. I was never right for it."

Arjan tried to study Kali's face, hoping to decipher whether he was being deceived. But Kali looked genuinely upset. Or he was a really good actor. But Arjan wasn't going to take chances. Kali had killed Ratri, Bali, Vikram, and so many others. He had driven Arjan and Kalki out of their village, their home.

He was Adharm.

He was the one Kalki had to kill.

I can just do it on his behalf.

"How did you do this?" Arjan asked.

"Long story, kid."

"Why did you do this? You have been nothing but horrible to me."

"Ah, well . . . I just told you. I thought I should do something nice for you. I had returned to reclaim the throne but then I observed how you were managing things. The city will prosper with you as its king. So I have given my support."

Arjan scoffed. *So he had returned with the aim of taking over the city.*

"Do the people know you have returned?"

"I intend to work in the shadows." Kali smiled. "If they know that you have been helped by me, they will not let you be king. You should see out there right now. They worship you. You are their god."

Why is he being so nice?

"You are hiding something."

Kali walked and stood in front of Arjan. "I am, in fact. A truth about us."

"Us?"

"You and me."

"I don't care what you say, Kali. I won't believe you."

"Not even the fact—"

"NONE!" He thumped his arm on the side table, breaking it.

Kali backed off. "I can see you are still as strong as when I last saw you. But now I know where this strength, this anger is coming from."

The Soma that Durukti gave me. Does he know now?

"It's in your blood," Kali said. He looked proud.

"I don't want your help. You and your giants need to leave,"

Arjan ordered. "I, the king, am exiling you. If my men find you in the city, you will not escape with your life."

Kali's face fell after listening to Arjan. "Sure, as you say, Your Highness."

An hour had passed and Arjan was still finding it hard to digest that Kali had *helped* him.

He hadn't gotten out of his bed and was blankly staring at the ceiling. Even though he hated Kali, he was curious to know what he had wanted to say to him.

Thinking of going out for a stroll, Arjan sat up on his bed when he heard a knock.

Who is it now?

"I'm sleeping!" he yelled at the door.

"It's me. Durukti," the voice said.

A smile spread on Arjan's face. *The very woman who destroyed my life and saved it as well.*

"Come."

Durukti entered the room and enveloped Arjan in a tight hug. Even in plain black clothes she looked beautiful. She was wearing a long gown, its neckline embellished with emeralds. Her lips had been painted red and her big, brown eyes were smeared with kohl.

"What a reunion, eh?"

Arjan held her hands. "How are you? Where have you been?"

Durukti lowered her gaze. "That doesn't matter. I heard you want us out."

"Your brother and his giants. You are very much welcome in the city."

"You know that I will have to leave with him. We are bonded because we are siblings." And then she looked away, as if she was hiding something. "All I can say is, Arjan, you need him. He has changed. Believe me if you don't believe him. He really wants to help you. He really wants to be there for you."

"Why?"

"Well, Kali wants to be the one to tell you why. And trust me, if you let him help, there is no doubt in my mind that you will win this war."

"What if he hurts any other of my friends?"

Durukti smiled. "I assure you, my friend, he won't. Things have *really* changed."

Arjan thought for a moment. "Let me think about it. By taking his help, I'll be staining the memory of my friends who were killed by him."

"He was different then. He was ill," Durukti responded. "I hated him too that time. But he has changed. He has clarity and he has power over the Danavs. He controls them through his mind. He can really help you."

And even though Durukti had not intended to, she had scared Arjan.

Controlled by his mind? Telepathic bonding. He had read about it. It was believed that some Ancients had been powerful enough to do it. And if Kali controlled the Danavs like that, they could turn on Indragarh in a second.

I wouldn't be able to do anything. What if he attacks? What if he hurts the innocents I tried so hard to protect, boys like Amar?

Durukti looked bemused, wondering what Arjan was thinking about so deeply.

I have to keep him happy until I come up with a way of dealing with him. Especially since I'm king now, I have to be diplomatic.

"Of course, Durukti. You all can stay." Arjan smiled. "Let bygones be bygones."

Durukti beamed and embraced Arjan, who instantly groaned in pain. "We'll see you tomorrow at the coronation. Can't believe you'll be a king. Gods, it seems like only yesterday I . . . I was awful to you, wasn't I?"

Arjan nodded meekly.

Durukti didn't say anything for an apology was not going to be enough. She turned to leave and was at the door when she said, "I'm glad I gave you Soma that day. It has really made you strong. Kali had grown mad after drinking it. Thank goodness you haven't been affected like that."

Arjan could see she was confused. It seemed like she was fighting the urge to say something.

And then she left.

From a cowherder to the king of Indragarh, Arjan had come a long way.

A long, scarlet, linen carpet had been spread on the pedestal. Arjan sat in the centre and beside him stood Nalakuvera and Rambha.

He had had to let the people believe in a lie to reach here. But he knew he was going to be a good king. He would lead the city into better times.

The crowd had gathered to see the coronation of their new king.

Arjan felt ecstatic. He was a king. The city belonged to *him.* If only his mother could see him right now, she would be so proud.

He beamed at the crowd as the crown was put on his head. There was a thundering applause. And in the midst of the crowd were three hooded people—Kali, smiling softly at Arjan, Durukti, grinning from ear to ear, and Arjan didn't recognise the third one. Her face was ghostly pale.

Arjan now looked at the nobles. Lord Amreesh was clapping reluctantly. His son, standing beside him, looked furious.

Arjan smiled a little.

But then his eyes met the sunken, dark eyes of Guru Narendra, the head priest who had rebuilt the temples in this city again after Kali had destroyed them. And in the entire assembly, he was the only one who wasn't clapping.

23

Padma had been imprisoned. And this was not her first time. Though unlike last time, she was outside. The prison was made of bamboo, and it was hard to break through.

She had looked around Macchanu's camp when she was being taken to prison—some raw food was being cooked outside the tents, the smell of copper hung in the air, a few of the men were forging weapons, and the tents in which the men were staying were tattered.

Padma, on her way to the prison, also noticed a large tent. Its flap was open. There were scrolls on the table. Rudras were standing around the table, discussing. Numerous charts and blueprints were scattered on the table as well.

Must be the planning zone.

But then she was taken away and pushed inside the prison.

Padma sighed audibly and sat on the ground. Ratna and Smrit worriedly watched her.

"So what now?"

"We give it a night," Padma said. "And then we escape."

"Any plan?" Ratna Maru asked. "We have no weapons."

Padma looked at Macchanu. He wasn't wearing his mask at the moment and was discussing something with his subordinates.

And at that moment, Padma came up with a plan.

She came forward, touching the bars as she shouted at Macchanu, "Hey, fake son! What's your plan for us?"

"What are you doing? He'll kill us!" said Ratna Maru.

"Great. I knew this was a bad idea from the beginning," Smrit added.

"FAKE SON!" Padma yelled again, ignoring her companions. "You do realise Lord Bajrang would send an army to get us if you don't kill us fast. What's your plan with us anyway?"

Macchanu stared at her. For a minute, Padma thought he was going to ignore her, but then he started walking towards the prison. "I won't kill you all. You seem useful. Crazy, following a hypocrite, but good. Following the hoofprints to discover our hideout, that was smart. Once my war is over, you'll be joining us."

War?

Padma wondered what Macchanu was planning to do. "Says the man who only has male guards."

Macchanu chuckled as he turned to face the officer standing on his side. He nodded at the officer who then removed the mask.

A Manav woman!

"My apologies. You cannot do this to Lord Bajrang though. He's a good man."

"I'll tell you a story, girl. Once upon a time there lived a woman. She was a poor fisher girl, completely alone in the world. A day came when she witnessed a grand event—the Avatar of Vishnu descending with his general, Bajrang. They wanted ships to travel to Lanka. The Vanars under Sugreev arranged them. But while they were preparing to leave, something happened. Bajrang fell for the fisher girl."

Lord Bajrang fell in love?

Macchanu continued, "The time came for Bajrang to leave but she begged him not to go. But he had to do his duty. Even so, he couldn't help but be drawn to her. Soon, the girl was with child. When Bajrang came to know about this, he thought about staying with her. But then, a terrible truth was revealed."

Padma's heart was racing.

"The fisher girl was no ordinary girl. She was one of the many followers of Raavan and she had been specifically placed there by the demon king to seduce Bajrang, so he would choose not to fight in the war. He was, in Raavan's opinion, stronger than anyone on the field. The girl had succeeded in her mission, but there was one problem." Macchanu looked into Padma's eyes. He had gotten dangerously close to her. "In the process of stopping Bajrang, she had fallen in love with him. But when Bajrang found out about the truth, he was horrified. Not only had he renounced his celibacy for a Rakshas, a *Rakshas*, mind you, but he had slept with someone from the enemy's army. So he *abandoned* her."

"What?!"

"She begged him to stay, telling him that she loved him. But he didn't care. He left for Lanka." Macchanu sighed. "She lived alone for the rest of her remaining life for Raavan thought of her as useless, and Bajrang didn't want her anymore."

Macchanu's eyes were glistening with tears.

"No one was there for her. Somehow, with the help of nurses, she managed to deliver a boy. But after giving birth, the girl grew weak day by day. She continued begging to feed herself and her son, but she died when the boy turned ten. But her son was different. He was physically strong, like his father. Though the boy was not immortal, he was ageing very slowly. After his mother died, he begged on the streets. He even stole sometimes when he was very hungry and had no money to buy food. This was how he survived for many, many years. After the Breaking, he searched for Vanar camps, hoping he would be accepted there. He was forty-five years old, but didn't look a day older than fifteen. No one believed his story. He was thrown out for being a liar and an opportunist. Unsure of what do to next, he wandered around aimlessly, until he found a group of men wearing strange masks—the Maruts. The Mahayudh had made them into Rudras. They had lost hope in gods, renounced their faith, and believed that violence was going to help them survive. That made sense in the boy's mind, for the gods had never been kind to him and his mother either." He clenched his jaw. "Your Lord Bajrang is a man of many qualities but he is also a coward. And cowards deserve to die. I've been trying to find him for so long. Then I heard from my men about a war taking place between Taar and Bajrang in Dandak hills. Honestly, I had thought Taar would win."

Padma couldn't believe what she was hearing. *Whatever I know about Lord Bajrang is a lie.* But could she believe Macchanu?

He is in tears. Why would he make all this up?

"What he started, I will end." Macchanu stomped his foot in anger. "I'll make sure Bajrang's followers are killed. But I don't plan to kill Bajrang. I plan to make him suffer. Just like my mother and I suffered because of him."

"I'm sorry," Padma managed to say, leaning on the bars.

Macchanu wiped the tears on his face and turned to leave. Padma sighed as she looked at him. The story reminded her so much of her relationship with her father—how he had backed away when she and her brothers had wanted to do something.

Lord Bajrang is the same as my father—a man one who leaves others in times of need.

"You don't believe him, do you?" Ratna Maru asked, sitting in the corner. Padma zapped back to reality, remembering that there were two more people in the cage with her. "He is trying to manipulate us."

"Maybe," Padma pulled out the knife that she had hidden under her tunic, "but I don't care about his story," she lied. "I had to get him close to take this weapon out of his scabbard without him knowing."

Ratna Maru laughed. "You are a fine woman, you know that?"

Padma smiled, gripping the weapon she had stolen.

"We wait for the men to fall asleep and then we escape," Padma said. She sat down on the ground, her mind filled with the story she had just heard about Lord Bajrang. The man from the legends, the man she respected, had turned out to be like her father.

How can I continue to serve him now?

24

"Concentrate. Breathe," Jambavan's voice came from the back.

Kalki took a deep breath, and tried to concentrate. He was sitting close to a cliff. A strong wind was blowing.

He took a few more deep breaths, but nothing happened.

He was finding it hard to concentrate. Bhargav's words were playing on a loop in his mind. He had said that Kalki was weak, that he always needed help.

Asking for help is not a sign of weakness.

Why was this bothering him so much?

Kalki began to hum a tune to distract himself. "What should I seek?" he asked Jambavan.

"Greatest strength. To control headache, control Channelling. One must learn where power comes from."

Kalki's eyes were still closed. "I know it comes from self-belief." *Something I'm lacking considerably.*

Jambavan smacked Kalki on the head. "Overconfidence so much. You know nothing. Self belief, important. Very important. But other factors, important too. One must learn others as well."

Kalki nodded. He took a deep breath letting the cold air seep in his body. He let his mind relax.

What is my greatest strength?

•

"If only one understood," a soft, familiar, silky voice said, "that strength is defined not by how much you weigh but by the choices you make, the world would become a merrier place."

Kalki opened his eyes. He was in a forest. The sky was clear, there were cherry trees and huge bushes all around. A few huts could be seen at a distance.

The place looked so familiar, and then Kalki realised where he was.

It's Shambala.

He knew this was just a vision in his mind, but it felt so real.

"You lived in a nice village," the voice said.

Kalki turned to see where the voice had come from. Behind him stood a tall man, wearing a saffron-coloured dhoti and a long scarf. His hair was matted and he was carrying a bow and arrows. His eyes were pure and soft.

Kalki knew who he was.

Lord Raghav.

"Yes, I did." Through Channelling, Lord Raghav had taught him how to use a bow and arrow and that had helped him kill the Brahmrakshas—Martanja. "It's nice meeting you after a long time. Your advice has helped me a lot."

"Have we met before?" He shrugged. "I don't remember. But I'm sure that advice given by others must have helped you as well. The world and the people in it have a lot to teach. Even so, you must learn to follow your heart, not what the others tell you to do. You must learn to forgive. You must know that war is not important; peace is." He sighed. "If only I knew this, my days would have been blissful after I defeated Raavan. I would have had such a simple life, but I let the society dictate my actions. That was my greatest weakness. I let others made me do things that I didn't even want to do." Lord Raghav looked at Kalki. "I don't want you to end up that way—miserable, unhappy, and filled with regret—

when all of this is over. You are the last one, Kalki. Your ending has to be better than all of us."

Lord Raghav looks so vulnerable right now. Kalki lowered his gaze and asked, "Why are we here?"

"I don't think you remember. This was the defining moment of your life." Lord Raghav turned to the pathway in front of them.

Kalki realised it was the same pathway that he and Lakshmi used to walk on, on their way to the gurukul.

But I don't remember anything life-changing happening on this day.

There were two kids walking on the pathway now—the boy looked weak but the girl looked healthy. They were holding hands.

Tears trickled down Kalki's face as he realised the kids in front of him were he and Lakshmi.

But what did I do on this day?

"I remember. I used to be weak. Though I was eating properly, I still got sick a lot. I was a victim of many illnesses—small pox, cold, fever. I don't understand why I was like this. If I had been given Soma when I was a child, why did I not become strong?"

"Giving such a potent drink at such a young age can weaken the individual. Even if you are an Avatar."

Kalki nodded. Lakshmi and his younger self were still walking on the pathway.

"I thought," Kalki confessed, "since I was so weak, I would die soon. That was why my parents were always so nice to me. Each day, I was so afraid that it might be my last."

"Fear," Lord Raghav nodded, "is important. It drives us to do things we think we are not capable of. The fear of not being able to save my wife drove me to fight the greatest Rakshas alive."

Kalki saw his younger self and Lakshmi being stopped by two men. They were tall, had greasy hair, and their eyes were fish-like.

"How do you do, kids?" one of them asked.

Lakshmi pulled young Kalki away. "Let's go. Mother says not to talk to strangers."

"But I'm not a stranger, child. I've been sent by your mother."

When Lakshmi didn't listen, the man grabbed her by the arm. "Why don't you come with us, child?"

Young Kalki was confused. He came forward and said, "Sir, please leave my friend alone."

"How sweet," the other man said, pushing young Kalki aside. "Why don't you leave, kid? We will drop her home."

"No!" Lakshmi screamed. But no one was around to save them.

"Come with us or die here." The man began to strangle Lakshmi.

And then, Kalki remembered what had happened.

Young Kalki was furious. His hands were clenched. And then he stormed towards the man. He rammed his head on the man's back. The man lost his balance and fell down, releasing his grip on Lakshmi.

The other man gasped and instantly attacked young Kalki, but Kalki stopped the man.

And then, the seven-year-old Kalki held the burly, heavy man in the air by his throat.

Kalki looked at his younger self in shock. And when he blinked, the scene had dissolved. He was back on the cliff, shivering in cold. Kalki sighed, looking at the majestic, snow-peaked mountains in front of him. Jambavan was sitting beside him.

"What see?"

"I saw my greatest strength." Kalki couldn't believe it.

"And?"

"I always thought it was . . . doing the right thing. Being good, selfless, was my strength."

"Was? What is your greatest strength now?"

Kalki felt power surging in him. He knew what he had to channel to fight his enemies.

"It's *anger.*"

25

Manasa's was feeling queasy in the vimana. She was sweating a lot, even though a strong wind was blowing, and she looked like she was going to throw up.

That's why Nagas prefer to remain on the ground rather than flying in the sky.

The last time she had been in the vimana was when she had thrown Kadru from it. Kadru had fallen into the abyss, disappearing forever.

Sometimes Manasa wondered whether she could have done something to change Kadru. Kadru was a good person at heart. She had somehow been corrupted by her greed for power.

She looked at Airavan, who was instructing the Suparn who was driving the vimana.

"We have reached," Airavan said.

Finally. We've been in the air all day.

Manasa looked down at the illuminated city of Varungarh. The streets were crowded with people even though it was late in the night. She didn't have a lot of information about the city except that Raktapa, the former truce maker and an ally to Kali, was ruling the city and was quite a nuisance. Vasuki and Manasa had met him once. He was a handsome but scary-looking Rakshas. And even though Rakshas were dark-skinned, he had a wheatish complexion.

And he loved gold.

"It's funny, you know," Manasa spoke, desperately trying not to throw up. "I had stopped Kadru from making Astras and now I'm seeking plans to make Astras myself. Maybe it's fate. Maybe if a certain thing is to happen, it will happen no matter what is done to stop it."

"Your Majesty," Airavan said, "we are close to the palace gates. Should we land there?"

Manasa held on to the vimana with her good hand. Her limp hand had been bandaged and gloved. "No, we land inside the palace."

"But what if Lord Raktapa attacks us?" Airavan asked. "There's only two of us."

Manasa ignored Airavan and came on her feet, rocking slightly as the vimana picked up speed. She told the driver, "Please head towards the palace and land."

The rider nodded and started lowering the vimana.

As the vimana reached near the palace, Manasa saw that a party was happening in the lawn. Delicacies had been placed on huge tables, and some Apsaras were dancing around the men. A couple of guards had been placed at the lawn's entrance.

"Drop us there."

"We are interrupting a party, Your Majesty," Airavan's voice rose in worry. "He will get angry."

"That's the point." Manasa liked the plan. "He has to see I'm not scared of him. Maybe then he will agree to help us."

"But—"

"Don't forget Rakshas admire people who have strength and courage. This is me showing them that."

And as the vimana landed, everyone on the lawn ran away. Shocked and confused, the dancers began to scream. The guards rushed towards the vimana, their swords at the ready.

Manasa got out, staggering on the grassy ground, her eyes on the huge chair on which the fiend was sitting. He stared at Manasa, his expression unreadable. But Manasa could make out what he was thinking—she was not welcome here in his palace, in his city. Standing next to him was his wife. She had turned eighteen this year. Her beautiful face was smeared with scars. It was common knowledge that Rakshas beat their women.

The guards surrounded Manasa and she raised her arms in surrender. So did Airavan. The guards took his sword.

Raktapa stood up, directing his men to back off. He walked towards Manasa, his shining black hair fluttering in the wind, with a smile on his face.

"What a delight. The Naga princess is here."

"It's queen now." Manasa forced herself to smile.

"You chose the right day to visit," said Raktapa, clapping his slimy hands. "It's my birthday."

Manasa drank the wine and leaned back on the chair. She was in the common hall with Raktapa. They were sitting opposite each other but Raktapa wasn't looking at her. He was busy playing with his dog.

"Thank you for the gold," he said, breaking the silence.

"That's not just gold, Lord Raktapa. That is my pledge of loyalty towards you. I want you to side with me."

He shrugged. "Ever since the Truce ended, I side with no one. I live quietly in my city."

Indeed. Things are calm in Varungarh now.

Varungarh was a beautiful, bustling city, surrounded by lakes and populated by the Rakshas. Manavs who worshipped Lord Varuna, the god water, lived here before Raktapa took over. Now, as per the wishes of its ruler, it was a land of Shiva devotees.

"Then there must be something I can do for you to side with me," Manasa said.

"I heard about what happened to Vasuki. My condolences. And now Kali has returned."

"Returned? When did he leave?"

"Ah," he chuckled, "you don't know what happened to your enemy. Kali had been defeated by a small girl. But now he has returned with Danavs."

When the hell did this happen? Now Raktapa won't help me. I don't even know what my enemy has been up to.

"It's wiser to side with someone who possesses mighty Danavs than with someone who has a treasure chest. I'm sorry, Manasa." Raktapa looked at her with pity.

"But your ancestor Raavan hated Asuras and Danavs," she said. "Aren't the Rakshas against them?"

"Oh, they are. Very much so. But you see," Raktapa stood up and started to walk towards Manasa, "times have changed. The creatures from the myths have risen. Kali has managed to do the impossible. I always thought he was . . . different. Strange. But cunning."

Manasa clenched her fist.

"You want my army to fight against him? Is that what you want?"

"I want the scroll," she declared.

Raktapa stopped abruptly. Manasa had surprised him.

"The scroll belonged to Lord Raavan and was passed down to Meghnad and so forth."

"What kind of scroll is this?"

"The one that outlines how to make Astras."

"Ah," he licked his lips, "interesting. You want to start a nuclear war, is it? You think using Astras against Danavs . . . will work?"

"I don't think. I *know*."

"Never thought of you as someone who believes in myths." Raktapa smiled. "The only reason I have not used the scroll to make bombs is because I don't want another Breaking. I don't want another Mahayudh."

He didn't sound like a Rakshas at all. Most Rakshas sought battles, while he was striving to maintain peace.

"I made sure to hide the scroll, so I gave it to my three most trusted scribes," he continued, his voice getting deeper, hoarser. "The scroll was handed over from one scribe to the other on a monthly basis. So if anyone ever tried to take it, they won't know which of the scribes had it. And if they kill the wrong one, the guards would be alerted that someone was trying to steal it. Now, you won't believe this, but many have tried to steal it. Many people still want to get their hands on Astras."

"Why didn't you just burn the paper if it was such an issue for you?"

"Burn a scroll that has been in my family for generations? What do you think of me? I am not *insensitive*," he exclaimed. "I am a lover of heritage."

"There won't be any Breaking. I promise. I just need to defend my army against Danavs."

Raktapa smiled. "I would have believed that." He walked to the main door of the hall and knocked on it.

Why is he knocking?

"You have revealed something very . . . interesting just now." Raktapa clicked his tongue. "If you wanted the scroll so badly, you should have just asked me rather than killing my scribes."

"Kill your scribes?"

The guards entered the room, their arrows pointed at Manasa.

"I didn't kill anyone." Manasa stood up. She hoped Airavan would intervene, but couldn't see him outside.

They must have gotten him too.

"Your assassin did," he said. "Two of my scribes have been poisoned by Nagas. I couldn't figure out how they had managed to enter the city. And now they have the scroll."

"But I didn't—"

"I don't know what you were thinking, getting my scribes

murdered by your men and then coming here in person to beg me for the scroll. But I am sure that you have a hand in this. Queen Manasa, you are under arrest for committing murder. And tomorrow, at dawn, you will be executed."

26

Arjan couldn't remember feeling as happy as he was this morning. Right now he was sitting on the throne.

The throne room was flooded with sunlight entering through the windows. Guards stood at the gate. And in front of the throne, a long, red carpet had been spread. It was a spacious room. Soon, the public would be coming in here to address their concerns to the king.

Me.

Arjan didn't know what to feel about that. His hands were stretched on the arms of the chair. He felt the power of a king.

"It feels good, doesn't it?"

Arjan looked over at Kali, who was standing at the door. He was in his usual black cloak, his head veiled under the hood.

"When will you attack the snake queen again? My Danavs are getting bored."

"I want to settle in as king before going to battle again."

"Seems fair. Usually kings don't fight in the wars, but you have turned into a warrior, haven't you?"

Arjan shot daggers at Kali. *Why is he talking like he knows everything about me?* He hated Kali. So many of his friends were dead because of him.

Arjan wanted to strangle him that instant.

But he controls Danavs. He might attack us if I do something.

He remained silent as Kali walked towards him. "I had become drunk on power. I know now that I was an unfit ruler. The crown looks good on you, my king."

"Urvashi and I took away your crown."

"No," Kali said softly. "It was my greed that made me lose the crown. But you are not like me. You are wise and kind. A good man."

Kali ascended the steps and stood in front of Arjan. He kept his hand on Arjan's shoulder, looking deeply into his eyes.

I can twist it and kill him.

"You are the king. And I'm your adviser."

"You are no one." Arjan jerked Kali's hand away. "The only reason I entertain you is because of Durukti. And because you helped us in need. Otherwise, I would have thrown you in prison."

"I know. That is why I helped."

Cunning bastard!

"This was your plan, wasn't it?"

"I did this to ensure that you won't kill me, Arjan. I just wanted to be safe. And I had to have people on my side, people that you hold dear, like Nalakuvera and Durukti, who you so dearly like even though she had destroyed your village. By offering my help through the Danavs I ensured that you'd be in my debt, that you wouldn't gut me the moment you saw me."

"I knew it." Arjan gritted his teeth. "You are nothing but a worm."

"But I did it for my safety. And for you. I genuinely believe that you will be a good ruler, Arjan. There's no hidden agenda. Believe me when I say this." His voice echoed in the gigantic throne room.

There is something he is hiding from me, from everyone. I can feel it.

And before Arjan could say anything, a Yaksha entered the room, panting. "My lord, Your Highness, we have an issue."

"What is it?" Arjan asked.

"Vandalism, Your Highness."

Arjan was wearing a dark grey coat buttoned up to his throat, a black dhoti, and golden slippers. A nice velvet satchel hung on his side in which his sickle had been kept.

Anyone would be able to tell that he was a king. He wasn't wearing a crown and yet he looked regal.

Why didn't Arjan wear the crown on his head? He didn't want to. He felt it didn't suit him. Moreover, he wanted to look like the people he served.

As he got out of the palace and outside the main gates, he saw a crowd had gathered in front of a wall. The people were whispering amongst themselves.

Nalakuvera was already there with three of his Yakshas guarding him, as if he was a god. And he was, in their culture.

When Nalakuvera turned to see Arjan, he asked him to come over to where he was standing. There was one word on the wall, written with bright red paint.

SODOMITE!

Kali came outside and stood behind Arjan. He looked distressed.

Arjan was fuming. The people gathered around the wall were staring at him.

Great. Now everyone will get to know about this.

"Get the men on duty in this part of the fort and question them. Interrogate them if you have to. How can they let this happen in broad daylight?"

"Already did, Your Highness," said Nalakuvera. "Apparently, Guru Narendra's followers were behind this. They don't like you because you are . . . well . . . what's written on the wall. I've imprisoned the guards for not doing their job properly."

"And what about Guru Narendra?" Arjan asked.

"We can't touch him. He is the head priest, after all. He has some very powerful men working for him. And many people still believe in the Vedic religion which Narendra follows and preaches. Going against him is like going against the people," Nalakuvera explained. "But I'll get more information about him." And Nalakuvera went back inside, his guards pushing the people away. The crowd dispersed.

Arjan looked at Kali, who was studying the wall. Once Kali and Arjan were inside the fortress, Kali said, "You can't show weakness."

"You are not my adviser, Kali."

"You can't show weakness," Kali repeated, ignoring Arjan. "Kill Narendra. I had destroyed the temples for a reason. All religion does is spread false belief and worship fake gods."

Arjan was tempted to agree, but he shook his head. *Every life is valuable. I can't turn back into a killer.*

"He's turning the people against you. You can't let him incite them. They fear you now. You don't want them to ridicule you behind your back, do you?" Kali asked. "I showed weakness once, when I was ill. It was after the Truce and it ended with people stabbing each other. Sometimes being a king means playing dirty."

No. I won't kill again.

Arjan stood rooted to his spot as Kali turned to leave. Suddenly, Arjan spoke up. "Why are you helping me? You hated me till now. What has changed since you left from here?"

There was silence in the room for a few seconds. Then Kali turned to look at Arjan. "You said whatever I say, you won't believe me."

Arjan remembered that statement. "Forget that. Answer me."

"Well, Arjan," Kali smiled, "the reason I am helping you and the reason I believe you'll be the greatest king out there is because . . ." his eyes shone with pride, "you are my brother."

27

The night had dawned. It was time to leave.

Macchanu had retired to his tent and his officers were guarding the cage. But it was late, and they were getting drowsy.

Padma was leaning on the bars of the cage when Ratna Maru said, "It's time. Let's leave." She began to tear through the ropes that bound the bamboo.

"To do what?" Padma snapped.

"Save Lord Bajrang and his people," Ratna Maru said matter-of-factly. "What's wrong with you?"

Padma sighed. "I don't know. I just feel . . . we have been led astray."

"I thought you were doing this because it was right." Ratna Maru gave the blade to Smrit, who began to cut the ropes. She came to stand beside Padma. "What's gotten into you?"

"I don't know. I was doing this for Lord Bajrang. I kind of looked up to him. But now that I know what he did, seeing the people he disappointed . . . I realise that he is—"

"Human," Ratna Maru completed her thought. "Look, girl, I don't believe a word of what Macchanu told us. I want to hear Lord Bajrang's side of the story. Then, if it turns out to be true, I'll pummel him."

Padma couldn't help but smile. She was feeling so messed up.

Smrit had managed to open up the side of the cage. The space was enough for a small-sized person to crawl out.

"Are you coming?" Ratna Maru asked. "Or do you want to be a part of the Rudras and fight Lord Bajrang for disappointing you?"

"What are you talking about?"

"The difference between us and Macchanu is . . . we do things because we feel they are right. We do things selflessly. Don't forget that it's not about Lord Bajrang right now. It's about the innocent people following Lord Bajrang. Their lives are at stakes. Macchanu wants to kill them."

Padma had forgotten about his devious plan of killing innocent Vanars. She had been so caught up in her emotions. What a fool she was being.

"For the right thing," Ratna Maru extended her hand.

Padma shook her hand and smiled.

And one by one, they got out of the cage. The guards had fallen asleep.

"Where to now?" asked Ratna Maru.

"I want to see what's inside the biggest tent in the camp—the one where they had gathered to plan in the morning. We have to sneak in and find out what they are going to do to the Vanars, so we can stop them," Padma whispered.

Ratna and Smrit went to take a few fire lamps from the guards' hands. They would need light to wade their way through the darkness.

And then Padma spotted Shuko flying in the sky. Instantly, she whistled to signal him to come over to her.

The sound woke the guards up.

Shuko flew down and started attacking one of the guards, while Smrit and Ratna Maru plunged the dagger in his body. Padma wrestled with the other guard. She didn't have a weapon, so she had no choice but to strangle him.

Both the guards lay dead on the ground. Everything had been

done so quietly that Padma got reminded of the way she used to operate when she was an assassin.

Padma and Ratna Maru took the guards' spears and Smrit carried the lamp, lighting their way towards the tent Padma had spoken of. Shuko was perched on Padma's shoulder.

"That was crazy." Smrit brought her hand forward for a fist bump.

Padma gave her a fist bump with a huge smile on her face.

"I hope you know that our coven is not limited to emancipated Apsaras," Ratna Maru added.

"I'll keep that in mind." Padma laughed. They had now reached the massive tent where Padma had seen Rudras discussing their plans.

Papers were strewn over a huge map on a table. Ratna Maru, Smrit, and Padma studied the map. There was a strangle symbol around Dandak Hills—multiple leaves combined into one large leaf.

What does this mean?

Padma looked at the charts scattered over another table. And then she saw one where the Vanar camp had been circled and crossed out.

Ratna Maru and Smrit came across a paper that had a detailed design of a shovel. It was much bigger than a normal shovel. They had all spotted some of these on their way to the cage. They found another paper on which was a detailed diagram of a large leaf. The word written on the top was 'Manchineel'. More information about the leaf was at the bottom—'potent, poisonous, another name is Hippomane Mancinella.'

"I think I've figured out what they are going to do," Padma whispered to Ratna Maru and Smrit. "They have planned everything. They have dug out the area outside Dandak Hills with these huge shovels."

"Why would they do that?"

"Because . . ." Padma shook her head, pursing her lips.

"Remember what they did with the farmers? Poisoning them with wolfsbane?"

"Oh yeah." Ratna Maru sighed.

"This is worse. Machineel is the world's most poisonous tree. Be it the root, bark, or leaves, every part of this tree is filled with toxins. Ingestion of its fruit can kill, and the sap from the leaves causes severe inflammation and burns on the body."

Ratna Maru and Smrit gasped.

"That attack on the farmers was a *test* to see whether the smoke would actually make them ill. This," Padma tapped on the paper, "is the execution of the test on a major scale. The entire camp of Vanars is going to be annihilated."

28

Night had fallen and Kalki was blissfully asleep, until he was woken up by the sound of someone munching food in the corner of the cave.

Kalki was in a dirty cot, wrapped under an even dirtier blanket. Although, lying in this filth was nothing compared to what he had gone through.

Jambavan was busy stuffing food inside his mouth when he saw that Kalki was awake. He picked up a fish and threw it on Kalki's blanket. "Take."

"No, no, it's all right." Kalki gingerly picked up the fish and kept it on the ground, feeling disgusted. He had never eaten raw food. "You got it from the village?"

Jambavan nodded. He took the fish back and began to eat it noisily.

"I had a conversation with one of the natives there," Kalki said, recalling his time with the stable master. "Instead of just taking food, have you ever talked to them?"

He looked at Kalki as if he was speaking an alien language.

"It's important to let them know you are there."

"I there. Protect them." He belched.

"But nobody there has ever seen you."

"Too flashy. Not my style."

Kalki sighed. "Well, they want see you, all right? They are scared because they think the deity they worship doesn't exist. It's important for them to know that you are looking out for them. Reaffirm their faith in you. As far as I know, that village is the only one that worships you. And all you do is sneak inside the village to take away food."

The bear-man scaratched his head, confused. "Responsibility?"

"Yes. Responsibility. Hiding inside a cave and eating your offerings is quite easy to do. But being there, helping them, being responsible is difficult. They want you there. And I'm sure they'll be very happy to see you."

Kalki waited for Jambavan to say something wise, or something that would show that he understood how irresponsible he was being. But instead he just got, "Errrp!"

Kalki was sitting outside on the same cliff he had sat on a few days ago. The wind was strong as always. He looked up at the night sky, a mixture of blue, purple, and red.

Kalki was sitting cross-legged, his hands resting on his knees. He felt good, peaceful. Slowly, he closed his eyes. Jamabavan was standing behind him. Kalki could hear him growling.

He asked his guru, "What should I look for now?"

"Your greatest weakness."

A chill went down his spine. He felt . . . afraid to know this. "Why?" he asked.

"Know your weakness, important. Protect yourself by knowing your weakness."

Kalki nodded. He took a deep breath and concentrated. After a few minutes, he caught a whiff of cherry blossom. He could feel the ground beneath him had turned grassy. He was in a different place now.

He had Channelled.

Kalki opened his eyes and saw that he was back in Shambala, but it wasn't the same place he had Chanelled to last time.

It was his home. His younger self was eighteen now. Arjan was present too. They were standing outside their hut. Vishnuyath, his father, looked furious.

I miss you, father.

Vishnuyath just boxed Kalki's ears, and he yelled in pain.

He has been dead for so long. And yet . . . it feels like it was only yesterday that I was getting scolded by him.

"Oh hello there, my friend."

Kalki turned to see Lord Vaman, the fifth Avatar of Lord Vishnu.

"What do we have here? My, my, someone is being scolded. Why is that?"

Kalki recalled what had happened this day. "I was supposed to guard the cows but I left to meet Lakshmi. When Arjan got to know of this, he took care of the cows but he," and he saw Arjan smiling in the corner as Kalki was getting an earful from his father, "was a tattletale. It was horrible."

"I can imagine, my friend. I used to be up to all sorts of mischief as well," Lord Vaman said, leaning on his flamboyant umbrella. "You know my father, Kashyap, was quite a nasty fellow. Beat me with a stick and made me do things I didn't want to do. When he got to know that I liked a girl, he laughed at me, said I was . . . erm . . . you know, not fit enough to be a husband. And that I was . . . tiny." He shrugged but Kalki noticed that Lord Vaman looked hurt. "I was jealous of tall people. But then I realised it doesn't matter how tall you are. What matters is that you are doing the right thing, that you have strength and courage. And courage, my friend, is not dependent on someone's height. Even a mouse can show courage in front of a cat and even an elephant can feel weak against a lion."

"Good advice."

"Thank you very much. I have a book full of it. I love to write, you see. Maybe I'll get it published one day." Looking at the eighteen-year-old Kalki, Lord Vaman said, "You look furious."

"I was," Kalki nodded, biting his lips. *But I don't remember what happened after that.* "I hated that Arjan was always better than me—more responsible, more studious. I tried to make him feel small by showing how strong I was. Though Arjan got hurt when we fought, I don't think he ever got jealous of me. He was comfortable with who he was, even if he lacked physical strength." Kalki sighed. "I hated him for that. He had been adopted, yet my father seemed to love him more. He was stealing my place. Oh, how naïve I used to be."

The scene began to change. Day turned into night and they were inside the hut now. Arjan was sleeping.

Kalki and Lord Vaman were standing at the corner of the room, watching Arjan sleeping peacefully. At that moment, he realised how much he missed his brother.

"What a peaceful face," Lord Vaman remarked.

And that was when Kalki noticed a shadow near the door. Someone had entered with a pillow in hand. The figure looked at Arjan for a few seconds and then pushed the pillow over Arjan's face. Arjan began to flail his arms, unable to breathe, trying to push the assailant away but the man was strong.

Kalki stared at the man in utter disbelief.

The man eventually fled without completing his job. And Arjan looked around confused as to what had happened. His younger self yelled and cried in the house, saying someone had tried to kill him.

"Oh dear, who was that?" Lord Vaman asked.

"It was me," Kalki said.

Kalki frantically paced in the cave. He had returned, but he felt restless. He felt . . . weird.

How can I forget about this incident?

Kalki had erased this incident from his mind completely. He remembered how horrified he had been at that moment, realising that he had been so close to taking his brother's life. That was when he had fled.

He was riddled with guilt.

I'm evil. I tried to kill my own brother. Oh god, how will I face Arjan now?

"Why do this?" Jambavan asked. Kalki had told him what he had seen during Channelling.

"Because . . . because . . . I was angry at him. I was foolish. I didn't know what I was doing. I just thought doing it would push my worries away." He shook his head, biting his thumb. "I was so—"

"Stupid? Weak?"

Kalki lowered his head, ashamed. He looked at the bear-man and said, "Jealous. I was jealous of him. Just like Lord Vaman was jealous of tall people."

"No," Jambavan responded, "you still are."

"No . . . I'm . . . not," he said, unsure, confused. "How does one combat jealousy?"

"By giving up on it," Jambavan said simply.

Kalki didn't have time to ponder over what Jambavan had said. A huge fiery rock had just hit the cave. They jumped outside, out of harm's way just in time.

Staggering on the snow-filled, rocky ground, Kalki saw dozens of white-cloaked men on horses. A catapult had been placed behind them. And at the front stood a large elephant clad in an armour made of iron.

So much to defeat two men. They must be really afraid of me and Jambavan.

And in the centre of the cloaked men, he saw the degenerate. Bhargav Ram.

29

"Spend the night thinking of your last wish, lady. At dawn you will be executed," the prison guard said and left.

Manasa plopped on the ground and looked around. Water was dripping from the ceiling and rats were scurrying inside their holes. Gleaming, slanting rays of the moon filled the cell with light.

Manasa sighed audibly, looking at her dishevelled attire. She could smell her own dirt. And she didn't like it.

It was a horrible plan. I should have just TAKEN the scroll from him.

Extending an olive branch through money was a mistake. But Manasa wanted to hurry back to her camp. She was frantic with worry when she thought of Danavs attacking her men.

What if Kali attacked today? I wonder if Vibhishan managed to lead the men properly. He would have to handle the war alone now. I will be executed tomorrow.

"What yer in for, lady?" the man in the adjoining cell asked, baring his rotten teeth. His face was soaked with dust, and he smelled horrible, like a dead rat.

On the other side, there was another prisoner—a blonde-haired man. He looked decent. Perhaps he was a soldier. "Leave her alone, Rustom."

"What's yer problem, Vinod? I'm just having a chat with the old lady."

Old lady? Really?

"Why they caught you?" Rustom probed.

Manasa didn't respond.

"They caught me because they think I run my slum like some lordship. What they don't know is I am not as corrupt as they are," he huffed, crossing his arms.

Vinod turned to Manasa and said, "You don't have to answer him."

Manasa was ignoring both of them.

"Bloody Rakshas! They think they can come here and disrupt our lives. I have been running my slum without any difficulty for years. And now, suddenly Raktapa has a problem."

"Yeah, well, you deserve to be here," Vinod said to Rustom. "You thought using your orphans to spy on people would be fine?"

"Well, I had received a lot of gold. What was I supposed to do? I had an employer. A bloody Naga like this one," he said, pointing at Manasa. "Had the same blue eyes."

The man had Manasa's attention now. "Who was this woman?"

"Oh, Your Highness is interested now, is she?" he laughed.

"Tell me about her."

"You wouldn't be able to make out she was a woman from her face, you know. She looked and walked like someone had beaten her to death. I guess I'm still not sure whether she was a woman. But let's call her a woman—"

"Can you come to the point?" Manasa snapped.

Rustom looked hurt. Manasa realised she had to quell her irritation. She batted her eyes, adding: "Pretty please?"

"Well," Rustom spoke up, appeased, "she bought some orphans from my slum. I didn't ask what she planned to do with them. Got to know later they were spying on people. Someone in Raktapa's castle."

Could this be connected to the scribes?

"What did your orphans find out?"

"Don't know, lady. Before I could find out, I was thrown in the prison."

Manasa wanted to ask more questions but before she could, a guard approached her cell. It was a different Rakshas this time. To Manasa's surprise, he opened the door and tossed her a blanket.

"Wear this around your face," he said.

"What's happening?"

"Airavan sent me."

Manasa couldn't understand how her general had managed this, but she was glad. She wrapped the blanket around her face and began to move outside. Once out of her cell, she turned back to see the surprised faces of Vinod and Rustom. "What if I want to know about these orphans?" she asked Rustom. "Where will I find them?"

"Just ask around for Rustom's Lair."

Manasa nodded. And then she followed the guard outside.

She didn't know where she was being taken. Everything was enveloped in darkness. She calmly followed the guard, all the while thinking . . .

The gods sent me to this prison. They wanted me to know this. This was predestined.

Manasa was relieved, thinking that she might be getting closer to finding the scroll. But the clock was ticking. She had to procure the scroll with haste.

The gods were on her side. They wanted her to win the war and were assisting her. She was sure of it.

There is a divine force helping me. It can't be a coincidence that I was in a cell beside the person who had conversed with the Naga lady.

As Manasa and the guard made their way outside through the narrow corridors of the prison, she began to wonder if she could call herself an atheist now.

They were about to reach the main gate of the castle, when Manasa spotted a man. He had a spear in his hand, but it was completely dark outside so she couldn't make out who he was. Two horses were standing a few steps away from the man.

The man lit the lamp he had kept on the wall.

Manasa raced towards Airavan and gave him a tight embrace. Airavan was surprised. He wrapped his arms around Manasa. Turning to the Rakshas guard, he said, "Thank you."

"I don't owe you anything now," the guard responded and hurried back to the prison.

"What did he owe you?"

"I was a bit of a gambler," he said, blushing. "And I was sort of on a winning streak against that Rakshas. He couldn't pay up, so I told him that one day I will come to take the money or something in kind."

"So you used that to save me?"

"You are the queen."

Manasa narrowed her eyes. "Or maybe you did it because you like me."

"I am supposed to like you." He smiled.

"Tell me, General, was my plan bad, stupid, and reckless?"

They had climbed on their horses and were making their way into the city. Both Airavan and Manasa had covered their faces.

"Your Majesty, you are the queen and you are always right."

"But still, it was bad, wasn't it?" Manasa probed. "Be honest."

"Well . . ." he looked at her, trying to hide his smile, "it was absolutely *horrible*."

And she laughed.

After a long time, she laughed.

Manasa and Airavan stopped a few steps away from the house at the end of the street. Guards had been placed outside it. The door and windows of the house were shut.

"This is one of the scribes' house."

Manasa looked at Airavan with a quizzical expression. "How do you know about the scribe?"

"When Raktapa was talking to you in the common hall, I was standing outside. I overheard everything. But when I realised he was planning to imprison you, I escaped. I had a few friends in the Rakshas army since I was here during the Truce with Lord Vasuki and General Takshaka. I hid inside the castle when you were being taken away. Through the help of my friends, I got out and then researched about the scribes."

"And?"

"They were poisoned by cobras. And cobras are dear friends of—"

"Nagas," she completed. "But we only worship them. No one keeps them as pets. Nagas used to do that in the past though."

"Whoever this person is knows how to control snakes," he said. "I couldn't find out anything else."

Manasa contemplated what this could mean. "Do you believe in destiny?"

"Your Majesty, that's strange of you to ask."

"Forget what I asked. Right now, we need to head to a place that will take us to the scribes' killer. Ask around for Rustom's Lair."

They rode around the city for hours and finally found what they were looking for—the slum.

Rustom's Lair was a gigantic building squeezed right in the middle of two decrepit buildings. There were a lot of children inside it. Some were talking to each other, some were eating, and some were playing.

Manasa and Airavan got down from their horses and came inside. The children looked at them, wondering who they were.

And then a boy started running away.

"Get him!" Manasa ordered Airavan.

While Airavan went after the boy, she observed the other orphans. They looked well-fed and were wearing proper, clean clothes.

Soon, she heard the wails of the boy. Airavan was dragging him inside. The boy was resisting. He even bit Airavan's hand, but Airavan was unfazed. He threw the orphan on the ground and brought a dagger close to his neck.

Manasa instantly gave Airavan a look, so he straightened up and kept the dagger inside his pocket.

"I apologise. My friend doesn't like children." Manasa knelt so she could be face to face to the orphan. "What's your name?"

There was no response. The boy just stared at her angrily.

"I'll give you gold." She took out her bangle. "Here. You can sell it in the market, but you have to tell me about the woman first."

His eyes shone as he looked at the bangle. "How do you know about her?"

"Rustom told me."

"He's a tyrant."

"I didn't like him either. But he led me to you, so I'm sure some good came out of it."

"We don't speak about our employers."

"This employer was like me, right? A Naga?"

He nodded.

"Tell me. I have more bangles just like this one. I'll give you all of them."

Manasa handed over the bangle to the boy. The boy quickly put it in his pocket and said, "She's leaving tonight."

"Who is she?"

"She goes by the name of Mother. And she has a lot of blue-eyed people who worship her. They believe she is a goddess."

"Do her followers have cobras?"

"I don't know."

"Why did she want the scroll?"

"I don't know why. We just spied on a few of the guards of the palace and overheard one of them saying that a scribe had been given the scroll this month. We also found out the addresses of the scribes and gave them to her. In return, we received food and some gold."

"Where is she right now?"

The boy opened his mouth, but then closed it abruptly. He looked scared.

"You won't be hurt, I promise," Manasa said.

He still didn't believe her.

She pulled out her golden bracelet studded in jewels and gave it to him.

The boy smiled. "She is camping on the outskirts of the city. We don't know the exact location since we were blindfolded whilst entering her hideout. But I counted the steps," he said proudly. "It's fifty steps to the east from the western gate."

"You remind me of someone." Manasa smiled.

"Who?"

"A girl. Her name was Padma."

"Ew, I am a boy."

And he scurried inside the building like a rat. Manasa looked at her general and said, "I will take over this city in the future and make this boy my spy."

"Sure, Your Majesty."

"Where is our vimana?"

"It's at the castle. They killed the Suparn driver."

"Can you get the vehicle?"

"My friends will help. Allow me to ride back and see what I can do."

"Great." She turned her gaze towards the western gate. "You leave to get the vimana. In the meanwhile, I'll go and find out who this Mother is."

"Alone?"

Manasa smiled. "General, I am quite capable of handling her, whoever she may be."

30

Arjan knew he couldn't avoid using Kali's giants. Especially after the talk they had had. Arjan had tried to forget about it, but it kept playing in his mind. Kali was a dishonest man, but Arjan couldn't detect any intent to deceive when Kali had confessed about Arjan being his brother. Arjan felt that the statement was true, but it had been spoken by an evil man. He pushed his thoughts away, and decided to focus on today.

At first, he had been adamant about not using Danavs in the war. But he realised that they didn't have enough men, and without the Danavs they would surely lose. So, begrudgingly, he had decided the day before that he would send some of them with his men in the war from now on.

Exasperated, Arjan ran his hand through his hair. He didn't want to owe Kali anything.

And on top of that, the man was claiming to be his brother.

Impossible!

He didn't want to think about that lie anymore. Kali had gone too far. Arjan felt stupid for allowing this monster to stay in the fortress. Moreover, he had made him his adviser.

The door opened and Nalakuvera entered. "You wanted to see me, Your Highness?"

"It is time to resume our war, Nala. Send our men and the giants to battle with our enemy."

"Understood. I will convey this to the men right away."

"Good. I will go get ready."

"For what, Your Highness?"

"To fight. Didn't you hear what I just said?"

Nalakuvera looked at Arjan in confusion. He opened and closed his mouth a few times, debating in his mind whether he should speak up or not.

"I don't think you should fight now, Arjan."

"Why?"

"Have you ever seen a king fight on the battlefield? What if something happens to you?"

Arjan got up from his chair and walked towards Nalakuvera. For a few seconds, they just looked at each other. Arjan took a deep breath, trying to quell the anger surging inside him.

With his face inches away from Nalakuvera's, he said, "Are you telling your king what to do?"

Nalakuvera was taken aback. He had never thought Arjan would talk to him like that.

"If you die, the city will be without a ruler again."

Something changed in Arjan's eyes. His face had softened slightly. Arjan went back and sat on his chair. He looked mentally exhausted.

"But we'll discuss this. If you want to fight, I won't stop you. And Arjan, I know about you and Kali. He had told me everything when he had come with his offer to help."

"I refuse to believe him."

"Can't you just accept that he wants to help you?"

Arjan was angry again. "He's not a nice man, Nala. He's anything but that. He always has tricks up his sleeve and he's . . . a killer." *Just like me.*

"So you don't believe that he's your brother?"

"I'm not an Asura. I am a Manav."

"But what if you are?" Nalakuvera went to stand beside Arjan.

"What if you really are a powerful Asura? Do you know that there is a prophecy that runs amongst Yakshas?"

Arjan shook his head.

"An Asura will fight and defeat the Adharm. An Asura will be the Dharm." He paused. "You're so powerful. Maybe you are the one our prophecy refers to."

"But," he sighed, "there is a Manav prophecy too. The one where the Dharm is a Manav."

"I choose to believe the prophecy of the Yaksha lore," Nalakuvera said. "You need to win over the army outside. And if you use Danavs, our victory is assured."

Arjan clenched his jaw. "You may leave." He didn't want to hear about Kali or his Danavs anymore.

Nalakuvera turned to head out. He was about to open the door, but he stopped. Looking back at Arjan, he said, "There is something you should know about Guru Narendra."

"What?"

"You need to kill him. Kali is right."

"Why?"

"He—"

They heard something crash outside. Arjan and Nalakuvera looked at each other in confusion. They sprinted down the hall and saw the ground floor was littered with men in saffron-coloured masks. The bodies of the fortress guards lay around the masked men.

"Narendra's men. They must have come here to create a ruckus and kill you." Nalakuvera looked at Arjan. "We need to leave. We should go somewhere safe and—"

Arjan didn't listen. Without a moment's hesitation, he jumped from the railing and fell on the floor below. Though he had leaped one story down, he was not hurt. Arjan rolled over and then stood up. Staring right into the masked men's eyes, he said, "You are not welcome here."

And then, Arjan began to knock the men out.

Nalakuvera had shouted for guards to come over, but till the time they arrived, Arjan would have to deal with them. One of the masked men headed towards Arjan with a sword, but Arjan swiftly slashed the man's throat with his sickle. And then, he plunged the sickle in another man's stomach.

The men kept coming one after the other. Blood was spraying everywhere as Arjan took the men's lives.

As he defeated his opponents with ease, he felt good. He felt powerful. He was invincible now. And this time, too, he had a reason for taking their lives. It was self-defense. These pious *bhakts* had come to his palace to kill him. Fighting back was necessary.

And then, one of the men remained. He began to whimper as he looked at Arjan.

"Leave before I kill you."

The man ran away outside, towards the main street. Arjan looked up on the first floor where Nalakuvera was standing. He looked proud. Arjan, then, scanned his surroundings. A pile of corpses lay in front of him, with the masked men's blood pooling on the floor.

"Serves them right," Nalakuvera said, laughing.

"I didn't think I would have to resort to this," Arjan spoke, guilt-ridden. He had calmed down now that his life wasn't in danger. "People should have the freedom to fight back a ruler they don't believe in. That's all right, but being violent about it and trying to kill the king is wrong."

"What's worse, Arjan," Nalakuvera spoke, "is that Guru Narendra is not a good man. He needs to be put down."

"But should I keep putting down people just because they oppose me?" Arjan asked him, perplexed.

"Yes. You have to be brutal." Nalakuvera leaned forward on the railing. "Just like you were tonight. These men got a taste of their own medicine. The last one you sent would tell people what happened here today."

"Why did he do this? This is treason," Arjan said, referring to Guru Narendra.

"Because," Nalakuvera shrugged, "if you confront him, he can just deny that he had a hand in this. He will say that those were not his men and you won't have any proof. That is his plan. And I think we haven't seen the last of him. He might be planning another attack, since his men have failed to kill you."

Arjan gritted his teeth. He didn't know what to do. *Being a king is not easy.*

"Also," Nalakuvera began, "he was behind something related to you. I did some digging and found out something about Guru Narendra, something connected to you."

Arjan's curiosity was piqued. *Narendra and me?* They were both poles apart and he had never met the old man before the council meeting.

"What?"

"He was the one who forced Urvashi into throwing you and Rudra in prison."

What? No . . .

"So that means—"

Nalakuvera nodded. "That means, my friend, he was the reason Rudra died."

31

Padma, Smrit, and Ratna Maru were riding towards Dandak Hills on the horses they had stolen from the Rudra camp.

The hooves beat against the snow on the ground. And when they finally reached the hill from where they could see the Vanar camp, they all saw that the ground around the camp had been dug up.

Padma had thought the Rudras were sleeping. But they had wasted no time in putting their plan into action.

The dug-up area was at some distance from the camp. And it was dead of the night; everyone was asleep.

They won't even know what hit them. They'll die in their sleep!

Padma and the others quietly made their way towards the camp, away from the hundreds of Rudras who were busy planting leaves inside the ground. Some Rudras had been tasked with carrying wooden buckets filled with hot water.

As soon as the leaves were put in place, the air around would fill with the deadliest poison known. The Vanars' bodies would burn, eventually killing them. Shuko flew towards Padma and perched on her shoulder after scanning the entire zone. "North! North!" he squawked.

Padma had sent him to look where Macchanu was. She had to stop him. Even if Lord Bajrang had abandoned Macchanu's mother, he had no right to kill the Vanars just because they followed him. They were innocent.

"You go and wake up Lord Bajrang," Padma said to Ratna Maru. She didn't want to face the Ancient right now. "I will handle his son."

"Are you sure you don't want to come?" Ratna Maru asked.

"Yes. Tell him and the Vanars about the Rudras' plan. They need to know what's coming for them. And they must gear up for a fight."

Ratna Maru pursed her lips and nodded. "Take care," she said, and headed towards the Vanar camp on her horse along with Smrit. Padma headed north to look for Macchanu.

"Wait," Padma whispered.

Ratna Maru and Smrit stopped, confused.

"What happened?"

Padma had wanted to say this for a while, so she just blurted it out, "I want you to come to Indragarh with me, after this is over. *If* there is an after for us."

Ratna Maru had not anticipated this. She looked surprised but happy. "Are you sure? I thought you wanted to go alone."

"I did," Padma smiled, "but you kind of grow on people."

"Well," Ratna Maru laughed, "I will keep on bugging you. Don't say later on that I didn't warn you." And then Ratna Maru and Smrit swiftly rode towards the main entrance of the Vanar camp.

Padma headed in the north direction but couldn't spot Macchanu anywhere.

Determined to find him, and kill if necessary, with a heavy heart she plunged herself into the unknown.

32

Kalki wondered if he would escape alive from here as he looked at the army of white-cloaked priests in front of him.

Though Kalki and Jambavan had managed to jump outside when the fiery boulder had hit the cave, Jambavan had been hurt. His face had been scalded. He was heaving, trying to withstand the pain.

Jamabavan can't fight. I will have to handle this alone.

Kalki took out his sword, ready to pounce at whoever came close to attack.

"You think you can defeat all of us, huh?" Bhargav yelled. "You can't save yourself. Even that wretched bear is down. He wouldn't survive for long."

"Stupid," Jambavan mumbled, weak and pale, "I am immortal."

Kalki couldn't help but grin.

"Remember . . ." Jambavan said, "courage comes from doing the right thing. Less training you had. But you will do well."

Kalki nodded. He looked at the army of priests and the elephant in front of him. Bhargav was leaning on his axe.

"I thought you didn't have enough people to help you," Kalki said, his sword shining under the blue light of the sky.

"Did I say that?" the old man asked. "I meant to say I don't have enough men to *spare* for a quick assassination. Moreover, you were coming to me without any hassle. But now with all this nuisance you have created, I feel it would have been easier to have my men bring you to me."

Kalki didn't waste any more time. Clutching his sword, he went towards the priests to attack. Deflecting their blades with ease, he began to slash and stab.

Kalki banged the hilt of his sword at one of the priests' head, and plunged his sword in another. As he swung his sword at the men in front of him, they died one by one, their white cloaks smeared in red.

He didn't need to use his newly-discovered strength. But still he closed his eyes and concentrated, letting the power surge inside him.

The moment he opened his eyes, he saw arrows coming towards him.

Kalki rolled away, and then aimed his sword with precision, Channelling the power of Lord Raghav inside him. He threw the sword in the air, directly at the arrows.

Bullseye!

"Oh, so you know now how to use your power."

"Of course." Kalki smiled but Bhargav wasn't looking at him anymore. He was glaring at the elephant. The elephant let out a deafening roar, swinging his trunk.

And the elephant was heading towards Kalki!

Right when the elephant was about to crush him under his feet, Kalki rolled away. He closed his eyes again, focusing on the strength inside him. And as the strength increased, Kalki realised that anger was surging inside him as well. Bhargav had hurt Jambavan, and now he planned to kill both of them.

They will die . . . just like Lakshmi . . . like Bala . . .

Kalki inhaled deeply and then opened his eyes. They were filled with wrath. He looked like an angry god.

Time to end Bhargav once and for all!

33

Manasa spotted the hideout from a distance. Just like she had been told, it was fifty steps away from the western gate of the city.

That boy was right.

She had a small dagger with her that Airavan had given to her, so she could protect herself if things went sideways. Right now, she was hiding in the bushes, observing what was happening in this camp.

Strange men in blue robes—the symbol of a cobra was etched on them—were loading their weapons and food in carriages. They were bald and had no brows, but their striking blue eyes, so deep and mesmerising, was the first thing that Manasa had noticed. She was sure now that these men were Nagas.

They are leaving.

Manasa couldn't see the Mother or any lady amongst the followers. She began to come closer, hoping to overhear something about the Mother or the scroll, when she heard a hiss.

Two huge cobras were behind her.

She must have kept them as guardians.

As the one of the cobras slithered towards her to bite, Manasa slashed it with her dagger. A moment's hesitation and she would have been poisoned.

The other cobra spun to attack her with its poisonous fangs, but Manasa dodged him. She held it down with her foot, and then plunged her dagger in the animal.

Manasa folded her hands towards the dead cobras. They were the products of Lord Shesh Naag who the Nagas worshipped. Closing her eyes, she silently prayed to the lord to forgive her.

When she opened her eyes, she heard multiple footsteps.

Three hooded figures were coming towards her, alarmed by the noise Manasa had made whilst killing the cobras.

"I thought you didn't have faith in gods," a gravelly, hoarse voice said.

It was so familiar.

No. It can't be.

The figure in the centre of the hooded figures had a hunched back and was leaning on a wooden stick. The figures on her side seemed like they were guarding her, ready to kill Manasa if she made a move.

"Why do you sound so familiar?"

"Why do you have to always come and ruin my plans?" the voice asked, yelling.

"Who are you?"

The figure didn't move or speak for a few seconds. And then, the hood was pulled back. Inside the hood was a wounded, bandaged, disfigured face of someone who once used to be beautiful. The nose was crooked, and multiple scars and bruises were on the face. One eye was covered in a bandage, and the other eye was slightly popping out.

But even in the worst possible look, Manasa could recognise this person.

The very person she had thrown from the vimana.

Someone who was supposed to be dead.

"Kadru," Manasa said, knowing very well that things had just turned from bad to worse.

34

Arjan knew he would be committing a murder. But he was okay with it.

That bastard is responsible for Rudra's death.

As he ventured down the street alone, his face wrapped in a cloth, he came close to the temple.

The very temple where Guru Narendra sat every evening to pray.

Arjan had his sickle with him as he walked in the empty, dark street. He stood close to the main gates for a few seconds. Two of the guru's followers were standing outside.

Arjan removed the cloth wrapped around his face. The men at the gates got alarmed but they could do nothing. Within moments, Arjan slit their throats. Their bodies dropped on the ground with a thud.

Arjan now headed inside, making his way towards the Vishnu idol where Guru Narendra was sitting. His followers were loitering in the temple, surprised to see Arjan. Some of them tried to stop him, but Arjan didn't want to waste time dealing with them.

Clutching his sickle, he swiftly killed whoever came in his way. Blood was flowing like water on the floor of the temple.

I have to kill him. And I don't care who else dies in the process.

Kali was evil but that didn't change the fact that he had been right. Arjan couldn't let anyone trample over him. *And if someone harms you, you harm them. An eye for an eye.*

Arjan finally saw the Lord Vishnu idol, and in front of it sat a bald priest, his hands folded in prayer. Guru Narendra was chanting loudly.

Nalakuvera had told Arjan that killing the guru openly would create problems. He had said that he could arrange for the guru to be killed in secret. If Arjan was going to be so brazen, the people of the city who revere the guru might revolt.

And Arjan had said, "Let them."

Arjan walked calmly towards the priest, covered in the blood of the people he had killed on his way. And then he brought the sickle close to Guru Narendra's throat.

The head priest stopped chanting. He turned his head to the side, looking at the sickle.

"I want you to die knowing it was me who killed you," Arjan said. "It is me who gets to kill you. And win."

Guru Narendra was silent for a moment. "But do you really win by doing this? Have you become the man you were supposed to be?"

There was a time when Arjan would've realised that killing this man wouldn't bring his lover back. He would've also realised that his brother, Kalki, would've never approved of such a thing. But that was the old Arjan. The Arjan of now could only remember how he had felt when he had burned Rudra's body on the pyre.

"No," Arjan said, bringing his sickle closer to the throat, piercing the skin, "I have become the man the world *forced* me to be."

35

Padma fell from her horse.

Her face smacked on the snowy ground. Blood oozed out of her nose as she yelled in pain. And behind her stood Macchanu.

They had been fighting on horseback, but then Macchanu had grabbed her and tossed her on the ground.

She still held on to her spear. Shuko was flying overhead. She was hoping that he would attack at the right time to distract him.

Macchanu's men weren't aiding him in attacking Padma. They were busy digging and putting the poisonous leaves in the dug-up area, over the dry ice. And Macchanu had specifically told them not to move until the work was over.

"You can't stop me, girl," he said loudly. "I will do the right thing."

"Killing innocents isn't right."

"Following Bajrang isn't right either. People should realise he's a hypocrite. He cannot save anyone."

"You have no right to take anyone's life," Padma said. "Listen, I know how you feel. I have gone through this. It was the worst time of my life. My father chose not to help me. He was a coward. But you have to live with it. At the end of the day, you have to realise that even if bad things happen to you, you must not let them shape you into a bad person. You must tell the world that no matter what you throw at me, I wouldn't lose who I am. I wouldn't lose the goodness in me," Padma yelled.

Macchanu got down from his horse and came at her with his thorned iron mace. He swung the mace to smack her but she managed to roll away. Unable to reach her spear, Padma just dashed towards Macchanu. She jumped on his back and shouted in his ears: "By doing this, you are proving to the world that it has been successful in making the worst version of you. I used to be like you. But I have realised I was wrong."

Macchanu grabbed Padma with his burly, hairy hands and hurled her across the ground.

She felt a searing pain in her back. Before she could muster the strength to get up, she saw the Rudra leader approaching her. Macchanu hovered over her, ready to kill.

As Macchanu swung his mace, inches away from Padma's face, someone jumped over him. Macchanu lost his balance and fell.

Padma managed to sit up, squinting her eyes in the darkness to make out who it was.

It was Ratna Maru! With the double-ended spear, she fought with Macchanu.

She will keep him busy.

Padma looked around. The Rudras were still busy arranging the leaves, and did not notice that Vanars were tiptoeing towards them.

When some Rudras turned to grab the terracotta jars filled with hot water, Vanars plunged their daggers inside them.

And pandemonium ensued.

The Vanars and the Rudras began to tear into each other.

As Ratna Maru and Macchanu battled in front of her, Padma got up and grabbed her spear. She toppled a Rudra, pushing him into the dug-up area. His body instantly began to burn as it came into contact with the poison.

Another Rudra tried to throw scalding hot water on her, but before he could, Shuko flew down and attacked him.

The terracotta jar fell from his hands as he tried to shoo the bird away. Padma thanked the bird and plunged her spear in his leg.

The Rudra howled in pain. Padma picked up the water jar he had dropped and poured the water on him.

But her relief was short-lived for at that moment, she heard a loud cackle.

Padma swivelled her head to see the scene in front of her—Macchanu was brutally smashing his mace on Ratna Maru's face.

"NOOOO!" Padma yelled.

Ratna Maru was bleeding profusely. Padma had to stop Macchanu or her friend would die. She looked around her, wondering where Lord Bajrang was.

And her gaze fell on the leaves.

Grabbing the gloves of the Rudra that lay dead on the ground, she stretched her hand towards the leaves and took some out.

This will be the end of you.

Macchanu's attention was on Ratna Maru's battered face. He didn't see who was coming at his back. Padma sprinted towards Macchanu and shoved the leaves inside his mouth and closed it.

Macchanu gasped. He couldn't breathe. His throat was burning and his eyes had turned red. And Padma heaved a sigh of relief. She then turned towards Ratna Maru, smiling at her friend.

Ratna Maru lay completely still. Her face was unrecognisable after the beating she had received. Her eyes gazed vacantly at the sky.

No.

Tears streamed down Padma's face as she closed Ratna Maru's eyes.

"It'll be fine," Padma said to herself.

But she knew that she wasn't fine. She had just lost the only good friend she had. Even as she grieved for Ratna Maru, she couldn't help but think, *Where the hell is Lord Bajrang?*

36

Red smoke was emanating from Kalki's body as he held on to the foot of the elephant. He was trying to push the animal away. The elephant was pushing back but couldn't move an inch.

Kalki took a deep breath, and gathered his remaining strength. And then he pushed the elephant back.

The animal lost his balance and fell on the ground.

Kalki leapt in the air and smashed the elephant's trunk with his bare hands. The animal cried in pain. He fell on the ground, unconscious.

Kalki turned to see the priests. Scared, they had scampered behind Bhargav.

Bhargav Ram was watching Kalki intently. He was still leaning on the axe he had brought with him. But now, there was fear in his eyes.

The Avatar of Vishnu walked towards Bhargav, his sword glinting in the light. He swung the axe towards Kalki, but Kalki stopped it like it was nothing.

"How . . ." Bhargav's eyes widened in horror. "How are you doing this? This was a gift from Lord Shiva. It was made by him. *HIM!* You know who Lord Shiva is? He will cripple you. He will destroy you. Who are you, eh?" he yelled.

"I'm Vishnu." Kalki smiled and threw the axe away. He grabbed Bhargav by the neck and pulled him up in the air. "You were right.

I'm no hero. But I don't try to be one as well. And perhaps, that's what matters most in the end."

"You can't kill me."

"I know. The only way I can do it is if I go back and get the Sword of Shiva and slaughter you." Kalki was disappointed. "But I don't want to. I still respect you." Kalki went to stand on a cliff, dragging Bhargav along. He could spot a frozen lake below them. "I really do." He held him close to where he could easily drop him. Bhargav was suspended in the air now. "What you did in the past has shaped you. And perhaps if it wasn't for the curse, you would have turned out to be the teacher I was meant to be with. But I promise you, I wouldn't let this incident tarnish your image. I will make sure everyone remembers you as my guru. Because I don't want the people to lose hope in the goodness of the great Bhargav Ram. I still want them to believe that you trained the Avatar of Vishnu, even though it's a lie."

Bhargav's face had turned red. "Do as you please. What do I care about what people think of me? Mark my words: I will return. I will crush you. I will make sure you die. You can't stop me."

"And I will fight you again. And again. And again."

"By not killing me now, you are risking the next Avatar to have the same fate. I will lie and deceive him as well."

"There will be no Avatar after me. I am going to kill every last evil. This Yug will be remembered as the Yug where evil died."

Bhargav looked down, worried. "Are you going to drop me? Is that it? That's your plan. I thought you didn't want to kill me."

"You won't be killed if I throw you, silly. You'll be hurt. And believe me," he released his grip and Bhargav screamed as his body fell on the frozen lake, "you deserve at least this much for lying to me."

37

"How are you alive?" Manasa snapped. "I saw you fall down. I saw you die."

"Fall down, yes," Kadru spoke, "but you didn't see me die. You don't know this, my dear sister, but I had had a little taste of the Somalata plant before fighting you. And unknowingly it gave me the power to defeat sure death, though I was hurt and broken. It also gave me the ability to talk to snakes. And luckily, my Children," she pointed at the bald men, "nursed me back to health. They believed in me. They knew I was their Mother. Since I had survived such a huge fall, they knew I was their goddess. I was the incarnation of Lord Shesh Naag."

"That's a lie."

"It's the truth. I am special." Kadru smiled, revealing rotten teeth and a slimy mouth. Manasa wanted to throw up right then and there. "I was going to look for you, but you have a habit of interrupting my plans. I might as well kill you today, then." She turned to her men. "Attack her from her right. She has a useless hand."

The Children nodded, moving towards her with blades in their hands, ready to pounce.

What do I do? I am outnumbered.

Manasa tried to defend herself, but she was not exactly adept at fighting with swords.

"What do you plan to do with the scroll?"

Kadru pulled it out of a pocket inside her cloak. "After this? I'll get the Soma and blow your army. Take what's mine. The usual, you know. I mean, I could get the Soma any time but the scroll wasn't accessible. So thought of getting it first, before letting anyone discover that it existed. I'm surprised that you know about it, Sis."

The Children got closer to Manasa. She tried to attack them but one of the Children grabbed her wrist. The weapon in her left hand fell on the ground.

She was weak and defenceless.

Manasa didn't know what to do in this situation. "You know, Kadru," she said to her cousin as the Children swarmed around her, "you are really a pain in the ass."

And that was when a strong gust of wind swept over them.

AIRAVAN!

He was on the vimana and he instantly drove it in Manasa's direction, hitting the Children and Kadru on his way.

The scroll fell out of Kadru's hand. Manasa dove towards it, picked it up, and jumped on the vimana.

"Aren't you going to kill her?" Airavan asked. "Kill them?"

She saw the so-called Mother as well as her Children groaning in pain. Some of them were carrying weapons and running towards the vimana.

Manasa knew that she and Airavan won't be enough to kill Kadru's army.

"No," she said as Airavan struggled to lift the vimana. Airavan looked hassled. He had little knowledge about these flying chariots. "Killing your family once is fine. Twice is just plain rude."

Airavan chuckled. And so did Manasa.

Kadru will have to be dealt with, but now Manasa must return to her camp. She was happy that she had managed to obtain the scroll.

Let's start bombing that damn Kali!

38

So many deaths . . .

Padma looked at the burning funeral pyres. She was standing next to Smrit, who had decided to step in and fulfil Ratna Maru's wish to emancipate the Apsaras.

The air was gloomy. Darkness had enveloped them even though it was a bright morning. Padma observed the people standing around. A lot of Vanars were gazing at the pyres, their heads lowered. Standing at some distance from the pyres, leaning against a demolished cherry tree stood Lord Bajrang.

He couldn't even look at the burning bodies of the Vanars who had died fighting.

Padma sighed. She asked the Apsara standing beside her, "Will you be coming to Indragarh with me?"

"No." Smrit wasn't crying anymore. Padma would always remember the painful, shrill cry Smrit had let out when she had seen Ratna Maru's dead body. "Ratna Maru was the leader. But more than that, she was my friend. I need to get used to the fact that she doesn't exist anymore. I need time to mourn her death. So I'm thinking of staying with the Vanars for some time."

She looked at Padma. "She came back for you, you know. She told me she wanted you to join us. That you would be a good warrior. Our sisterhood would be stronger with you by our side."

Padma smiled. "You are strong, just like Ratna was. You people never needed me."

Smrit smiled back. Gazing at Ratna Maru's burning body, she said, "She wanted vengeance. She was planning to kill Nalakuvera. And the sad part is that I just received a raven from one of our Apsara scouts in Indragarh saying that Nalakuvera is over there. He is managing the treasury. It would have been perfect for us to go there, free the Apsaras, and kill Nalakuvera." She shook her head. "Ratna Maru died without doing that."

Padma didn't say anything. She patted Smrit on the shoulder and began to move. Shuko was perched on her shoulder. Padma walked past Lord Bajrang, ignoring him.

Lord Bajrang turned to her and asked, "Where are you going?"

"Leaving."

"Are you okay?"

Padma stopped and looked straight in his eyes. "You had a son."

Lord Bajrang's eyes softened. "It was a moment of . . . weakness. I shouldn't have broken my celibacy vow."

"I don't give a shit if you broke it or not. That's not what I'm angry about." Padma gritted her teeth. "I want you to know that if you have done something, you should stand by it rather than just leaving it behind. I prevented the deaths of hundreds of Vanars yesterday in a fight that started because of *you*. You made Macchanu into what he was. He was your son and *I had to murder him*!" she exclaimed, unable to control her anger. They were standing at some distance from the pyres, so no one else heard what she said. "And where the hell were you when we were fighting?"

"I couldn't bring myself to face him. I'm sorry, Padma. I told you I'm not perfect. Leaving the fisher-girl behind was one of my biggest mistakes, an act I deeply regret." He paused. "I didn't know it would come to this. But I'm grateful for what you did."

"My lo—, Bajrang," Padma corrected herself, "you have the ability to help this world, but you just hide in your hole. You should be fighting. Kalyug is upon us and Kalki will need you and your army when he returns." Padma squared her shoulders and stared right into Lord Bajrang's eyes. "But you won't go because you don't give a shit, do you? And I lost my friend protecting your ass. Guess what. You owe me one."

Padma left the dumbfounded Lord Bajrang and went on her way. She had never thought that she would be so disrespectful to someone like him—a legendary Ancient who had fought with an Avatar by his side.

But what's the point of having so many accolades if you can't even stand by the people who need you.

She didn't care about him anymore.

As she came close to her stallion, ready to leave for Indragarh, she told Shuko, "Go to Kalki. Tell him about Ratna Maru. Convey to him that I am on my way to Indragarh. I need to meet Arjan."

The parrot squawked.

"I know Kalki wanted me to be with you. But I want you to go. I feel he needs you right now. Don't worry. Nothing will happen to me. I can protect myself. Hell, I just killed an Ancient's son." She smiled sadly. "Good luck, friend. Hope we meet again soon."

Shuko nodded and then flew away, disappearing into the clouds.

Padma climbed on her horse and began to ride down the hill. Her mind was filled with the thoughts of her dead friend. There was a reason behind sending Shuko away. If he would've accompanied her to Indragarh, he would have noticed what she was about to do there. And Shuko would have definitely informed Kalki.

Padma didn't want anyone to know.

She wasn't going to Indragarh to just meet Arjan.

She was also going to *kill* Nalakuvera.

39

Kalki was a few steps away from the cave, or what was left of it.

He looked at the snow-peaked mountains. The sun was about to set and the sky was tinged in a beautiful mixture of red and yellow.

Jambavan got up and walked towards Kalki. He was feeling much better now. Kalki had fetched some herbs he had asked for, ground them, and made a paste that he had then applied over Jambavan's wounds.

"Need to throw bodies," he said, referring to the mangled corpses of the white-cloaked priests. "No place, so throwing in the frozen lake only."

Kalki laughed. Now that he had taken care of Bhargav and affirmed that he was not weak, like Bhargav had proclaimed, Kalki was feeling much better.

"How are you feeling?" Kalki asked, concerned.

"Fine, I will be. You worry about yourself."

Kalki nodded. The burns would heal completely with time. *Jambavan will be all right.* "I should leave for Indragarh and stop Kali."

He shook his head. "The Sword of Shiva. Get it."

"Do I really need it? I am stronger now. I feel like I can handle Kali."

"Sword of Shiva *only* way to kill Adharm," Jambavan said. "*Only.* Remember that. Sword of Shiva kills immortals and Adharm.

But not Dharm. Happened once. Won't happen again. Gods won't allow."

"Really? Who got killed by the Sword of Shiva?"

Jambavan smiled. There was sadness in his voice when he said, "That's a story for another time."

"Sure." Kalki looked at the road ahead of him and asked, "Where should we go?"

"Up. Find the Shiva temple. The Rta will guide you."

"Rta?"

"Natural order that coordinates the operation of this universe," he explained. "The Chakras from which your powers come are made from the fragments of Rta."

"I still have so much to learn," Kalki admitted. Even though he had defeated Bhargav Ram, managed to grow more powerful, and received training from Jambavan, there was still so much he didn't know.

"Let's go, then," Kalki said. "Where's your horse? Or you prefer walking?"

Jambavan frowned and then shook his head. "This journey you must complete yourself."

"Thank you for guiding me, my lord."

"I've done it many times," Jambavan said, referring to the previous Avatars.

"Where will you go?"

"Where I should have, long back." Jambavan sadly lowered his head. "My people. My village. Right, you were. Very right."

Kalki smiled. It was time to leave. But he wanted to pay his respects to Jambavan. Kalki got off Devadatta, walked towards Jambavan, and touched his feet. The Rakshas lord blessed Kalki with a long life.

Kalki climbed back on his horse and started riding ahead.

Where to, boss?

Boss? I thought I was 'human'.

Na, you beat that old whiny man's ass pretty well. You get some respect from me, at least for now.

Some? Kalki smiled. *Well, my friend, we are going to the Temple of Shiva. To find the Sword which will kill the Adharm.*

PART SIX

THE END OF AN AGE

40

Durukti had another brother.

When Kali had told her that Bali was alive, she had been elated. She had been quite young when the fire had happened. How heartbroken she had been to learn her little brother had died. She had refused to speak to Kali, or anybody else, for weeks. But Kali had been equally devastated. With time, she had learned to accept what had befallen them.

And then, about a month ago, Kali had told her that their little brother was alive. And he was none other than Arjan.

Durukti had stared open-mouthed at Kali. *Arjan?* Thank goodness she had given Soma to Arjan before his fight with Kali that time. Otherwise, Kali and Durukti would have been complicit in killing their own brother.

She had wondered how Arjan would react on learning that he was an Asura, that he was related to them. Kali had broken the news to him gently, and even offered to help Arjan fight in the war. These days, Kali had turned over a new leaf. Durukti had never seen him like this—emotional, selfless, and just plain nice. Perhaps, the fact that his brother was alive had made him look at things differently. It seemed to Durukti that Kali was trying to protect Arjan.

And Arjan . . . was being Arjan. He had chosen to bury his head in the sand. *Maybe he can't accept the fact that he is the brother of a killer.*

Durukti thought about Arjan as she took off her black robe. Kali said they had to conceal themselves, so she covered her head at all times. But she was getting sick of hiding all the time. She had voiced her exasperation to Kali, who had pacified her by saying that they will reveal themselves when the time was right. And Durukti knew that would be when Arjan defeated Manasa's army.

Durukti plopped down on her bed. She had been given a small room in Nalakuvera's fortress. The room opposite to hers belonged to Kali and Alakshmi.

There is something wrong with her.

The woman gave her the creeps. Durukti shivered in fright whenever Alakshmi was nearby. She also had to be wary of the hyenas that prowled around Alakshmi, following her wherever she went. And Durukti never forgot that the hyenas were under Alakshmi's control. One whistle from their master, and the animals will not hesitate to tear into Durukti's flesh.

Durukti knew that Kali was planning to bear children with Alakshmi and the thought scared her. She was sure that Alakshmi wouldn't be a good mother.

She couldn't understand why, but she also felt that Alakshmi was hiding something.

Durukti got up. She wore her slippers and made way to Kali's room, hoping to catch up. Koko and Vikoko, his trusted guards, weren't standing outside his room. *Maybe they have gone to eat. Kali doesn't need protection inside the fortress anyway.*

She was about to knock, but then she heard someone mumbling.

"Why do you want me to do this?" Kali asked.

"Help your brother? He's the perfect ruler," Alakshmi replied in her raspy voice.

"No, he's not. Believe me, I want to help him. But I don't think he's ready to be a ruler. That wretched guru ordered his followers to attack him today, but still Arjan is not doing anything. I think I can manage this situation better. Arjan can take the throne once my reign is over."

"Is the throne more important than your own brother, my lord?"

Kali didn't know what to say.

"You have more pressing issues to worry about."

"Like?"

There was a pause. "The Adharm rides back."

"Kalki."

Durukti still couldn't digest the fact that Kalki was evil. As far as she knew, Kalki had never done anything that would be considered wrong. Unlike her brother, he hadn't enjoyed killing people. *I wonder where Kalki is right now.*

"He will seek the throne, my lord, just as Shukra had predicted. And do you know what he will do to get the throne?"

"He will kill Arjan," Kali responded.

Kalki will never do that. This wretched woman has brainwashed my brother.

Alakshmi hissed, "Yes, yes. He will kill him."

"But they've been brothers all their life, even if Arjan was adopted."

"But what will he do when he learns Arjan's an Asura? Will that not make him feel like he has been betrayed? He will be angry and will not hesitate to murder your brother, the brother you've united with after so long."

Durukti heard someone stomp their foot on the ground. "Yes, you're right. I can't trust that village boy. He toyed around with Durukti as well. And he killed Martanja, my ally."

"Yes, indeed," Alakshmi hissed again. "Let your brother rule. And keep advising him, like you have done till now. And protect him when the time comes."

Kali and Alakshmi were silent for a few seconds.

Durukti cautiously opened the door and peered inside.

Alakshmi was massaging Kali's head with oil. They were sitting in front of a mirror.

"We need to bear children, my lord. The Asura race must continue. It must grow and prosper like it did in the past."

"Yes." Though Kali had agreed with her, Durukti could tell that he looked uncertain. He even seemed slightly afraid.

And before she could hear any further, someone whispered in her ear, "I didn't know you liked eavesdropping, Lady Durukti."

There was a sharp intake of breath when Durukti saw who had just spoken to her.

It was Rambha, Nalakuvera's wife. Even straight out of bed, with her hair in a simple bun and nothing but a translucent robe on her body, she looked beautiful.

Rambha was watching Durukti intently, her face expressionless.

Is she angry? What should I do?

"Lady Rambha," Durukti said, blushing. "I was just um . . ."

"I'm not a lady. I'm a tool to give pleasure to my husband . . . a very special tool. Follow me."

What? That's how her husband treats her? And she is okay with it?

Durukti had heard of how Yakshas treated women. It was despicable. Yet, Rambha seemed like she had no problem being treated like an object. Durukti was confused. She thought about all this as she followed Rambha down the hall, away from the people she was spying on. She tried to come up with a good reason as to why she had been eavesdropping, but before she could even utter a word, Rambha said, "I can understand. You don't trust the new woman."

"Yes, yes. I don't. How did you know?"

"I don't trust Asuras, my dear," Rambha said, ignoring her question. "Even you. But you are just an idiot while she . . . she's just insane."

Durukti didn't know whether to be relieved or upset. *Better not say anything.*

They walked down the stairs and soon stood outside the basement. A Yaksha was standing guard.

"Why have we come here?"

"Do not be hasty, my dear. For now, understand that I'm trying to help you."

Rambha nodded at the guard. The Yaksha lighted the lamp and led the way inside. They walked for some time, and then reached a hall filled with cages. The prisoners inside had been handcuffed in iron chains.

All the prisoners were women.

"What . . . what is . . ." Durukti couldn't believe her eyes. The fortress had a dungeon in the basement. Clearly, these girls were slaves. And some of them looked so young. She eyed the girl in the cage at the front. *She doesn't look a day older than twelve!*

All of them were beautiful, extremely so. That's when Durukti realised that they were Apsaras. They were clinging to the bars of their cages, curious to see who had come with Lady Rambha.

"This is my husband's favourite place," Rambha said. "He plays around with every girl here."

Great. My brother and I are staying in the fortress of a pervert.

"Why are they in cages?"

"Because then they wouldn't be able to escape, silly. Many do. I don't know why. We give them food, let them exercise to maintain their amazing physique. And when my husband comes to play with them, we inject an aphrodisiac in the girls' bodies. So everyone has fun."

Durukti was speechless. There was so much she wanted to say, but she had to remind herself that she was in a dark basement, alone with Nalakuvera's wife and a Yaksha guard. Rambha could easily order the guard to execute her, and no one would ever know what happened.

"All right," Rambha said, smiling, "here's how I can help. The girls are not here just to pleasure my husband. Some of them are brilliant spies. You can hire any one of them and instruct them to find out about Alakshmi. You can grant them a reward. Just don't give them too much food. Nala doesn't like them fat."

Durukti looked at their faces. They seemed eager to get out. *It's unfortunate that I can only choose one.*

She spotted a girl who was sitting inside the cage, her eyes downcast. Unlike the other girls, she didn't seem interested in getting out. The girl was busy making some sort of drawing on the ground with her finger.

"I want her."

Rambha opened the cage and roughly pushed the girl in front of Durukti.

"What's your name, girl?" Rambha asked.

"Meera."

Rambha smiled. "Well, Meera, Lady Durukti wants you to do something really important for her."

Meera nodded and then looked up at Durukti.

Well, I guess I have a spy now.

Durukti, Rambha, with Meera behind them, ascended the stairs and came out of the basement. As they reached the common hall, Durukti spotted Kali and Nalakuvera talking to each other. Some Yaksha guards were standing around them.

Durukti walked towards Kali and asked, "What happened?"

"Guru Narendra has been murdered," Nalakuvera said flatly. "His throat was slit by our very own king, tonight."

A chill ran down Durukti's spine. *Arjan has killed someone?*

She looked at Kali. He was grinning from ear to ear. "Well, I'm glad. That man deserved to die," he said.

"You are glad," Nalakuvera said, trying to control his anger, "but what will we do when riots start happening, huh? And things are only going to get worse now. Arjan won't stop even after killing the head priest. He plans to close all the temples in the city. The people who practise the faith . . . they will lose their mind. I bloody told him to be careful, to be discreet."

Kali put his hand on Nalakuvera's shoulder. "It's all right, friend. I'm sure our king has thought everything through."

"Doesn't seem like it," Nalakuvera said, shaking his head. "You should have seen him. He was covered in blood from head to toe. If I didn't know any better, I would say he is becoming a monster." Nalakuvera sighed. "And on top of all this, he's going to enter the battlefield tomorrow."

"Kali, I'm worried about Arjan," Durukti said to her brother.

"It's all right, my dear sister. He will be fine. Our king is going to battle with the Danavs at his side." Kali embraced Durukti and whispered in her ears, "He's finally showing the colours of a true Asura."

41

The king of Indragarh was battling along with his army like a soldier. Arjan had just thrown his spear at a Naga. He didn't want to use the sickle he had received from his mother. It was precious. He didn't want it to be sullied with blood.

The spear reached its target, piercing the Naga's chest. Blood gushed out of Arjan's enemy, spraying like a fountain.

He headed towards the dead man to retrieve his weapon. The air was thick with the smell of fresh blood. It made Arjan feel . . . strong . . . powerful.

He pulled out the spear and began to attack the enemy soldiers. Two Nagas were about to finish off some of his men. Arjan charged towards them. He kicked one of the Nagas, and slashed another's throat.

The remaining Naga yelled in anger. He ran towards Arjan, wielding his sword.

Arjan blocked him with his shield.

While Arjan held him off, another Naga ran towards him at his back. He was inches away from killing Arjan with his sword, when Arjan swiftly moved away. The Naga ended up killing his own comrade.

Arjan didn't waste another second. The Naga lay dead on the floor, Arjan's spear lodged in his throat.

He helped his men stand up.

At that moment, Arjan saw a volley of arrows aimed at him. He managed to save himself through his shield, but his men were only carrying swords.

These bloody Suparns.

Manasa's army was winning. Arjan looked around and everywhere his men lay either wounded or dead. Some were still battling, but the Nagas were monstrously strong.

And now we should retrieve.

Arjan's plan was to go with his foot soldiers in the beginning to fight. After a little while, they would head back to their camp. The Danavs will take care of the enemy as Arjan and his men relaxed and drank ale.

The Danavs appeared on the battlefield now. They crushed the enemy soldiers on the ground and smashed the Suparns flying in the air.

Arjan smiled as he looked at the giants. Even with just two of the Danavs, their victory was assured for the day.

The victorious king of Indragarh had arrived at his camp. The enemy had chosen to retreat once the Danavs had entered the battlefield.

The war, according to Arjan, would be over very soon. He had decided to set up a camp near the open area where they had battled. He could have just left for his palace, but he wanted to stay near the battlefield and make sure that everything was well in place.

He was being tended to by two Apsaras. They were massaging his body. A shaman was checking to see if there were any wounds or scars.

"How is it possible that a man goes to war and doesn't get hurt? How many did you kill, Your Highness?" the shaman asked.

"Around a hundred," Arjan replied casually. "I was covered in blood. Have you washed it off my body?" he asked the Apsara. She nodded.

"Fascinating," the shaman commented. "My fellow doctors and I want to study how your body works, to see where you get your strength."

"From the idea that if I kill one, I save ten," Arjan said.

"No, scientifically, Your Highness."

"There's no science that can measure my strength, doc. I possess magic."

"Is that why you have closed all the temples?"

Arjan shot him a look. "I chose to close them because our religion was propagating false values."

"But some people aren't happy about this."

"Eventually, they will understand that I closed the temples for everyone's good." Arjan stood up, crackling his knuckles. He turned to the general of his army and asked, "What do you think, General? Will we win this war?"

"Of course, Your Highness."

"Great. Wonderful." Arjan clapped his hands. "Prepare a feast for all the survivors. Do the giants eat anything?"

"Uh . . ." the general scratched his head, "I have never seen them eat anything."

"I'm not sure either." Arjan was silent for a few moments, thinking. "Perhaps they don't."

"Perhaps." The general shrugged. "Your Highness, a messenger has arrived from the Vanar camp, demanding to meet the king for some important matter. We don't believe she's really a messenger."

"Why?" he asked.

"For one, she isn't a Vanar."

Vanar camp? He had read about them in Kali's archives after his coronation. It was customary to read who the previous kings and queens did dealings with, to be informed about them.

Arjan had come to know that Kali had sent a few of his soldiers to aid General Taar some time back.

Have they come to ask for more soldiers?

"What's her name?"

They had begun to move towards the tent where the messenger was waiting. And when Arjan entered, his eyes saw a bruised, wearied girl.

He knew this girl very well.

The girl smiled softly as she looked at Arjan and flung herself in his arms.

"Padma." Arjan smiled, embracing her back.

She pulled away after a few seconds. Though Arjan had seen her only a few months ago, she somehow looked much older. She had a wide grin on her face as she looked at Arjan and said, "Who knew that the man I'd left at Vedanta's fort would one day becoming king, huh."

42

It had been over an hour. Durukti was waiting on the terrace for Meera but there was no sign of her. With every second that passed, Durukti's worry increased.

She peered down at the lawn. Alakshmi and Kali were standing together, talking. Their guards were standing a few steps away from them. Durukti saw Alakshmi teaching Kali to whistle like her, to control the two hyenas.

Durukti wanted to talk to Kali, wanted to convey that she didn't trust Alakshmi. But after what she had overheard, she felt afraid of her brother. She just couldn't understand what he was thinking. *Does he really care about Arjan?*

She got tired of waiting.

I should just go to my room.

Sighing, Durukti went down the stairs and walked in the empty corridor. A few guards had been stationed here. They bowed when they saw her.

The Yakshas in the fort knew about them—the three Asuras staying together with Nalakuvera. They didn't question their king for he was their god and you can't question a god.

A god . . .

As Durukti came near her room, her mind began to fill with thoughts of Arjan. He was becoming more and more like Kali.

Kali had smashed the temples when he had been king, and now, Arjan had closed all of them down. *Does he realise the enormity of what he has done?*

Durukti was about to enter her room when she smelled something.

A putrid stench was wafting from Kali's room. The door was ajar. Durukti opened it and peered inside.

And inside was a corpse. The body lay flat on the ground. Blood was seeping out of it on the floor. And over the corpse, a hyena was busy chewing the flesh. Durukti gasped in horror as she looked at the dead body's face.

Meera! My spy.

She must have come to this room to find something on Alakshmi, but ended up meeting her death.

Durukti screamed, panicked. The sound alerted the hyena. It bared its bloody fangs, looking at Durukti.

Within a second, it lurched itself towards Durukti. Durukti ran outside, slamming the door in the hyena's face. She held the door handle to prevent the animal from getting out.

For a few minutes, the hyena kept growling. But soon, the growling stopped. The animal gave up. Wiping the beads of sweat on her forehead, Durukti wondered what to do. She prayed to god to spare her life. Asuras were atheists, but Durukti didn't care about that right now. And then she let go of the door handle, and ran towards her room.

Poor Meera. She died because of me.

Durukti knew there would be questions about who the trespasser was and what she was doing in Kali's room. She would have to pretend that she knew nothing about what had just happened.

It had been an hour. Durukti hadn't been able to sleep. And then she heard footsteps. Alarmed, she got up and quietly opened her door. She saw Koko and Vikoko entering Kali's room.

Kali was standing outside, next to Alakshmi, looking confused. Nalakuvera and Rambha were present as well.

"How did a bloody trespasser enter my room?" Kali scowled, looking at Nalakuvera. "I thought your soldiers were alert."

Nalakuvera looked perturbed. He was gazing at the dead girl. "Kali, I don't know what to say. And I feel . . . as if I've seen—"

"She's an Apsara. Maybe she wanted to steal something," Rambha suggested, eyeing Durukti. She had noticed Durukti peeping from her room. "It happens. No big deal. But the creature shouldn't have killed her for it."

"My pet sensed danger from the girl. It reacted like it should have," Alakshmi said coldly. Don't you agree, dear?" she asked Kali.

"Absolutely. Thievery is as bad as murder. Koko," he ordered his general, "take the body and call a bunch of nurses to wash this room."

Nalakuvera added, "I will make sure that the room is cleaned properly, Kali."

Everyone dispersed. Durukti calmly and silently closed the door. She heaved a sigh of relief. She had been so afraid that the others would find out the truth.

I should have never done this in the first place. I can't be so reckless.

There was a knock on her door. Durukti immediately got up, startled.

"Durukti?" It was Alakshmi.

Durukti opened the door and the onyx-haired Alakshmi entered. She had a smile on her face.

"What?"

Alakshmi came closer to Durukti, her face inches away.

"I know it was you," Alakshmi said, still smiling. "My hyenas told me."

43

Manasa had arrived at her camp a week ago with the scroll in her hand. She had informed Vibhishan about what had happened, about how she had managed to procure the scroll to make Soma bombs.

She had immediately gathered the Suparn engineers and told them what was to be done. The engineers had been trying to make the bombs, but for some reason, they weren't working. Making the mixture was tricky, they had said.

For seven days, she had fought with Kali's army. And every day, she had been forced to retreat as her men were trampled on by Danavs.

But today, the engineers had called Manasa to see the testing of the bombs. They were hoping that they had gotten the mixture right.

Manasa climbed on her chariot with Vibhishan as they headed south of the war camp, where the forest was. Soon they were surrounded by tall, towering trees, enveloped in darkness.

"Do you think it'll work?" Manasa asked, afraid of the answer.

Vibhishan shrugged. "I have no clue, my dear."

They rode in silence for a few minutes.

"Do you regret not killing Kadru?" Vibhishan had been thinking of asking Manasa about her cousin.

"I don't care about her. That day when we were fighting, I should have made sure she was dead. Who knew she had consumed some of the Somalata plant that day. Now, she has gone mad and refers to some overgrown Naga followers as her Children. But she doesn't scare me."

Vibhishan said, "Then why do you sound so worried?"

Because, deep down, Manasa couldn't ignore the fact that Kadru was still out there. And she wouldn't sit quietly.

They were almost at the end of the forest when they spotted Naga guards. And in front of them stood Airavan.

The chariot stopped. Vibhishan and Manasa stepped down and joined the general. Airavan led them towards the engineers.

"As you know, Your Majesty, the Suparns have been trying to make bombs for a week now. They were preparing Astras as per the instructions on the scroll you gave, but they just wouldn't blow up."

Manasa looked at the catapult which had been stationed there. There was no depression anywhere on the ground near it.

"But they say that they have been very careful in making the concoction for the bombs. They should have positive results today."

"We better. One more attack by the Danavs and we are dead. Get the Astras on the catapults."

Airavan nodded. He looked at the Suparn engineers and began to shout orders. The engineers loaded the Astra on the catapult. It was glowing with a bluish liquid inside.

As the Astra was placed on the catapult, one of the engineers scampered to Manasa. "Your Majesty?"

"Yes?"

"We followed the instructions written on Lord Raavan's scroll, but the Astras weren't working. So we have altered the quantity of the substances used. But this is still a trial. We don't know what the result will be."

"That's fine. Let's keep our fingers crossed and hope for the best."

"Thank you. The scroll specified that the Soma liquid extracted from the Somalata plants had to be mixed with the ground weed—"

Manasa snapped at him. "You don't have to tell me all the ingredients. Just get on with the testing."

The engineer nodded.

Vibhishan, Airavan, and Manasa moved towards the side, looking at the field where the Astra would be thrown.

"All right, Your Majesty. Just to let you know, the Soma we have used today is much less than the quantity that will be actually put in the bombs. Since we are just testing right now, we don't want to blow up too much," Airavan said, and then ordered the engineer to shoot.

The engineer fired the bomb and the moment it came into contact with the ground, a deafening explosion occurred. There was a blinding flash of light. Manasa and the others had to close their eyes and cover their ears.

When Manasa opened her eyes, she saw that all the trees around them had blown up. There was a huge depression on the ground where the Astra had hit.

"What the . . ." Manasa couldn't believe this.

In fact, none of them could. The engineers looked happy though. Their efforts had borne results. Vibhishan had almost fainted. He was wiping the sweat on his forehead.

Manasa bit her lip as she turned to Airavan and asked, "How much Soma did you *use*?"

"Your Majesty," Airavan turned to face Manasa, "we used a tablespoon of it."

44

In the week that Padma had spent with Arjan, she had realised that he was a changed man now. Right now, they were sitting next to each other in Arjan's tent.

Arjan's army had won the battle again. And like every day for the past week, he had organised a feast for the soldiers. Some of them were enjoying their drinks, discussing the fight that had happened during the day. Though many of them were still in the infirmary, recuperating after the fight.

"Let's walk for a bit."

Arjan and Padma walked away from the feast area and made their way towards the open ground, just outside Arjan's tent. As they walked in silence, the sound of flutes and harmonica receded.

People were bowing to Arjan. It was a sign of respect but Padma noticed the fear in their eyes. *I wonder what the people of Indragarh really think of their king.*

"Kalki thought you needed saving." Padma smiled, shaking her head. "Clearly, he was wrong."

"Even so, Padma, it's good that you came here. I was wondering what you were up to all this time. I remember that day when I helped you escape, and . . ." Arjan suddenly grew pensive. "I used to be so naïve. I used to think that doing good and being good was the most important thing. Look at me now."

"Yes, you have changed."

Arjan closed his eyes, as if trying to push away the thoughts he was having. "But you have had quite a journey. Fighting the Pisach, helping the Vanars, and meeting Lord Bajrang. Dear me, I thought he didn't exist, but he very much does."

"And he's not what you expect." Padma frowned.

Arjan and Padma stopped as they saw the Danavs on the ground, snoring. He and Padma had walked quite a distance.

"We should head back," Arjan said. "I have a palace now. I'll set up a room for you. You know most of what happened with me but we still have a lot to catch up on."

"Yeah, you fought Kali, almost defeated him, then helped Vedanta's daughter take away his throne, and now," she looked up at the giants, "you are taking help from him to defeat the snake queen. A lot has changed."

"Who knew that I, a mere villager, would be king one day."

"Well, Indragarh is going to prosper under your reign. I have no doubt about it and—" The rest of Padma's sentence was drowned out because of the Danavs' snoring.

"I still can't believe they actually exist," Padma said. "I thought they were a myth created by the Asuras to scare the rest of the Tribes."

"I have trouble believing it too. But they are here, and they only listen to Kali. I was thinking of getting rid of them before, but I need them for winning this war. Manasa slaughtered my people."

"Your people, huh?" Padma couldn't help but smile. "Gods, you have been on the throne for merely ten days and you're already speaking like a true king."

Arjan laughed without restrain.

Suddenly, Padma clasped his hand. They used to be soft but now they were filled with scars and cuts. "I just want you to know . . . that day when you helped me escape, I wanted to come back for you. But I thought you had died. I'm sorry, I should've—"

Padma couldn't finish her sentence. Arjan had pulled her into a tight hug.

"You did what I told you to do—help my brother. I will be eternally grateful for that."

Padma smiled. *Maybe he hasn't changed that much.*

"When will he come back here?" he asked.

"He will return soon." *I hope he does.* She hadn't heard anything from him since he had left to see Bhargav Ram.

"I want to see him, talk to him."

"He misses you too, Arjan."

Arjan smiled at Padma. They were on their way back to the camp. Neither of them spoke for a few minutes. But then, Padma mustered up the courage to speak. She had to know.

"Something has been on my mind, Arjan," Padma began. "For the past week, I've been hearing people say that you killed the head priest of Indragarh." Padma had also overheard people worrying about the riots that had broken out in the city. Arjan's decision to close all the temples had bred unrest and anger in the city.

"Unfortunately, those aren't rumours."

"You *killed* him?" spoke Padma, incredulous. "You do realise the repercussions, right?"

"Rudra *died* because of that man. Narendra represented a religion that looked at my love for another man as filthy, as a disease. The city doesn't need a religion like that," Arjan said, panting. He paused, trying to calm down. "I've let people trample over me all my life. Not anymore. People need to wake up and realise that they shouldn't be looking up to people who worship false gods."

"I understand, Arjan. But you are a king now. Your people are unhappy. They are protesting in anger. You have taken away their faith."

"What?"

"Faith," she repeated. "Faith gives us hope. People of Indragarh had faith in the religion practised there. I have heard that in one of the sermons, a priest had advocated that even if the world we live in is corrupt, people should still strive to be good. The darkness can always be vanquished through the light. Isn't that a good thought?"

Arjan looked surprised. "You have changed."

"I think we both have changed."

They had entered the camp by now, and were walking towards Arjan's tent.

"I don't want a room in your palace, Arjan. I know my way around the city."

"But—"

"I have some . . . unfinished work."

Arjan must not find out that she was hoping to figure out a way to kill Nalakuvera. After all, she had just told him that he had been wrong to murder Guru Narendra. *I'm about to kill someone for revenge, just like Arjan.*

Padma gave her friend a tight hug and climbed on her horse.

"Also," she said, "I didn't know you were fighting the men of Bhanmati as well."

Arjan looked at her, bemused. "They have sided with the Naga queen. Never thought Bhanmati was ever going to be a part of any war."

"Yeah, looks like he isn't spineless anymore."

"Who?"

Padma looked up. "Don't tell anyone, but my father is Lord Vibhishan, the king of Bhanmati."

And before Arjan could react, she rode towards the city.

45

Kalki passed by a huge Vishnu idol. He wanted to stop and pray, but he was itching to get his hands on the Sword of Shiva. And he could see the temple from where he was. He was almost there.

I shall return to it once I get the sword.

Devadatta galloped up the mountain without stopping. Soon, Kalki arrived at the Temple of Shiva. He stared at the majestic temple before him without blinking.

The temple's walls were incredibly high and rocky. No normal person could climb them to enter inside. The iron entry gate was radiating a blue light. Kalki could see the garden from the entrance—there were gigantic trees filled with fruits, bowed down by their heavy branches, bushes filled with never-seen-before flowers, and the tall grass was sparkling under the moonlight.

After the garden, there was a stairway leading inside the temple.

There was something in the air around the temple. The place *felt* ancient, as if it had been here for decades, guarded and hidden in the midst of the Mahendragiri Mountains.

But when Kalki got off Devadatta and came near the temple gates, he was surprised to see that there were spears on the ground, and leaning on them were . . . people.

They were strange-looking men in black robes. Their mouths resembled a sparrow's beak. They were looking down, had not even acknowledged Kalki's and Devadatta's presence.

This doesn't look creepy at all.

Kalki moved closer to one of the cloaked men, to see whether they were even alive or not. He gazed into his glassy eyes. They were crystal blue, but not like Naga blue. Even when Kalki came close to the man, he didn't turn to look. All the men were staring into space.

"They call themselves the Sunyavadis," a voice came from inside the temple.

A seven-foot-tall old man appeared outside. There was a huge scar on his forehead. He was smiling at Kalki. Locks of dishevelled white hair were falling on his face. He was wearing a long, furry coat. Kalki looked at the white tunic the man was wearing underneath. It was covered in blood. The man put on his sandals and began to descend the stairway.

"Who are you?" Kalki asked. "And who are Sunyavadis?"

"Worshippers of the void. Basically, they are the undead. They have been on this earth for a very, very long time," he said. As the man walked down the stairs, Kalki noticed that there were bruises all over his throat and hands, as if he was . . . a leper.

"They came into existence when time was invented and assist those who are the harbingers of the ending."

"The ending?"

"Yes, when an Age is on the cusp of ending, the Sunyavadis come to life to assist the people who will bring about the end. They don't do much except for looking creepy, though," he sighed, "and talk about the True Prophecy."

"And what's that?"

"In every Yug, there are false prophecies propagated by multiple Tribes. Each Tribe has one, you see. But they are not real. The Sunyavadis know the actual prophecy."

That means the Sunyavadis knew about him and Kali. He looked at the man and asked, "Who are you?"

"You are here for the sword, right? Come along," he said, and the gates swung open on their own. The Sunyavadis still weren't looking at Kalki, but they slowly moved to the side to let Kalki enter.

Kalki reined Devadatta to a tree and began to head towards the man.

You are going to leave me with these freaks, Devadatta shrieked.

You'll be fine.

Easy for you to say, human.

I don't think they'll hurt a horse.

Well, all right, just don't rein me tight. I want to be able to run if they chase me.

Kalki sighed. *Sure.*

Human?

Hmmm?

The man is strange. Be alert. I smell what I smelled from Bajrang.

What?

The smell of an Ancient.

Kalki entered the temple.

There wasn't anything interesting inside the temple except for a few portraits on the wall.

"This temple used to be a shrine. It had been built by an Asura for Shiva," the old man explained.

"Asura?"

"I know. Weird, right? And if my memory serves right, I believe this temple belonged to Lord Virabhadra."

"That's another name of Lord Shiva."

"You might think so but to the Sunyavadis, there were multiple Shivas. They believe that 'Shiva' was just a war title given to different people."

"So Lord Virabhadra was given this temple?"

"Oh yeah. Awesome, right?"

The old man stopped. They had come near a huge casket. Charred skeletons were lying around it on the ground.

"Don't be afraid. They were thieves who tried to steal the sword. But the sword burned them. Only an Avatar is allowed to wield it."

"Someone told me that it had been used once to kill an Avatar. Who was he?" Kalki asked, curious.

"Beats me," the man shrugged, "now it can only kill the Adharm, and possibly immortals."

"Are you like its guardian or something?"

"No. There's no guardian. I searched for this sword for a long time. Not many people knew about it then," he said, and opened the casket.

Inside was a skeleton wearing an armour. In his left hand was a Trishul and in his right hand, he was holding the Sword of Shiva. It was radiating in the dark room. Kalki instantly felt something, as if his body and spirit had just established a connection with the object in front of him.

"After Lord Govind cursed me, I roamed around in a forest for a very long time. And one day, as I was walking, I saw these tall, snow-peaked mountains. I began to journey towards them, almost in a trance. Before I realised it, I had reached the temple. The sword was lying in this very casket."

The man paused and looked around the room.

"You know, Raavan was a Shiv bhakt. He built this temple."

"Why didn't Raavan take the sword?"

The man pointed at the skeletons. "Because he knew he wasn't an Avatar."

"But who made the shrine?"

"An Asura, I told you." The man smiled. He gazed at the sword and said, "It has been waiting for so long. Not even Raghav knew of its existence. Raavan had not told anyone about the sword. He couldn't risk Raghav knowing. If he had gotten hold of the sword, it would have made him invincible. And by the time Govind came to know, it was already too late."

"So it has never been used by Dharm?"

The man nodded. "The sword cuts flesh like butter. Even the mighty Danavs don't stand a chance against it. And it forms a bond with its user. It will even recognise the Adharm. If he picked up the sword, he would be immediately incinerated."

Kalki couldn't wait anymore. He raised his hand and grabbed the golden hilt. The skeleton's hollow eyes lighted up. It moved its head towards Kalki. For a second, Kalki thought it would come alive and attack him. But the skeleton just loosened its grasp, and Kalki picked up the sword.

The sword was incredibly heavy. As he struggled to lift it up, Kalki felt the sword become one with his hand, with his body. And now, it was as light as a feather.

He was about to sheath the sword when the old man stopped him. "Don't. You have one more thing to do," the man said and came to his knees.

"Kill me."

"Wait, what? Why?"

"Because I'm the Cursed One. I am Ashwatthama. I was the one Symrin was working for." His eyes had softened. "And I am the one who orchestrated everything to bring you here."

Kalki couldn't believe it.

"It was me who brought about Kalyug," Ashwatthama said.

46

Durukti knew she was in trouble.

She had been jittery all day, scared that Alakshmi would rat her out to Kali. But Alakshmi had not said anything. She had just been watching her, following her everywhere.

Finally, it grew dark. Durukti made an excuse of not feeling well and locked herself inside her room. She lay on her bed for hours, thinking of what to do.

There was a sound of footsteps. Durukti got up and peered outside. Alakshmi was heading out alone. There were no guards with her. She had not even taken her hyenas.

Where is she going so late at night?

Durukti had to find out. She quietly opened her bedroom door and tiptoed outside, behind Alakshmi.

Alakshmi was walking ahead, oblivious to the fact that she was being tailed. And then, all of a sudden, she turned.

Instantly Durukti hid behind a column in the hallway.

"Who's there?" Alakshmi asked, but there was no response. She cast a look around her and then resumed walking.

Durukti continued to follow, biting her lips in anticipation. Alakshmi was out of the fort now. She was heading towards the watchtower. There was no one there today.

Alakshmi began to climb the staircase.

Careful not to make a noise, Durukti silently crept up the stairs. Soon, she reached the top.

Alakshmi was looking at the site in front of her—the entire city of Indragarh.

Why is she here? Who is she meeting?

"You can stop following me now," Alakshmi said calmly, without even turning to look at Durukti.

Durukti froze.

No.

Alakshmi whistled and instantly Durukti heard something—two hyenas were growling behind her.

"Come closer, dear, or they will eat you."

Durukti gulped nervously as she walked towards Alakshmi. She wanted to run away. But one step back, and she would end up being the animals' chew toy.

"How did you know?"

"Because I made sure you followed me." Alakshmi turned to face Durukti. "I went past your room a couple of times until you were disturbed, and intrigued."

"You *wanted* me to follow you?"

"Absolutely. This is the place where you will, unfortunately, commit suicide."

"What do you mean?"

Alakshmi looked down. "I'm sure your head will crack when you fall from here."

Durukti stared at Alakshmi. "In other words, you are going to kill me, and tell everyone that I committed suicide?"

"Yes, my dear. I feel like you will become a problem if you stay around any longer."

Alakshmi whistled and the hyenas started getting closer to Durukti. Durukti was forced to move away from them, and nearer to the edge.

"No one will believe you," Durukti yelled.

"Sure they will." She smiled. "I can make up the most absurd story, and Kali still wouldn't doubt me."

Durukti clenched her jaw. "What do you plan to do with Kali? At least let me know this before I take the leap," she said, peering down, almost losing her balance. *If I fell down from here, I wouldn't survive.*

"That's none of your business. Kali is part of a grand plan that Shukra and I made."

"He's dead."

"I know. I was surprised that Kali chose you over him, even though you practically betray him at every chance you get."

"Please, Alakshmi, tell me what you are planning to do to my brother. It's my last wish."

"Fine. He's the instigator."

"Instigator of what?"

"Of Kalyug."

"So I was right. He's not Dharm."

Alakshmi laughed. "Who knew Kali would believe such crap. He thinks he's so great that he should be the hero. Well, Shukra and I thought . . . we'll let him believe that he was a hero."

"And now what? Kill him?" Durukti knew that Alakshmi wouldn't do that. But she was just trying to keep her busy. While talking, Durukti was thinking of what to do to get away safely. She was also hoping to get Alakshmi to spill some vital information about Kali and her plans for him.

"Of course not. Like I told you, he's the Asura instigator, just like the Yaksha Nalakuvera, and I'm sure there is some Manav instigator as well. The instigators push the Dharm and Adharm to fight the final battle, the battle which will determine whether good will win or evil."

"How did Shukra know all this?"

"He could converse with the Sunyavadis, worshippers of the void," Alakshmi said. Durukti had no idea who they were. "They know the True Prophecy."

"You are lying," Durukti snarled.

"What? I'm not!"

"If Kali isn't Dharm or Adharm, how was he able to raise Danavs? Shukra said that only the Dharm could do that."

"Well . . ."

"It was a lie, wasn't it?" Durukti couldn't believe it. "It was a lie because anyone could have risen the giants."

"Yes, but Asura blood had to be sacrificed. Shukra died instead of you, unfortunately. We had to stroke Kali's ego, so we gave him a false hope of being Dharm."

"But how does he control them?"

"He doesn't control them. They *serve* Adharm. That's why they are helping Kali. The day the Adharm would embrace his destiny, the Danavs would answer to him."

Poor Kali. He will be crushed when he learns the truth. "You did all this much to help the instigator. Why didn't you help the Adharm in becoming Adharm?"

"Because the prophecy states that only the instigator can do that. And I must say that Kali is doing his job well. If things proceed according to plan, the Adharm will awaken fully, very soon."

"Who are they? WHO ARE DHARM AND ADHARM?"

Alakshmi whispered the names.

A shiver ran down Durukti's spine. And then, Alakshmi came forward, raising her hand to push her down.

But Durukti caught hold of the hyena woman and pushed her down instead.

Alakshmi wailed as she fell from the watchtower.

The body smacked on the ground. Alakshmi's head burst like a watermelon.

She was dead.

Durukti took a deep breath, trying to contain her happiness. She turned to face the predators—the hyenas were looking at her with a confused face. They didn't know what to do now that their master wasn't with them. They simply ran away.

She couldn't believe she had just murdered Alakshmi.

But at least Durukti knew the truth.

The truth about the Dharm and Adharm.

And she had no idea whether she should tell Kali or not.

47

Ashwatthama was still kneeling, hoping that Kalki would strike him.

But Kalki stood rooted to the spot with the Sword of Shiva in his hand, unable to grant the old man's wish.

Kalki still couldn't believe what was happening. "Why are you doing this?"

"You don't understand the curse of an immortal."

"Oh, I think I do." Bhargav Ram's face flashed in his mind.

"No, no," Ashwattahma shook his head, "you don't. When I was cursed by Govind after killing the Pandav children—"

"Yes. Infanticide. You invented that."

"And I live with that guilt every day." Tears fell down Ashwatthama's face. "But my curse was supposed to be lifted. Everyone thinks Govind had cursed me to live forever, that death won't come to me even when I wished for it. But that's not how it is. Govind told me that I can be killed, but only in Kalyug by the hands of the last Avatar of Vishnu, through this sword. That is why I couldn't come to you earlier. You were not an Avatar. But you are now. You radiate. You are the strongest of them."

Kalki flared his nostrils. "So you let my friends die, you let my family rip apart, just so I would reach here to get this sword and kill you?"

"It was only a matter of time. I have been so, so patient." Ashwatthama sighed. "And I'm guilty. Oh dear, I am so guilty."

"If you hadn't intervened . . . I would still be at Shambala."

He nodded. "But you would not have been able to seize the opportunity to be this . . . hero of Kalyug."

"Do you think I care about that? So many people I loved and cared about are *dead*!" Kalki grabbed hold of Ashwatthama's throat and lifted him up with ease. Ashwatthama didn't even try to stop Kalki. "Because of you, Lakshmi died. Because of you, my father died. Because of you, I don't even know what my brother is up to."

"Listen, even if I hadn't done anything, the Sunyavadis would have appointed another instigator to make you come here. It was supposed to happen. Everything happens according to the True Prophecy."

"And what does this prophecy say in the end?"

"That you kill the Adharm."

A question popped in his mind. "And what if this . . . this True Prophecy is not fulfilled?"

"I don't know. Perhaps the cycle would never end. Perhaps we would remain in Kalyug forever."

Kalki tightened his grasp and Ashwatthama began to choke. He looked at the bloody scar on the old man's forehead.

That's where the Mani used to be.

"Kill me. Kill me. I cannot live anymore."

He wanted him to kill him.

He would like that.

But should I?

Kalki thought for a moment. He knew what to do now. "You have done so many wrong things. You deserve to die. But you know what . . ." He loosened the grip and threw Ashwatthama on the floor.

Ashwatthama coughed vigorously, gasping for air.

Kalki walked down the stairs and towards the front gates to leave. "Your biggest punishment," he said, "for inciting this entire event, this entire Kalyug would be to *not* kill you. You deserve to suffer even more."

He heard Ashwatthama's shrieks as he walked out of the temple and he saw the Sunyavadis had changed their stance. They had aligned themselves in neat rows, one behind the other, and were now kneeling next to their respective spears.

They were *bowing* to him.

Kalki passed by the Sunyavadis, out the front gates, when he heard something.

The sound of footsteps was coming from the back. Kalki spun, dodging a sword attack from none other than Ashwatthama. He was using Kalki's old sword which he had left inside the temple.

"If you won't kill me, then save yourself from me. You would have to eventually."

And he tried to strike Kalki in the face, but he dodged the attack like an acrobatic, zooming in the air and rolling behind.

"You can't force me to kill you."

"See me try!" And then Ashwatthama tried to ram the sword in Kalki's shoulder. He missed, and the sword only grazed it, but Kalki howled in pain as blood started pouring out of his wound.

Control your rage. You must not use it against the fallen.

Ashwatthama continued to attack. He brought the sword forward to pierce Kalki's chest, but Kalki deflected this attack with the Sword of Shiva.

The sword in Ashwatthama's hand began to shake, and within seconds, it turned to ashes.

Kalki looked at his own sword, surprised by how powerful it was. Though he knew by now that it had the ability to incinerate other weapons, to see it first-hand had been something else.

Ashwatthama looked at his burnt sword, utterly desolate. "Please, I beg you. I did everything so you would kill me. Release me from this wretched life!"

Kalki and Ashwatthama were standing in the midst of the Sunyavadis, who were still on the ground, bowing.

Ashwatthama now balled his hands into fists, trying to punch Kalki. Kalki dodged him easily. He didn't need to use his sword. The fight was clearly one-sided.

Kalki punched Ashwatthama in the gut. The immortal felt pain surge in his body. He fell down, coughing up blood.

"I do not have time to waste on you. This sword will now be used to end Adharm, to end Kali," Kalki said as he began to move towards Devadatta, leaving Ashwatthama behind. "It's funny that you planned so much, you assumed you had thought everything through, but there was one thing you didn't account for—my decisions. You thought I would give in to my anger, that I would kill you, but my anger is my strength. And it cannot be used on foolhardy individuals like you. You and Bhargav are strange men—one wants immortality, the other wants to get rid of it. The only decent person out here is the one who eats raw fish. This journey has taught me a lot."

Kalki climbed on his horse and began to move.

"I will return . . . I will—"

Ashwatthama couldn't finish his sentence. He couldn't move a step forward. Kalki turned his head and saw that the Sunyavadis were clinging to Ashwatthama, preventing him from going after Kalki.

"NO! LEAVE ME! LEAVE ME, YOU LITTLE—"

Kalki couldn't understand why the Sunyavadis were helping him. But then he thought about it and he realised that Ashwatthama was just the instigator. He was supposed to lead Kalki here, but now his work was over. The Sunyavadis live to see an Age end. They want the True Prophecy to be fulfilled. They don't want Ashwatthama to harm the Dharm.

"You trusted the wrong people, apparently." Kalki smiled. "Will send a raven when I'm done killing Kali."

"You don't understand," Ashwatthama shouted, laughing at the same time.

"What?"

"The True Prophecy didn't say that Kali would be the Adharm. He's just an instigator, like me." He continued to laugh hysterically.

Kalki was taken aback. "What do you mean? If he isn't Adharm, then who is?"

Ashwatthama's face lit up. His lips curved into a malicious grin.

"It's your brother, Kalki," he roared.

Kalki's face grew pale.

Arjan?

"And to fulfil the True Prophecy, and end Kalyug, you know what you have to do?" Aswatthama cackled, still trapped in the Sunyavadis' icy grasp. "You have to *kill* him."

48

Kalki didn't know what to do with the information he had now. He was thoroughly confused. Riding away from the Temple of Shiva, away from Ashwatthama, he couldn't stop thinking about his brother. He rode in silence, not letting Devadatta enter his mind.

I travelled all the way to the Mahendragiri Mountains to be trained . . . to be strong . . . so I can kill my own brother?

The very thought of Arjan's death was making Kalki hyperventilate.

As he rode down the hill, he spotted Lord Vishnu's idol that he had passed by on his way up. He had to stop and pray. Perhaps, the mighty god would give him some answers.

Kalki knelt down to pray. There was not a soul in sight. Other than the chirping of birds and rustling of the leaves, there was no sound. It was quiet, peaceful.

Kalki's eyes shot open when he heard a loud squawk above him. Shuko was flying overhead, and finally came down and perched on his shoulder.

He was happy to see his old friend again. The quirky parrot had been with Kalki since the beginning of his journey.

How ya doing?

I'm fine.

You seem troubled, kid. Is everything all right?

Kalki didn't know what to say. He looked at Lord Vishnu's idol for a few seconds, and then touched his feet.

As he began to walk back towards his horse, he asked the parrot, *Why are you here?*

Your girlfriend sent me.

Padma? Why?

She said she will be fine. That I should help you now. But I think she might be up to something.

Why? What happened?

While Kalki got back on Devadatta and resumed his way down the hill, Shuko told him everything that had transpired at Lord Bajrang's camp. Kalki figured out what Padma was about to do. *She's going to take revenge.*

Could be.

I have no doubt in my mind that she will kill Nalakuvera. Thank god Arjan will be there. Kalki stopped thinking. He was filled with an unexplainable dread and anxiousness. He just could not digest the fact that Arjan was Adharm.

Kalki remembered how meek, how shy Arjan had been as a child. And the Adharm was supposed to be *evil.* How could Arjan be evil?

And to be Adharm, he had to have Soma. *Did he consume it behind my back? When? Where did he get it?* The Soma in their village was burnt long time back.

There were so many questions going through Kalki's mind. Deep down, he desperately hoped that Ashwatthama was wrong, that the True Prophecy was wrong. Arjan was his brother. No matter what, Kalki couldn't bring himself to kill him.

He looked at Shuko. *Ratna died, eh?*

Yeah. It was pretty sad.

I wish I could have saved her.

Even the mightiest heroes can't save everyone. You must understand that.

Kalki closed his eyes as he touched the hilt of the Sword of Shiva. Ratna Maru's face flashed in his mind.

The sword deserves to be dedicated to Ratna.

On an Apsara, human? Devadatta asked.

On a woman who valiantly fought for her mission. On a woman who didn't hesitate to jump in to save her friend. On a woman who wasn't chained by her identity, by her Tribe. She deserves to be respected, and immortalised, for her bravery.

He unsheathed the sword and said, "From now, I claim thee, the Sword of Shiva, to be the Ratna Maru."

Kalki put the Ratna Maru back in the sheath. He looked at the path in front of him. The path that he would take to reach Indragarh.

Towards Kali. Towards Arjan.

Finally, it seems like your journey will be over soon, Devadatta said.

It better be. Too much has happened, Shuko said.

Kalki smiled. He clutched the reins of his white horse as it picked up speed. And on they went.

Here we go.

49

Padma raced through the rooftops.

God, how I miss living in a city.

She had been on the go for so long. And she had had to tolerate the harsh winter during her time at the Vanar camp. So, right now, Padma was enjoying the gentle, warm breeze wafting in the city.

It was the dead of night. The city was asleep. But there were a few people huddled outside their houses, whispering.

Riots had broken out after Guru Narendra's death. The closing of all temples had not been received well by some people either. And Nalakuvera had ordered some of the soldiers to hunt down the revolutionaries.

Poverty was rampant in the city now. The money in the royal treasury was supposed to be used for the city's development, for the betterment of the people. But Indragarh's king had decided to use that money for forging and repairing weapons used in the war against the snake queen, and to throw lavish feasts every night for his soldiers.

It really *was* Kalyug.

Leaping from one building to another, Padma finally arrived in front of the royal palace. It was the tallest structure of the city, visible from every building. She took out her dagger to take care of any guards that would obstruct her way inside. But she didn't know she would not need to use it today. All the guards were huddled in front of a watchtower around a corpse, away from Nalakuvera's fortress, on the right.

She silently climbed on the gate and made her way inside the palace ground.

And Nalakuvera was right there, looking at the dead body. His wife, Rambha, was standing with him.

Too many guards are around him. If I attack now, there is very little chance that I'll survive.

Deciding to wait for her chance, she slowly tiptoed her way inside the fortress.

And then she heard a familiar voice.

It was Kali. He looked shaken and confused.

Someone has died in the fort. But that's not my concern.

Arjan had told her about Kali, and about his Danavs. Not many people were aware that Kali was in Indragarh, living in the royal palace.

Padma had never liked Kali.

She had confided a lot in Arjan. She had even told him about her father. But now that she thought about it, she suspected that Arjan may have told Kali.

No, he wouldn't tell anyone.

As Padma walked inside the fortress, she searched for the door that would lead to the basement. In the week that she had stayed in Arjan's camp, she had heard rumours that the Yaksha king was keeping the basement of his fortress full of Apsaras.

She was going to free the Apsaras, just like Ratna Maru wished to.

Unless . . .

And Padma came up with a plan—a surefire way for her to kill Nalakuvera.

As she walked in the halls of the fortress, she came across a door from which she could see a stairway leading down.

Bingo.

This was her lucky day. No guard had been placed outside this door. They were all busy dealing with the corpse outside the watchtower.

She took out a pin from her hair, and unlocked the door. As she descended the staircase, careful not to make a noise, she was enveloped in complete darkness.

Light flooded in the long, narrow corridor, at the bottom of the staircase. There were fire lamps hung on the wall. She proceeded to walk and eventually reached a spacious room.

It was filled with cages. Apsaras were trapped inside. And a guard, short in height and pot-bellied, was dozing peacefully on his chair.

Tiptoeing, she passed by the guard and looked inside the cages. Even though it was the dead of the night, all Apsaras were awake. They had heard loud voices from the floor above them, a few hours ago. Another dead body had been found in the castle grounds.

"I'm here to save you all," Padma said to one of the Apsaras, her voice barely above a whisper. "Can you tell me where Nalakuvera is? We need to sneak out, and if he comes down here, we're going to get in trouble."

"The Yaksha king comes once every day," the Apsara whispered. "Sometimes he is alone and sometimes he comes with his vile wife. But he won't come down in the middle of the night."

Perfect.

"Where's the key to the cages?" Padma asked.

"That drunkard has it," the Apsara said, pointing at the guard, "who's sleeping away to glory."

Padma nodded. She moved towards the guard, pulled out her dagger, and was about to slit the guard's throat.

But she stopped.

If I kill him, they'll know something is amiss.

Padma took a deep breath and stepped back. She then spotted the keys in his hand. Carefully, she opened his hand and took away the keys. The guard grunted. And for a moment, Padma thought she had woken him up. But he didn't open his eyes and continued snoring.

Padma grinned as she began to open the cage.

"Thank you so much, girl," an Apsara exclaimed. The other Apsaras began to excitedly talk amongst themselves.

Padma nodded, but when she opened the door, she didn't let the Apsara out. Instead, she went inside and then manouvered her hand out of the cage, locking it from outside. She then tossed the keys on the floor towards the guard. "Why did you throw them away?" the Apsara said, incredulous. Padma casually went at the back of the cage and sat down. "You could have helped us. And why in the world did you cage yourself?"

Padma didn't respond.

She would help them. But only after killing Nalakuvera.

Padma ripped apart her tunic to make it more revealing. She even torn her pants to make them look like shorts. And then she removed the band tying her hair.

She then clutched her dagger, and hid it at her back, inside the clothes.

The moment Nalakuvera would come to take an Apsara, she would volunteer.

And then she would stab him and escape.

50

Arjan had a splitting headache in the middle of the battle.

He was fighting a Naga one moment and in the next, his head was about to explode.

He heard voices in his head. But so many people were speaking at once. Arjan couldn't make out what they were saying.

Arjan instantly clutched his head. The Naga was about to kill him, but he, somehow, managed to defend himself.

The Suparns fired a volley of arrows in his direction. Arjan protected himself through his shield, but the Naga died on the spot.

Arjan raced through the field with his shield in one hand, and spear in the other. The sickle was strapped to his belt. He was about to throw his spear at one of the Suparns, when the headache returned.

The pain was unbearable. Arjan fell on the floor, dropping the spear and shield on the ground.

YOU'RE LATE! WE CANNOT WAIT ANYMORE! the voices screamed.

"WHAT DO YOU WANT FROM ME?" Arjan yelled.

CHANNEL YOUR PAST!

What?

Arjan didn't understand what he was supposed to do. *Whose voices are they?* Before he could even could even think about it, a

Suparn came flying towards him. Arjan tried to kill him with his spear, but couldn't even manage to lift his weapon. The pain in his head was excruciating.

Arjan was helpless. The Suparn easily held him and soared in the air. When he had reached high enough, he released his hold. Arjan plummeted down on the ground.

Is this how I will die?

But Arjan's body didn't hit the ground. He was in a hand—huge, dirty hand of a Danav who had saved him from falling to his death.

The Danav bowed.

COMMAND THEM! the voice screamed in his head again.

The Danav turned to move back to the camp when a thick fireball was launched by the Nagas from a catapult. The fireball hit the Danav.

A huge puff of blue smoke spread in the air. There was a blinding flash of light, and a deafening explosion.

The Danav fell on the ground. Arjan opened the giant's hand and jumped out. Some of Arjan's men and some enemy soldiers got crushed under the giant's body.

He was dead.

Oh god! No!

Arjan raced to the head of the Danav. That was where the fire ball had hit him. It was a deep wound. Blood was gushing out of it. Arjan could even see the Danav's bones.

They have found a way to kill our greatest allies.

"FALL BACK!" Arjan yelled.

They had to retreat. Danavs couldn't be used anymore. And without their help, they were dead men. *What is this strange blue ball that they have fired?*

CHANNEL YOUR PAST!

The screams weren't stopping.

"How should I?" he asked himself. His army was obeying his command. Everyone had begun to fall back to the camp.

BY LOOKING FOR IT!

Arjan slammed his goblet on the floor.

The glass rolled over towards the feet of his generals. Arjan had called them to his tent to talk.

"What the hell?" Arjan said, looking at the men standing in front of him. A fire lamp had been hung inside. The light of the lamp gave an eerie glow to Arjan's face. In the partial darkness, he looked menacing. There were deep scars on his chest. "What the hell happened outside?" He gritted his teeth. "We lost a Danav. Do you know that? A giant! How the hell were they able to defeat him? With one hit! ONE!" he yelled.

His head was throbbing again, but the pain had ebbed considerably by now.

One of the generals said, "Our apologies, Your Highness. We should have anticipated it. It was strange that the enemy had just thrown a small battalion in the field to fight us even though we had a Danav amongst us. Now we realise why they had done it."

Arjan shot him a look. The general lowered his head, afraid to speak.

"They knew that bomb will create a huge blast that would not only kill the Danav but the people around it as well. So many of our men that were near the Danav, died instantly," another general said. "It is a miracle that the blast didn't affect you."

"It wasn't a miracle, General, but I don't expect any of you to understand that." Arjan stood up and walked towards the generals. "If only we had thought of this earlier," he turned to the one who had just spoken, "this wouldn't have happened. We need to make sure that we figure out the strategies that the opposition is using on the battlefield."

"Yes," the general said, nodding vigorously.

Arjan nodded to himself and then instantly punched the general in the gut. He fell on the ground, moaning. "It was your job to study their strategies. And if you don't, we pay the price for it."

"I didn't antic—" the man cried but was interrupted.

Arjan yelled, "THEN YOU SHOULD HAVE ANTICIPATED! It's what you are supposed to do, you little shit. Will I have to teach you that?" He looked at the other generals. "I think I broke his ribs. Take him away."

The generals carried their hurt comrade out.

Arjan sighed, exasperated. He picked up the goblet from the ground and wiped it. An idea came to him that instant. *What if I send a spy to the enemy camp?*

The spy who no one would doubt.

The spy who was the enemy king's daughter.

Let's hope Padma agrees to this.

51

"Say it again, please." Kali had already heard it once, but he still couldn't believe it.

He stood rooted to the spot. Of late, not much was going according to his plan. His soon-to-be wife had been murdered hours ago by god knows whom. Kali thought that it might be the same person who had sent the Apsara in his room.

And Kali was frustrated that he had to keep on hiding himself. No one in the city knew that he was back. He used to be Indragarh's king and now he was mooching off a Yaksha.

His brother, Bali, was king now, but he was not ready to believe that Kali was his brother.

Nothing is going well.

He had wanted Arjan at his side, but Arjan detested him. And on top of everything, his sister was now making atrocious claims about himself, about who he was.

"You are not Dharm," Durukti said again. "Nor Adharm. You are . . ."

She didn't want to speak any further. But Kali understood what she was going to say.

I'm nothing.

"Who are Dharm and Adharm then?"

"Kalki is Dharm, and Adharm is our brother, Bali."

Kali looked thunderstruck. His brother.

I don't deserve this. I can't be a nobody.

"How do you know all of this?" he snarled, his eyes widening.

"Alakshmi told me on the day she died. She . . . came to my room and confessed everything. She was feeling guilty for manipulating you," Durukti said, lowering her eyes.

She always averts her eyes when she's hiding something.

"But why did she come to you? Why not confide in me?"

Durukti froze. She was silent for a few seconds, and then she said, "Alakshmi was scared of what you would do to her after learning the truth. She claimed she didn't want to lie to you, but Shukra had made it very clear that it had to be done. She was only following his instructions."

"Why did they bring me all the way to the bloody Black Ocean? If Arjan is Adharm, then why was I chosen to raise the Danavs?"

"Because you are supposed to *push* him to become Adharm. And I think she was right. Arjan began to change ever since we got here. Alakshmi said that you did your job well."

"Indeed." Kali slumped in his chair, running his hand through his hair. "I played right into that woman's hands."

When he had been told that he was Dharm, he had been so happy. He thought he finally had a purpose. But now, he had nothing.

"Are you okay?"

"Yeah, I'm fine. Alakshmi got what she deserved."

Kali felt Durukti's hand on his shoulder as he looked outside the window.

"I know. You are a good man, Kali."

Kali kept his hand over Durukti's.

"Do you think we can believe what Alakshmi told you? What if she was lying again?"

"She was telling the truth. I connected the dots after she told me." Durukti sighed. "You went mad, just like any normal person would after consuming the Soma. If you were Dharm or Adharm, your mind would not have been affected."

Kali chuckled. "I guess I should have believed less in myself."

"No, you are still great and strong and—"

Kali grabbed Durukti by the throat. He dragged her towards the wall and pushed her up against it.

It was so sudden. Durukti couldn't breathe. She struggled weakly, trying to loosen Kali's grip on her, but Kali held her up with ease. "Don't patronise me, my dear. I'm nothing, all right? Nothing! I'm not Dharm or Adharm. I was just a pawn to Shukra and that bitch." Anger burst out of him like hot lava.

And then, he released her. He was angry at what she had said, but he didn't want her to die because of it. Durukti fell on the floor, gasping for air.

He knelt down and kept his palm over her cheek. "Apologies, my dear sister. I was angry."

"I could have died, you bastard!" Durukti said, pushing him away. "I was being nice to you!"

Kali sat back in his chair and poured himself some wine. "Frankly, my dear, I feel you are not being completely honest. You have betrayed me in the past."

"Whatever you want to feel," Durukti leaned on the wall, still clutching her throat, "feel. I don't care. I'm *done* being nice to you. One moment you were patiently listening and the next you try to kill me! What kind of mood swings are these?"

Kali didn't know what was what anymore. He had acted on an impulse. Unsure of how to respond, he just gulped down his wine.

There was a knock on the door. Kali opened it and a Yaksha entered inside.

"My lord, there's been an incident."

"Yeah?"

The Yaksha looked at Durukti. Her face was ashen. She was struggling to stand up.

"Eyes up here, Corporal," Kali said.

The Yaksha instantly straightened up. "Yes, my lord. So um . . . King Arjan sends a message. A Danav is down."

"Down? What do you mean?"

"It has been killed by our enemy."

Kali couldn't believe it. What kind of sorcery had the opposition used?

"He just wanted to let you know—'

"Get out," Kali yelled.

The Yaksha bowed and left.

"Oh yeah," Durukti rasped, "just so you know, the Danavs serve Arjan, not you. He can control them. He just doesn't know how to do that yet. So the one weapon you have against everyone, doesn't belong to you as well."

Kali growled at her as he picked up his black cloak, the one he always wore when he went out in public.

But he stopped.

Why am I hiding when I'm no one?

Kali walked with his head held high in the streets of Indragarh. The night was about to end. The people were still in their beds but a few drunks and homeless people could be seen here and there. And they stared as the previous king of Indragarh walked past them. But Kali didn't care.

He had his two bodyguards, Koko and Vikoko, behind him. And in front of him, prowled two hyenas. After Alakshmi's death, they had been wandering in the palace garden. When Kali spotted them in the bushes, he whistled, just like Alakshmi had taught him to. And they had come running.

The whistle controlled the hyenas and made them do the whistler's bidding. And there were different kinds of whistles to command them—a shrill whistle to stop them from attacking, a short but loud whistle to make them chase someone, and a long whistle to summon them.

Well, Alakshmi was a liar, but she taught me something useful, at least.

Kali had never felt anything for Alakshmi. He had only agreed to marry her to further the Asura Tribe. In a way, it was a relief that she had died.

As he walked out of the city towards Arjan's camp, the people lurking about stared at him, wondering who he was. He bore an uncanny resemblance to their previous king.

Kali made his way towards Arjan's tent. The camp was quiet; the soldiers were still asleep. When a Yaksha guard tried to stop Kali from entering, he whistled and the hyenas began to growl and started advancing towards the guard. Afraid, the guard backed away.

Arjan came outside to see what was happening. He and Kali looked at each other. Kali whistled again and the hyenas stopped in their tracks.

"What are you doing? The man doesn't know who you are." Arjan paused, looking at Kali. "And where's your cloak?"

"I don't need it anymore," Kali said. His eyes softened as he looked at Arjan, who was his brother Bali, the one he thought had died when he was a child.

Arjan invited him inside. Kali instructed his guards to stay outside, and tethered the hyenas to a tree.

The brothers were sitting opposite each other now.

"What is it?"

You're Adharm. The Dark One. The source of all evil in Kalyug. But you're my brother.

Kali knew that as soon as Kalki reached Indragarh, he would not hesitate to kill Arjan.

Can I let that man do this to Arjan?

"I heard a Danav died today."

"Yes." Arjan looked down, ashamed. "I'm sorry one of your giants died. I don't know what we should do now. The Danavs are important for winning this war."

"Do you know how they did it?" Kali asked.

"The shamans have studied the powder used in the bomb they threw at us. They say it was Somalata plant mixed with weed and pig fat."

"What? The opposition has Soma?"

"Apparently."

Manasa had the Suparn army on her side, so it made sense. Suparnika was the only place that had Somalata plants now.

"Great." Kali shook his head. "Now what?"

"We cannot use the giants. So I don't know." Arjan held his head in his hands.

Arjan is just a poor, young boy who has been given too much responsibility. He can't be king. I have to help him.

Kali knew what he had to do now.

He looked at Arjan and sighed. "Will you listen to me?"

"What do you suggest?"

"I think we should attack. Full on. Immediately. Send all the Danavs into the battlefield and annihilate the enemy. This war has been going on for too long."

Arjand was flabbergasted. "Are you sure?"

"Of course. Finish them once and for all." Kali paused as he noticed that Arjan looked conflicted. "I know you don't trust me, Arjan. But I believe I know about war more than you. You should accept that and—"

Kali stopped when his eyes met Arjan's. He was close to tears.

"If we don't attack with all our force, we will only lose more men. And eventually, we will lose the war. You can't let the snake queen take over Indragarh. You must protect the city. Believe me, if we attack with all our force, the enemy won't stand a chance."

Arjan mulled it over. "What if they attack again with these Soma bombs?" He paused. "There's also another way. I have a friend in the city. Her name is Padma. She is King Vibhishan's—Manasa's ally's—daughter."

Kali narrowed his eyes. "What do you plan to do with her?"

"Send her as a spy. She can steal or burn the Somas so they can't be used. It's the perfect plan."

Arjan was getting desperate. Kali could see it.

Desperation often yields worst results.

"And she would agree?"

"She hates her father. She told me once."

"I see. But I don't think we can put the fate of this big war on one woman." Kali noted the fact that this girl was the snake queen's ally's daughter. *She can be useful later on.* "Let's send some men to the enemy camp right now. They can sneak inside and damage the catapults. That way, the bombs will be useless. And at the crack of dawn, we attack them with the Danavs."

Arjan nodded. "Makes sense."

Kali extended his hand. "Let's finish this war, brother."

"I'm not—" Arjan stopped. "Fine. Let's do it."

They shook hands. Kali smiled. He thought he had no purpose, but he did . . .

He had to save his baby brother from the madman, Kalki, and he had to ease the burden of kingship.

And if it meant being cruel, pretending to be evil in front of the world, he would do it. He wouldn't let anyone know that Arjan was Adharm.

Don't worry, Bali. Everything is going to be all right soon.

52

Kalki was supposed to be back in Indragarh by now.

But he was so confused. What was he supposed to do once he reached the city? Find his brother and *kill* him? Why was Arjan Adharm? Was he a changed man now?

So many questions were running in his mind. Afraid and overwhelmed, he had chosen to stop for the time being. Devadatta needed to rest as well.

Kalki walked around the forest nearby, and then sat down under a large banyan tree. He closed his eyes and concentrated. Soon, he was Channelling.

As he opened his eyes, the forest disappeared. Instead of the trees, Kalki saw a lake in front of him, filled with blood. The sky was a dark grey, filled with thundering clouds. And on the other side of the lake were corpses. Innumerable dead bodies filled the air with a putrid stench. The ghastly scene before him reminded him of Kurukshetra.

"Why have you returned?" a voice came from the back.

Kalki turned to see an old man with a white greasy beard and a crown on which a peacock feather was stuck. He looked frail, exhausted. Blood was oozing out of the wounds on his body. The old man was leaning on a sword that was dug in the ground.

"I think I know you," Kalki said.

"Of course you do, kid." The old man smiled. "I met you once."

"Are you . . ."

"I am Govind. And this is Dwarka."

Kalki was stunned and speechless. He had never heard what Lord Govind was like during his last years. He had never bothered to read about it in gurukul. But now, here he was, the aged Lord Govind, standing right in front of him. "What is this? What happened?"

"Karma," he responded. "But that's not important right now. You Channelled because you wanted to know something. Tell me, why are you here?"

Kalki gulped nervously. There was a bright flash of lightning in the sky. "I got to know something about my brother and it has been troubling me." He paused. "My brother is—"

"I know. All Avatars know. And you don't believe it?" Lord Govind asked.

"Of course not. It's absurd. Even if Lord Vishnu came down to tell me this, I wouldn't believe him."

"Doesn't matter whether you believe it or not. What's written is written."

"I can't kill him." Kalki stepped forward.

"Why?" The old man looked up at him. His eyes were a beautiful sapphire blue. "Why can't you?"

"He's my brother."

"He's Adharm first, then your brother."

"But not for me."

"You are being stupid!" exclaimed Lord Govind. He walked and came close to Kalki. "Imbecile! You can't save one to let millions die."

"I know Arjan. He would never hurt another soul."

Lord Govind chuckled. "Do you really know him? It has been months since you saw him. A lot has changed. He has gone through a lot."

"How do you know?"

"We know everything," said Lord Govind simply.

Then he raised his fist and slowly began to move his index finger in a circular motion. The scenery dissolved.

Kalki saw a plain land in front of him. Corpses were piled one upon the other across the entire battlefield. Corpses of children, of women and men.

The people who weren't dead, were being killed.

By hyenas.

By leopards.

Kalki began to heave as he witnessed the massacre. He saw the ferocious animals were being controlled by someone—a boy with long onyx hair. He had strange inked designs over his face. And his eyes were red.

The boy had a long whip in one hand and a sword in the other. He was covered in blood from head to toe.

Kalki knew the boy.

Arjan.

"What is this?" Kalki asked. "How did you do this?"

"As Avatars, we can show you a vision of the future," Lord Govind said.

"This can't be true."

"It's going to happen soon. He's going to end the world if you don't kill him. What's written shall happen."

Kalki's eyes welled up with tears as he saw Arjan killing the people around him. He couldn't believe his baby brother would become . . . a monster.

He couldn't bear to look at Arjan anymore.

When he opened his eyes, he found himself back in the snowy

hills. Devadatta was resting nearby, and Shuko was perched on Kalki's shoulder, waiting for him to say something.

Kalki didn't want to kill Arjan. He was his brother.

But if Arjan would end up becoming a killer . . . I may have to kill him.

53

The night had passed uneventfully. The Apsaras were suspicious of their new inmate. Some just thought she was mad. Who would choose to lock themselves up in a dungeon? Come morning, Padma heard people in the fortress yelling. Everyone was alarmed.

"What is going on?" the Apsaras murmured amongst themselves.

A guard came down the staircase and entered the chamber. The Apsara in the cage beside Padma's asked him, "What is it? What has happened?"

"Shush, girl!" the guard yelled. "It doesn't concern you."

"But we are worried. We are afraid something is happening."

Padma noticed that the guard looked stressed. "It's just a riot. Some people are protesting against our king and Lord Nalakuvera is trying to calm them down. And they are trying to enter the fort."

Of course. This has been happening ever since Arjan killed that priest.

Padma looked up as she heard more voices. Someone was cackling. And by the sound of footsteps, it seemed like a lot of people were inside the fortress.

The guard looked up, confused.

Instantly the doors of the basement opened and dozens of Yaksha guards entered with a woman leading them. She was breathtakingly beautiful.

"Lady Rambha, you shouldn't have come."

"Nonsense. I don't want the people of my Tribe to perish. They are all coming with me," the green-eyed Apsara said. "Are you sure Nala will follow us later?"

"Yes, my lady."

"Good. Open their cages," Rambha said to the guard.

The Apsaras began to line behind Rambha and followed her outside. Padma was walking ahead, close to the woman leading them out the fortress.

"It's absolute mayhem outside. The gates have been breached." Rambha looked concerned. Beads of sweat had appeared on her forehead.

They were going towards the back of the fort.

"We need to leave." Rambha addressed the Yakshas and said, "Men, you need to help Nala hold the intruders off. But I want four of you to stay with me. Protects us till we reach the back gate. It's not safe here anymore." She now turned towards the Apsaras that were following her, "Once we are out of the back gate, we must mount the chariots and leave."

"Where will we go?" an Apsara asked.

"I know a place where no one will find us."

She could have left these women behind. But she cares for the people of her Tribe.

"I don't understand what they are rioting about. And why are they going after Nala's life?" Rambha wondered aloud as they came out of the fort and into the bright sunlight.

Padma looked around her. She was in the midst of twenty Apsaras or so, all of whom were walking in a straight line. Four guards, carrying spears, were running along with them. And leading all of them was the beautiful Rambha.

"Who is this woman?" Padma asked the Apsara beside her.

"Lord Nalakuvera's wife."

What?

"They think Lord Nalakuvera advised the king to kill Guru Narendra," Padma heard a guard tell Rambha.

"But he didn't—" Rambha shrugged. "What's the point of telling you? You are just a stupid guard."

They were a few steps away from the back gate now. The guard moved to the back of the group.

Padma had to think fast. She could try to escape and go back to the fortress. She may get a chance to kill Nalakuvera. He would already be busy battling the intruders. But the guards accompanying the Apsaras were watching them vigilantly. There were four of them.

I won't make it to the fortress.

A guard pointed at a figure standing outside and said, "There's Kali's general out there. She will be escorting you to a safe location."

Kali's general is here?

"Why the hell is she here?"

"The general says she is accompanying Lady Durukti, who will be travelling with you. Both of them are already outside, waiting in the chariot."

"All right," her voice softened. Rambha didn't mind if Durukti tagged along.

They were close to the gate, when Padma made her way towards Rambha.

I may not be able to get my hands on Nalakuvera. But I can kill his wife. That Yaksha is going to suffer, just like Ratna Maru suffered.

As Padma came forward, she whispered in Rambha's ear, "Regards from Ratna Maru," and then swiftly slit her throat with her dagger.

For a moment, no one noticed. But then blood began to gush out, and Rambha collapsed on the ground. The guards ran towards her, and the Apsaras yelped, horrified.

"RUN!" Padma yelled.

The Apsaras pushed the guards away and moved out the back gates. Dumbstruck, the guards could do nothing but watch as the women ran away.

Someone lightly thumped Padma on her back.

"GOOD WORK!" an Apsara yelled at Padma. "SHE WAS A TYRANT!"

Padma grinned. She had finally done something right. And she felt good.

She felt free.

The chariots stood outside. As the women ran outside in all directions, the charioteers looked around, unable to comprehend what was happening. The guards having recovered from their shock were following the Apsaras, trying to drag them back inside.

And in the midst of this pandemonium, there stood a familiar figure.

I have seen her somewhere.

Padma couldn't recall where she had seen this woman. She locked eyes with the woman for a few seconds and then sprinted towards the nearest alley, away from the chariots.

The woman in the centre was standing still. She was tall and slender, and her long, braided hair were as black as the night.

The woman began to chase Padma.

Padma could have stopped to fight. She still had her dagger. But her instinct was telling her to run away from the woman as fast as possible. She was at the end of the alley when the woman caught up to her.

The woman landed a blow on Padma's head. And Padma couldn't help but crouch on the ground, clutching her head.

The tall woman was towering over Padma. Weakly, Padma tried to slash the skin on the woman's foot, but the woman simply stepped away.

"WHO ARE YOU? WHY ARE YOU AFTER ME?"

The woman didn't say anything. She grabbed Padma and tied her hands with a bamboo rope. She took out her sword and put it near Padma's throat. "Move," the woman said coldly.

"Why me? I'm just an Apsara."

"Don't fool me, girl. I know who you are," the woman said. "My lord told me all about you. He described to me what you look like, but he didn't have to. After all, we have already faced each other once."

Padma squinted to look at the woman properly. And her gaze fell on the golden irises of her attacker.

No.

"Vasuki's assassination . . . you were trying to kill me." Padma drew in a sharp breath. "You are—"

"General Vikoko, Lord Kali's right hand woman," Vikoko had a devious grin on her face, "and believe me, he has grand plans for you, *Princess* Padma."

54

Arjan had gone inside the war again. His bronze armour was glistening in the light and his weapon was tinged in red with the blood of the Nagas.

This is my day.

Things had gone as planned. Arjan's men had snuck in the Naga camp and destroyed all the catapults. There had been only two. And at dusk, the Indragarh army had proceeded to attack.

Beside Arjan stood Koko, Kali's general. Kali had instructed him to help out in the fight. It was an all-hands-on-deck situation.

At least, that's what Arjan thought. He didn't know that Kali had also instructed his general to watch out for Arjan, and kill whoever came close to harming his brother.

We will win this war.

Arjan was sure that he would emerge victorious today. He looked at the men fighting the Nagas with all they had. The nobles had given Arjan some strong, able men. The Manavs had been assigned to fight on foot, and on horses. And today, even the Yakshas were present on the battlefield—they were functioning as archers, bringing down the Suparns. The Danavs were standing near the battlefield, waiting to be ordered to enter the fight.

There is no turning back now. It's all or nothing.

Kali had made Nalakuvera call all the Manav nobles of Indragarh to the camp to see the moment of their victory, the moment their enemies will be slaughtered.

Perhaps he REALLY has changed.

Arjan couldn't believe he was thinking something good of Kali. He smiled at the foolish thought.

As Arjan made his way towards the Yakshas along with Koko, he witnessed countless dead bodies of the Suparns on the ground. But he could see many of the Nagas fighting relentlessly. Arjan saw many of his men struggling to kill them.

Time to kick things up a notch.

Arjan ordered the Yakshas archers to steer their arrows towards the ground, at the Nagas.

The Nagas' lifeless bodies fell on the ground.

Arjan's entire army was overpowering the enemy. And at that moment, Arjan could see Kali's brilliant plan working. Arjan surveyed the scene in front of him with satisfaction . . . until he saw men on chariots making their way towards Arjan, killing his men on the way.

Arjan picked up a javelin from the ground and aimed at the man in one of the chariots. But the javelin missed its target.

Arjan turned to Koko and said, "Order the Danavs to enter now."

Koko didn't say anything. He continued watching the war happening in front of him.

Arjan waited for Koko to respond. On the battlefield, the men on the chariots were massacring his men.

Koko still wasn't saying anything.

"Will you send the Danavs now? Otherwise, we will end up losing a lot of our men."

Koko didn't even look at Arjan.

"Order the Danavs, General."

Finally, Koko turned to look at Arjan. "I'm sorry," he said.

"What?"

"It is *his* plan. And with time you will realise that he is right."

Arjan looked at him, puzzled. His army was beginning to lose. He now looked up at the Danavs. They stood where they were, not even moving an inch.

Arjan gritted his teeth.

GAHHHH! KALI! SHOULDN'T HAVE TRUSTED HIM!

Arjan turned to enter the field when he felt strong arms wrapping around him and pulling him away.

"It's not worth it. He's doing it for you," Koko said to the struggling Arjan.

"What is he doing? Killing my people?"

"The Dharm returns. You need to be safe when he does."

"Kalki? Why do I need to be saved from my own brother?"

Arjan tried to escape but Koko was very strong. Before he could push him away, he felt a handkerchief wrap around his mouth. Arjan smelled something toxic and nauseating.

"Don't worry. I am not going to kill you. It's just chloroform. You'll be fine. He wants you to be saved."

Arjan continued to struggle but soon he could no longer keep his eyes open.

Before fainting, he managed to ask, "Where . . . where are you taking me?

"Some place safe," the voice said as it began to fade, "some place where no one can hurt you . . ."

55

"We are quite excited to know you have returned. That Urvashi was a bloody tyrant, I tell you. Where have you been?"

"On a vacation. Now I have returned, and important work has to begin."

"Please. We are being ruled by another tyrant. Things were fun when you were around," Lord Amreesh said to Kali. He then moved towards an empty chair, near to where the rest of the nobles were sitting.

Kali had asked Nalakuvera to bring the nobles together. They were feasting in Arjan's luxurious tent. The table in front of the nobles was laden with sumptuous, extravagant dishes and wine. Apsaras were sitting on the laps of some of the nobles, who were busy stuffing their mouths with food.

Nalakuvera was sulking in the corner of the tent, sipping his wine. There was a scar on his cheek. This morning, he had been inches away from being killed. But his guards had killed the intruders at the right moment. The citizens who had infiltrated his fortress had been dealt with. His wife, however, couldn't be saved. The body had been found near the back gates of the fortress.

Kali walked up to the Yaksha king, glancing at the entrance of the camp where Vikoko stood. "I hope you are okay."

"Yeah." Nalakuvera smiled sadly. "It's good that Arjan is listening to you now. He will finally win the war."

"In the beginning," Kali said, looking at Nalakuvera, but he knew every noble was listening in, "I thought Arjan would be a great king. Letting him rule was the right decision, so I had offered help." Kali paused, sighing. "But you know, I was wrong. He's a kid. A villager. He has much to learn. All he has managed to do is increase his physical strength."

"What do you mean?" Nalakuvera asked. "He has been managing fine."

"No, he hasn't. He has made mistakes. Just look at the city. It's plunging in chaos."

"What? But I'm handling the people—"

"I'm sorry for your loss. I will avenge Rambha. I liked her."

Nalakuvera was perplexed. "She was assassinated by some Apsara in the fortress. How would you even know who she was?"

Kali looked at him and said, "I know everything, Nala." He put his palm on Nalakuvera's shoulder and gave him a kiss on the cheek.

And then he stood up, looking at all the nobles.

Kali was wearing a black dhoti and buttoned-up coat that had the design of an owl standing over fire. It was his symbol when he had united the Tribes against the Manavs.

"Everyone!" he addressed the nobles. "I hope you enjoyed the feast. I organised it to celebrate our victory today. But I must inform you that we haven't won yet."

All the nobles were confused. Some laughed nervously.

"This is serious. Your entire army is at stake. Last night I had convinced the king to sacrifice it."

"But the Danavs are there," one of the nobles spoke.

"Are they?" Kali laughed. "I specifically instructed them not to intervene."

"Wait." Nalakuvera stood up, furious. "That can't be true."

"But it is!" he said. "It is! And I have your bloody balls in my hands. Now your entire army will die." He pulled up the flap of the tent. Everyone could see the battlefield. Nagas and Suparns were killing the men of Indragarh. Manasa's army was winning. "And the king is dead. I made sure he died."

Nalakuvera marched towards Kali and yelled, "Why the hell did you do that? He was the saviour!"

"Not really, no. I am. Lord Kali."

The nobles looked at each other, unsure of what to do. Indragarh's ruler had been killed. Again. Their men were out in the battlefield; most of them would be dead by now.

Kali began to circle around the frightened nobles and said, "I have called you all here to declare that I wish to rule the city again. All you esteemed noblemen have a seat in the council. Let me be king."

"Why should we do that?" Lord Amreesh asked, pushing the Apsara away.

"Because if you don't, you will be left with no one to protect the city. My Danavs wouldn't help till I tell them to. The army would be slaughtered. And then the snake queen will come for all of you."

Nalakuvera looked at him, shaking his head.

Kali snapped his fingers. Vikoko entered in the tent with a long scroll. "I asked a lawyer to set this up. By signing on this paper, you all will agree that since the current king is dead, you all feel that I should take things over. Do that, and my Danavs will save your army."

"This is blackmail," one of the nobles said.

"Congratulations! You are quick to learn." Kali slow-clapped.

Everyone looked at the scroll, confused.

Kali whistled. Slowly, the growling hyenas came inside the tent, staring at the nobles and Nalakuvera.

"And yes, if you don't sign the scroll, you'll be eaten alive," Kali added. "Just wanted to add a little motivation, you see."

Vikoko came forward with the scroll and quill in his hand. The nobles got up, one by one, and signed.

Nalakuvera didn't move from his chair. Kali took the scroll and quill from Vikoko and presented it to the Yaksha king. He knelt to whisper in his ear, "Don't worry. I will never forget your hospitality. You gave us a roof, fed us, and even asked your men to guard us. I will take care of you, for sure. You will hold more power. I promise."

"I don't believe you," Nalakuvera said.

"Why? I can give it to you in writing. I will make you prime minister."

"Do whatever you want," he said and signed the scroll. "I don't believe the saviour is dead."

"I can assure you, Nala," Kali said, scowling, "he will not *return*. I have made sure of that."

For a moment, Kali thought Nalakuvera was going to attack him. But then, he just slumped back in his chair, as if he didn't care about anything anymore.

"Thank you, everyone. You all are safe now."

So was Arjan, as Kali had hoped. Kali's purpose now fulfilled, he was ecstatic to be king again. He loved having power. He *loved* winning.

Kali walked towards Vikoko and handed her the scroll, and instructed, "Notarise it." He then looked at the nobles who cowered under his gaze. Nalakuvera, who was quietly watching Kali, said, "What's your plan . . . Your Highness?"

"My plan is simple. I will stop this war."

"How?"

"Involve the Danavs for today." Kali nodded at Vikoko, who went out the tent, towards the battlefield. "And then, we call a truce."

"A truce?" a noble exclaimed, appalled. "Why would the snake queen agree to a bloody truce?"

Kali smiled. "Because I have something that she would definitely want."

56

Manasa knew from the beginning that something was wrong.

Ever since the battle had begun, the Danavs weren't doing anything. They were just standing at the periphery of the ground, near enemy camp. Though Manasa rejoiced that her side was winning, she was growing more perturbed by the second.

What is Kali up to? Why is he not sending in the giants?

Not that Manasa was complaining. Their catapults had been destroyed last night. So they wouldn't be able to use the Soma bombs on the Danavs. Some Suparns had already been tasked with repairing them. But it was taking time.

But then, a few hours into the battle, the Danavs entered the battlefield. The enemy infantry and cavalry had fallen back to their camp, and the Danavs were standing in a line in front of Manasa's army, ready to attack if the Nagas or Suparns advanced.

Airavan had instructed the men to retreat.

Manasa was observing the Danavs from the watchtower. She looked down and spotted Airavan. "Have the catapults been adjusted?" she yelled.

"The men need some more time, Your Majesty."

We don't know what the enemy is planning. Kali might ask his Danavs to attack any minute.

She climbed down the ladder and walked to Vibhishan's camp. The Manav soldiers were resting. Some were getting their wounds treated. Others were heating up their food.

They have done a fine job.

She saw Vibhishan outside his tent, talking to his generals. When Manasa approached Vibhishan, they bowed and left them alone. Vibhishan's lips curved into a smile. "Oh dear, we had almost got them."

"That was their entire army, according to my stats. I guess they realised that they would lose without the Danavs. But I don't understand what's going on. Why are they just standing?"

"I wish I knew, my dear. All we can do, in the meantime, is recuperate. Let the soldiers rest, so that they have the strength to fight what's coming next."

"I suppose."

Vibhishan and Manasa entered the tent. He sat on his bed, and gestured to her to sit on the chair beside it.

"Are you okay, my dear?"

Manasa didn't know how to respond. She had been so close to defeating Kali's army. Hot, boiling anger surged inside her as she thought of Kali.

But taking vengeance wasn't the only thing on her mind. She was going to steer Naagpuri into better, stronger times, once the war was over. Maybe she could do the same for Indragarh after she killed Kali.

"Let's make this world a peaceful place. Where Tribals and Manavs live together in harmony."

"But no city in Udaiyas will ever accept a Tribal as their ruler."

"Then we shall make a Manav king sit on the throne," Vibhishan said, smiling.

Is he referring to himself?

"And you can finally focus on your own kingdom in Dakshini."

Manasa smiled. The idea was good.

"Let's strive to make the people of our kingdoms prosper," Vibhishan said, "no matter how this war ends."

Manasa said, "I'm sure we will win. They lost a lot of their men today. And as soon as we have the catapults fixed, their Danavs won't be a problem either. Though they can enlist more men if they approach Raktapa and ask for his Rakshas army. But I feel Raktapa will stay aloof, as always. His Rakshas are a problem though. They will have to be dealt with once this war is over."

"Let's not be too ambitious."

Vibhishan and Manasa laughed. He began to pour some wine for her when Airavan entered the tent. He looked worried.

"Your Majesty?"

Manasa and Vibhishan turned to look at him. "What is it?" she asked.

"There's a messenger here."

"From?"

"Kali."

"Kill him, as I instructed." Manasa didn't want any truce offerings or any conversations which would unnecessarily stall a winning war.

"That was what I had been going for," Airavan said, "but this messenger has a very important message for you both. Especially you, my lord," Airavan said, turning to Vibhishan.

The king of Bhanmati wiped the sweat on his brows and asked, "What happened?"

"It concerns your daughter, apparently," Airavan said.

Manasa could see the colour draining from Vibhishan's face.

"My daughter is dead."

"No," Airavan shook his head, "Kali has her imprisoned. As proof, he has conveyed through his messenger that her name is Padma."

Manasa looked at Vibhishan. He was leaning on a pole inside the tent. His eyes were brimming with tears.

Padma? The assassin I hired? She is Vibhishan's daughter?

"Is he correct, Vibhishan?"

The king nodded.

Damn it.

"What should we do, Your Majesty?" Airavan asked.

"What does he want?"

"He wants Lord Vibhishan to forfeit his alliance with you and in return his daughter will be given back to him."

"NONSENSE!" Manasa shouted. Vibhishan's men made up one third of her army right now. And unlike the Nagas and Suparns, many of these Manavs were healers and blacksmiths. She needed them to nurse the injured soldiers, and repair weapons.

"He has sent a scroll with the messenger and needs Lord Vibhishan's stamp over it. Once he receives the scroll, he will send Padma to the camp."

"Listen, Manasa—" Vibhishan began in a quivering voice, but Manasa raised her hand, stopping him from speaking. She turned towards Airavan and said, "Bring in the scroll. Vibhishan will stamp it."

"Your Majesty?" yelped Airavan.

Vibhishana looked at Manasa, thunderstruck. "But, Manasa, what if he's bluffing?"

"We can't take that chance. It's your daughter, Vibhishan." Manasa clasped her friend's palm. "You said to me you regret not helping her."

"Yes, my daughter and sons wanted to fight Vedanta. They wanted to abolish monarchy."

"I don't want you to lose out on another chance of helping her. And if Kali is bluffing, and this is a trap . . . we will respond in kind."

"But if I forfeit the alliance, your army won't last for even a week."

"I'll figure something out." Manasa smiled. "Rescuing your

daughter is more important." Manasa didn't want to lose her only ally, but she had no choice. She wanted to help her friend.

"Thank you," said Vibhishan, and embraced Manasa.

Manasa turned to Airavan. "Let's do this bloody transfer, as fast as possible."

57

There was a loud bang outside. Arjan woke up with a start.

What is this place?

He knew he was no longer in the camp. It was an ordinary room. Arjan was lying down on a cot. A small plate of food had been kept on the ground, along with a jug of water.

Arjan's gaze fell on the window. He had to steady himself when he stood up, for he was feeling dizzy. But he managed to walk to the window and peer outside. There were bars on the window, and all he could see was grass and a few plants outside. Arjan even tried to break the bars, but his effort was in vain.

Arjan sighed as he looked outside. The sun's light had begun to fade. A warm breeze rustled the leaves of the trees.

How long have I been here?

Arjan walked towards the door to try to open it, but a greenish liquid had been poured over the doorknob.

Poison.

The door itself was made of metal.

Exasperated, Arjan punched the wall, again and again, till his fists began to bleed. A crack on the wall appeared, but it didn't break.

"You mind, buddy? I'm trying to sleep," a familiar voice came from the other side of the wall.

"Hello? Who is this? Hello!" Arjan desperately called out to the voice. "This is Arjan. Can you hear me?" He banged on the wall. "I'm the King of Indragarh. Can you hear me? Please save me."

"Arjan?" the voice said. "It's me, Padma." The voice was clearer now. Padma was speaking whilst standing close to the wall.

"Why have they trapped you?" Arjan asked, confused. Though he was relieved that he wasn't alone.

"Kali knows that I am a princess. I wonder how he got to know that," she said with a hint of sarcasm in her voice.

Arjan bit his tongue. "I'm sorry. I should have been careful. But I had begun to trust Kali and I wanted his opinion on my ideas. Oh god. Because of me, you are in trouble."

"I don't even know what he plans to do to me," Padma said. "You were an idiot to trust him. He killed all of your friends, Arjan. He tried to kill *you*!"

"I know." Arjan ran his hand through his hair. Everything had come crashing down. "I'll help you. I promise. I'll help you escape—"

And then they heard footsteps. Arjan peered outside and saw a lot of soldiers marching.

"They are here," Padma said, her voice barely above a whisper. "THEY ARE HERE TO PICK ME UP! THEY ARE TAKING ME AWAY!"

Arjan frantically punched the wall, trying to get to the other side. But he couldn't do it. He was exhausted. His energy had been drained and he felt drowsy.

Arjan heard the door close on the other side close.

The only question that was in his mind was, *What are they going to do with her?*

58

Kali got down from his charcoal black stallion. He looked over at the snake queen's army that was standing at a distance.

And behind him stood Indragarh's entire army. The sand on the battlefield had turned a bright red. They had been fighting and killing each other for days. A vulture hovered over the people. Kali took out his binoculars and peered in the enemy's direction. Manasa, the snake queen, was standing at the back of her force.

Kali had figured out now why this war was happening. Because of him. He had killed the snake queen's brother and tried to assassinate her as well.

People just don't understand politics.

Beside Kali were his two generals, Koko and Vikoko. They sat atop their horses, looking at the enemy soldiers. Their hands were on the hilt of their swords, ready to attack if someone harmed their lord. And in front of Kali stood two hyenas, growling.

"They seem hungry, my lord," Koko said.

"Feed them once we are done handing over the princess."

Nalakuvera was sitting on his horse at the back, with his Yakshas. And the usually happy Yaksha king looked morose.

How things change. I was living in his fortress like a leech. Now, I am king.

"Are you sure this is the right thing to do?" Nalakuvera asked.

"Of course," Kali responded. "Once Vibhishan leaves the camp, it'll be easy for us to kill Manasa."

"Hate to say it, but it makes sense," Nalakuvera said. "But I'm still mad at you. I believed in Arjan. A little more guidance from us, and he would have made a fine king."

"Oh, I know that," Kali said under his breath.

His guards brought Padma and pushed her to kneel in front of Kali. Her hands had been tied at the back. The hyenas began to growl at her. Padma shrieked at the sight of the monsters and then looked at Kali.

Kali had expected Padma to beg for her life. But she just spat on Kali's feet.

"You deserve this, you runt. Because of you, Ratri died."

Kali chuckled. He remembered that. That traitor. He felt no remorse on killing someone who had betrayed him. *But Padma should realise that.*

"I hope you will be happy to see your father. I heard you don't like him."

Padma glared at Kali.

Kali waited as a messenger from the enemy camp rode towards him. He took out the agreement that had Vibhishan's stamp on it.

"Great. Send her away."

The messenger grunted. He grabbed Padma and put her on the horse. Padma turned her head towards Kali and gave him a dirty look.

They rode off in the direction of Manasa's camp.

"Your plan has succeeded," Nalakuvera said, impressed. "Can't believe I'm going to say this, but we may win the war because of you."

Kali took out his binoculars and looked at the enemy again. The snake queen had a smile on her face now.

What is the meaning of this?

Kali observed the enemy's army. The general standing in the front had a huge grin on his face.

He turned to Koko and said, "We've been played."

"My lord?"

"What do you mean?" Nalakuvera asked.

"The scroll means shit." He tore the paper. "The moment the girl reaches there, they will resume the fight."

"But they stamped on the agreement."

"War has no rules, chump," Kali confidently said. "Just like *I* have none."

Kali whistled. The hyenas began to race in the field towards Padma. And now, he would wait and look at the beautiful, chaotic show in front of him.

59

Padma's instinct was telling her that something was going to go wrong.

As she was nearing Manasa's camp, she could see two people at the back of the soldiers. She had thought she would never see them again—her father and her previous employer. It had been so long since Padma had been with Lord Vibhishan. She still disliked him, but she had missed him dearly. She wanted to tell him that she had been foolish to leave to fight Vedanta. Her brothers were dead because of her. And then Padma looked at Manasa, the queen who had hired her as an assassin.

Father allied himself with Manasa. Does that mean these two are friends? I had no idea.

Both of them had wide smiles on their faces . . . until they heard a loud whistle.

What is happening?

Manasa and Vibhishan were not looking at Padma anymore. Horrified, they were staring at something behind her.

Padma turned and saw Kali's hyenas running towards her. One of them bit the horse's leg. The horse neighed loudly, and flung his legs in the air, dropping Padma and the messenger on the ground.

Whilst Padma tried to get up, one hyena lurched at the messenger, gnawing at his throat. The other one was advancing towards her.

Manasa and Vibhishan's frantic yelling reached Padma's ears. They were telling their guards to go and help Padma. But Padma knew that even if they rode towards her at breakneck speed, they won't be able to reach her on time.

I have to save myself.

Padma backed away from the hyena. She was going to run, when the hyena jumped on her.

Padma screamed. The hyena had bared her fangs. She was about to dig them in her throat. Having finished killing the messenger, the other hyena was heading towards Padma as well.

This is it. This is my death.

I can't die like this. Not without killing Nala. Not without meeting Kalki. Not without meeting my . . . father.

Padma saw the monstrous eyes of the hyena as it opened its mouth wide . . . and dung fell inside it.

The hyena began to choke. The other hyena stopped advancing towards Padma. It was looking in the direction from which the dung had been flung.

And then, a familiar green parrot perched on Padma's shoulder . . .

It was Shuko.

"What are you doing here?" she asked. "I sent you to—"

The parrot squawked happily. Time stood still as the two armies gawked at the spectacle in front of them.

The hyena near Padma's feet was still looking at something in the distance. Padma followed its gaze.

There he was.

Kalki.

He was sitting on a horse, wielding a glowing sword.

"He's back." She mumbled and then turned to face Kali, who looked white as a sheet. "HE'S BACK! AND HE WILL KILL YOU ALL."

Devadatta galloped towards the centre of the field where Padma was lying. Kalki pulled out his sword and swiftly sliced the hyena near Padma's feet into two. The other hyena had choked on the dung and died.

Kalki got down from his horse and extended his hand to Padma. And that's when Padma noticed something. She didn't know why but red smoke was emanating from his body.

Padma grasped his hand and got up.

"Are you okay?" Concerned, Kalki knelt down and looked at her bruised leg.

"Oh god, you came at the right time. You have no idea how happy I am now that you are here."

"Because I saved you or because you actually missed me?"

"Oh shut up." Padma wrapped her arms around Kalki and gave him a lingering kiss.

"Uh, okay then," Kalki said, smiling from ear to ear.

And then he turned to look at Kali. Kali calmly met his gaze.

"Don't kill him now," Padma whispered, still in Kalki's arms. "He has Arjan."

Kalki looked taken aback. He opened and closed his mouth, as if debating something in his mind. But then he just nodded and said, "Let's take you to a safe place, shall we?"

They both climbed on Devadatta and headed towards Manasa's camp. Even though things were far from over, for now, Padma was happy.

60

Padma had woken up after a long nap.

She got up from the cot and opened the flap of the tent. It was dark outside.

It took her a few minutes to realise that her leg had been bandaged. She walked back to her cot and saw Kalki sleeping on the chair beside it.

Padma smiled as she spotted her father sitting in the corner of the tent. When Vibhishan saw Padma go back to her cot, he got up and came to sit beside his daughter. He couldn't look her in the eye, unsure of what to say.

Padma remained silent as well.

After a few minutes, Vibhishan looked at Kalki and said, "Whoever this boy is, he seems important. You had fainted after that traumatic encounter with the hyenas. This boy carried you to this tent and refused to leave your side. While you were resting, my dear, Manasa and I spoke to him about the war that has been happening here. After listening to everything we had to say, he suddenly declared that he was going to sleep. I think he just wanted to be near you."

Padma smiled, playing with her hands.

"Do you love him?" her father asked.

"What?"

"Do you love him?"

"Why do you ask?"

"Because he clearly loves you." Vibhishan chuckled. "And the way he easily killed those monstrous creatures . . . people were saying that he looked like a god."

What if I tell you that he is a god? But Padma didn't say that. "How have you been?"

"Fine. You?"

"I have been . . . good."

"Manasa told me you used to work for her."

Padma hung her head in shame. She had hoped to hide the fact that she used to work as an assassin, from her father.

"She told me what she made you do. You were an errand girl, right? Running off to get milk and stuff."

A sigh of relief escaped Padma's lips. "Uh, yeah, sure."

"I thought you were dead," Vibhishan spoke softly. "My dear, I am so sorry. I should have been there with you."

"No," Padma shook her head, "I was stupid. I went with my brothers, believing what we were planning to do was noble, that we were going to help build a utopian society. How foolish I was to think that killing a king would be the end of monarchy. Another king was crowned after Vedanta died. And now Arjan sits on the throne. Your sons and I were so naïve."

"Well, they were my sons," Vibhishan mumbled. "Are they . . ."

"Yes." Vibhishan wanted to know for sure what had happened to his sons. After all, the daughter he presumed dead was sitting with him right now. "They were not rescued. I tried to avenge them, but eventually lost hope. When I came here, Arjan told me that Vedanta was beheaded by Kali for treason." She paused, smiling to herself. "You can be saved from a twenty-year-old girl but you can't save yourself from karma."

"I suppose so," Vibhishan said.

Padma lay down on the cot again. As she combed her fingers through her hair, she realised there was sand stuck to her scalp.

Vibhishan looked at her and laughed. "I will ask my men to fetch you some water to clean your head. Your hair is a beautiful shade of silver now."

Padma touched her hair. "Thank you. I dyed it to hide from Vedanta."

"I see. So what's your plan now, my dear?"

"I want to fight with your men, but I also want to save my friend, Arjan. Kali has captured him." *And kill Nala.* Padma will have to take care of that Yaksha king first. Arjan was strong enough to protect himself, and Kali will be dealt with now that Kalki had returned.

"Sure," Vibhishan said, "do what you have to do. It's good to have you back. By the way, Manasa has called a meeting and wants all of us to attend. We will strike at Kali's army tomorrow and must be prepared."

Padma liked the fact that Vibhishan was treating Padma like an adult now. She wanted to hug him, but perhaps, it was too much for now.

"Will be there."

Padma and Kalki stood on one side of the round table. Manasa, Vibhishan, and Airavan stood opposite them. They were discussing the strategies to employ in tomorrow's attack.

"So," Manasa began, "we have the so-called chosen one amongst us. The Avatar of Lord Vishnu himself, born to kill the Adharm. The last I saw you was when you were being tried for hurting Kali's ridiculously sensitive sentiments. And you wanted to kill him. I'm glad the latter part hasn't changed since then." Padma had filled in Manasa and Vibhishan about Kalki. "You know, some people were saying that they are afraid of you. And some think you have come from the heavens."

"I came from Mahendragiri. If that's heaven, I can't even imagine what hell would be like," Kalki joked.

Everyone laughed.

Padma liked this. She was in the company of like-minded people who had come together to achieve the same goal: to destroy evil.

"So what's the plan?" Kalki asked.

"In all fairness, Avatar of Vishnu, shouldn't you be the one to lead us?" Manasa asked.

"Never thought you'd ever believe in the prophecy," Vibhishan remarked.

"I've seen things that made me believe there is a god and he wants us to win," Manasa confessed. "And now, that this god is here with us, I would like to make use of him."

Padma looked at Kalki's face. She thought he would be annoyed but he was just laughing.

He appears so calm but I can't help but think of how he reacted when I told him about Arjan.

Before heading to Manasa's tent for the meeting, Padma had sat with Kalki and told him what had happened at Lord Bajrang's camp, and about her time at Arjan's camp. Kalki had mutely stared at her when she had told him about Guru Narendra's murder.

"I am not a king," Kalki said, looking at Manasa. "I am a warrior. I can fight but when it comes to strategising, I don't know what to do. So you tell me and your men what to do. And I will follow and execute as you command."

Manasa nodded. "Okay, here's what we should do. My men will fight on foot. But I'll have Suparns focus their attention on the Danavs. They will aim their arrows at the Danavs' eyes, which will impair their sight. And then, I am hoping Kalki can finish them off."

"Padma told me everything about these creatures. I'll handle them."

"Great. I will keep a check on things from the camp. Will be observing everything from the watchtower," Manasa said and then she turned to Padma. "I think you should go and rest."

Padma shook her head. "I don't need to rest. I am fine. I plan to rescue Arjan," she said, turning to face Kalki. For a moment, she thought he would say that he wanted to come along. But Kalki didn't say anything. His face was impassive, revealing nothing.

She didn't know why, but she was sure Kalki was hiding something from her.

What is he hiding?

"You're going to Indragarh? People will recognise you," Manasa said.

"I'll make sure they don't. I can be quite discreet. I'll find where he is and save him."

"But why are you going to save Arjan? He is our enemy."

"No, he's not. He has been influenced," Kalki said defensively. "And he's my brother. If you don't let her go to save him, I won't fight for you."

"Is that a threat, boy?" Manasa said, barely managing to conceal the anger in her voice. "Are you trying to bully me?"

"I'm not bullying you. Just putting it out there," Kalki said.

There was complete silence in the tent for a few minutes.

"Fine." Manasa sighed. She looked at Padma and said, "Save your friend but stay alert and protect yourself, Padma. You know your father and I will be constantly worried once you leave."

"Roger that."

"Now," Manasa pulled out a chart, "I plan to use these strategies since we have lost a lot of men—"

And then they all heard the boom of a huge blast. Manasa got out and saw the soldiers running around, confused and scared.

We are going to die!

61

The first thought that Manasa had when she heard a blast from inside the tent, was that Kali had come for her. He had somehow made past the guards at the entrance and was going to kill her now.

But when Manasa came outside, determined to not cower before her enemy, what she saw took her by surprise.

Men, covered in black cloaks from head to toe, were plunging their knives in the soldiers' bodies. The blast had blown up many tents. And some of these strange men were burning their stock of food and wine.

Kalki came out and surveyed the sight before him. He and Manasa looked at each other, each wondering who these men were and why they were attacking their camp. They wordlessly stared at each other for a few seconds, and then Kalki took out his sword. He began to attack a bunch of intruders that were chasing Nagas. Padma wanted to come out and fight, but Vibhishan dragged her back inside the tent with him.

Manasa couldn't just stand and see her men die. She turned to Airavan and said, "Give me a weapon."

"Your Majesty, you should stay back," Airavan cautioned. He was standing in front of Manasa, his shield at the ready.

Manasa pulled out one of the two swords that Airavan was carrying. "You are protecting the wrong person, General. Fight with me."

Airavan pulled out his blade, and reluctantly added, "As you command, Your Majesty."

"You are a good general, Airavan."

They were standing back to back when the cloaked men ran towards them.

One man sneered at Manasa as he aimed his knife at her. But Manasa dodged the attack and swiftly stabbed the man with her sword. Another man came at Manasa, but she struck her attacker's knee. The man fell on the ground, howling in pain.

Manasa wanted to see his face. She pulled away the hood and saw a bald, hairless man, and his eyes were blue, just like . . .

Nagas.

At that moment, she heard one of her soldiers shout, "SERPENTS! SERPENTS!"

Snakes were crawling on the ground. Manasa noticed that Kalki was seconds away from being bitten by one. Luckily, he noticed the snake near his feet on time and killed it with his sword.

Manasa turned to face Airavan, who was busy defending himself. "It's the Mother. It's Kadru. She has found us," Manasa said, panicking.

I should have killed her when I had the chance.

While Manasa was lost in thought, cursing the day she had chosen to let her monstrous cousin live, she didn't realise that an attacker was speeding towards her.

"MANASA!"

Airavan's voice jolted Manasa out of her thoughts. The attacker was inches away from piercing his knife in Manasa's back.

But Airavan came between her and the hooded man. The blade went right through him.

Manasa screamed as the attacker pulled the blade out and then severed Airavan's head. And then, strangely, he picked it up, wrapped it in a white cloth, and ran away.

And that was the moment, all of the hooded men ran towards the back of the camp, towards the forest.

Manasa couldn't order her men to go after them. She was numb. She couldn't look away from Airavan's headless corpse. Kalki tried to follow them, but couldn't keep up.

He returned to Manasa's tent after a few minutes. "I'm sorry. They ran away so fast. After a point, I couldn't even see them. It was as if they had vanished into thin air."

Manasa wept as she knelt to hold the hand of her general, her friend.

"The back half of the camp is pretty burnt out. It was a planned attack. We lost a lot of nurses," Kalki said.

Anger began to bubble inside Manasa.

"Kalki," she said, still looking at Airavan, "I trust you to handle the Danavs in the attack tomorrow. Inform my men about what we discussed in the tent. I want to find my cousin. Her men don't have any magical powers. They haven't vanished into thin air. I suspect they are hiding in the forest. And once I find them, I *will* kill each and every one of them."

62

Embrace yourself, the voice inside of him repeated.

"I don't know what you mean," Arjan said, and immediately felt stupid for talking to himself.

But what else could he do. He was alone, and he kept hearing voices in his head. No matter how much he tried, they just didn't stop.

Have I become delusional?

Arjan had no idea how much time had passed since he was locked up in this dingy, small room. And he was sure he was being drugged. Even though he didn't feel tired, he would fall asleep for hours after having the food laid out for him.

Being unable to do anything was driving him crazy. There were cracks on the wall now. He punched it whenever he felt frustrated.

I am a prisoner and I don't even know where I am.

All Arjan could make out was that there was a garden outside this prison. For all he knew, he might not even be in Indragarh right now. *But Kali doesn't need to throw me out. I am sure he is planning to kill me so he can be king.*

You have delayed too much. Embrace! the voice screamed again.

"What should I embrace?"

Yourself!

"I have done that already!"

No! You have not embraced the real you. Close your eyes. And feel the Chakras in your body. Seek yourself. Your past self. And learn from him.

Arjan didn't know what the voices were getting at. His past self? Was the voice asking him to remember his childhood?

Once you embrace your true self, you shall be able to escape from here.

Arjan desperately wanted to escape. He couldn't bear being in this prison anymore. So he obeyed the voice and closed his eyes, trying to remember who he was. He emptied his mind, and focused on his breath.

Nothing happened for a few minutes. Just as Arjan had begun to doubt the voice, he felt the ground shake.

Show me the way to embrace my true self.

Arjan felt himself rise from the ground. He was suspended in the air for a few seconds, and then gently landed on the ground beneath him. But the ground wasn't rocky and cold anymore.

When Arjan opened his eyes, he found himself in a lab.

Jars and test tubes lined the shelves on the wall. A man was standing in the centre of the room, carefully mixing two liquids in a beaker. The man had a long white beard, and striking blue eyes. He was wearing a crown. Though the man was clearly old, Arjan noticed his toned, strong arms.

Arjan was gazing at the tattoos on the man's torso, when the man turned to him and said, "Finally made it here, eh?"

"Who are you?"

"You must ask where you are."

He led Arjan to the corner of the lab, and opened the mosaic window. Arjan noticed that it was pouring outside. But the rain had not dulled the beauty of the iconic buildings. The sun was shining brightly, and a rainbow arched in the sky. On the road, children were happily dancing and splashing in the water.

"Welcome to Haihayas Kingdom, the greatest empire after the Golden Age of the Asuras," he proclaimed proudly. "I inherited this beautiful kingdom after my father died."

"Haihayas . . . it sounds familiar."

Arjan and the old man stared at each other for a few seconds.

"This was what the kingdom was like before Bhargav destroyed it."

"You are . . ." Arjan narrowed his eyes, trying to recall the old king's name from his textbooks. "You are Kartavirya Arjun, the king who had a thousand arms."

"Well, me having thousands arms," he said, raising both his hands in the air, "is an exaggeration. But yes, I am Kartavirya."

Arjan had read about him in gurukul. He was one of the strongest emperors of his time. There were different stories about how he had captured Raavan. And he had been finally defeated by an Avatar of Vishnu—Bhargav Ram.

"You must understand, Arjan," Kartavirya said, "that it is imperative that you stop the Avatar of your Age. Look what happened here. So many innocent citizens of my kingdom perished because my Age's Avatar thought that everything was fine as long as he managed to defeat me."

"What do you mean?"

"I know power got to my head. But did I have to die for that? Did my people deserve to die for that? An Avatar is not a god, my boy. He can make a mistake. And I know I did some . . . questionable things, but there needs to be a balance of both good and bad forces for there to be stability in the world." Kartavirya paused suddenly and looked at Arjan with pity in his eyes. "The Avatar of my Age destroyed me, and the Avatar of your Age will kill you."

"Why would he do that? Unlike you, I am not drunk on power. I didn't kill—" Arjan couldn't finish that sentence, for he knew that that wasn't true.

"My kingdom flourished under my rule," Kartavirya announced. "Evil is always considered bad. Speak what you will about me, but there is evil in every person. Do you think you are perfect? Do you think anyone is? When you killed Guru Narendra, it sent a clear message to the people about what will happen to those who mess with you. It was a good move; people began to fear you and that is essential to avoid dissent. And what happened when you were trying to do good? You looked weak and desperate in front of Kali, and that resulted in you landing in a prison."

Arjan bit his lip.

He is right.

He felt furious as he recalled his moment of weakness. As his anger began to rise, golden smoke began to emanate from his body.

"Let your pain and anger empower you, boy," Kartavirya said. "Just like you did when you killed Urvashi. You remember that day? You remember how powerful you had become? Believe me, if you channelise your pain and anger, your powers will increase tenfold."

Arjan was quiet for a few minutes, thinking over what he had just heard. He asked, in a low voice, "Why does the Avatar want to kill me?"

The old king's gaze narrowed. He put his arm around Arjan and gave him a sad smile. For a moment, Arjan was awed by how striking Kartavirya looked. He couldn't believe that all this was happening, that he was talking to an Ancient.

"Kill you? He wants to incinerate you. The White Horse Rider wants nothing but your death," Kartavirya said. "And if you aren't prepared, he will get what he wants. You must not let him harm you, Arjan. You are important. Very important. After all, you are Adharm."

Arjan's heart skipped a beat.

"No, I am not," Arjan said, forcing the king's arm away.

"Yes, you are. Embrace your true self."

"You are lying!" Arjan screamed. And then it hit him. He shuddered as he said, "Wait. Was it you screeching in my head all this time?"

"Amongst others."

"There are others?"

"Other Adharms, who embraced themselves. You can unlock great power from your pain and anger, Arjan. But first you must accept yourself."

The White Horse Rider . . .

Kartavirya was referring to Kalki. Arjan had once heard Kripa say that Kalki was destined to ride the White Horse. *But Kalki would never want to kill me, no matter what the old, lunatic king is saying.*

"I am not evil. I know I've killed people, but I had rea—"

"Being evil isn't all bad," Kartavirya said, shaking his head. "How can I make you understand? Your goodness has only created problems. Imagine, if you had killed Urvashi in the beginning, when you had seen how poorly she was ruling, then Rudra would have been alive, right?"

"Yes."

"Now replace Rudra with the country of Illavarti and Urvashi with the White Horse Rider," Kartavirya said. "What do you think will happen?"

Arjan understood instantly.

"Kalki will rule. And then what will happen? Your kingdom will perish. He is a warrior, not a king. You are ruling well. Continue to do so," Kartavirya said.

"What should I do?"

"Embrace your true self, and you will be able to defeat the White Horse Rider."

Arjan sighed. "All right. I will embrace my true self."

It was a lie. Arjan was still finding it hard to believe that he was evil incarnate. But Kartavirya's other arguments were making sense. So Arjan had just spoken to make the old king stop going on like a broken record.

Kartavirya smiled.

"What happened when Bhargav Ram tried to take over your kingdom?"

"That's a story for another day. All you need to know is that I was a good king, no, the greatest king this city could have. The time I reigned has gone down in history as the golden age of Haihayas kingdom." Kartavirya smiled. "No one knew that I was an Adharm because I was a Manav. No one suspected, except for Bhargav Ram. I am the only Manav to become Adharm. The gods chose me although usually an Asura is chosen to be Adharm, like you."

"I'm not."

"Yes, you are," Kartavirya stressed. "Better start believing in your true lineage. It's important."

And then Arjan was zapped back to reality. Panting and sweating, he opened his eyes and blinked. The wall of his prison stood before him.

He couldn't believe it had happened. He had had a conversation with a mighty king who had died long ago.

Arjan knew what had to be done.

If it was for the betterment of his country and his people, he may have to be the evil one. No matter how twisted Kartavirya was . . . he was beginning to sound right to Arjan.

63

"He has returned!" Kali yelled, ramming his fist at the table.

The papers fell down. The lamps on the table shattered.

Kali surveyed the room with his bloodshot eyes. In the farthest corner stood Durukti, silently gazing at him. There was hope in her eyes. She was glad that Kalki had returned. In another corner lurked the sulking Nalakuvera, leaning on the wall, blowing on his nails. Koko and Vikoko were standing beside Kali, their faces impassive.

"Who is this *he*?" Nalakuvera asked.

"He is the worst thing that can happen to us right now. He's Adharm and we need to put him down." Kali had to lie. He was scared that Kalki knew the truth about Arjan. And who knows what Kalki had been up to all this time. From the way he had protected Padma a few hours ago, he looked even stronger than when Kali had last seen him.

Nalakuvera frowned. "So what do you want to do?" he asked.

"Durukti, you may leave," Kali ordered his sister.

Durukti stared at Kali, confused.

"My dear, you must be tired. Why don't you retire to your room and rest? Lord Nalakuvera and I will strategise on what is to be done," Kali said, hoping Durukti would agree. If not, he would have no choice but to force her to leave. They were going to decide how to deal with Kalki. And Kali didn't trust his sister would keep quiet if she came to know of their plans.

Kali could see the angered face of his sister before she stormed out the room. Sighing, he sat back on his chair and scratched his chin thoughtfully. "Here's what we do. I stay at camp. Koko and Vikoko," he turned to look at his strong generals, "you be at the battlefield. I have told the Danavs to listen to your commands. Make sure you keep hitting their defences until they are broken. And Nala," Kali looked at the Yaksha king, "your father had mentioned to me once that you are quite a performer."

"Indeed I am," Nalakuvera straightened, a bright smile appearing on his face. "I am an actor."

"An actor, huh. You know what moves people? A good play. It is entertaining, and a way to subtly convince people to believe what the writer believes." Kali got up from his chair and walked towards the window. He saw a street splattered with blood. The people were going crazy. Their king had died again, and now the previous tyrant had returned to rule them. He had not even taken the public's vote into account. The people were even more outraged. "I want you to write a play that would portray me in all my glory as the greatest ruler of Indragarh. Show the people that all their previous rulers were megalomaniacs, but I am righteous. I do not want any issues within my own city. At this rate, if something isn't done, I will have no subjects by the time I win this war."

Nalakuvera looked doubtful of the plan. Kali could see him in the mirror beside the window. *Great, I'll have to lie to convince him now.* "Do you know who killed Rambha? My general told me that it was the snake queen's assassin."

"Are you sure?"

"My general was there when she was killed."

Nalakuvera's hands had balled into fists. He had a determined look on his face.

Kali walked towards the Yaksha king and kept his hand on

his shoulder. "Will you be able to move the people in the city to support me? You need to act your heart out."

"I will write a good play," he said. "But what if there's a revolt during the performance?"

"I'll supply you with enough men so you won't have to worry about a riot. Anyone who attacked the actors on stage will be dealt with. Your play must happen. I want the civilians to celebrate the fact that I am their king now."

Nalakuvera nodded.

"You are relieved," Kali added.

Nalakuvera left the room. And as he did, Kali turned to Koko and Vikoko. "Have you sent the raven?"

"To Lord Raktapa, my lord?" Koko asked. "Yes, we have."

Cracking his knuckles, Kali responded, "I hope he accepts the alliance again. We do not have much to give but I have promised him a few villages around the city in return."

"But that's not all you offered, my lord," Vikoko added. "You also offered to give him Lord Nalakuvera's stronghold in Alakpur."

Kali knew that the city wasn't his to offer. And he knew if Nalakuvera got to know about this, things would get messy. *I'll cross that bridge when I come to it.* He wanted the Rakshas army to back him up. Kali knew that Manasa must have gotten the catapults repaired by now. The enemy had weapons against the Danavs, and they also had Kalki now.

And as much as he hated to admit, he knew that Kalki was a fine warrior.

Kali was about to head to his room when there was a knock on the door. Without waiting for an answer, the door swung open and something was thrown inside.

The generals got alarmed. Pulling out their weapons, they instantly stood in front of Kali. Kali remained impassive as he saw what had been thrown in—a human head. The man's hair was filled with beads. He had blue eyes. His face was pale, his tongue was out, and his eyes were glassy.

The generals firmly clutched their weapons as a slim, hooded, hunched figure entered. It was wearing a black cloak.

Kali, unperturbed by the presence of the figure, simply asked, "Who are you?"

"A person who makes a dramatic entrance, Lord Kali."

"How did you enter my palace?"

"My Children helped me."

Kali narrowed his gaze. "What kind of sick joke is this?" he said, pointing at the severed head. "Who is he?"

"The general serving under Manasa."

Though wary of the person in front of him, Kali couldn't hide the elation he felt on hearing this. "You attacked Manasa?"

"Yes, I did, and I give you this head in return for an alliance with me."

"Who are you?"

The figure removed the hood, revealing an almost hairless head and a dark, disfigured face. "I am the Mother."

"Mother of what?"

"Snakes. You'd be glad to know that I am considered Lord Shesh Naag's gift to the world. I cheated death. My Children worship me."

"I don't worship anyone, god or human."

"You don't have to." She walked around the room as the generals pointed their blades in her direction, ready to kill if she attacked. "I come here because I have issues with Manasa. I think both of us will benefit once she is dead, so I've decided to give you my support. While you brazenly attack her with your army, I will infiltrate her camp and attack her men when she least expects it."

"How exactly would you do that?"

"Just like how I entered this well-guarded palace." Her grim, dark face lit up. "I have a garrison hidden at the outskirts of Manasa's camp. I will strategise when to attack the camp next. I won't attack her soldiers, just their resources, the stuff her men survive on—grains, medicines, food, and whatever else can be found."

"So you will destroy it from within," Kali mumbled. *The plan is interesting.*

"Yes. My Children are strong. Whilst Manasa is fighting you, I will make sure that her camp is depleted of everything. As the food disappears, her men will fight over what is left. And when the medicines vanish, her injured men will die. Soon, she will have no choice but to surrender."

Kali couldn't believe his luck. *This woman looks disgusting, but if she managed to enter my palace without getting caught, who knows what she will be able to do at Manasa's camp.*

"Consider us allies now, Mother. Is there anything you want in exchange for lending your support?"

"Yes." She walked towards Indragarh's king and looked him in the eye. "When she surrenders, *I* should be the one to kill her."

64

Kalki stood at the back of Manasa's army. On his left stood Lord Vibhishan. Manasa was on his right, keenly observing the battlefield in front of her.

Men would die. Death was inevitable. This was war, after all.

But Manasa was still grieving over the loss of her general. She had badly wanted to go after Kadru but she couldn't just leave her men. Their general had died three days ago. Manasa had to appoint another general from amongst her men to take Airavan's place and command the soldiers on the battlefield. She had been observing how he directed the soldiers and handled himself during fights. But today, finally, she had decided that the new general was a capable man and she would venture to the back of the camp after the battle, and go after the woman that got Airavan killed.

Kalki looked at Manasa's army standing tall in front of him. Nagas were the infantry, armed with swords and shields. Vibhishan's men were the cavalry, sitting atop their horses, ready to swing their swords. And the Suparns were armed with arrows, hovering in the sky. Shuko was flying overhead the battlefield. Devadatta was gearing up to gallop.

And on the opposite side, Kalki could see Kali's army.

Everyone was prepared.

Kalki unsheathed his sword and yelled, "Attack!"

The infantry of both the armies clashed. Manasa then released the cavalry to attack the enemy from the right.

"I should be inside of it," Kalki said.

"No," Manasa said, firmly. "Like I've been saying for the past two days, you go in only when it's absolutely necessary. You don't need to fight from start to finish every day. You may exhaust yourself and when we really need you, you'll falter."

Both sides had lost many men in the previous two days of battle. Kali and Manasa's armies had fought all day. Both the days, Manasa's men had managed to overpower Kali's men. Towards the evening, when Manasa observed that she was close to victory, the enemy would send in the Danavs. The Danavs would trample on Manasa's men and crush the Suparns in their giant hands. And as soon as Manasa's men threw bombs, and Kalki was sent in the battlefield to finish the giants off, Kali's men retreated.

This was the third day of battle. And Kalki was getting antsy.

Shuko dove down and whispered to Kalki, *Left side is defenceless*, and then he flew away.

Kalki grinned when he noticed that no one was at the left flank of the enemy's army.

"Why aren't we attacking from the left?" Kalki asked.

"Because . . ." Manasa paused, thinking. "They have . . . wait . . . hold on . . . they are defenceless on the left, aren't they?"

"Oh yeah. Is this a mistake or a strategy?" Kalki wondered.

"Maybe they just forgot to guard that side in their haste to attack." She looked at Vibhishan. "Get a part of your men to attack from the left."

Vibhishan signalled to the captains and then pointed at the left side. The captains nodded, and ordered their men to follow them.

"You are risking it? It may be a trap," Kalki said.

"War, much like life, is a gamble."

Vibhishan's captains led a part of the cavalry to the left side and attacked the enemy soldiers, taking them by surprise.

"Well, I guess they really had been hasty." Kalki smiled. "Your gamble paid off."

Manasa didn't smile back. And before they could celebrate, a Danav entered. Only one. He went towards the left flank, aiming to crush Manasa's cavalry.

"GET THE CATAPULTS!" she yelled at her captains.

Kalki cursed under his breath. He didn't like this at all. Manasa had been using Soma bombs to kill the Danavs. *If this continues, this war will turn into the Mahayudh. I won't let history repeat itself.*

"No," Kalki said, turning to face Manasa.

"What do you mean 'no'?" Manasa looked at Kalki with a puzzled expression.

"You can't use bombs."

"Why not?"

"Because it's wrong!"

"I don't have time to consider whether I'm being ethical or not. This is a war. I need to win. The Danav can't be stopped without the bombs."

Kalki pursed his lips. "Oh he will. *I* will stop him. You hold on to those bombs till I return."

And with that, Devadatta neighed and rode into the battlefield with his rider.

Kalki and his horse stood out amongst Manasa's men. He made his way towards the Danavs, turning to ash whoever came in his way through his mighty Sword of Shiva.

He was riding towards the Danav at breakneck speed and he realised how *big* it really was. One foot of the giant was equivalent to five soldiers. As the giant moved closer to the left flank, Kalki stood up on his horse.

Ready, human? Devadatta asked.

They were coming close to the Danav. Devadatta was galloping towards it, and when he passed by the giant's leg, Kalki lurched from the horse and clung on the giant's ankle.

Carefully, with the sword's hilt in his mouth, he began to claw his way up. The giant stopped moving and looked at Kalki.

Kalki stopped climbing, unsure of what to do. The Danav was staring at him. And then, slowly, the Danav moved his hand to grab Kalki.

Kalki held on the Danav's skin with one hand and clutched his sword in the other, slicing the Danav's fingers without difficulty.

The Danav bellowed. Everyone on the battlefield looked up to see what had happened.

Come on, you can do this.

Kalki managed to climb to the chest of the giant, whose other hand was coming towards him.

But Kalki didn't waste time. He took a deep breath and looked at the red smoke emanating from his body as he plunged his sword deep inside the giant's chest and then slid down, slicing the entire torso.

Dust swirled in the air as the Danav fell on the ground. It looked down at its body as blood and guts spilled out.

And it fell on its own army.

The Nagas and the Suparns cheered loudly. Kalki sheathed his sword and waved at the soldiers.

And the red smoke filling the air under the bright light, looked white . . . so white . . . he was looking like an angel.

He looked at battlefield and spotted two dark figures in the distance—the generals of Kali. They were staring at Kalki, mounted on their individual scythed chariots. Their weapons were glistening under the bright light, and one of them pointed their blade in Kalki's direction. Kalki just smirked.

You are going to die next.

65

Padma had changed her hair from silver to black. Kali was king now. His men might be prowling around the city. She couldn't risk looking so distinctive.

She had to be careful.

Padma ran her hand through her hair as she walked on the street. She didn't feel like herself in the black hair, but that was the point. To not be herself. To hide amidst the crowd and disappear.

The street she was walking on was deserted. Padma remembered a vibrant bazaar when she was here last. Instead of the shopkeepers trying to attract the customers by their cries of cheap prices and exquisite products, there were only beggars walking. People chose to stay in their houses, their door and windows shut most of the time. Riots were happening daily. Some people were angry at their current king, some were angry at their previous king, and some just didn't want monarchy. The city had become unsafe. Kali's men were patrolling the streets, ready to round up any revolutionaries they found.

It made Padma feel like it was the end of the world.

Soon, Padma entered a narrow alley and made her way to a tavern. The place was stinking horribly. Men sat around consuming liquor. Some were drinking alone, and some others were clanging their mugs together.

Padma looked at the barkeep—a young, short-haired, violet-eyed girl. She was cleaning a table and then went to stand behind the bar. A wide cabinet was placed at her back, displaying a wide range of suras and wines.

The eyes of the men in the bar followed Padma as she walked to the barkeep and said, "I would like some moonshine."

The girl looked at Padma, and her eyes widened in horror.

"Hello, Reena." Padma smiled viciously. The woman tried to escape, but Padma grasped her hair and dragged her out of the bar.

"You ratted me out, didn't you?"

"She threatened me. What could I have done? I had to tell her that you stopped by and were on your way to Lord Nalakuvera's fortress."

Padma punched Reena so hard that a few teeth broke and fell out of her mouth. "You could have refused to tell her anything. We were friends. We stayed together after the revolt in Indragarh during Vedanta's time. You had even talked about supporting my brothers. Why the hell did you betray me?"

People began to circle around Padma and Reena. Irritated, Padma took out her dagger and aimed it at everyone. Darting her eyes frantically at the people, she said, "Move one bit closer and you will be next."

The people stepped back, scared.

Padma directed her attention on Reena. "Now, why did you?"

"Times have changed."

"And your fate has changed too. You will die now." She brought the blade close to Reena's throat.

"NO! NO!" Reena pleaded. "I can help you. I can tell you anything. I have contacts *everywhere*. What do ya wanna know?"

Padma put the dagger back. *How can I forget? Reena always stayed informed about who was where doing what.* "What is Kali up to? Where does he hold his captives?" Padma asked. She had been blindfolded when she had been thrown in the prison, and when she had been taken out. She had zero idea about the location.

"Lower your voice," Reena said, looking around them. Most of the people had dispersed, but a few were still lurking in the street. "Man, I don't know what the king is up to. People are scared to even discuss about him in their homes. I don't know where he holds his captives. But you could try the palace prison."

"Kali might keep the normal prisoners there, but the person I'm looking for must be well-hidden. Which means, you have been completely and utterly useless." Padma took out her dagger again.

"Wait, wait, wait. I know one thing."

"What?"

"Well, I may not have any intel on our king, but I know something about the Yaksha king. Will that help?"

"What about him?" Padma asked, aiming the dagger at Reena's throat.

"He has just hired a theatre troupe. At the west of the city, he has been allotted a building so that he and the actors can practise there. One of the actors of the troupe told me that they are looking to hire more people to play extras and props. Lord Nalakuvera has written a play on the story of Indragarh or on King Kali, I'm not sure which."

Padma smiled. *I know what I have to do now.*

"The actor also told me that all theatre performers had been given masks which they wore while practising."

"Masks?"

"Yes, colourful masks."

"I see."

Padma left Reena on the ground, and walked away, beaming.

Please stay alive, Arjan. I need to deal with Nalakuvera first. Then, I will come back for you.

Padma looked at the building in front of her as she thought about her plan.

She had heard the people whispering that the play would show Kali as the great supreme leader. Many civilians were planning to create mayhem, but the performing area would be heavily guarded.

When planning to assassinate someone, always assess the situation.

She had to enter the building. There was a chance that Nalakuvera might be practising with the other actors. If he was inside, she would take her chance and kill him. If not, she would find a way to stay in the building till he came. And if he didn't come, she would find a way to participate in the play and kill him when she got the chance.

Padma walked towards the main door confidently when two Yaksha guards stopped her.

"Where do you plan to go, miss?"

"To meet the theatre coordinator," she calmly responded.

The two Yaksha guards looked at each other and laughed. One of them said, "The coordinator will come to you. No outsiders are allowed."

"Tell the coordinator that the best actor of this country is standing outside."

The guard, taken aback, nodded and walked inside. After some time, a tall, lean man came out to see her.

"Best actor?" he blurted with an impeccable accent. The brows on his oval-shaped face were furrowed, and he kept adjusting the scarf around his neck, which was dark red in colour. "What nonsense is this? Who are you?"

"I want to work for Lord Nalakuvera," Padma said. "I really look up to him. And I'm a talented actor, who won't take no for an answer."

"The extras have been hired. You are late!" he shouted. "Don't waste my time."

I have to enter the building.

Padma fell flat on the ground and grovelled in front of the coordinator. "Please, Sir, please let me do it. I beg of you, Sir. I beg of you. I want to eat something. I am famished. I am an orphan, and haven't had even a morsel of food for days."

The coordinator recoiled in disgust. "Leave my fine shoes and stand up."

Padma stood up, close to tears.

Wringing his hands, the coordinator said, "All right, all right. If someone falls ill, you'll play their role."

"Sure, Sir."

"And till then," he picked up the mop lying on the ground inside the building and handed it to her, "you clean floors."

Padma forced a smile. This was beneath her. But she had to get in the building. She had to find a way to kill Nalakuvera.

"All right," she took the mop, "whatever you want, Sir."

66

The new general appointed by Manasa had apprised her of what was happening in the tents at the back, near the forest. So, as the sun was about to set, she went to look at the scorched, tattered tents at the back of the camp.

After Kalki had killed a Danav with such ease, the enemy had chosen to retreat. Manasa had called back her army as well. Many of the soldiers had been wounded in battle. They needed rest, and some needed to be treated immediately. But her new general had informed her how the tents where soldiers were to be treated had been burnt.

Manasa cursed under breath, sure of who was behind these attacks.

Kadru and her Children.

She dismounted from her horse and began to walk towards the three infirmaries, closely followed by her guards.

Two infirmaries had been burnt to a crisp. She walked inside the only remaining one. The victims who had narrowly escaped from the fire in the now-burnt infirmaries had been placed here along with other wounded soldiers. The tent was completely filled. There was hardly any space to even stand.

"I want to see the head shaman," Manasa said to one of the nurses. She nodded and left the tent.

Manasa waited for a while. One of her guards volunteered to go out and get the shaman but she told him to stay beside her.

The shaman may be busy saving someone's life. He, and the nurses, are heroes.

Later, the nurse came back and guided Manasa to the shaman's tent. The shaman was a bald-headed, white-bearded, old man. He was going through some papers, signing them, and giving them off to the nurses going in and out of his tent.

"Well, Your Majesty, what a sight for sore eyes. You have come here to see a small establishment of ours," he softly said.

Manasa could see how fatigued he was. He was a fellow Naga. He had been at the back of the camp, saving lives since they had camped here, and she didn't even know his name.

"What happened? Can you tell me?"

"It's those bloody hooded creatures. They wear their hoods like a cobra wears its skin." The shaman sighed. "And we don't have enough guards here at this part of the camp, you know, Your Majesty. So we haven't been able to fight back properly. We had to put the burnt infirmaries' patients in the one that remains now, and the doctors managing those infirmaries were injured, so they are our patients as well. These creatures . . . they are vicious . . . and strange, I feel. I saw one up close, and honestly, his eyes were sort of unfocused, as if he had been hynotised."

"They worship someone malicious," Manasa told the shaman. "I wouldn't be surprised if she actually had hypnotised them. But don't worry, she will be dealt with soon." Manasa paused for a second, looking at the pile of papers on the shaman's desk. "You are doing a fantastic job, doctor. I am so grateful to have you in the war camp."

A queen doesn't focus only on winning fights. She cares for her people, the people of her Tribe, of her kingdom. Manasa had forgotten that in her quest for vengeance. And now, seeing the shaman and nurses work so hard, she wanted to make amends. *It takes guts to fight on the battlefield, but there is bravery and nobility in saving lives. The soldiers aren't the only heroes of this war.*

"My dear friend," she said, "I am adding guards here at the infirmary, and my men are scouting the area as we speak, looking for any clue as to where the attack came from."

"I know that, Your Majesty. Thank you." He respectfully bowed. "I suspect they are hiding in the forest. That's where they disappear to once we chase them. And I'm not sure why but they are quite enamoured by our Ayurvedic medicines. They didn't only burn the infirmaries; they also stole medicines from my office."

At that moment, one of the men Manasa had sent to scout the area entered inside and whispered something to her.

"My men have found no camp in the forest," Manasa said, disappointed.

The shaman didn't know what to say. He just leaned back in his chair.

They are around here somewhere. I can feel it.

"Did you only come to inspect the burnt infirmaries, Your Majesty?" the shaman asked.

Manasa shook her head. "I have a dangerous proposition for you. You know we have to catch them, right?"

"Of course. My friends have died because of them."

"Good. Please listen to my plan."

He leaned forward. "A plan that involves a simple doctor?"

"Not just involves but centres around a doctor."

And a smile spread on her lips.

Night had fallen.

The shaman's tent had been shifted close to the forest entrance. There was no one in or around the tent except for the shaman. He was busy reading some papers, and behind the shaman, a lot of Ayurvedic medicines had been placed.

A perfect bait.

Manasa was hiding in the bushes nearby, squinting her crystal blue eyes in the depths of darkness. Behind her stood her guards, their weapons at the ready.

"Your Majesty, you didn't have to come. We could have handled this," one guard said.

"No. I have a personal grudge against these shits."

The flap of the shaman's tent had been purposefully left open. Manasa saw as the shaman got up, stretched, and lay down on his cot. Soon, he began snoring.

What an actor!

If the Children were around, they won't be able to resist coming and stealing from the shaman's tent.

When Manasa was a child, her father had taught her how to trap bees. They had to be given an illusion that there was honey, when in fact, her father had placed glue that the bees would stick to. Vibhishan had called it a honeytrap.

Well, this is my honeytrap.

As the shaman pretended to sleep, Manasa and her guards stood waiting.

Hours passed. The men were exhausted. Some had sat on the ground, some were sipping water, trying to keep themselves awake. Manasa's eyelids had begun to droop. She was about to fall asleep when she noticed shadows around the shaman's tent; she was wide awake in an instant.

"Remember my instructions," Manasa said to her guards.

Manasa suspected that the Children would not kill the shaman. Like they did the previous day, they will aim to steal the medicines. And once they run away, she and her guards will chase them and discover their hideout.

As Manasa expected, the Children were going through the

cabinets, taking the Ayurvedic creams and tablets, and stuffing them into their rucksacks.

"How did you know they would not attack the shaman, Your Majesty?" the guard whispered.

"My cousin is very predictable," Manasa responded and that was enough justification. "Let's go."

Manasa and her guards moved, their feet crushing the leaves on the ground. They crept behind the Children at a safe distance as the Children tiptoed into the forest, carrying their rucksacks.

All of them walked behind the Children, careful not to make a sound. But then, one of Manasa's guards accidentally stepped on a twig. There was a loud crack.

No.

The Children looked back and instantly sprinted ahead.

Manasa began to chase them without caring about the fact that if she was attacked, she wouldn't be able to defend herself. She had no weapon. The guards behind her began to dash after the Children as well.

Manasa caught up with two Children that were running ahead. She swivelled her head and saw that her guards were picking up speed and were now running beside her.

She had looked away for a second, and in that second, the Children swiftly jumped inside the earth. Manasa couldn't comprehend what had just happened. They had vanished right in front of her.

Manasa carefully stepped forward and walked to the area where the Children had disappeared. Her guards stood alarmed, their weapons at the ready.

And there she saw—hidden under thick branches, twigs, and leaves—a hole. It had been carefully dug.

They are hiding under the ground?

Manasa couldn't hide her shock. The hole was massive. She drew the conclusion that the Children must have been digging for a while. They might have come right after the incident at Varungarh.

A smile came on Manasa's face as she realised that she had just found Kadru's hideout. *I won't let this opportunity go. I have to burn this place as quickly as possible.*

67

When Arjan Chanelled again, he found himself in front of a burnt house. It stood adjacent to a dense, dark forest. The fragrance of roses and jasmine permeated the air, along with the smell of charred wood.

Why does this feel familiar?

He walked inside. The air inside the house was nauseating. Arjan took a deep breath and coughed loudly. He detected the smell of iron, of . . . fresh blood. And there was dust everywhere—on the floor, on the broken and burnt furniture, on the paintings. And in the centre, Arjan saw a man looking at six corpses—one woman and her five children.

The man had a thick bushy moustache and oily hair. He was weeping. Wiping his tears, he turned to see Arjan, and let out a sigh.

"People worship the good," the man began. "Or who they believe is good. History is written by the victors. But where is our version? Where is our story?"

Arjan was trying to figure out who the man was. From his attire, Arjan knew that he was royalty, but he couldn't figure out the man's identity.

"Who are you?"

The man sighed. "Do you know what an Avatar does to the world? Do you know how he corrupts without knowing?"

"What do you mean?"

"They killed innocents," he said, pointing at the corpses. "Children."

Arjan immediately understood where he was. He looked around. "This is the lacquer house built to kill the Pandavas. Kauravas had hoped to burn them alive but Pandavas escaped through a tunnel and—"

"Vidura invited the Nishads and their mother to enter the house and die in their place, so everyone would think that the Pandavas had died. My friend Purochana died in his sleep," the man said, referring to the architect of the house. "They killed these children. And an Avatar sided with these murderers." He flared his nostrils.

"You are . . . Duryodhan." Arjan couldn't believe he was speaking to the man he had secretly looked up to. When Arjan had got to know Duryodhan's story in one of the classes at gurukul, he had told no one that he had sympathised. Duryodhan was the rightful heir of Hastinapur.

Tears streamed down Duryodhan's face. "I didn't even know till the end that I was an Adharm. I was only doing what I thought was right." Duryodhan grew quiet for a few seconds, and then, all of a sudden, he shouted, "He could have supported me! People have been spreading wrong stories about me. They think I asked for Govind's men, but I asked *him* to support me. But Arjun massaged his ego so cleverly. Arjun was standing at his feet, bowing. This is the only reason he chose to support him!" He looked at Arjan, his eyes bloodshot. "I am not evil. I was loyal to my allies, to my friend Karna. I was good till the end. I fought for what was right. Now, tell me, is Govind a good man? During my battle with Bhim, he egged him on to strike my thigh. And Bhim did that, even though the rules of the fight state that one must not attack below the belt!"

Arjan didn't know how to respond. Duryodhan's anger was justified.

"If Govind hadn't interfered, I would have defeated Bhim,

you know," Duryodhan said, morosely looking at the burnt house they were standing in. "And there would have been peace in the kingdom, in *my* kingdom," he said. "But no. They killed me. And then they died one by one. And Govind . . . you know what happened to him, right?"

"He was killed by an arrow?"

"Yes. But I'm talking about the time before that. Before he was assassinated." There was fury in Duryodhan's eyes. "Dwarka was submerged. The Yadavs eventually killed each other. Govind lost everyone, even his son. At the end of the day, karma gets to you. And then the Breaking happened. The entire world was enveloped in all sorts of illnesses," he said. "Today, the White Horse Rider is using Astras, just like Govind had used them in the Mahayudh. And he will bring about another Breaking. Do you want that?"

"He would never do such a thing," Arjan mumbled under his breath, unsure. It had been so long since he had seen Kalki. *What if he has changed?*

"Embrace your true self. You must do that, or the Avatar will bring about an era of darkness," Duryodhan said, as he started to fade. "Being Adharm does not mean being evil. You are just standing opposite the Avatar, not believing in the things he considers right. He needs to be put down, Arjan. I should have aimed to kill the Avatar long ago, but I didn't. I don't want you to go down a similar path. Just be careful. He carries a powerful sword. Embrace your true self, and you will be able to defeat him."

And then, he faded away completely.

For a while, Arjan stood frozen at his spot, looking at the corpses on the floor.

Then he closed his eyes. When he opened them, he was back in the prison. This time he was not panting or sweating. He quietly curled up on his cot as thoughts began to enter his mind.

He recalled how he and Kalki used to run outside their hut, how they would sit together and watch the sunset on the highest hill in Shambala. Arjan remembered a conversation he had had with Kalki about how he wanted his funeral to be.

Many years ago.

"I don't want to be burnt," Arjan said. "I want to be buried, so that I am one with the soil, with the earth. That way I will be at peace."

Kalki chuckled. "You want to go against what our religion prescribes?"

"It's my body. I should decide what's to be done with it."

Kalki put his arm around Arjan. "No matter when or how we die, I know we will be remembered as heroes, as great men."

"Where do you want to die?"

"Me? Well, certainly not here. Perhaps in the fancy palace I'll own one day." Kalki grinned.

"You are such a show-off."

"Ah, well, you know I wouldn't change for the world." Kalki hit Arjan on the head. "And stop talking about death on such a good day. Let's celebrate life."

Present.

Tears brimmed in Arjan's eyes.

I can't kill him.

But perhaps . . .

I will have to.

68

Another day. Another battle.

But for some reason, Kalki could feel that the war was going to end soon.

Kalki was waiting to go in. He and Vibhishan were looking at the battlefield as their own infantry and cavalry clashed with the enemy force. Shuko was flying overhead as usual.

And there was no sign of a Danav, which was good since Kalki didn't want to face another one. Even though he had cut the last one fairly quickly, it had taken a tremendous amount of effort and resulted in a lot of pain.

From his binoculars, Kalki could see his army getting crushed in the centre.

"I wish Manasa were here," Kalki said to Vibhishan.

"I'm sure we'll manage fine in her absence, son," Vibhishan responded. "I trust you. Manasa needs to rest, and plan what to do tonight as she enters the forest."

Vibhishan isn't as uncaring as Padma claims. Here he is, encouraging me, believing in me. Kalki closed his eyes and concentrated on communicating with Shuko.

What's going on? Kalki asked the parrot.

They are annihilating the soldiers in the centre.

That's what I thought. Do you see any weak point? A poorly-guarded side that we can send our soldiers in, to attack?

There was a pause.

The centre of the field is being efficiently guarded. And I see drummers too, directing the enemy soldiers.

Do you see any reserve army?

Nope. And no giant is nearby.

Kalki opened his eyes. He had come up with a plan. But he didn't know whether it would work. He turned to the captain next to him and said, "Tell the extreme left and right squads to create a tight circle around the enemy in the centre."

"What if they use their reserve army to attack us?"

"I have just received information that they have no reserve army," Kalki said. "Tell the squads to create a circle, so when they try to move back, they wouldn't be able to. They will get stuck, surrounded by our army."

The captain grinned. "Sounds like a great plan."

"Also," Kalki said, "there are drummers guiding the enemy soldiers. Since the generals are commanding a lot of men, they are using drummers to indicate where and how they should attack our men. Let's kill them. Once they are out of the picture, their attacks wouldn't be this organised."

"He's right," Vibhishan said, turning to the captain. "Order the Suparns to fly to the centre of the field and kill the drummers."

The captain nodded and headed in the battlefield. Soon, Kalki saw the horsemen running towards the centre of the battlefield, cutting whoever came in their way. He saw the drummers die one by one as the Suparns aimed their arrows at them. The enemy soldiers were taken aback by the strategy.

"It's working," Vibhishan said, thumping Kalki's back. "You said you are only a warrior, yet you strategised well."

Kalki didn't say anything. He had gone red with embarrassment after receiving the compliment. He was looking at the battlefield when he noticed two chariots emerge from the enemy camp.

And behind the chariots, walked a Danav.

"Oh dear." Vibhishan sighed. "They are not happy."

"I know. I think it's time for me to jump in."

And then Devadatta neighed. Kalki pulled Ratna Maru out and he went to battle, focusing on the two chariots that had entered the field.

Koko and Vikoko.

We will fight at last.

69

Padma had been with the theatre troupe for two days but hadn't seen Nalakuvera. This morning, she had heard that he had been in the building, giving tips to the actors, but by the time Padma had woken up, he was gone.

She was mopping the floor, unsure of what to do next. She had to find a way to be in the play. *That may be my only chance to kill him.*

She had seen the actors rehearse yesterday. Nalakuvera wasn't present, but an actor had been practising the scene where Nalakuvera, who would be playing Kali in the play, fake-stabs a masked woman who was supposed to be Manasa. She had been portrayed as the evil snake queen.

Padma knew what she had to do. She smiled to herself, as she went about mopping the floor.

It was the next day; the day of the performance. And the woman playing Manasa had fallen ill.

Padma was washing the window when she saw a small group of people had gathered around the poor woman, who was shivering because of the fever she had. The coordinator looked worried. He was praying, hoping that the woman would recover in time for the play.

But the coordinator knew there wasn't going to be a miracle. After a while, he came over to Padma and said, "I hope you are prepared. You have been watching our practises. You just have to lie dead for a scene. Will you be able to manage that?"

Padma meekly nodded.

The coordinator left the room.

Padma walked to the woman and looked at her—she was sweating and coughing.

"How ya feeling miss?" Padma asked.

"Bad," the woman said, and began to cough again. "Hand me some water."

Padma nodded, pouring some in a cup and helping her drink. When she was done, Padma walked to the end of the bed and said, "You are not tucked in properly. Can I help?"

"Yeah, sure, do whatever you want. Just get rid of this smell. Oh gods, get an incense stick, would you?" she said and soon, dozed off.

Padma tucked her in, looking at the object the smell was coming from. Last night, when this woman had gotten drunk, Padma had helped her to bed. The woman had been knocked out. She had no idea that Padma had put onion slices under her armpits. The night had passed peacefully, but the woman had caught a cold and fever. Just like Padma had planned.

She slowly pulled the onion slices out.

"Sleep," Padma said, glad that her plan had worked. She had to do this. There was no other way for her to enter in the play.

It was showtime.

Smirking, she grabbed the woman's coloured mask and wore it on her face.

70

Manasa brought her men to the forest, where the hole was. She had not been able to wait till the battle with Kali's army was over. Sending a messenger, she conveyed that she needed a bunch of Nagas and Manavs to go with her to the forest. She trusted Kalki and Vibhishan to take care of the battle for the day. She *had* to take care of Kadru first.

Unlike yesterday, today she was carrying a weapon and she had more men with her. Along with the Nagas, she had also commanded the Manav soldiers to come with her.

The Children will put up a fight, but my men will deal with them.

The men circled around the hole and asked, "What should we do, Your Majesty?"

"Distract the Children," she said, giving him a sly smile, "while I go inside. Two of you," she pointed at the Nagas, "follow me when I go. Let's do it."

And when they were about to jump inside, Manasa stopped them and said, "I am proud of you all. Thank you for fighting alongside me."

The soldiers were taken aback as the queen expressed her gratitude. As they were about to jump in, a few Children suddenly appeared and jumped on the soldiers' back.

With two Nagas beside her, Manasa saw the scene unfold. The Children and some of the soldiers were fighting.

Manasa pulled out a sharp knife and jumped. The two Nagas jumped after her, and then the rest of the soldiers followed. Some of them had to stay on the ground to prevent the Children from chasing Manasa.

She landed under the ground with a loud thud. Groaning, she gathered her strength and stood up. Her men fell on the ground a few seconds after her. They were inside a tunnel leading to a cave.

As Manasa and the men began to walk, one of the Children jumped at her. She stabbed him with her knife and threw him away.

As she walked to the cave, more Children began to leap on her, but not even god could stop Manasa from getting to Kadru today. That was how determined she was to kill her cousin. She simply stabbed the Children and walked swiftly ahead. Her men had to deal with the Children attacking them from the back.

As she entered the cave, she noticed that medicines stolen from her camp had been kept on the floor, near the walls. On and on Manasa walked, till she reached an area where a fire lamp was burning, giving a ghostly glow to the person sitting on the ground.

Kadru.

There were Children around her, who leapt to attack Manasa, but her men came running to help her. They swung their maces and battered the Children.

Manasa made her way to Kadru, who was still sitting calmly. She was a few steps away when she heard the hiss of cobras.

I hate these things.

There were two of them. Manasa backed away slightly, knife in her good hand. She jumped to the side as a cobra tried to attack her. And then she dodged the other one.

I can't keep moving away.

Taking in a deep breath, Manasa yelled and aimed her knife at one of the cobras. It went through its body. The cobra lay dead on the floor.

Manasa smiled, but her relief was short-lived. The other cobra began to crawl towards her.

And Manasa was without a weapon.

She thought of running away, but Kadru was right in front of her. She had to take a chance.

As Manasa moved inside the cave, towards her cousin, the cobra bit her on her arm. She yelled in pain.

I've been poisoned. I'm going to die. But I will take Kadru with me!

She walked towards Kadru, who stood up, surprised. She hadn't expected that Manasa would be alive till now. Before Kadru could even utter a word, Manasa stuffed her poisoned palm inside her mouth, letting her poisonous blood drip inside her.

The already weak and broken Kadru began to cough as the blood, and the venom with it, trickled down her throat. She dropped on the ground, wanting to hurl. Manasa knelt down and punched Kadru.

"Please! Please help me!" Kadru pleaded.

"I hate you so much."

Manasa saw a stone lying on the ground. She picked it up and smacked Kadru's face with it. Her nose broke even more.

And then she smacked it again.

Blood sprayed on Manasa's face.

And she smacked it again.

She continued to hit Kadru till her face was completely covered in blood.

"I will make sure you don't return again, you psycho!" Manasa said, unable to stop hitting her cousin.

Her men arrived after dealing with the Children. They looked at her worriedly.

"Your Majesty, she's dead," one of them said.

Manasa looked at Kadru's face, or what was left of it. She wiped the blood from her own face and heaved a sigh of relief. "Hand me a box of the medicines kept on the ground. I need to take something that might prove effective in removing the poison from my system."

And as she walked back after having the medicine, the only thing she said was "Finally."

71

The chariots were headed towards him. Kalki was still in the centre of the battlefield.

He knew he had to deal with Koko and Vikoko fast since the Danav was reaching for his army. And they would all die if he didn't kill the Danav.

I asked Manasa to not use the bombs. Their deaths would be on me.

Kalki wielded his sword as he saw Koko and Vikoko's chariots move around him in a circle.

They were moving so fast that Kalki didn't have time to move away as Vikoko's chariot passed him by. The scythe on its wheels cut his shoulder. Vikoko laughed, joining her brother.

Kalki began to move towards Vikoko, but Koko steered his chariot and struck his sword at Devadatta's back.

These humans are irritating, Devadatta said.

We cannot kill one at a time, Kalki said. *It has to be together.*

So what's the plan, boss?

Kalki took a deep breath, assessing the situation. He narrowly missed getting cut by the scythed chariots. The twins were laughing at him.

On my command, you run towards one of them, while I'll run towards the other, Kalki instructed his horse. Devadatta nodded.

And then Kalki yelled, "Come at me!" Vikoko instantly steered her chariot towards Kalki. She gripped the sword in her hand, and confidently raced towards him, knowing that when Kalki attacked, Koko would attack from the back.

But Kalki wouldn't let that happen.

"RUN!" he yelled and leapt from the horse.

Devadatta rushed towards Koko, stopping him from making his way towards Vikoko. And Kalki jumped on Vikoko's chariot. He snatched the reins from her hand and with a quick movement, pierced his sword in her stomach.

Blood gushed out her mouth as Kalki pulled his sword out. Pushing Vikoko on the ground, he looked over at the other chariot, and saw the surprised and distracted face of Koko.

Devadatta hit the horses and Koko lost control of the chariot. As Koko tried to calm his horses down, Kalki threw his own sword, aiming it at Koko. The man died instantly.

Kalki jumped out of the chariot and ran towards Devadatta, who was glad to have him on his back. The horse rode towards the sword, which was still attached to the dead Koko. Kalki picked it up and made his way towards the Danav, who was about to crush his men. The soldiers had panicked and were trying to run away to their camp.

Come on. Just hold on for me.

Devadatta was as fast as lightning as he galloped towards the giant's feet. Kalki jumped from his horse, stuck his sword in the ankle of the giant, and slid down, tearing the giant's leg apart. When he was close to the heel, he dropped down on the ground. In an instant, Devadatta arrived and Kalki mounted him again.

The sword cut flesh like butter as always. The giant lost his balance and knelt on the ground, clutching his injured leg.

As it tried to get up, Kalki circled around it on his horse. He jumped and landed on the Danav's arm. Kalki carefully but quickly reached his shoulder, and managed to ram his sword in one of the Danav's eyes.

The Danav let out a deafening roar. He noticed Kalki and turned his head to growl at him. His hand was coming towards Kalki, ready to crush him, but Kalki easily sliced his fingers.

The Danav howled in pain again as blood gushed out of his palm.

Clutching the skin of the Danav, Kalki stood on his chest. He took deep breaths as red smoke emanated from his body. Gripping his sword, he yelled furiously as he sliced the Danav's head off.

Everyone stopped fighting and looked up at the headless giant as his body collapsed. They all watched in fear as Kalki stood atop the corpse with his sword tinged with the Danav's blood.

72

Padma was waiting behind the curtain with the other masked actors. Her eyes were focused on her enemy, her target—Nalakuvera. He was performing his part well. The crowd was watching in awe. The actors were enacting a war scene right now.

Padma casually waited for her turn, tapping her feet, when she heard the coordinator yell, "WHERE'S THE CORPSE? WHERE'S THE CORPSE?"

Padma raised her arm.

"What are you doing? Your scene is up next."

Padma hadn't realised that. She was so close to her goal.

Let's hope nothing goes wrong.

A cot was brought in front of her. Calmly, she lay down on it and the stagehands brought her where the play was happening. Her heart was pounding in her chest as her cot was placed near Nalakuvera.

He was the only one not wearing the mask. A dummy knife made of rubber was in his hand. He brought it close to Padma's chest.

"Now," he announced, "I shall kill my adversary—the evil, dark queen of Nagas. No serpent shall harm my people anymore." Nalakuvera knelt down beside the cot. He had a huge smile on his face as he whispered to Padma, "I know it's you."

A chill went through her body.

What?

"Did you think I wouldn't recognise you because you changed the colour of your hair? The coordinator had informed me about the cleaning lady he had hired. I saw you days ago, sleeping peacefully in the room given to you in the building," he continued to whisper. "But don't worry, I want a dramatic show, and killing you in front of everyone will achieve that. Just like mother wants. After all, she believes the city should know that I fear no assassin from the enemy."

Nalakuvera brought the blade closer. He kept his thumb on it, and that's when Padma realised that it wasn't soft. It was not made of rubber. It was a real blade.

The blade was inches away from Padma's throat when there was a commotion in the audience.

Confused, Nalakuvera turned his head to see what was going on. The guards had caught some people with rotten eggs and tomatoes. Some were even carrying stones. The people were pushing the guards, shouting that the city would flourish without any ruler, be it Kali or anyone else, and that all kings were corrupt, and didn't give a damn about the citizens.

"No, this was not supposed to happen," he mumbled. "Kali said the guards would handle it if there was a riot."

This is my chance.

Instantly, she pulled out the knife hidden under her sleeve and plunged it deep inside his neck. Nalakuvera's eyes protruded in shock. Padma pushed him away and got up.

"Wh-why? Did . . . Manasa . . . send you?"

Padma knelt next to the dying man as she said, "No, it was Ratna Maru." She grabbed his hair as Nalakuvera struggled to speak. "Remember her?"

"Who is she?"

"Your brother's wife."

"But . . . but . . ." Nalakuvera's face turned ghostly white.

"I'm doing a favour for a friend. And now my job is done." And then she pulled out the blade from his neck.

The blood gushed out and Nalakuvera whimpered.

Padma looked at the crowd. The Yaksha guards no longer bothered to manage the crowd. They were advancing towards her.

I have to move.

She leapt into the frantic crowd. The Yakshas were trying to follow her, but there were so many people blocking their way, pushing and pulling each other.

Padma threw away her mask.

Grinning slyly, she walked away as the Yakshas tried to search for her. But they couldn't even find her shadow.

Time to consume a copious amount of alcohol, and then return with Kalki to find Arjan.

73

Things had turned bad for Kali in the past couple of days. The city was plunged in darkness. The play had not been received well by the people. Nalauvera had been assassinated. Their army had reduced considerably, including the Danavs. The secret garrison that the Mother had was dead too. Kali and Durukti had been depressed ever since they had been given the news of Koko's and Vikoko's death.

Durukti was wondering what was going to happen now. She had reached the door of Kali's room when she saw a guard leave in a hurry, leaving the door ajar.

Durukti entered inside. She could see how exhausted Kali was as he leaned on his table, reading the letter he had just received. And then, he ran his hand through his hair. *Is there more bad news?*

"You can come closer, Durukti." Kali turned to face her.

For a moment, she froze, surprised that he had noticed her even though she had been careful to not make a sound.

And then she firmly told herself, *I should stop getting scared of him.*

She took a deep breath, and walked towards her dark, crazy brother. He looked as handsome as ever.

"I just wanted to see how you were doing," Durukti said.

"It's all right," he said, slumping down in his chair. "Have you ever thought about what you want to do with your life? I mean, other than just being my sister, being here."

Durukti responded, "I've always dreamt of opening a gurukul and teach children."

"A gurukul headed by an Asura woman?" Kali scoffed. "That will be acceptable only in an ideal world, my dear."

"I believe such a time will come soon," she paused, lowering her gaze, "when we will have a utopian society, where women of all Tribes will be considered equal."

"Hmmm. Interesting. How's Bali?"

"Good. How long do you plan to keep him imprisoned?"

"I don't know. I am afraid to let him out. I am starting to feel like I shouldn't have taken hold of the city. It's gone mad. The public still hates me. And I may lose the war. So many of my men have died, and I have lost three of my giants. Only one remains. My only ally has been killed as well." Tears started to well up in his eyes. "And you know, I was just wondering what started all this."

Durukti froze.

"You," he pointed at her. "You had to go to that darn village. If you wouldn't have, we wouldn't be here."

"I was trying to save you. Don't you dare pin this on me. The city burns because of you."

"What does it matter what you were *trying* to do. Look at the result. You brought me something that made me crazy. What is happening now is because of you. You started everything."

Durukti flared her nostrils. *He's a coward; can't even own up to his mistakes. I should've never tried to save him.*

He picked up the goblet on his table and drank the liquid in one go. "I got a response from Raktapa." He showed the letter to her. "His men have arrived."

Durukti looked dumbstruck. "He accepted?"

"Yes. The men are waiting for my orders." Kali smiled. "I want Manasa and Kalki dead. We'll attack tonight. Destroy them fully. And for Raktapa's generosity, I have decided to give him something to make it clear how grateful I am for his help."

"What?"

"You."

For a second, Durukti thought Kali was joking. But Kali looked dead serious. She took a few steps back and turned to run away, but a guard was standing behind her.

"I don't even know if he wants to get married but I'll make sure this wedding happens because, frankly, my dear, I want you to suffer," he said, smiling deviously. "I want you to be treated like a Rakshas wife. That will be your punishment for spying on me, for betraying me, and for starting a chain of events that led us to our DOWNFALL!"

"You are mad. You have gone crazy again. You said you were sorry—"

"GAH!" Kali punched the wall in anger. "I was weak. But no more!" Kali threw the goblet on the floor, and walked towards Durukti. "You will be his from tomorrow."

"You wish." Durukti spat at him. Quickly, she drew the sword from the guard's sheath and plunged it inside the guard.

And then without looking back, she ran.

74

Kalki held Padma's hand.

They were sitting in front of Manasa's tent, looking at the stars. Hours had passed as they had talked, but to Kalki and Padma, it had seemed like seconds. Kalki could hear music being played in the distance. He could see Vibhishan laughing like a buffoon with his soldiers while Manasa sat beside him, smiling awkwardly with a drink in her hand.

Though the war was not over yet, she knew that they will win. And she had managed to finish off the woman that had killed her general, her friend. So, today, she was celebrating.

But for now, Kalki and Padma were immersed in each other. They had shared what had happened with each of them since they separated.

"So you lied about saving my brother?" he chided her. Kalki wasn't angry. Padma was being honest, after all.

"I didn't lie. I tried to find out about him, but nobody knew where Kali kept his prisoners. And I knew Kali must have kept him somewhere no one will be able to find him, so it won't be the palace prison. Tomorrow, let's leave for Indragarh and find him, all right?"

Kalki grinned. "I still can't believe he became a king. Once Kali is dead, he will get the throne back."

"Yeah, we'll see to that."

Kalki nodded. So much had changed. He hoped that Arjan was the same. "Let's go tomorrow. We are at the cusp of victory. But before that, my brother must be saved."

Padma smiled, slowly planting a kiss on his lips. "Of course, my love."

"You made me believe you can fall in love twice." Kalki smiled.

"Well," she shrugged, "I am just lovable, you know. And I'm glad that I've managed to do what I came here for. And that we are—"

The rest of her sentence was drowned out by the sound of horns.

Kalki and Padma got up. Manasa kept her goblet aside and walked towards Kalki. The people stopped dancing around the bonfire as guards appeared, and instead of going to Manasa, they went to Kalki.

"Lord Kalki," the guard said, "there's a messenger."

"Who?"

"Goes by the name of Durukti. Said she is Kali's sister and knows of the attack he's planning."

Padma and Kalki glanced at each other, confused. *Durukti ran away?* Before he could say anything, Manasa spoke, "She's lying. Behead her."

"No," Kalki said, louder than he had intended to. "Durukti is the good one." He looked at the guard. "Bring her in. She must have some vital information to give us."

As the guard left, Manasa glared at Kalki. "What are you doing? This is my war. I can't let you order my men around."

"This is not *your* war, Manasa. This is *our* war," Kalki said. "All of us are fighting together. And our goal is to get rid of Kali. Durukti might have some crucial information. We should at least hear her out."

Manasa still looked unsure of letting her enemy's sister enter inside her camp, but she knew if anything untoward happened, the sister will be killed without hesitation. "I know," she responded in a low voice. "I know that too."

A few minutes later, the guards brought in Durukti. She was panting, and was covered in a black cloak from head to toe.

She removed her hood and gazed at Kalki. It had been so long since Kalki had seen her. He had hated her at a time. She had destroyed his village, but he had later come to realise that there was goodness in her.

"Lady Durukti," he said, bowing.

"Please, no lady. I kind of renounced that title by coming here." She chuckled nervously as she looked around. Every person's eyes were on her. "How are you, Kalki?"

"I am . . . great," he said awkwardly. "How are you?"

"I am . . . uh . . ."

Padma intervened. "Can we cut this chit-chat and ask what information she has for us?"

Kalki smiled. *Is she getting jealous?*

He looked at Durukti. She cleared her throat, looking a bit flustered, and began to speak loudly. "Kali plans an attack now. I left the palace, hoping to bring you this news. He has got Raktapa's army and he plans a night combat."

"Rakshas?" Manasa stepped forward. "They fight like monsters. My men are strong, but people of their Tribe are brutes."

"We have Kalki," Vibhishan added.

"Don't worry," Kalki said, gripping the hilt of his sword that was dangling on his belt. Shuko, who had been flying in the air, swept down and perched on his shoulder. "We will be safe. I promise. Has he followed you?"

"I don't know."

And then he heard Shuko say, *They are here, kid. And there's a lot of them.*

Before Kalki could warn the others, the emergency horns resounded in the air.

"ATTACK! ENEMY ATTACK! AND THEY ARE COMING CLOSE TO THE CAMP! TOO CLOSE!" a guard yelled.

75

Kalki knew that this was the beginning of the end.

They didn't get a chance to save themselves as the Rakshas army rammed into their camp. The enemy soldiers roared as they destroyed the little speck of happiness that Manasa's army had built. The Nagas, Suparns, and the Manavs ran around, panicked. Some were quick to draw their weapons, others had to run to their tents to get them. Durukti rushed inside the nearest tent with Vibhishan while Manasa left with her guards to fight.

Wielding his sword, Kalki whistled for Devadatta. The horse made his way to him, avoiding getting burnt in the explosions.

Kalki bid farewell to Padma, who was battling a Rakshas with two swords, and hopped on his horse. He spotted a Rakshas about to kill a Naga. Kalki clutched the reins and galloped towards the them. While riding, Kalki swung his sword and cleanly beheaded the Rakshas. The Naga ran away.

Kalki got reminded of the last days of battle at Shambala when the Rakshas had attacked. But unlike last time, he was stronger now. Swinging his sword around, he began to kill the Rakshas who were frantically running away from him.

He observed that some of them were burning the tents. Kalki rode towards them and knocked them down through his sword.

"GET AWAY FROM ME, YOU MONSTERS!"

Vibhishan was trying to keep the Rakshas from entering the tent he and Durukti were in. Kalki rode towards them. *They don't know how to fight. I must take them somewhere safe.*

He dismounted from the horse. The Rakshas had punched Vibhishan and was about strike him, when Kalki ran towards him and plunged his sword in the Rakshas' back. Blood spurted from the Rakshas' mouth as his lifeless body fell on the ground.

Vibhishan heaved a sigh of relief. Durukti hesitatingly stepped outside.

Kalki looked around him. The fire had spread; the tents were burning. He saw Padma battling two Rakshas at the same time. Manasa was using her dagger with her good hand, stabbing whoever was attacking her.

"Let's go," Kalki said, turning to Vibhishan and Durukti. "You'll be killed if you stay here."

They both nodded and hopped on Devadatta.

As they rode towards the back of the camp, Kalki swung his sword at the Rakshas that came in their way.

The three of them rode close to the forest. Kalki spotted an empty tent. The Rakshas hadn't reached this far back in the camp. He asked Devadatta to stop and directed Vibhishan and Durukti to go inside.

Before entering the tent, Durukti turned towards Kalki and said, "Listen, I'm sorry. I'm sorry I destroyed your village. And I was mad to save Kali. He has been wrong all along. I was just too naïve to see it. I hope you have it in your heart to forgive me."

"I forgave you a long time ago." Kalki smiled. "Now go inside."

And instantly, her eyes protruded in shock. Kalki didn't understand what had happened until he saw an arrow lodged in her back. She fell on the ground.

Kalki dismounted and ran to Durukti. He held her tightly in her arms.

"Wait . . . no . . ." He looked up to see where the arrow had come from.

And then, he saw *him.*

It was Kali.

He was smiling, brushing his hand on his crossbow.

"It is only fitting," he spoke loudly, "that one who stabs you in the back, gets stabbed in the back."

Kalki looked at the trembling body of Durukti as tears welled up in his eyes.

"I'LL KILL YOU!" Kalki yelled, flaring his nostrils.

"You wish, Kalki. I came here to make sure that my sister died. And now, you will die as well." Kali shot an arrow from the crossbow again.

Kalki held the arrow in mid-air, and then twisted it. He gently placed Durukti on the ground, wiped his tears, and glared at Kali.

With anger surging inside him, the red smoke began to emanate from his body. He rushed towards Kali and rammed his head in Kali's stomach.

They both rolled on the ground. Kalki was about to take his sword out, but Kali smacked Kalki's hand with his crossbow.

Kalki howled in pain as he struggled to get Kali off of him. He used his uninjured hand and wielded the sword but Kali quickly pulled out a knife and slashed Kalki's wrist.

The sword dropped on the ground.

"You are still weak! People say you are a great warrior, but when it comes to it, you can't even protect yourself. Take a good look at my face, Kalki. It's the last thing you will see before you die!"

And the knife was plunged in Kalki's chest. He could feel the blade hitting his bones. Kali was laughing like a madman.

"I wanted to kill you the moment you laid your eyes on my sister," Kali said. "And look what you made me do. Kill her. Just like her, you will die too."

Kalki didn't say anything. He was gritting his teeth, battling the pain he was feeling.

"You are wrong," Kalki said as began to pull the knife out, surprising Kali. "It's not me who'll die today. It's *you*." And then, Kalki stabbed Kali in the chest.

Kali fell on the floor, surprised that Kalki still had the strength to attack.

Kalki's anger was mounting. A lot of red smoke was coming out of his body and filling the wound on his chest.

Within seconds, he was completely healed.

And then, Kalki did the unthinkable. He closed his eyes and let the sword speak to him. And instantly, the sword rose from the ground and came to him, drawn to its master.

"How are you doing this?" Kali said, growing pale. "It's . . . it's . . ."

"It's the Sword of Shiva and I'm the Avatar of Vishnu." He brought the Ratna Maru close to Kali's throat. "And I pass the judgement of execution."

Kali laughed. The knife was still inside his chest. "You think things will be over once you kill me? There will be more evil people out there, just like me. And, right now, you'll be killing the wrong person."

"I'm killing an evil man."

"Arjan is Adharm!" Kali laughed. "*He* is evil. Gods, you are killing the wrong man."

"And for some reason," Kalki smiled, remembering the faces of Bali, Ratri, Durukti, and all the friends he had lost, "it feels *right*."

Kalki raised his sword and was about to strike Kali, when Kali rolled away and started to run towards the front of the camp, shouting as he pulled the knife out of his chest.

"You can't kill me so easily," he screamed. Blood was gushing out of his chest. Kalki saw him tear a part of his garment and tie it around his wound. *The knife must have missed his heart. If only I had plunged it deeper!*

And at that moment, he saw a Danav enter the camp along with more Rakshas.

"I came prepared," Kali shouted, smiling.

He is running away.

Kalki was confused as to what he should do—deal with the Danav or follow Kali?

I have to end him, once and for all.

He trusted Manasa's men to take care of the surprise attack. Kalki quickly sheathed his sword and began to chase Kali.

This is the end.

76

Arjan was so happy. He had Chanelled to a place he had been missing so much—Shambala.

And he could see his home. Tears brimmed in his eyes as he looked at his home. It was dark outside. It was peaceful and quiet, as if the battle of Shambala hadn't happened at all.

He walked inside the hut, hoping to see his mother, but instead he found a strange man, wearing a hard, golden armour. The man was twirling his moustache. His irises were golden, and he had a huge crown on his head.

He was looking at Arjan.

"Who are you?" Arjan asked. "What are you doing in my house?"

"I'm here to show you the truth," the man said. "The truth about how our own blood betrays us."

"What do you mean?"

The man didn't respond. He just signalled Arjan to follow him. They reached Arjan's room. He saw his younger self sleeping.

"Do you remember this night?" the man asked.

"No."

"This is the night an intruder attacked you."

"Yes, a thief."

"A thief who didn't steal anything but tried to kill you," the man continued.

Arjan nodded. He had never understood what had happened that night. "Who are you?"

"I'm Hiranyakashyap, the man who was betrayed by my own blood—my son. He was supposed to worship me!" he said, balling his hands into fists.

And before Arjan could respond, he saw someone enter the room with a pillow in his hand.

This person stuffed the pillow on young Arjan's face. Arjan tried to remove the pillow, but couldn't. Eventually, the person ran away.

Hiranyakashyap and Arjan followed the figure. Arjan was curious to see who it was. And when the figure came outside, the moonlight illuminated his face.

It was Kalki.

No.

"He tried to kill you once," Hiranyakashyap said. "And he failed. Do not give him another chance."

Arjan's blood ran cold. Anger was bubbling inside him. Hiranyakashyap stood next to him and kept his hand on Arjan's shoulder. "Embrace who you are, and command the fallen ones."

"The Danavs?"

"Yes."

"And then what?"

"Kill the Avatar."

77

Padma didn't know what was worse—watching another woman flirt with Kalki or battling the Rakshas. For now, Padma chose to focus on fighting the Rakshas.

With swords in both her hands, she began to kill them without a hitch.

Two Rakshas came howling towards her. She swung her blades and cut their heads.

Rakshas were big, unfortunately, so she had to be extra careful while dealing with them. And they were so many. She had been killing them non-stop, but they wouldn't stop coming at her.

Padma went to help Manasa. A Rakshas was sitting on top of her. He was about to strike her when Padma pierced her sword right in his gut and kicked him away from the Naga queen. She extended her hand forward, and Manasa held it and stood up.

"You haven't changed much since I hired you," Manasa said.

"You clearly have. When did you learn how to fight? You always said that you could only strategise. And thank you for not telling my father that you had hired me to kill people."

"I have not learned anything. But I can't hide in my tent while my people are dying. I have to do something. And as for not telling Vibhishan about hiring you as an assassin, well, he would stop being my friend if he knew that," Manasa said as she looked around. "This won't end. We are losing, Padma. We need to leave."

"But the war?"

"It's lost." Manasa sighed. "My men and I are fighting but the Rakshas invasion was not something we expected. Sometimes it's better to know when to step back and for now—"

Two Rakshas appeared in front of Manasa and Padma. As they came forward, a man came in between them.

Padma couldn't see who it was. She squinted her eyes as she noticed that there was fur on the man's body.

Oh dear!

"Get lost, you two. You don't want to deal with an Ancient."

The Rakshas looked at each other in confusion. Before they could do anything, Vanars came at them. They swung their maces on the Rakshas' heads.

Padma saw more Vanars enter the camp, and they began to fight the Rakshas. They climbed on top of them and smacked them with their maces.

Lord Bajrang smiled as he turned to look at the two stunned women behind him.

"Looks like I made it in time."

Padma didn't wait to embrace him.

"All right then," Lord Bajrang patted her on the back. He turned to Manasa and said, "Your Majesty, my army is at your disposal. Soon, we will kill the Rakshas. And we apologise for coming late since . . . you know . . . asking thousands of Vanars to leave their comfortable home was tough."

Manasa simply stared at Lord Bajrang for a few seconds.

"My lord, Padma and Kalki told me about their time with you. I am so honoured to have you here. Thank you so much for coming to aid me," Manasa said, respectfully bowing. "But who called you, if you don't mind me asking?"

"She did," he said, pointing at Padma.

Manasa nodded and bowed again before going to aid her soldiers.

"Padma, I apologise for everything," Lord Bajrang said. "You were right. I refused to come out of my cocoon at Dandak. The world needs me; it needs my people. And you and Kalki need me. I am sorry I couldn't arrive any earlier. I knew that if I didn't come here, you both might end up resenting me, just like Macchanu. I am not going to abandon anyone."

Padma couldn't help but smile as tears streamed down her face.

Just then, the ground beneath them shook. Lord Bajrang and Padma looked up to see a Danav swinging his huge arms, uprooting the tents of the camp, and beating his chest.

"I'll deal with him," Lord Bajrang said.

But before Lord Bajrang could even move, the giant stopped, for some reason.

And then, to everyone's surprise, he turned to walk out of the camp.

"What just happened?" Padma quizzically looked at Lord Bajrang, who looked grim. "Did he just realise we will win, so he has lost hope?"

"No," he shook his head, "it's not that. I think he's being *called*."

"But by whom?" Padma asked.

"I remember how the Danavs had behaved when they were being controlled by Raavan." Lord Bajrang responded. "My guess would be that the Danav is being called by the Adharm."

78

Kalki was on Devadatta, and Kali was riding ahead on his horse. They had both whistled for their horses on their way out of the camp and towards Indragarh.

Kalki's speed had reduced since he had had to bat away the Rakshas that blocked his way. But he was catching up now.

Soon they entered the city. Kalki moved past the same gates through which he had entered with Lakshmi. They had been trying to get weapons to fight against Mlecchas. At that time, the security around the gate had been tight. Today, however, there was no one guarding the gates.

Kalki looked back. He had seen the actual war taking place in the camp on his way out. He wanted to help his friends.

I want to go back, but I have to end Kali first.

He shook his head. He had to have faith that they would be all right. With determination, he galloped towards Kali.

Kalki looked around him. The streets were completely empty. It was the dead of the night. People were asleep in their homes.

"KALI!" Kalki shouted. "You can't run away from me. Not anymore."

Suprisingly, Kali stopped. He got down from his horse, groaning as he tightened the cloth around his wound. The cloth was wet with blood.

"I don't plan to run away, my friend," Kali said, smiling.

Kalki, I don't have a good feeling about this, Devadatta's voice boomed in Kalki's head.

Kalki got off his horse. He took one step and an arrow came flying towards him, searing into the skin on his arm. Kalki didn't even flinch. Calmly, he pulled it out and looked in the direction from which it had come. A soldier was standing on the terrace of a nearby building.

Kalki narrowed his eyes. He took out a knife from his belt and threw it at the soldier. The blade reached its target, and the soldier fell down the building.

"Is that what you planned for me, Kali?" Kalki asked, looking at the Asura king. "A soldier with a weak crossbow!"

"Do you think I am that predictable?"

And then, Kalki felt pain in his right arm, where the arrow had hit. Within a few seconds, the pain gave way to numbness.

Kalki couldn't move his right arm anymore. "No! My sword arm—"

"Has been poisoned, yes," Kali said. "The arrow had been dipped in a liquid that immobilises the body part it comes into contact with. I got it extracted just for you. I knew I couldn't defeat you if we fought. But this," Kali pointed at Kalki's arm, "will make you weak."

Kalki tried to move his arm, but in vain. He looked at his sword as it hung loosely on his belt. He couldn't wield it in his left hand. The sword had just become useless.

As Kali advanced towards Kalki, his path was blocked by Devadatta. The horse ran towards Kali, but Kali smacked him on his head, and pushed him to the side.

Devadatta fell on the ground, bleeding.

Kali sprinted towards Kalki and punched him hard on his face. Reeling from the attack, Kalki fell down. Then he tried to get up, but Kali kicked him in the gut. Blood spurted from Kalki's mouth as he fell on the ground again.

Kali pulled him up by the throat, choking him, and said, "Like I said, you are still weak. Just like you were the first time I saw you."

Kalki struggled to remove Kali's hands from his throat.

"Enough of this," Kali said, and dropped Kalki on the ground. Kalki gasped for air. "I have done my part. Now, I will sit back and relax as my men tear you from limb to limb."

Kalki looked up and saw a dozen soldiers behind Kali. They were wearing sturdy armours and carrying maces. Kali snapped his fingers and the men began to advance towards Kalki, ready to end him.

"I had to lure you towards the city . . . away from your friends so that they won't rush in to help. Now I have you right where I wanted. My men and I are going to have fun with you."

Kalki didn't have the energy to stand. As the men came closer, he wondered what to do.

I need to Channel. I might get an answer.

He closed his eyes and concentrated. And then, he felt something. He opened his eyes to find someone touching his arm. It was a young Lord Govind.

Govind is here. In Indragarh. How?

"You'll be fine." Govind smiled as he touched Kalki's arm. Light went from his palm to Kalki's. And immediately Kalki felt the numbness going away.

With a surge of energy, Kalki stood up and backed away from the soldiers. Lord Govind was standing beside him, in a spirit-like form.

Kalki looked up at Kali. He looked confused, and then, horrified. Kali gasped as he looked around Kalki.

On Kalki's left and right side, Avatars had appeared—Lord Raghav with a bow and arrow, Lord Vaman, who was smiling, Lord Narasimha, who was growling, ready to claw at anyone who attacked, and Lord Varaha wearing his boar-like cap, with a club in his hand.

"How are they even here?" Kali was confused.

Kalki didn't know, but he was glad that they had all come to him.

"We are projections of your Channelling. You have been internally conversing with us for so long. Your powers have grown and enabled us to externally project ourselves," Lord Govind explained. "We might not have the same powers as our real counterparts, but we can take out his men while you deal with him."

"What does this mean?"

"It means you have embraced the truest and fullest power of an Avatar." Govind smiled as he pulled out his sword and got ready to attack Kali's men.

Kalki grinned as his eyes fell on Kali. "Let's do this."

The Avatar projections began to battle with Kali's men. Lord Raghav was firing arrows with precision. Lord Vaman was a tiny man, so he was plunging a dagger in the soldiers' feet. Lord Narasimha was angrily clawing at the soldiers. Lord Varaha was hitting the soldiers with his club. And Lord Govind was tricking the soldiers into fighting each other.

Now that his sword arm was all right, Kalki wielded his sword and sprinted towards Kali. Frightened, Kali backed away, turning to run.

But Kalki didn't waste time. He grabbed Kali by the throat and lifted him up.

Kali struggled, trying to kick Kalki in the gut, but couldn't.

"You can't win. Even if you kill me, the Adharm will make sure that you die."

"Where is he?" Kalki asked.

"You don't want to know. It doesn't matter."

Kalki tightened his grasp. "TELL ME!"

Kali still didn't answer. And Kalki didn't want to waste any more time. He pushed the blade inside Kali's chest. Kali screamed as his insides were gutted. Pulling the blade out, Kalki threw Kali's lifeless body on the ground.

He looked back at the Avatar projections. They had done the job. Kali's men had been killed.

It's over.

And then he thought about Arjan.

Where could he be?

79

Kalki returned to the camp and saw that Manasa's army was safe.

The Rakshas had been beaten with the help of Lord Bajrang and his Vanars. The fire had been extinguished. The injured men had been rushed to the infirmary and were being tended to. But there was one person who had died in the chaos ensued by the Rakshas.

Kalki was standing next to Durukti's lifeless body. It had been moved to Manasa's tent. Padma was trying to comfort him. Just then, Manasa, Lord Bajrang, and Vibhishan entered inside and stood around the Asura's body.

"She was a brave woman. She did what my father had done for Lord Raghav," Vibhishan said.

Kalki fought back tears. "She cannot die. I can't let her."

Lord Bajrang closed his eyes and kept his palm on her chest. "Her spirit has not left her body yet."

Hope sprung in Kalki as he looked up at the Vanar king. "What should we do?"

"You can endow her with immortality."

"Endow?"

"Yes. Just like I was Endowed by Lord Raghav."

"And my father was," Vibhishan added.

"Lord Raghav was special, so he could Endow twice," Lord Bajrang added. "He was the perfect man. But I don't know how many times you can do that. If you want her to come back to life, Endow her."

Kalki closed his eyes and concentrated on the chakras in his body. In a few seconds, he began to glow. He felt warmth spread in his entire body. Slowly, he placed his hand on Durukti's forehead and said in his head, *I ENDOW YOU FOR YOUR COMMITTMENT, FOR YOUR HONOUR, FOR YOUR TRUTH. YOU WILL LIVE FOREVER.*

He repeated this in his mind for a few minutes. When the warmth began to fade, Kalki opened his eyes. Nothing had changed in Durukti.

Her eyes were closed . . . her body was cold.

And then, a second later, she opened her eyes and looked around her, confused.

Finally she looked at Kalki, who was grinning from ear to ear. He enveloped her into a tight hug.

A nightmarish night had given way to a bright, clear morning.

Shuko perched on Kalki's shoulder as he looked at the barren field in front of the camp. He could see the Danav's footprints on the ground, heading north. Padma had told Kalki about the Danav that had abruptly left the camp in the midst of battle. He agreed with Lord Bajrang. The Adharm must have called it to him. And he knew what lied in the north—his village, Shambala.

At that moment, Manasa came out. She wrapped a shawl around herself and headed towards Vibhishan's tent. Kalki had heard that she had offered to help build houses at Dandak Hills and give woollen clothes to the Vanars, as a gift to Lord Bajrang for helping her in the war.

Manasa had decided to move back to her kingdom, Naagpuri. She would rest for a few days and then confront Raktapa. She hadn't forgotten that he had tried to get her executed. And Vibhishan would return to Bhanmati. As to who will rule over Indragarh, Manasa and Vibhishan would sit down to discuss soon. Neither of them wanted the throne; they had their own kingdoms to deal with.

Padma came out of her tent. She smiled when she saw Kalki and came to stand beside him. "Are you okay?" she asked.

"I don't know," Kalki said. "I'm worried about Arjan. You know he is—" He stopped speaking. He didn't want to tell her. She considered Arjan her friend. *What if she comes to hate him after learning that he is Adharm?*

"He'll be fine. Just bring him back." Padma kept her head on Kalki's shoulder. "Some people think you'll be a great king."

"Some people?"

"My father and Manasa."

Kalki chuckled.

"Hey, if you want to marry me, you have to be a king. Otherwise, my father will get some snobbish prince."

"Look who's talking," Kalki retorted playfully. "I thought you were going to stay an assassin all your life."

"I have changed, Kalki. I want to live a peaceful life now." Padma smiled as her hands wrapped around his scarred body. "I want to be happy. I want to be with the person I love. What about you?"

Kalki caressed her face. "Of course. If I have to be a king to be with you, then so be it. But don't think I wouldn't be snobbish. You have no idea how snobbish I can be."

They laughed.

And Kalki wanted to stay with her, but he couldn't wait to see his brother.

"Do you want me to come?" Padma asked.

"I will find him. Don't worry." Kalki didn't know what was going to happen. If it came to it, Arjan and Kalki might end up killing each other. And Padma shouldn't have to see that.

And then he whistled for Devadatta. He mounted his horse and started riding north, back to the place where it all began.

80

The sun had risen when Kalki reached Shambala.

A normal stallion would have taken days to reach this place, but Devadatta was no ordinary horse. He was strong and powerful. Running three times faster than a normal horse, he had taken only a day to reach the village.

Kalki couldn't help but feel nostalgic. The village seemed so calm and serene. It had been built back after the attack.

Shuko was in the sky, searching for Arjan.

Kalki roamed in the lanes of Shambala. Some villagers were up and about. They looked at him and his white stallion in awe. And as Kalki rode ahead, he saw three kids sitting in front of a hut—one boy was being scolded by his father, the other boy's nose was buried in his book, and the girl was snickering at the boy getting scolded.

And for some reason, it reminded him of Lakshmi, Arjan, and himself, when they were kids.

Kalki smiled at them. A moment later, Shuko came down and told him, *He's up on the highest hill in the village.*

What's he doing here?

Just sitting, staring at the sight before him.

And the Danav?

Nowhere to be seen.

Kalki nodded as he rode towards the hill, leaving the kids behind. Then he remembered that it was the same hill they had sat on many times to watch sunsets.

There he is. Arjan was sitting cross-legged, looking at the rising sun. Kalki got off Devadatta, and said to Shuko and the horse both, *Stay back.*

Why? Devadatta asked.

I want to talk to him in private.

The parrot and the horse stayed put as Kalki walked up the hill, his sword dangling on his belt.

Arjan was looking at the breathtaking scenery in front of him. He seemed calm.

"You don't have to kill me yet, Kalki," Arjan said, smiling as he turned to look at his brother.

"You knew I would be coming?" *He looks so different.* Arjan's hair had grown so much. His body was ripped, and he had huge scars on his chest.

"I called the Danav for a purpose. I hoped that you, or Manasa's men, would see the Danav heading north," Arjan said. "I wanted you to come here and see this."

"Where is it now?"

"I killed him. He's nothing but ashes now. Apparently, I can control his demise too," Arjan confessed.

He took a few steps towards Kalki, and Kalki immediately kept his hand on the hilt of his sword.

"I am not going to kill you." Arjan looked hurt.

"Why?"

"Because," Arjan said, "I realised how stupid that would be. You are my brother. I won't kill you, even though you tried to kill me once."

"It was a mistake, Arjan," Kalki said defensively. "I was stupid."

"You're still stupid." Arjan chuckled. "I am not going to lie though. For a moment, I thought about killing you. I actually thought that the Adharms of the past were right. But in the end, they made me realise something. The Avatars they had faced were different. You are not a megalomaniac like Lord Govind. You don't follow what the society dictates, like Lord Raghav. You don't have anger issues like Lord Narasimha. You are a good man, Kalki. And I used to think I was too, but I'm not so sure anymore."

Tears streamed down Kalki's face as he came forward to hug Arjan. The sword was within his reach, but he didn't need to use it.

"You *are* a good man, brother. Don't ever doubt that," Kalki said, "So what now?"

"Will you show me your sword?" Arjan asked.

Kalki nodded, handing it to him.

"Before coming here, I Channelled to know what will happen if the True Prophecy of the Dark Age isn't followed," Arjan said, moving his hands over the inscriptions on the Sword of Shiva, "I asked multiple Adharms. All of them said that if the prophecy isn't fulfilled, the world will descend into chaos. Darkness and evil will spread and the concept of time will be no more. You know we can't let that happen."

"What are you saying, Arjan?"

"You know *I* can't let that happen," Arjan said. "Some things *have* to happen; we can't stop them. We can't change our fate."

Kalki froze. Arjan was gripping the sword tightly. Kalki had, without a thought, handed the mightiest sword to exist, to Arjan. It was Kalki's only weapon.

He's going to kill me.

And then Arjan pointed the hilt of the sword towards Kalki. "Hold it."

"What?"

"Hold it!"

Kalki took the sword, confused. *What is his plan? What is he trying to do?*

And then, before Kalki could do anything, Arjan pulled the blade towards himself . . . towards his stomach.

He wants me to kill him?

"I know what you're trying to make do, but let me be very clear about this. I *won't* do it. And I won't let you do this either!" Kalki yelled, and yanked the sword away from Arjan's grasp.

The movement was so sudden that it took Arjan by surprise. He and Kalki both lost their balance and fell.

Arjan angrily rammed his fist on the ground. Kalki dusted himself off and stood up.

"Brother, please. Things have changed. I am not the same Arjan you remember. I've killed people in anger. *I've taken lives and I'm not sorry that I did*," Arjan yelled, holding back tears. "If I am not killed, I'm afraid I will become even worse."

"It doesn't matter, Arjan. You can change. I forgive you for all the bad things you have done till now. *I'll* make sure that you don't become evil. You don't have to die!" Kalki said.

Arjan grimaced. "You don't understand. You are just being idealistic. We are not living in a utopian world."

"That's where you are wrong, brother. I know things seem bad, but I *will* steer you on the right path. Just come with me, and things will get better. I promise."

Arjan's expression changed. He coldly looked at Kalki and said, "I am your brother, but I'm Adharm first. And I promise you, Kalki, if I am not stopped, I *will* kill more people. Whoever opposes me, whoever doesn't follow my orders, shall die by my hands."

"I don't believe you," Kalki said.

Arjan sped towards Kalki, as fast as lightning, and landed a punch on his face. Kalki reeled from the impact. *When did he get so strong?* Massaging his cheek, which had grown red, he shook his head and stood up.

Arjan hurled himself forward and grabbed Kalki by the hair.

"Kill me; otherwise I will kill you." And then he pulled Kalki's sword towards his chest, while Kalki gripped its hilt. "Do it."

"No," Kalki said, coughing as blood trickled down from his mouth. "Don't make me do this."

Kalki didn't want to kill Arjan, but then he remembered what Lord Govind had shown him—what Arjan would become if he wasn't killed.

"Do it, Kalki. The world will be a better place without me. Do it!"

For a second, Arjan recoiled in shock. And then, a sad smile appeared on his face as he looked down at his body.

Kalki had pierced the sword right into Arjan's heart as tears trickled down his cheeks.

And then, Arjan fell down, and Kalki closed his eyes.

As the sun rose, the Adharm took his last breath.

Kalki held Arjan as he cried his eyes out. "You forced me. We didn't have to follow the prophecy, Arjan. We didn't have to!" he yelled in agony.

Arjan smiled. "I . . . couldn't . . . take . . . the chance," he said his last words to his brother.

Kalki saw golden wisps of smoke release from Arjan's body, and tears flow down his eyes as they closed. Forever. He pulled the blade out and held on to the lifeless body of Arjan.

The Adharm was dead. And the Dharm was crying for him.

EPILOGUE

A few months later.

Kalyug was over.

Kalki had reached the Bajrang temple to take his mother away with him.

He was happy to see his mother after such a long time. Sumati burst into tears as she saw her son. She enveloped him into a tight hug.

"You don't know how much I've missed you. Where's Arjan?"

"Let's go, mother," Kalki said, avoiding her question.

Sumati nodded, wiping her tears. "Sure, let me just get back the bags." She turned to go inside, but then turned back, confused. "But where? Back to Shambala?"

"No, Ma. To Indragarh."

"Why?" She looked at Kalki quizzically. "Young man, we are villagers, not cityfolk."

"But the king has to be where the throne is," Kalki said matter-of-factly.

"King?"

Kalki pointed outside the temple. Sumati gasped as she saw a huge army standing around the garden. The men were waiting for their king and his mother. And in front of them stood Padma.

"I didn't let them come up here because," Kalki looked at the people walking in the temple, "I thought they will feel threatened."

"Are you really my son?" Sumati joked. "You have changed so much."

"No, Ma. I'm same." Kalki smiled. "I will never change. And there's your daughter-in-law," he said, pointing at Padma.

Sumati boxed his ears. "How dare you get married without the blessings of your mother!"

"Ow, ow, ow, no, no. I'm *going* to marry her. I came here for your blessings."

"Good boy. You have found such a beautiful girl. Now, I'm going to go get my bags, and then you can tell me where Arjan is."

Sumati went inside the temple.

Tell her, kid, Shuko said to Kalki.

Yeah, tell her the truth, human. Break the heart of your mother. That's what the dumbo says.

Hey, who you calling dumbo, you horse? Shuko squawked.

Oh wow, what a comeback. I'm hurt, Devadatta said.

Kalki looked down, debating what to do. No one except Shuko and Devadatta knew the truth. To everyone else, Kalki had lied, saying that Arjan died fighting Kali's men, that Arjan had been ambushed when he was trying to escape. No one needed to know that Arjan was Adharm. Kalki didn't want his image to be tarnished. The only person alive who knew about Arjan's true identity was Durukti. And she had sworn to not tell anyone.

A few minutes later, Sumati came outside with her bags.

Kalki put his arm around Sumati as they went down the stairs.

He was glad. Things had worked out well.

Manasa had gone back to Naagpuri and taken control over Varungarh, as was her plan. With the help of Lord Bajrang and his Vanars, defeating Raktapa and his Rakshas had been an easy task. Vibhishan was happy sitting in his peaceful kingdom in Bhanmati.

He and Padma were still awkward around each other, but Kalki knew things between them would smooth over with time.

And as for Durukti, Kalki was glad he had made her immortal. She was healthy as a horse, and had realised her dream of opening a gurukul. He had seen her a few weeks ago as she was taking her first class. She had hired other women to teach at the gurukul as well.

And thinking about all his friends, he remembered the ones that had lost their lives. He saw the faces of Bali, Ratri, Lakshmi. They were smiling at him.

And then he saw the face of his beloved brother. Arjan was sitting cross-legged on a hill, smiling playfully at Kalki. He had always loved this smile of Arjan's.

Kalki had buried Arjan, just like Arjan had wanted. He had buried him on the highest hill in Shambala where he and Kalki watched the sunsets together, where they had fought months ago.

"Ma," Kalki said, looking at Sumati, "You want to know what happened to Arjan?"

Sumati nodded. In her heart she had guessed what had happened to her boy. If he had been alive, he would have come to see her. But as she waited for Kalki to speak, she desperately hoped that her instincts were wrong.

"He is dead, Ma. But he died to save the world. He died a hero."

THE END
OF
KALKI'S JOURNEY

TRIBES

RAKSHAS – Intelligent humanoids, born in the South on the island of Eelam, are strong in combat and have tougher skin compared to other Tribals. Their average height goes above six feet. They have a patriarchal system and their culture, regardless of their furiousness, is quite backward. Most of them worship Lord Shiva, but are often considered by others as atheists. They have black skin and oiled hair.

NAGAS – Royalty and aristocrats living in the city of Naagpuri which floats on a lake. Nagas worship Lord Shesh Naag and Lord Vishnu. Nagas are diplomats more than warriors, but have grown their military system over a period of time. Women are respected in their culture. They are said to have blue eyes and fair skin.

YAKSHAS – Short in height and mischievous. They are considered the least threatening, but are very good in finances. They worship only their king and not any god. They lack military and political skills. Yakshinis, the female counterpart of the Yakshas, are rare. They live in Alakpur which is in the midst of a desert. Their Tribe is considered the richest of all.

ASURAS – Extinct race. Not much is known about this Tribe. They were considered to be the reason behind all the evil in this world. There was a great hunt of this Tribe where many Asura children, women, and men were slaughtered and hanged due to the superstitions about them. Some survived and have been wandering. They are atheists.

DANAVS – Brothers of Asuras, they are supposedly as tall as trees and as huge as mountains. They were the arch-enemies of the gods and had been put to sleep for their walks could create tremors. They are grandly fantasized during bedtime stories and many have not seen them since the Breaking.

PISACHAS – Cannibals. Live over swamps in Daldal Lands. They worship the 'the fittest'. They believe in karma and they ink their bodies with each crime they have committed. They are considered to be mentally unstable and only a fool would cross their lands.

VANAR – They live in Dandak Hills. They are considered to be vastly knowledgeable. They have hairy bodies which are sometimes ridiculed as being defected. They have gone underground and they choose not to be friendly towards visitors. They worship their protector Lord Bajrang who is considered an immortal and their king.

NOTE: *There are other tribes that are not in the list. They are yet to be researched and documented.*

– Ved Vyas.

ACKNOWLEDGMENTS

Since this is the last book of Kalki trilogy, I would like to thank some very important people who have helped me make this series a bestseller.

First off, I want to thank my parents. They encouraged me to pursue writing, and have always believed in my books.

Thanks to my invaluable mentor, Mr. Anuj Bahri from Red Ink Literary Agency. He guided me on how to turn my writing into a career.

Thank you my publishers, Gaurav Sabharwal and Shikha Sabharwal, who worked really hard to make this book a bestseller. Their involvement is priceless.

I would like to express my gratitude to the Fingerprint! team, starting from the editorial—Pooja Dadwal and Garima Shukla helped me make this book better. Garima suggested that I change the ending, and that led to a major impact on the story.

Thanks to the marketing team—Neeraj sir and Yola, who assist me a lot, and Mayank, who makes sure that the book sells well on Amazon. And thanks to the sales team—Mahesh sir, Rajaram sir, Nihar sir, Surendra sir, and Nataraj sir.

A big thank you to my design team at Arthat Studio, which has consistently given me great covers. Without them, the books won't be where they are today.

And thanks to Bijit Sinha, my editor and my good friend.

Kevin Missal wrote his first book at the age of 14, and at 22, the St. Stephens graduate is bestselling author and a full-time writer, with the first two books in his Kalki trilogy being runaway successes. *Dharmayoddha Kalki: Avatar of Vishnu* and its sequel *Satyayoddha Kalki: Eye of Brahma* have sold one lakh copies in under a year.

Kevin loves reading fantasy fiction and has always been a fan of mythology. His books have featured in newspapers such as *The Sunday Guardian*, *The New Indian Express*, and *Millennium Post*.

He lives in Gurugram and can be contacted at kevin.s.missal@gmail.com.